PRAISE FOR MARIAH STEWART

~ The Wyndham Beach Series ~

AN INVINCIBLE SUMMER

"*Oh* my. This book was simply *gorgeous*! Each of the characters we're introduced to leaves a mark on your heart. The love that was both lost and found is enough to turn the biggest skeptic on to the idea of everything happening for a reason, and in its own time. All in all, it was a wonderful cast of characters with varied lives that are intriguing, heartbreaking, and uplifting in equal parts."

—*Satisfaction for Insatiable Readers*

"This is my first by this author, and it certainly won't be the last. Her writing is extremely engaging, and the author really brings to life the dynamics of longtime friendships and relationships and all the ups and downs that come with them. I couldn't help but fall in love with this book."

—*Where the Reader Grows*

"A multigenerational storyline, an idyllic setting, and a new series from one of my tried-and-true authors? Yes please! As much as I loved the setting and the premise of this one, the characterization is where it really shines. Maggie and her two lifelong friends were all such lovely, authentic women."

—*Novelgossip*

"This story hooked me from the beginning and kept me dangling all the way through: cheering, crying, and just absorbing the decisions as Maggie finds her path to true happiness. A wonderful story I just fell for!"

—*A Midlife Wife*

"What makes this book so readable are the relationships and how the past ties into the future. Isn't that the way it is for all of us? *An Invincible Summer* is a fast-paced, easy-to-read story delving into the relationships we have in life and how they both break and sustain us."

—*Books, Cooks, Looks*

"I really loved these characters and this story. The characters just felt real and flawed in the best of ways. I found myself caring about each of the characters, which has me really excited that this book is just the beginning to a series. I will definitely be continuing on, as I want to see what happens with some of these other characters. I just want more, if I'm being honest! Read this book if you are a fan of women's fiction, contemporary fiction, or are looking for a great summer read."

—*Booked on a Feeling*

"This book was raw and real. Stewart crafted beautifully imperfect characters that allow us to see ourselves in their struggles. I spent the majority of the novel on the edge of my chair, cheering for Maggie and her daughters. This book also gives off what I'd consider Virgin River vibes, so if you like that series, grab this one and give it a try."

—@stumblingintobooks

"What a down-to-earth, heart-filling, and sentimental read. Full of friendships, forgetting, and moving forward. The relationships and characters are realistic, charming, and the plot is a bit elusive to keep you on your toes. A very enjoyable read about love, loss, and second chances, and it is a page-turner."

—@momfluencer

"This novel by @mariah_stewart_books is what a women's fiction novel is all about. There's a bit of romance, friendship, and complicated relationships. I really enjoyed how this book highlighted the messiness that life can be, but [it was] done in a lighthearted way. And the overall theme of learning lessons from the past and the courage to move forward onto new phases of one's life was endearingly told."

—@tamsterdam_reads

"There is so much I loved about this read. The setting of Wyndham Beach is gorgeous. I could smell the sea air, feel the warmth of the sun as the women took their coffee and sat watching the horizon. I could feel Maggie's pull to return to her roots. I loved the female relationships in the book. Maggie is a strong but supportive mother who brings her children through crises but holds out for her own choices, and the independence of her own life. The gatherings with her friends are glorious—tattoos, rock concerts, and the warmth of conversations between women who really know and understand each other. This was such a celebration of life and especially of women of *all* ages."

—@salboreads

~ The Hudson Sisters Series ~

THE LAST CHANCE MATINEE

"Prepare to fall in love with this amazing, endearing family of women."
—Robyn Carr, *New York Times* bestselling author

"The combination of a quirky small-town setting, a family mystery, a gentle romance, and three estranged sisters is catnip for women's fiction fans."

—*Booklist*

"If you like the Lucky Harbor series by Jill Shalvis, you will enjoy this one. Stewart's writing reminds me of Susan Wiggs, Luanne Rice, Susan Mallery, and Robyn Carr."

—*My Novelesque Life*

THE SUGARHOUSE BLUES

"A solid writer with so much talent, Mariah Stewart crafts wonderful stories that take us away to small-town America and build strong families we wish we were a part of."

—*A Midlife Wife*

"Reading this book was like returning to a favorite small town and meeting up with friends you had been missing."

—*Pacific Northwest Bookworm*

"A heartwarming read full of surprising secrets, humor, and lessons about what it means to be a family."

—*That Book Lady Blog*

THE GOODBYE CAFÉ

"Stewart makes a charming return to tiny Hidden Falls, Pennsylvania, in this breezy contemporary, which is loaded with appealing down-home characters and tantalizing hints of mystery that will hook readers immediately. Stewart expertly combines the inevitable angst of a trio of sisters, a family secret, and a search for an heirloom necklace; it's an irresistible mix that will delight readers. Masterful characterizations and well-timed plot are sure to pull in fans of romantic small-town stories."

—*Publishers Weekly*

"Stewart [has] the amazing ability to weave a women's fiction story loaded with heart, grit, and enough secrets [that] you highly anticipate the next book coming up. I have read several books from her different series, and every one of them has been a delightful, satisfying read. Beautiful and heartwarming."

—*A Midlife Wife*

"Highly recommend this series for WF fans and even romance fans. There's plenty of that sweet, small-town romance to make you swoon a little."

—*Novelgossip*

"These characters will charm your socks off! Thematic and highly entertaining."

—*Booktalk with Eileen*

~ The Chesapeake Diaries Series ~

THAT CHESAPEAKE SUMMER

"Deftly uses the tools of the genre to explore issues of identity, truth, and small-town kinship. Stewart offers a strong statement on the power of love and trust, a fitting theme for this bighearted small-town romance."

—Publishers Weekly

DUNE DRIVE

"Rich with local history, familiar characters (practical, fierce, and often clairvoyant centenarian Ruby is a standout), and the slow-paced, down-home flavor of the bay, Stewart's latest is certain to please fans and add new ones."

—Library Journal

ON SUNSET BEACH

"Mariah Stewart's rich characterization, charming setting, and a romance you'll never forget will have you packing your bags for St. Dennis."

—Robyn Carr, New York Times bestselling author

COMING HOME

"One of the best women's contemporary authors of our time, Mariah Stewart serves the reader a beautiful romance with a delicious side dish of the suspense that has made her so deservingly popular. *Coming Home* is beautifully crafted with interesting, intelligent characters and pitch-perfect pacing. Ms. Stewart is, as always, at the top of her game with this sensuous, exhilarating, page-turning tale."

—Betty Cox, *Reader to Reader Reviews*

AT THE RIVER'S EDGE

"Everything you love about small-town romance in one book . . . *At the River's Edge* is a beautiful, heartwarming story. Don't miss this one."

—Barbara Freethy

"If you love romance stories set in a small seaside village, much like Debbie Macomber's Cedar Creek series, you will definitely want to grab this book. I easily give this one a five out of five stars."

—*Reviews from the Heart*

Goodbye Again

The Mercy Street Series (Suspense)

Mercy Street

Cry Mercy

Acts of Mercy

The FBI Series (Romantic Suspense)

Brown-Eyed Girl

Voices Carry

Until Dark

Dead Wrong

Dead Certain

Dead Even

Dead End

Cold Truth

Hard Truth

Dark Truth

Final Truth

Last Look

Last Words

Last Breath

Forgotten

The Enright Series (Contemporary Romance)

Devlin's Light

Wonderful You

Moon Dance

Stand-Alone Titles
(Women's Fiction / Contemporary Romance)

The President's Daughter

Priceless

Carolina Mist

A Different Light

Moments in Time

Novellas

"Finn's Legacy" (in The Brandywine Brides)

"If Only in My Dreams" (in Upon a Midnight Clear)

"Swept Away" (in Under the Boardwalk)

"'Til Death Do Us Part" (in Wait Until Dark)

Short Stories

"Justice Served" (in Thriller 2: Stories You Just Can't Put Down)

"Without Mercy" (in Thriller 3: Love Is Murder)

Goodbye Again

MARIAH STEWART

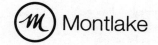
Montlake

Published by Montlake, Seattle

www.apub.com

Amazon, the Amazon logo, and Montlake are trademarks of Amazon.com, Inc., or its affiliates.

ISBN-13: 9781542033077
ISBN-10: 1542033071

Cover design by Caroline Teagle Johnson

Printed in the United States of America

For Kate Collins Curnin
May 11, 1969–January 12, 2021

Prologue

On the day she turned sixteen—when she was still Lydia Hess, the *Bryant* still seven years into her future—Liddy thought she knew how it was all going to shake out. She and her two besties—Emma Harper and Maggie Lloyd—would finish college and return to their hometown, Wyndham Beach, on the lower coast of Massachusetts, to live their happy-ever-afters with the to-be-determined loves of their lives and raise their families. Maggie, of course, would marry Brett, her high school love, but wouldn't move back home until his professional football career was over (no one in the entire states of Massachusetts and Rhode Island doubted Brett Crawford would be drafted by a pro team, but they all, naturally, prayed he'd go to the Patriots). The three of them—Liddy, Emma, and Maggie—would always be best friends, and their children would play (and be BFFs), too. They'd live out their best lives together, grow old together, and support each other in whatever life might throw their way.

At fifty-nine, Liddy was in turn amused and chagrined by her younger self's naivete when she considered her bold predictions hadn't even been half-right once it was all added up.

Liddy and Emma did return to Wyndham Beach after college graduation (University of Rhode Island and Smith, respectively), Liddy to marry Jim Bryant, son of the town's most successful insurance agent, who had the policies for all the local properties, autos, and businesses locked up. Emma had married Harry Dean, who was older by thir-teen years and the son of the president of the First National Bank of Wyndham Beach (and destined to follow in his grandfather's and his father's footsteps to the bank's big corner office). Maggie had strayed most from the script, having (shock!) broken up with Brett after his sec-ond season with the Seattle Seahawks, and instead of coming home—where Liddy and Emma could have supported her through whatever heartbreak she must have been enduring, had she taken them into her confidence, which inexplicably she had not—Maggie had stunned everyone by up and moving to Philadelphia, where, two years later, she married Art Flynn, a Philly lawyer, and settled into a life that had been step one in totally blowing up Liddy's life plan.

Maggie had lived happily on Philadelphia's Main Line, raising her two daughters and teaching in the private school they attended. Grace, her older daughter, had gone to law school and joined her father's firm, Flynn Law, after passing the bar. She married the man she'd thought was her one true love, but that hadn't worked out so well. Natalie, the younger of Maggie's daughters, taught English at a community college in a Philly suburb and was the single mother of four-year-old Daisy. Both Maggie's girls had made some questionable decisions over the past few years—mostly where men were concerned—but then again, Liddy conceded, who hadn't at some point in their life? Three years ago, Art died from a cancer diagnosed only months before his death, and Maggie's seemingly happy life had come to a screeching halt.

Emma and Harry had one son—Christopher—who'd been a joy to Emma but a source of contention to Harry from the day the boy discovered music. Harry's vision for their son's future had had Chris following in his footsteps straight to Harvard and eventually to the office of the president of the bank, but once the boy learned to play the guitar, it was all over. Chris had set his sights on becoming a rock star, and that was exactly what he'd done, becoming the international voice and face of DEAN, the band that had its humble beginnings in the

Wyndham Beach garages of their ever-changing teenage participants. Nine years ago, Harry had had a sudden heart attack and died without ever reconciling with his son. Since then, Chris and his wildly successful band—the final lineup having solidified in college—had traveled around the world several times, leaving little time for trips home to visit his lonely mother. So much for Em's happy ending.

Liddy's blueprint for her own future hadn't quite held up, either. She and Jim had bought the house his great-grandfather had built in Wyndham Beach, and they'd planned on renovating it and filling it with children. After years where she'd suffered a series of miscarriages and a stillborn son, Liddy had become mother to a healthy baby girl, Jessica, who'd been the center of Liddy and Jim's universe from the moment of her birth. Jessie had grown into a remarkable young woman, kind and beautiful and blessed with amazing artistic talents, and who, at twenty-nine, with no apparent warning, had taken her life. A year to the day later, Jim had asked for a divorce, and the collapse of Liddy's world had been complete.

So much for happy-ever-after.

Chapter One

Every morning upon waking, Liddy's first thought was of her daughter, and the choice she'd made to end her life without ever confiding in her mother the intent or the reason. Four years after the fact, Liddy was still searching for answers.

In the solitude of her quiet house, Liddy spoke aloud to Jessie several times over the course of each day. Sometimes it might be merely a quick, "Morning, sweetie." Other days it might be a little more complex, as when Liddy wanted to buy the town's only bookstore from its retiring owner. She'd gone over all the pros and cons with both her lawyer and her accountant, then later, at home, with Jess. In the end, remembering how her daughter had loved going to the shop and searching for the perfect book, Liddy had followed her heart and signed the papers, jumping in with both feet, taking possession of the building and the business. If nothing else, the prospect of turning the closed, run-down bookstore into a lively, thriving business had put a new bounce in Liddy's step. The plan for the renovation—however intimidating it might be—had lent new purpose to her days.

As she walked toward the center of Wyndham Beach on a late August morning, the chorus of the last song she'd heard before she'd left the house still playing in her head (Sting's "Fields of Gold"), Liddy mentally ran through the day's agenda: remove all the books from their shelves and box them up, then move all the bookcases to the center of the shop so the walls could be painted. The floors needed refinishing, but she had no idea how that could be accomplished given the limitations of the shop itself. Where would everything go while the work was being done? She'd have help with the packing of the books and the painting, but still, the logistics of it all were daunting. There was much more on the overall to-do list, but if she thought about the work in its entirety, she'd exhaust herself. Probably pass out from the stress right there on Front Street. People coming into town to shop or mail letters or meet friends for breakfast would step over or walk around her prone body. She could hear them complaining about her lack of consideration: "Humph. You'd think Liddy'd at least have had the courtesy to pass out on the grassy strip between the sidewalk and the street instead of right in the damned middle of everything."

Amused, Liddy smiled as she pushed open the door of Ground Me, the local coffee shop boasting the best brew in town, a claim not unfounded. Liddy waved to Brett Crawford, the chief of police and Maggie's former and present love. He was deep in conversation with two members of the town council (what was *that* all about?) and his wave was uncharacteristically perfunctory.

"Good morning, Miss Lydia." The young man behind the counter greeted her with a winsome smile. Blond surfer-boy hair flopped onto his forehead as he pushed up the sleeves of his light-blue button-down shirt, which, along with khaki shorts, made up the shop's preppy uniform. "What will it be today? The usual, or shall we walk on the wild side?" He leaned closer and lowered his voice. "I could fix you a large dark roast latte with extra cream and sugar. Top it with whipped cream and a touch of caramel." He waggled his eyebrows.

Liddy laughed. "Get thee behind me, Satan. I'm sticking with the same old, same old, but thanks for asking."

"You got it." He turned to prepare her coffee, and she tried to remember his name. He was the grandson of someone in town, but she couldn't remember whom. When her drink was ready, he handed over her order. "So it's my last week here before I go back to school. You gonna miss me?"

"Of course I will." She smiled as his name bounced back into her head. "Remind me what college you go to, Ryan."

"University of Connecticut," he replied.

"Oh, right. Well, good luck this year. Come see us over your winter break." She paid for her coffee and winked as she turned to leave. "Go Huskies."

Once outside, Liddy stopped on the sidewalk to take a few sips of her coffee. Regular medium blend. Half-and-half. One artificial sweetener. "Perfect, as always," she murmured. "I will definitely miss that boy."

The light was green at the three-way corner where Front, Church, and Cottage Streets merged, so she hustled across toward her destination. It was a perfect end-of-summer morning, sunny but cool with the promise of a decent beach day that afternoon. She knew crisper weather was ahead and for a moment wished she could take the day off. Just this one before the days grew shorter and cooler and there'd be no more hours spent lounging on the beach until next year. But her list was endless, and if she wanted to open the new-and-improved bookshop by the time Alden Academy—the private school that stretched along the harbor not far from the center of town—reopened for the fall term, she had to use every day to the maximum. She'd wanted to bring the shop back from the dusty, dingy, poorly organized state it had been in when she'd bought it, and she'd already made great strides toward that end. Her goal was to open the first Tuesday in September, and that date was just around the corner. Before she knew it, it would be Labor Day, and the next day cars would be pouring into town from all over New England to drop off the sons of the families who could afford the steep costs associated with a tony prep school like Alden.

Liddy unlocked the door to her shop, pausing to catch a quick glimpse of her reflection in the front bay window. She was a tall woman who carried a few extra pounds on her large-boned frame. Her salt-and-pepper hair hung over her left shoulder in one big, fat, long braid. She'd be hard pressed to deny her age, though the lines on her face weren't *that* bad, and her wide-set eyes were still crystal blue. She wore old, bright-yellow J.Crew rubber flip-flops, a faded light-blue T-shirt with URI (in honor of her alma mater) in white on the front, and a pair of olive-green cargo pants, which she'd bought online months ago. Once they'd arrived, she'd decided something even remotely trendy didn't suit her usual style (most days that being aging flower child), and she'd meant to send them back. But the pants slated for return were forgotten in the midst of the hullabaloo over the summer with Maggie moving back to Wyndham Beach and Liddy discovering the reason Maggie hadn't married Brett all those years ago (oh, the deliciousness of the drama!). Since Liddy was stuck with the pants, they'd become an integral part of her gardening, cleaning, painting, all-things-messy go-to outfit.

Once inside, she turned on the overhead lights. They were neon and harsh, but there wasn't much she could do about them. Maybe she'd replace them someday, but the estimate she'd received from the electrical contractor was mind-blowing, so she'd moved that item to the bottom of the list. Earlier in the week she'd lowered the front window shade and decided to leave it down. The natural light would be lovely and welcomed, but no need to let the entire town know what she was doing until she was ready to show them.

For a very long moment, she stood at the front of the store, remembering a time when trips to this shop had been so routine she'd barely registered their importance. Now she lamented the irreclaimable beauty of those lost days, when they'd walk from their home, Jessie's hand in hers, her daughter chatting endlessly about whatever popped into her mind, Liddy hardly listening to half of what Jess was saying. How many times had she replayed an argument with Jim or the plot of the previous night's favorite TV show in her head while Jessie had been sharing a story she was making up as they ambled along? The memory turned Liddy cold inside. She'd give anything for one more sweet morning walk with her child.

She could almost see an enthralled Jessie sitting on the story rug in the children's section at the back of the store, eyes wide as she listened to an animated Alma Jo Lattimore, the late wife of the previous owner, read aloud at Tuesday morning story time. Liddy closed her eyes, and for a brief flicker in time Jessie was running to her, face shining, clutching the book she'd desperately wanted. All those books purchased over the years remained in the bedroom of Jess's apartment in the carriage house behind Liddy's home, the old structure she and Jim had renovated to give their daughter a place of her own. As a struggling artist, she couldn't afford to rent an apartment but needed space where she could live and work with some degree of privacy. Jessie had created her best work in her three years there, work she'd stockpiled without having shared with anyone. Neither her boyfriend nor her parents had seen her last paintings, which, in retrospect, offered only the most subtle hints of the pain she'd been hiding from everyone.

Liddy blinked away the memory and tucked it back into the corner of her heart where she kept such things, and forced her feet to move. She had plenty of time to look back when she was home alone, but right at that moment there was work to do.

She dropped her handbag on the counter next to the ancient cash register, a beautiful relic from another time: a bright-red 1950 National Cash with the Coca-Cola logo above the keys. Carl Lattimore, the son of the previous owner, had assured her it still worked but admitted his father had used a five-year-old Casio for all transactions in the store. She still hadn't decided what to do with it. Liddy patted the vintage machine as she walked past. It had long since been dubbed Big Red, and she'd expressed surprise that Fred Lattimore, who'd owned the shop for as long as Liddy could remember, hadn't taken it with him.

"I thought about bringing it home," Carl had told her. "But I'm afraid seeing it will remind my dad of the bookstore, and he'd take off, thinking he needed to go to work. Alzheimer's is a terrible thing, Liddy. The register needs to stay in the shop. Everyone in town knows Big Red."

So for now the antique remained on the counter, which itself showed its age.

"Yeah, well, showing one's age isn't a crime," she muttered as she looked around, feeling overwhelmed, not for the first time in the course of the store's renovation.

She'd been as aware as the next person the town's only bookshop had room for improvement. Lots of improvement, from its physical appearance to the selection of books it offered and the way they were displayed. Fred Lattimore's decline had begun sooner than any of his store's patrons had realized. Of course, they knew he sometimes—okay, frequently—forgot to order the latest books from their publishers, which meant if you were really craving that new tell-all autobiography or women's fiction or thriller, you had to drive to New Bedford to a brick-and-mortar store or order online. Once inside Fred's store, the books had been arranged with seemingly no thought to how customers might find them. His random shelving had made locating a particular title somewhat of a scavenger hunt. There were those in town who had grown tired of trying to think like Fred. Of course, older residents had forgiven him his idiosyncrasies—"Oh, that's just Fred's way"—but more often than not, over the past two years, even Liddy (who thought she'd cracked Fred's shelving code) had often left without a book in her hands.

The profit and loss statement Fred's accountants had given her told a grim tale of no profit and much loss. Even Liddy's accountant had advised against her purchasing the business, pointing out she had no business experience herself.

"But I have common sense," she'd told him. "And I've been a reader all my life. I know books, and I know what people want in a bookstore, because they're the same things I want. The same things my bookstore will have."

He'd shrugged and given Liddy his blessing and reminded her he was there to help when she needed to bail out. She'd thanked him with a tight smile on her face and a promise to herself there'd be no bailing.

Liddy reminded herself of that conversation as she took in the scene before her. Books piled on the floor, walls that hadn't been painted since the nineteen sixties, and area rugs worn and buckled and bearing the scent and scars of countless pairs of muddy feet.

In her mind's eye she knew exactly how she wanted the store to look and how she was going to run it—and no one had better get in her way.

She paused and looked around at the chaos surrounding her. "It's going to be great when it's finished, Jess," she said softly. "You're going to love it."

Her list for the day was specific and detailed, and she'd stick to it, come hell or high water.

"Get moving, Liddy. Those books aren't going to box themselves."

She started in the front of the store, carefully placing the books into the cartons she, Emma, and Maggie had put together the night before. She'd filled four boxes when she heard the front door open.

". . . but I told him I was really busy, and I'd rather they send the lawyers up here to take my deposition," Grace Flynn was saying.

"Will they do that?" Maggie strolled in behind her daughter. Petite and blonde, she'd dressed much like Liddy, in an old T-shirt and work pants.

"I'm pretty sure but probably not till late fall. I think they'd like me to be as nonhostile as possible." Grace laughed. "As nonhostile as someone can be whose entire life was blown apart by their client."

Liddy stood up and moved the box she'd just finished packing to the side of the aisle. "So they're really prosecuting that woman for hacking into your computer?"

"You betcha. That bitch not only stole my husband, she ruined my career." Petite like her mother, dressed in denim shorts and a tank top the color of lemons, Grace took off her sunglasses, placed them on the counter near Big Red, and pulled her ponytail a little higher.

After Zach, Grace's husband, left her for one of their paralegals, she'd anonymously started a blog, *TheLast2No*, where she'd let rip her feelings about her ex and Amber, his girlfriend. Soon readers who'd been similarly dumped by their significant others had gathered to whine and rant and bitch without fear of judgment. When Amber had hacked into Grace's computer and discovered Grace (screen name Annie Boleyn) was the mastermind behind *TheLast2No*, she'd contacted a reporter and tipped her off. The following day, Grace was exposed as Annie and became the laughingstock of the Philadelphia legal community for her inability to gracefully bow out of her ex's life, the consensus being she was unstable and unprofessional. Leaving Philadelphia and her legal career behind, Grace had moved into the house her mother had purchased in Wyndham Beach, but she was still getting her feet on the ground and trying to reinvent herself. In the wake of the discovery of Amber's illegal hacking, the FBI had been notified, and Amber had been taken into custody.

"But she's out of jail, right?" Liddy walked to the door and locked it. She didn't want any unexpected visitors.

"So I heard through the grapevine. Zach had to bail her out." A sly smile crossed Grace's lips. "He's started his own firm out in Chester County, since no one in Philly would hire him once word got out. Amber is his only employee, because no one wanted her, either. Paralegal, receptionist, assistant, gofer. Karma can be a beautiful thing."

"So they tell me." Liddy tossed her an empty box. "How 'bout you box up some of those books in the children's department?"

"Sure." Grace caught the box with both hands.

"I'll take nonfiction," Maggie said. She grabbed a few boxes that were still flat and carried them halfway down the aisle, where she proceeded to unfold them.

The three worked in silence for several minutes before Liddy called to Maggie, "I saw Brett at Ground Me a while ago. He was with a couple of town council members. Looked like they were having a meeting."

"Oh, yeah. He mentioned he was getting together with a couple of guys for coffee this morning. Something about people complaining about kids drag racing out on Darby Road in the middle of the night." Maggie sorted through the books on the shelves in front of her, placing some into the open box but leaving others on the shelves. A moment later, she said, "Liddy, there are some really old books here, some with missing, torn, and marked-up pages. Maybe you ought to go through them. A few should probably be tossed, but you might think about selling others online instead of having them take up space in the shop. Who knows how long they've been there? Once you rearrange things, you're not going to have room for books that aren't likely to sell."

"Like I have time to run an online business," Liddy replied. "Just toss the ones aside you think are ready for the scrap heap. I trust your judgment." She paused as if reconsidering. "Maybe make a list of those you're throwing out. There could be newer editions we might want to bring in."

"Good idea." Maggie came to the front of the store and picked up her bag. Opening it, she took out a small notepad and a pen.

"I can set up online sales," Grace called from the back of the long room. "I've finished most of your website already. I can work up an online store for you. Easy peasy. Just set aside those books you think should go, Mom, and I'll inventory them. When new titles are brought in, we can add them, too. Many brick-and-mortar bookstores have online shops."

"Thanks, Gracie," Liddy said. "You're hired."

"I accept." Grace looked at her mother. "Do I know how to ace a job interview or what?"

"Where would you keep the books you want to sell?" Maggie walked back to the shelves where she'd been working.

Liddy stopped for a moment to consider. "Well, I have two floors above the shop. I need one for storage." She stepped to the counter and took a sip of coffee. "Grace, you could set up an office for yourself on the second floor and work out of there. We can work out some sort of remuneration schedule once I get this place in order."

"Sounds good. I'm happy to do that. I have lots of time on my hands," Grace reminded her.

"Did you sign up to take the Massachusetts bar exam?" Liddy took another sip before setting her coffee back on the counter.

"Not yet. I don't know what I want to do. I don't even know if I want to be a lawyer anymore." Grace stood at the back of the room, her hands on her hips.

"You worked really hard in law school. You've spent almost ten years as a practicing attorney. A *successful* attorney." Maggie stepped into the aisle to face her daughter. "Are you sure you want to leave that behind?"

"I'm not sure of anything right now. I didn't say I'd never practice law again. I just don't know if, when, or where. I can take the Massachusetts exam anytime. I don't have to decide right now." Grace turned her attention back to the books.

"Besides, I'm having fun creating websites," she added. "I have three clients lined up, and I'm going to work on the mayor and the council to update the town's website. Have you ever looked at it?" Without waiting for a response, she went on, "It's woefully dull and unimaginative and doesn't do justice to this pretty town. Wyndham Beach should have a much more robust tourist business. It's well located, totally charming, has beautiful beaches, good—some truly great—restaurants, pretty B&Bs. But tourists? Not as many as we should have. Why do you suppose that is?" Grace emptied one shelf and moved on to another. "People like to check out websites before they make decisions like where they want to go on vacation or long weekends. They want to be able to look at their choices of where to stay and where to eat. The website we have now is pathetic. No pictures of the cute shops in the center of town or the beautiful historic district. The charming B&Bs are busiest when the academy has a weekend that brings in families. And"—she paused—"the only photo of a beach on the website is of the 'Beach Closed to Swimmers' sign next to the lifeguard stand on the Cottage Street Beach. How inviting is that?"

"And you would do what?" Liddy asked as she emptied the table of bestsellers, noting the newest was six months old.

"Show off the town's strengths, its beauty. Photos of the harbor with the sailboats. People fishing at Cottage Street Beach—who swims there anyway? Drunken teenagers in the middle of the night? The beaches they should focus on are Island Road and Ellis. There should be all sorts of info about places to stay, places to dine, places to shop, including pictures from every season. The shops on the Stroll are fabulous, but who knows about them other than people who live in Wyndham Beach? Oh, and the occasional Alden parent who sticks around for more than the amount of time it takes to watch a lacrosse game. We should be marketing what the town has to offer to those parents, give them a reason to stay here when they visit their kids. There's so much, and yet you'd never know it from looking at the website. I realize our proximity to the Cape could be part of our problem—who doesn't love Cape Cod?—but there's no reason we shouldn't be able to attract people who don't want the crowds on the Cape."

"So are you working up a proposal?" Liddy asked.

"I will as soon as I finish the Meehans' new websites. Separate sites for each of their shops—Ground Me, Dazzle Me, Dress Me Up—and one big site linking those to each other and then to all the shops on the Stroll. I'm having the time of my life."

"Sometimes a change of scenery, a change in routine, is good for the imagination," Maggie said.

"It's sure worked out that way for me. All the years I practiced law, I never thought about changing careers, and I never thought of myself as an especially creative person. But then came the big *boom* in my life, and here I am, and I'm having fun. I guess sometimes you just need to trust in providence or God or fate or whatever you believe in." Grace turned her back and returned to her book sorting.

"It's wise to keep all the doors open," Liddy said. "You never know what might come through next." She directed her gaze to Maggie. "Take your mother, for example."

Maggie and Grace both laughed.

"Yeah, Mom kept the doors open, all right," Grace said, a glint in her eyes. "And look where she is now. Back with her old boyfriend, reunited with her lost son. Even found a couple of grandkids she hadn't known about. If Joe and Natalie hadn't sent their spit into the same genealogy site, Mom, chances are he never would have found you or Brett."

"Well, that would have happened even if you'd stayed in Pennsylvania," Liddy reminded her.

"True." Maggie nodded. "Natalie and Joe had been communicating for several months before I knew anything about it. And I guess at some point Brett and I would have been talking once Joe made it clear he wanted to meet us. But without Brett and I both being here in Wyndham Beach, I don't think we would have developed a relationship again."

"Yeah, if you'd stayed in Philadelphia, who knows? You might have met someone else," Liddy noted.

Maggie shrugged. "I like to think things play out the way they're supposed to, you know?"

Not really, Liddy could have said. *Why was Jessie dying the way it was supposed to be? Why did my husband leave me when I needed him the most?*

The women worked in silence for several minutes. Finally, Grace said, "I have the kids' books packed up. What are we doing with the boxes?"

"I was thinking we'd just lug them all into the middle of the room," Liddy told her.

"Wouldn't it have been easier to leave them on the shelves while the walls are being painted?" Grace asked.

Liddy shook her head. "No, because while the walls are being painted, the bookcases are going to be painted as well."

"Huh." Grace stepped into the aisle to inspect one of the bookcases she'd just emptied. "What color?"

"White. The books will stand out better against a white background."

"But the shelves will get dirty and show wear faster on white," Maggie pointed out.

"You have a better idea?" Liddy dropped the book she'd been holding, and it fell into the box with a thud.

"I kind of like the natural wood." Maggie ran her hand over the shelf she'd just emptied. "I think just cleaning them would improve the appearance."

"Hmmm. Maybe." Liddy considered the option.

"Or maybe you can have them sanded and refinished in a light stain," Maggie suggested.

"I don't have the time nor the inclination to sand down all those shelves and then stain them in addition to everything else I need to do. I want to open right after Labor Day."

"Hire someone." Maggie joined Liddy at the front of the store.

Liddy finished the last of her coffee. "I guess I could give Shelby's a call. See if they can fit me into his schedule and how much he'd cost me."

"Who?" Maggie asked.

"Emmett Shelby? We called him Tuck? He was three years ahead of us in school," Liddy explained. "He's got a contracting business here in town. Did a lot of work on my house over the years. You remember him?"

"Oh, sure. He was on the football team the first year they went to the state championship," Maggie recalled. "He was a lineman or something. He and Brett were friends."

"Right. Anyway, I'll give him a call and see if I can fit him into my budget."

"Liddy, did you get the paint for the walls?" Grace walked toward them, brushing her hands on her shorts and leaving dusty smears.

"Yup. Paint, brushes, rollers, painter's tape, and some tarps. You about ready to roll?" Liddy grinned. "Pun intended."

"I am. Let's just leave the boxes of books where they are. Help me move everything away from that back wall, and I'll get started first," Grace said. "I love to paint."

"Well, you've come to the right place."

"Is Tuck Shelby any relation to Lincoln Shelby?" Grace dragged a box of books farther from the wall.

"He's Linc's father." Liddy turned to Maggie. "Tuck married a girl from Fall River, had Linc and a daughter. His wife died years ago. Maybe twenty or so?" Liddy told her. "Tuck's supposedly semiretired, but he still seems to work a lot. Linc has taken over a lot of the business. They still live on Shelby Island—Tuck's dad's still alive, but I heard he's not expected to be around much longer. He's gotta be in his late eighties, early nineties by now."

"How'd he get the name 'Tuck'?" Grace called from the back of the shop.

"Oh, something to do with him never tucking in his shirt when he was little, so his mother was always yelling at him to *tuck it in*," Liddy said. "It stuck."

"I remember his sister, Angelina, used to call him something that rhymed with Tuck," Maggie reminded Liddy. "Whatever happened to her, Lid? Do you know?"

"Moved out west somewhere back in the nineties. As far as I know, she's never been back. No idea what she's been doing out there all this time. Don't even know if she's still alive." She paused. "Though I guess if she'd died, I'd have heard about it. Now, Tuck's daughter—"

"Okay, ladies, if you're all done gossiping," Grace interrupted. "Let's get these bookcases moved away from the wall and get the tarp down. If we get paint on the floor, we could have a problem."

Liddy nodded. "Excellent point. I'd been thinking I'd have the floor refinished, but it's not practical at this point. I think maybe a good cleaning will do the trick now."

"Could you grab the other end?" Grace stood next to the side of one of the bookcases from the children's section. "We can start painting back here and move around the room and go section to section." She pushed on the bookcase, but it remained in place. "Damn, this thing is heavy."

Liddy took hold of the end of the bookcase opposite Grace. "On three . . . one, two, three."

The bookcase didn't budge.

"This sucker is heavier than it looks. Maggie, give me a hand on this end." Liddy took a step to the right to make room for Maggie to work with her. "Okay. Once again . . . one, two, three . . ."

Despite their collective efforts, the bookcase didn't move.

"Ahhh, Houston, we have a problem." Grace blew out a long breath. "We need brute strength."

"Well, it looks like it's solid oak, so yeah, it's going to be heavy." Maggie glanced at Liddy. "We're not going to be able to do this ourselves. Brett's on duty right now, so he can't help us. Anyone we can call?"

Liddy groaned. "The only person I can think of is Tuck. Maybe if he's free sometime today, he could stop in and give us a hand."

"Is his number on your phone?" Maggie asked.

Liddy tapped the side of her head. "It's in here. I've had to call him so many times over the years the number has been imprinted on my brain."

"Oh?" Maggie raised an eyebrow.

"Like I said, he did all the work on my house. Get that look off your face. It was strictly business."

Liddy went to the front of the store and searched her bag for her phone. Finding it, she tapped in the number she knew by heart.

"Damn. Voice mail," she grumbled. "Tuck, it's Liddy Bryant. I'm down at the bookstore—" She paused. "You know I bought the bookstore, right? 'Cause Fred Lattimore was retiring? Anyway. I'm trying to move some bookcases out of the way so we can paint the walls, and we just can't get them to budge. We think they're solid oak. So I'm calling to see if you might have some time to stop by and maybe give us a hand. Call me when you get a minute, please."

It took Tuck less than a minute to return the call.

"Liddy? Sorry I didn't pick up right away."

"Hey, Tuck. Thanks for calling back," she said.

"So you bought yourself a bookstore." Tuck chuckled.

"I did," she said with no small amount of pride.

"Now, why does that not surprise me?"

"I don't know, why doesn't it surprise you?" Smiling and maybe feeling just a teensy bit flirty, she leaned on the counter.

"I'm guessing you're bored with all that volunteer work and all those town boards you're on. I'm not surprised you'd be wanting to do something for yourself. And I did know Carl was going to sell his dad's store, and it did cross my mind not too long ago you might be looking for someplace to put all that energy of yours. Besides, the bookstore suits you."

"Well, lately the only volunteer work I've been doing is at the art center when Emma needs a hand. But you're right. I needed something that was all mine, and this opportunity came at just the right time."

"I sure wish you much success, Liddy. I hope you have a heck of a time and enjoy your new venture. Now, what can I do for you? Something about moving some bookcases around?"

Liddy explained the situation.

"Sounds like you need some muscle," he said after she finished her rundown. "I can send a few guys over right after their lunch break." He paused. "If I get a few of my men over there within the next hour or so, you'd be good?"

"I'd be ecstatic, are you kidding me?" Liddy gave a thumbs-up to Maggie, who grinned. "Thanks, Tuck."

She hung up and told Maggie, "He's sending some guys over in about an hour to give us a hand. I should probably leave the door unlocked for them." Liddy tossed her empty coffee cup in a nearby trash can. "I never expected those shelves to be so heavy. I'm lucky Tuck's on a job today and is willing to lend us a few hands."

"Nice of him," Maggie said.

"Yeah, he's a good guy."

They resumed culling books from the shelves and boxing them up, occasionally commenting on a title they came across.

Moments later, Liddy went to the door and peered out. "One of Tuck's vans just pulled up out front." She glanced at her watch. "Damn, that was fast, guys," she said as she opened the door. "I'm so happy to see you. You're saving the day."

Three burly young men in their twenties shuffled into the shop. They all wore dark-blue baseball caps, dusty jeans, and dark-blue T-shirts with Shelby & Son on the front, their faces partially covered by sunglasses.

"Boss said you had something you wanted moved?" the first in line said.

Liddy nodded and pointed to the bookcases, which lined the walls of the shop from front to back. "I need those all moved away from the wall so we can paint."

"And who's going to move them back?" a deep, familiar voice boomed from the doorway.

Liddy turned around and smiled without realizing she was doing so. "I thought maybe I'd head out to Route Six and flag down a few truckers. Or I could give my cousin Ron a call. He's a guard out at Barnstable County Correctional Facility. Maybe he could bring me a few buff inmates for a day."

"That would be against the law, Lydia," he said solemnly. "We'd have to report you."

"We'd hate to see Brett take you off in handcuffs." Maggie stepped out from behind a bookshelf.

"Hey, Maggie." Tuck beamed and extended a hand. "How's it going? Long time."

"Going great, Tuck." She joined him and Liddy near the counter and shook his hand. "You?"

"No complaints. Well, none worth talking about, anyway." He glanced around the shop. "You planning on leaving the store set up the way old Fred had it?"

"Not planning any big changes just yet," Liddy said. "For now I just want the walls painted and something done with the bookshelves. I'd thought about painting them but then Maggie thought I might be better off leaving them natural."

"Maggie's right. Once you paint them, you'll have to keep up with it. Why make more work for yourself?" He ran his hand along first the side, then the back of the nearest shelf. "Yeah, solid oak. Nice grain." He wet a finger with saliva and rubbed it on the shelf. "I wouldn't bother sanding. They're already stained. I'd just give them a good cleaning. Dust them first, then a little damp cloth will do just fine. Much more practical and very low maintenance."

"Okay. Thanks." Liddy stuck her hands into her pants pockets. "One less thing to do."

"So show me what needs to be moved and where you want it to go," he said.

"I think your guys are already on it. In the back there . . ." She pointed and he headed for the back of the shop.

"He's looking good," Maggie whispered when Tuck was well past.

"Yeah, he is," Liddy whispered back. "But he's just a friend."

"I bet he could be more if you wanted." Maggie waggled her eyebrows up and down. "Weren't you lamenting not too long ago you had no sex life?"

Liddy pretended to ignore her and followed the voices to the children's section, Maggie laughing softly as she joined her.

"You know, Liddy . . . ," Maggie began.

"Shut. Up." Liddy walked a little faster. Yes, Tuck looked great. The short sleeves of his gray tee barely contained his biceps, and he looked as if he could still play linebacker, a testament, she supposed, to forty-some years of physical labor. His salt-and-pepper hair was still thick, more pepper than salt. All in all, he did, in fact, look pretty damned good for a man who'd turned sixty-two that year.

"Yes, thank you. That's perfect," Grace was saying to the borrowed work crew. "You don't need to move the bookcases any farther. We just need enough room to set up the ladder to reach the top of the wall when we start painting."

"That's a lot of wood trim." Tuck stood with his hands on his hips, surveying the job. He turned and addressed Liddy. "You sure you're up to all that?"

Liddy pointed to Grace. "There's my painter. Ask her."

"I'm up to it," Grace told him.

"That's Grace Flynn, by the way," Liddy told Tuck. "Maggie's daughter."

"Well, Grace Flynn, that's a lot of wall, and like I said, a lot of woodwork. You going to be calling me in a few days when your arms are aching?" he asked, a smile in his voice.

Mariah Stewart

Grace shook her head. "Nothing I haven't done before. It might take me a while since the room is so large, but I'll get it done. And Mom's good with a roller, so I'll have help."

"Let me know if you want a few extra hands, all's I'm saying. We can send in reinforcements if you need them. Liddy's been a good customer and an even better friend for just about all the years I've been in business." Tuck draped an arm around Liddy's shoulders. "I'm happy to be here when she needs a little help."

Liddy turned her head just as Maggie mouthed, *You're blushing.*

Behind his back, Liddy made a one-fingered gesture in Maggie's direction just as the front door opened and closed. She stepped away from Tuck and into the aisle to see who'd come in.

"Hey, Linc," she called to the young man who peered around the first of the bookcases. "We're all back here."

"Is my dad here? I saw the truck out front." Linc Shelby walked toward the gathering at the back of the store. He was taller than his father but just as solidly built. His hair was almost black and his eyes chocolate brown, his face rugged and handsome.

Liddy and Maggie both tried not to stare.

"Right here, son," Tuck called out. "You done over at the Prentiss place already?"

"I need to pick up a few more panels of drywall," Linc said as he surveyed the scene. His eyes fixed momentarily on Grace. "Hey, Grace."

"Hey, Linc," Grace returned the greeting. "If you wouldn't mind," she said to the three young men moving furniture, "pull the others away from the wall so we can work all the way to the front of the store."

Tuck's crew did as they were directed.

"What's going on?" Linc asked.

"Liddy needed a few extra hands today, so we're taking a little break from the job to help her out," Tuck told him.

"Your break is probably over," Liddy said.

24

"I'm not concerned about the time." Tuck watched his men move bookcases away from the wall. "Guys, leave enough space between them so the shelves can be wiped down."

After they'd moved the last one, he turned to Liddy. "That enough room?"

"More than enough. Thank you, boys."

"Anything else we can help you with?" Tuck asked.

"No, thank you. You've done more than enough."

"You sure?" Tuck asked. She nodded, and he turned to his crew of three, who were standing around awaiting orders. "Guys, looks like we're done here. Go on out and get in the truck. I'll be out in a minute."

The three men filed out of the store.

"Tuck, I don't know what we'd have done without you. The three of us pushed and shoved and those damned things wouldn't move an inch." Liddy placed a hand on his arm. "Now, what do I owe you?"

"Consider this a shop-warming gift."

"No, seriously," Liddy protested. "I feel like I'm taking advantage of our friendship. You interrupted your own job to help us out. You should let me do something for you."

Tuck's lips turned up in a broad smile. "Well, then, I'll think about that and let you know. I could probably come up with something."

Behind him, Maggie's eyebrows shot up almost to her hairline, and she grinned at Liddy, who did her best to ignore her.

"Linc, I'm shoving off," Tuck called to his son, who was helping Grace set up a ladder near the back wall.

"I'll see you later at home," Linc called back.

"After you finish up at the Prentiss house, stop on over to the job on Allen Street. We could use you," Tuck said.

"Can't." Linc pulled the step side of the ladder so it opened up fully. "Gotta pick the kids up at three, and Duffy has a soccer game at three thirty in Fairhaven."

"I thought that was tomorrow." Tuck frowned.

"Nope. Today."

Tuck shrugged and glanced at Liddy. "Gotta keep up with the grandkids, you know?"

Liddy didn't know, but she smiled anyway as Tuck left the shop.

Linc straightened out the legs of the ladder. "It's a little wobbly, but it should be fine. It might not be tall enough, though." He seemed to gauge the height of the wall. "Give us a call if this one doesn't work out for you. We can bring you a taller one."

"Thanks. We'll do fine." Grace began to arrange her painting supplies.

"Well, you might want to . . ."

"No, really. It's fine. But thank you."

"Well. Okay, then." Linc brushed his hands off on his shirt and told Liddy, "I'm looking forward to seeing this place when you're done. I'm sure it will be a huge improvement."

"Sweeping the floors would be a huge improvement," she replied and walked him to the door. "But we're hoping to do better than that."

"You need anything . . . ," he said before he opened the door.

"I know who to call. Thanks, Linc." Liddy closed the door behind him and locked it. She returned to the back of the room, fanning herself. "Anyone else notice the temperature in the room go up a few degrees when Linc came in?"

Grace ignored her, but Maggie laughed.

"If I were half a lifetime younger," Liddy said.

"You'd still be too old for him," Maggie teased. "But yes, he really is handsome. Coal-black hair and deep brown eyes. What a combination."

"Looks a lot like his daddy did when he was young. Only Linc is more settled than Tuck was. I think Tuck was still riding that old Harley of his up until a few years ago. Then he wrecked it out on Calhoun Drive. Damn near killed himself." Liddy took a bottle of water from her bag, opened it, and took a long drink. "I guess he figured it was a sign from God he should move on to something safer. Didn't even get the bike repaired, just let the insurance company keep it."

"I guess that would be sobering," Maggie said.

Grace joined them at the front of the store and reached for the bottle of iced tea she'd earlier left on the counter. "Ugh. It's warm," she said after tasting it.

"What do you think, Grace? Thumbs-up on Linc?" Maggie asked.

Grace shrugged and took another sip of iced tea.

"Something wrong with your eyes?" Liddy was clearly skeptical. "That boy's everyone's type."

Grace dismissed the subject with a wave of her hand. "I'm going to run across the street and pick up some lunch. What can I bring you guys?"

"We'll meet you over there. I think we could all use a break right about now," Liddy announced.

Maggie nodded, straightened up, and rubbed her back. "Best idea you've had all day."

"I'll get a table. Don't be too long, okay?" Grace left the store without waiting for a response.

Liddy and Maggie stared at the closed door, then at each other.

Liddy picked up her bag. "Think maybe your daughter needs glasses?"

"One might wonder," Maggie said.

"You'd think a newly divorced woman would be really happy to meet a guy like Linc."

"Yeah, you'd think." Maggie took her sunglasses from her bag and slid them on. "I've about given up trying to understand my kids. The only one who is pretty much out there with his feelings is Joe, and I didn't raise him. We're still getting to know each other; maybe that's why he's so open." She held the door open for Liddy. "Nothing can make you crazier than your kids."

"Tell me about it," Liddy muttered as she dug in her purse for the key to the shop door. She paused in the doorway, then glanced over her shoulder to the back of the long room to the children's section. The reading rug, now worn in places and so dirty the colors were no longer clear, lay folded and forgotten. She tried to call up the tableau she'd seen earlier, but Jessie was no longer there.

Liddy softly closed the door behind her and locked it.

Chapter Two

Liddy eased herself into the tub of hot water, submerged to her chin, and uttered a soft sigh. Over the past week, she'd discovered muscles she hadn't known she had, and every one of them was screaming for mercy. Her nightly hot baths had gone a long way toward relieving the pain, but she wished she had one of those lovely deep tubs with rushing, whirling water to sink into. Like the one Maggie had in her master bath. Liddy'd come *this close* to asking if she could use that tub just one time, but it was too weird a request to make even of your best friend. Besides, she reminded herself, Brett was at Maggie's just about every night, and it would be even more weird to lounge in someone else's bathtub while that someone's boyfriend waited to use the shower. Even the thought of all that hot, swirling water around her aching limbs couldn't bring Liddy to put herself into that scenario.

And she knew for a fact Brett was at Maggie's most nights because Grace had told her so in a confidential semi-rant yesterday morning.

"Where's your mom?" Liddy had asked when Grace ducked into the shop alone, water from an unexpected storm cascading from her wide-brimmed hat.

Grace had rolled her eyes. "It's Brett's late day. So they sleep in. Or whatever it is they're doing."

Liddy had nodded knowingly just before a wave of unbidden and unwanted memories crashed over her. Mornings when she'd awaken to an arm snaking around her waist, soft breath against her neck, whispered words of love. Hot kisses along her shoulder. Days when she and Jim had "slept in."

Bitterness had swept through her to banish the images. The same man who'd once made her feel loved unconditionally had left her to cope with loss so fierce she still could feel it in every bone in her body. Jim had walked out on her quietly and without drama when she'd needed him, without offering an explanation, regardless of how lame it might have been. She still didn't understand why he hadn't needed her as much, or why he'd left, but she did know she'd never forgive him.

Liddy had taken a deep breath and wiped away the ghosts of her marriage. "Well, so, are they loud? Is that the problem?"

"Loud . . . ? Oh, gross. That's my mother we're talking about." Grace had gone past her to the rear of the shop and taken off her raincoat at the back door. She'd stepped out onto the small porch, shaken the water off her coat, then hung it inside on a hook. "I'm thinking maybe I should look for a place of my own. Something small and not too expensive. I feel like one of those people the television folks make fun of all the time. You know, the thirtysomething-year-olds who are always the butt of jokes, like guys who live in their parents' basement and spend all their time on their computer."

"There aren't many apartments in Wyndham Beach, and I doubt any of them are cheap," Liddy had said. "And those few are probably rented. But if you're serious, you can look on the bulletin board at the general store. People place all sorts of notices there." She'd set the papers she'd been holding on the counter. "Are you serious about moving out?"

"I don't know. I think so." Grace had sighed. "On the one hand, Mom deserves to have this time with Brett. She doesn't need her grown daughter hanging around all the time. If she and Brett are ever going to work things out, they need time alone to be together. On the other hand, it's a big step for me to commit to renting a place here when I'm not sure what I want to do in the long run."

"Most rental places are going to require a one-year lease."

"I don't know where I'll be in six months, let alone a year. Of course, if I found a place I loved, that could change."

"Well, if I hear of anything, I'll let you know," Liddy had offered, and they'd gone about their business, Grace painting the front wall, Liddy washing down the bookshelves.

The bathwater had chilled while Liddy replayed her conversation with Grace. Immediately after getting out of the tub, she grabbed the closest towel and wrapped it around her. The evening air was cool, and she cursed having left the bedroom window open. She wrapped a second towel around her shoulders as she went to the window and closed it. Nearby her phone pinged to let her know she had a new voice mail waiting to be heard. She listened to the message on her way back to the bathroom.

"Hey, it's Emma. I have something for you I know will put a big smile on your face. I'm coming by to drop it off. Be there around seven fifteen or so."

Liddy checked the time and noted she had half an hour before Emma arrived. She lightly towel dried her long hair, then wrapped it atop her head and secured it before pulling on a pair of white cotton ankle-length pants. She reached for a vintage Blondie T-shirt. It was half over her head when she reconsidered, pulled it off, and exchanged it for the tee Emma's son, Chris, had made to mark the occasion she, Emma, and Maggie had traveled to Charlotte, North Carolina, to see Chris's band, DEAN, in concert. Liddy smiled as she pulled on the shirt, which sported an image of a shaggy-haired Chris. The three old friends had danced in the aisle that night, singing along with the much-younger crowd. They'd laughed when Maggie had tossed a package of Junior Mints onstage to Chris while women around them tossed their underwear. (Chris had pocketed the candy and ignored the rest, possibly in deference to his mother, who was seated in the first row.) They'd shed a few tears when Chris had introduced Emma to the crowd via a lovely tribute before jumping from the stage to hug his mom. The next day, they'd gone to a tattoo parlor and gotten matching tattoos—three curling ocean waves—to commemorate their lasting friendship. All in all, it had been a grand weekend, one they hoped to repeat when Chris's concert schedule allowed.

Liddy made her way downstairs to the kitchen with twenty minutes to spare. She sliced some cheese and washed some grapes, arranging them on a pretty plate. She added apple wedges and wheat crackers and had just set an unopened bottle of wine and two glasses on the counter when the doorbell rang.

"Come on in." Liddy opened the door and stepped aside to allow her friend to enter.

Emma was petite, just a few inches over five feet. She wore her dark hair in the same style she'd always worn it—a neatly trimmed pixie with deep bangs—and she hadn't gained an ounce since high school. She wore pearls with just about everything except her bathing suit (*With jeans? Yes, and so Emma!*), and they never looked out of place. Even Liddy, whose own style tended more toward comfortable than stylish, admired the fact Emma could wear anything, and it always looked perfectly Emma. Tonight she wore a cotton shift in pastel colors and blue leather sandals. And, of course, a short strand of pearls.

"Nice shirt." Emma's eyes were shining as she waved an envelope at Liddy. "I couldn't wait to come over to give you this. Honestly, it's been burning a hole in my pocket since this morning. I would have brought it right to the bookstore, but there was no one else at the art center until late this afternoon, and we had classes going straight through till six."

"So hand it over." Liddy grabbed the envelope and headed for the kitchen, Emma keeping pace. A glance at the raised return address made Liddy's heart skip a beat. The Toller was the big-time art gallery in Boston where Emma had arranged for a showing of some of Jessie's work. She took a deep breath and came to a standstill. "Should I be sitting down?"

Emma nodded. "Not a bad idea." She took Liddy's elbow and steered her into the kitchen to the U-shaped nook overlooking the backyard. "Sit. Then open. Then happy dance."

Liddy slid onto the banquette seat. Before pulling out the envelope's contents, she glanced at Emma, who sat across from her. Emma was grinning ear to ear.

"Oh, for God's sake, Lydia, look at the damned thing," Emma demanded.

"I'm looking." She then raised her eyes to meet Emma's. "This is real?"

"Of course it's real. The gallery sold the five paintings we sent them, and if you read the letter, they're looking for more. So whenever you want, I can send a few more from the canvases we have at the art center, as long as you're okay parting with them. I'll contact Malcolm Toller and let him know when you decide."

"This is amazing," Liddy said, still in slight shock. "I figured a few hundred for the big ones, but . . ."

"Oh ye of little faith." Emma grinned and tapped the envelope. "There's a breakdown there on the second sheet of the letter, showing how much each of the works sold for. I was very optimistic when we agreed to send those paintings to the Toller—they have a reputation of only handling what they consider sure things—but I have to admit, the numbers surprised even me. I mean, I did consult with them when they were pricing the work, but it's not unusual for there to be a certain amount of negotiation when it comes to sales." She reached for Liddy's hand. "Oh, my friend, I'm so happy for you."

"I can put a new roof on the bookstore if it needs it," Liddy murmured. "I went up to the third floor yesterday after the storm and found water dripping down the wall. I damn near died. The last thing I need is another big expense outside what I'd already budgeted. But this . . ." She happily waved the check. "This gives me some breathing room." She squeezed Emma's hand. "Thank you so much for arranging this for me. I don't know how to thank you." She paused. "Actually, I do. You're acting as my agent, so you should receive an agent's cut. What would that be?"

"Don't be ridiculous." Emma waved a dismissive hand. "I was merely acting as your friend who happened to know someone who knew someone at the gallery."

"That *someone* you knew is your son, and we both know he personally contacted the gallery owner to inquire if the Toller had any of Jessica Bryant's work on hand. That sparked the interest in the showing here in Wyndham Beach."

Emma shrugged. "Chris and Jessie were friends. He recognized her talent a long time ago. He welcomed a chance to bring her work to the attention of others. I wouldn't be surprised if he'd bought one of those paintings himself just to get the ball rolling."

"I'd have given him any he wanted," Liddy said, remembering the night of the concert in Charlotte how Chris had pulled her aside and shared a memory of growing up with her daughter and expressed once again how sad he was she was gone, how much he missed her when he came back to Wyndham Beach. She met Emma's eyes across the table and quoted her friend's understated praise of her son. "He's a good boy."

Emma laughed good-naturedly. "I know you and Maggie get a kick out of repeating that mantra of mine, but he is indeed a good boy."

"Well, I owe that good boy big-time. Let me know when he's coming home again. The least I can do is cook his favorite meal for him." Liddy slid the check back into the envelope. If the bank were open, she'd have been putting on her shoes and heading out the front door.

"I wish I knew when he'd be home," Emma said wistfully. "He travels so much. And . . ."

"And what?"

"I think he's seeing someone."

Liddy laughed. "Em, honey, your boy is always seeing someone. He's an international rock star."

"No, I mean I think he's seeing someone special. I think he has a girlfriend," Emma confided.

"*A* girlfriend? As in, just one? That would be news." Liddy got up and poured wine into the glasses she'd earlier set out, then handed one to Emma. "What makes you think that?"

"Just a feeling." She appeared to think it over. "I can't put my finger on anything in particular. Just little things like he said he wasn't taking a date to the music awards."

"So?" Liddy brought the cheese and fruit to the table.

"So he always has a date for those award things. He never goes alone."

"Did you ask him about it?"

Emma shook her head. "I don't want to be the mother who constantly pries into her kid's life. He's in his thirties. He doesn't have to answer to me."

"If he had a girlfriend, he'd be taking her, right?" Liddy thought aloud. "So maybe he's just taking a break from, you know, *dating*. Whatever that means these days."

"Maybe." Emma sounded unconvinced. "Or maybe his girlfriend wasn't available for some reason."

"What woman wouldn't be available for Chris Dean?" Liddy scoffed. "Unthinkable."

Emma shrugged. "I guess."

"He'd let you know, I'm fairly sure, if there was someone special, and he'd bring her home to meet you. Despite being who he is, he's still a good boy." Liddy grinned.

"And yet again, you mock me." Emma laughed.

"Nope. Just agreeing with you. You raised him right, Em. He's still the polite, respectful young man we all knew when he was growing up."

"God, I hope so." Emma expelled a long breath. "All I really want for him is to find the right girl and be happy."

"And live happily ever after right here in Wyndham Beach. And have lots of kids for you to spoil," Liddy teased.

"What's wrong with wanting your family nearby? Or wanting to be a grandmother?"

"Nothing. I'm just teasing." Liddy topped off their wine. When Emma began to protest, Liddy reminded her, "You're not driving. You're walking less than two blocks. You can handle it."

And at least you have the prospect of becoming a grandparent, which I do not, Liddy could have said, but she held her tongue. It wasn't Emma's fault. It was just one more thing Jess's suicide had taken from her.

Time to change the subject.

"So it looks like Maggie and Brett have picked up where they left off, lo, those many years ago," Liddy said.

Emma nodded. "They belong together. They always have. It was inevitable they'd find their way back to each other. It's good they have time to spend together, now she's moved back home."

Liddy raised an eyebrow, and Emma asked, "What?"

"I have it on good authority they're spending *a lot* of time together."

"You say that as if it's a bad thing."

"No, I say that as if they're practically living together." Liddy picked up a cracker and took a bite.

"Well, she did mention he stayed over a few times."

"More than a few. It's, like, practically every night."

"Did Maggie tell you that?"

Liddy shook her head. "Grace did. She's thinking about looking for a small place to rent so she can move out and give the lovebirds some space."

"Was she serious? About moving out?" Without waiting for a response, Emma said, "I wonder how Maggie would feel about that."

"I think Maggie would be okay about it, but I don't think Grace has discussed it with her, so don't say anything unless Maggie brings it up."

"Oh, I wouldn't. So I guess Grace is planning on staying in Wyndham Beach at least for a little while. Is she looking for an apartment here in town?"

"She said she isn't sure where she wants to go or what she wants to do in the long run, but for now she's staying, and yes, she's looking. She's built up quite a nice business creating websites. She's very creative. She's doing a lot of work for me, including setting up online book sales; plus she'll be working in the shop a few hours every day once we open. So I hope she stays around. I'd hate to have to find someone else who can do all the things she's doing. She spends almost as much time at the shop as I do."

"Good luck to her finding someplace reasonable to live. There's not much available in terms of rentals, and I understand those few are quite expensive."

"I did caution her, and I suggested she check the bulletin board at the general store."

"I was in there this morning and I checked out the board—force of habit, you know. No one goes in or out without checking the board. The only rental notice I saw was for a room on Allen Scott's third floor."

"Which is probably unheated, and comes with the possibility of that old coot popping in unannounced. I will make certain she knows not to follow up on that one."

Emma appeared about to say something, but did not until Liddy asked, "What?"

"I was just thinking. You have the carriage house with a full apartment in it, and . . ."

"The apartment is Jessie's," Liddy snapped.

"Of course." Chastised, Emma looked down into her wineglass. "I shouldn't have . . . I'm sorry."

Liddy sighed. "*I'm* sorry. I shouldn't have jumped on you. For one thing, I doubt Grace would want to live in the apartment where her friend took her life. For another, and it probably sounds irrational, I can't bear the thought of cleaning all of Jess's things out of the apartment and filling it with someone else's belongings. I'm not over it, Em."

"And you shouldn't be." Emma got up and, gesturing for Liddy to scoot over on the bench seat, sat next to her and put an arm around her shoulder. "No one should ever expect to 'get over' losing a child. You do have to move on with your own life, and I must say I'm so proud of you for doing that, even in the wake of Jim's leaving and your divorce. Buying the bookshop was a brilliant move on your part, and I love you're doing it. But your moving on doesn't mean leaving Jess behind."

"She's with me every day." Liddy searched her pockets for a tissue as tears began to flow.

"Of course she is. She always will be. I don't know if I could go on if something happened to Chris. I worry about him all the time, and I pray for him every morning and every night." She smiled weakly. "I have my entire family praying for his safety."

Liddy forced a smile of her own. "Nothing like having a family of ministers on your prayer chain."

"Yup, my dad and my brother are on the case." Emma got up and retrieved the box of tissues from a nearby counter and placed them in front of Liddy.

"I had no idea you were so worried about Chris." Liddy pulled a tissue from the box and wiped her face, took a second, and blew her nose.

"He performs in all these big stadiums. He flies everywhere around the world. I worry about some fanatic setting off a bomb, like what happened at that concert in England a few years ago—that suicide bomber?—or smuggling a gun into the arena and shooting up the place."

Emma visibly shivered. "Why does anyone do that batshit crazy stuff?"

Emma's use of *batshit crazy*—an expression not normally in her vocabulary—was a clear indication she had some serious anxiety issues.

"And plane crashes," Emma went on. "I worry about hijackings and faulty engines and wings falling off. I know it's excessive. And it's probably all unfounded. But he's all I have."

"I understand," Liddy told her. And she did understand. Still, Emma's anxiety seemed over the top. "But you might want to talk to a counselor. It might help. You know, talk out your fears."

"I just did that."

"I meant with a professional, someone who might have some constructive suggestions to help you cope."

"I am coping just fine."

"Of course you are." Liddy hoped she didn't sound sarcastic or patronizing. "Have you let Chris know how you feel?"

"Are you kidding? There's nothing he can do about it except change his life, which he isn't about to do, nor should he, just because his mother conjures up the worst possible scenario every time he announces a trip."

"I guess all this has something to do with the fact you're hoping he does actually have a serious girlfriend, so he'll maybe settle down in one place for a while. Preferably in Wyndham Beach."

"I can't deny it's crossed my mind. But you know, he only dates these high-profile women who live in Manhattan or LA or Paris or Rome or London. Models. Actresses. Other singers. I can't see any of them wanting to live here, in this little out-of-the-way beach town, where the Fourth of July parade is the most exciting thing that ever happens."

"Have you met any of these women?"

"No," Emma admitted.

"Then maybe you shouldn't judge. Maybe they're more down to earth than you give them credit for."

Emma rolled her eyes.

Liddy ignored the eye roll. "Look, Chris is a smart boy. When the time comes for him to choose a life partner, he'll pick right."

"Oh, of course he will. I should have more faith in him. And I shouldn't let my imagination carry me off to dark places." Emma gave Liddy's arm a squeeze. "Thanks. I feel better now."

"You're welcome." Liddy sniffed back what she hoped would be the last of her tears that night.

"Getting back to Grace. If I hear of anything for rent, I'll let her know," Emma said.

"I guess I could offer to let her stay in my guest suite." Liddy rolled a grape on the table from one hand to the other. "Then again, having Grace stay in my house and work in my shop might be a bit too much togetherness." She paused as a thought occurred. "But there is the little house."

"The little house where Jim had his insurance offices?"

Liddy nodded. "I haven't thought about that place since Jim left and took his business with him. It's at the back of the property—actually, it's on a separately deeded lot, like, where another big house would have been built if they'd wanted to—so it's private. Hmmm. Something to think about."

Liddy topped off their wine, and they sat in silence for a few moments. Finally Liddy motioned for Emma to get up so Liddy could get off the banquette.

"I want your opinion on something." Liddy went to the refrigerator and brought a wedge of cheese back to the table. She cut a few more slices and placed them on the tray. "You remember those greeting cards Jess used to make? The ones she made for birthdays and holidays for family members and friends?"

"Of course. I was the happy recipient of several of those beautiful cards. She was always so thoughtful." Emma settled back onto the seat opposite Liddy.

"Well, I'm thinking about framing some of them and hanging them on the walls of the bookstore."

"That's a great idea. I still have every birthday card she made for me. I bet Chris kept his as well. And, of course, those Christmas cards." Emma swirled the wine around in her glass. "They were so unique and fanciful. Everyone who received one felt special."

"If she sent you one of her cards, you were special to her." Liddy swallowed yet another lump, remembering how every year Jessie designed her holiday cards and sent the same one to everyone on her list. But birthday cards were always one of a kind, designed especially for the recipient. It still amazed Liddy so many people had kept them, as if they knew how much love had gone into each one.

"Oh, you know the ones she made with the little animals on them? The little bears and the monkeys and the baby tigers? I loved those," Emma recalled. "Wouldn't they be perfect enlarged to poster size for the children's section of the shop?"

"I hadn't thought of that, but yeah. That would be . . ."

"Posters!" Emma was visibly excited at the thought. "The ones with the flowers would be just lovely behind the counter. Oh, and you could display some of them at the art center. I bet we could sell them."

"Hmmm." Liddy hadn't thought of that, either.

"Oh! You could have them reproduced as greeting cards. You could sell them at the shop and even take orders online. Grace could add them to the online store she's setting up."

"That's definitely something to think about." Liddy frowned. "Would that be exploitive, do you think? You know, taking advantage of my dead child's talent?"

"I just sold five of Jessie's paintings for several thousands of dollars. How is that any different?"

"I don't know. Maybe because Jess always hoped to sell her paintings, but as far as I know, she didn't have any plans to do anything with her cards."

"Doesn't mean she wouldn't have. Who's to say someone—like maybe me, even—wouldn't have suggested it to her at some point?"

"Maybe. I'll think about it." Liddy pulled a grape from the cluster on the tray and popped it into her mouth.

"You do that. It's a great idea. Not just another source of cash for you but another way to get Jess's name out there, let more people become acquainted with her work and her name."

"There is that." Liddy was going to have to give the idea some serious thought. Getting her daughter the recognition she deserved was important to her.

And, of course, she'd have to talk it over with Jessie, see how she felt about the prospect.

Emma was so intrigued by the thought of all they could do with Jessie's greeting cards, she took off, leaving a half-empty glass of wine on the counter.

"I can't wait to get home to find those cards. I saw them somewhere recently but don't remember where, and it's going to bother me until I find them." As she stepped onto the front porch, she added, "And I'm going to call Chris and see if he still has his and if he knows where they are."

Liddy stood in the doorway for a few minutes, even after Emma disappeared at the end of the block, watching the lengthening shadows as dusk crept in. She locked up, then went into the kitchen, where she grabbed the check from the table and tucked it into the pocket of her pants. Taking her glass of wine to the back deck, she lowered herself onto one of the comfy lounges and momentarily closed her eyes, savoring the gentle breeze laden with the scent of the last of the summer roses blowing across the yard. She finished the wine and set the glass on a nearby table. Her body was tired, and she easily could have fallen asleep, but her mind was racing, reliving the conversation with Emma.

She looked out across the yard, where the white flowers she'd planted in the garden beds here and there glowed in the growing darkness. The path to the carriage house was illuminated by the solar lights she'd installed at the beginning of the summer. There were nights when sleep would not come, nights when she'd followed that path and unlocked the side door, slipped inside, and climbed the steps to the second-floor apartment, where Jessie had lived for the last three years of her life.

"I want to move home, Mom." Jessie had unexpectedly appeared in the kitchen early on a Saturday morning when a curious Liddy had followed her nose to the scent of coffee she had not made. She had found Jessie sitting at the table, her hands wrapped around a mug she'd bought for her father years before on a trip to New York. She'd twisted her long silver-blonde hair in one hand and let it fall over her left shoulder. "I want to paint full-time. Unfortunately, having not sold a damned thing, my art isn't supporting me, so paying rent is a problem."

"Of course you can come home, Jess. You don't even need to ask. Your room is always there for you."

"I was actually thinking of the carriage house."

"You mean the second floor? The apartment?"

Jessie had nodded.

"Oh, honey. No one's lived there for over a decade. I haven't even been in there in at least five years. I'm sure it's a total mess. God knows what kind of critters may have moved in."

"So I can clean it up, fix what needs to be fixed." She had grinned. "Move the wildlife out if necessary. It'll be fine."

"Right now, there's no water, no heat, no utilities of any kind."

"But all that can be hooked up, right?"

"Yeah, but what's wrong with living here in the house?"

"Well, for one thing, I'm almost thirty, and that's too old to be living under the same roof as your parents." Before Liddy could comment, Jess had added, her eyes shining, "And if memory serves correctly, there's that big room across the back with all those windows and all that perfect light. I could set up a studio there. I could work there."

"You could work there and still live here. You don't have to . . ."

"Yeah, Mom. I really do." Jess had fisted her right hand and placed it in the middle of her chest. "I need time to find out if I really am as

43

good as I think I am. I keep feeling like it's now or never. Like time is running out. Like I'm wasting my life waitressing six days a week to make enough to pay the rent. On my day off, I have a million errands to run and I'm exhausted. I've been trying to paint, but I know I can do better. I figured I could get a part-time job here doing something—doesn't matter what—just so I can make enough for food and to pay you and Dad for whatever utilities I use. But if I don't have that rent payment hanging over my head at the beginning of every month, maybe I can do some decent work."

"Your work is more than decent, Jess. You're exceptionally talented. Everyone recognized that long ago."

"Thanks, Mom. But I'm having a hard time supporting myself and finding time to paint. I tried everything I could think of. I had room-mates, but as you may recall, that hasn't worked out so well."

Liddy had recalled. Two party girls who played loud music and entertained their friends four or five nights out of seven.

"I tried living with Cal for a while, but he didn't understand bound-aries. I need to be left alone to work, but he thought when I was home, I should be there for him. The apartment I'm in now is really small, but it's the only thing I could afford on my own. Paying for it eats up all my time and most of my energy, so I'm not getting much done. I could have stayed in that nice town house with Laurie and Sharon, or I could have stayed with Cal and played house, and I'd have as much work to show as I do now. Mom, I need to be by myself. I can't focus when someone else is around. It's like other people's energy gets in my way. If I'm under your roof, as much as I love you and Dad, it would be hard for me to tell you to please go away and let me paint."

Finally, Liddy had nodded. "I get it. I do. And you're right. You need your space."

"I hate to impose on you and Dad, but . . ."

Liddy had held up a hand. "You're not imposing, Jess. This is your home. We're your parents, we love you, and we will always support you, no matter what. But I'm afraid the apartment needs so much work."

Jim had come into the kitchen dressed in his usual weekend garb, worn jeans and a Brown University sweatshirt. "Hello, pumpkin. How's my silver girl?" He'd sung a line from an old Simon and Garfunkel tune—"Bridge over Troubled Water"—and kissed the top of his daughter's head. "Nice surprise, finding you here. What's the occasion? And what apartment are we talking about?"

He'd poured himself a cup of coffee. "And why are we talking about apartments? Are you looking to move again?"

Jim had joined Jess and Liddy at the table and listened as Jess repeated what she'd told her mother.

"Of course you can live there if you feel that's the best place for you. I don't remember the place being all that bad, but we can go take a look." He'd smiled across the table at Liddy. "And we'll fix whatever needs fixing to make it comfortable. Your mom and I have always believed in your talent, Jess. You deserve the time to explore and see where it takes you. Let's get some breakfast; then we'll walk out back and take a look at the old place. See what shape it's in and we'll take it from there."

They'd ended up investing several thousand dollars in updates, but in the end, Jess had gleefully danced through each room, finally declaring, "It's perfect. Everything is perfect." She'd launched herself onto her parents, embracing them both. "I can't thank you enough. You guys are the best!"

"Just be happy. Do your best work," Jim had told her. "Here's your chance to prove to the world you are a serious artist. Time to show everyone what you've got, kiddo."

The feelings the memory of that day brought back rolled themselves into a ball and settled in Liddy's chest, making it hard for her to breathe. She rose from the lounge and went inside for the keys to the carriage house.

When Liddy had first handed over the keys to Jessie, she'd secured them on a metal ring to which she'd added several little charms. An artist's palette. A small green watering can. A kayak. An open book. Jim had teased that some night Jess was going to walk home after having a few drinks at Dusty's and try to unlock the door with the kayak.

Liddy juggled the keys, tossing them up and catching them in her right hand as she followed the long, winding path to the carriage house's side door. She turned on the outside light, fit the key into the lock, swung open the door, and stepped inside. The climb to the second floor was steep, and she was slightly winded by the time she reached the top. She hesitated before snapping on the switch for the overhead light in the kitchen.

Jessie's favorite coffee mug—covered with quips from the old *Seinfeld* TV show—sat on the counter where she'd left it that last morning or the night before. A dish towel carelessly tossed onto the round butcher block table lay where it had landed. The bulletin board next to the door held reminders for a dentist appointment Jess would never keep and the receipt for some art supplies ordered from a shop in Boston. A photograph of Jessie and Pugsly, the dog they'd found running loose on the beach one morning without tags and for whom they'd been unable to find owners. Eight-year-old Jess had been convinced the dog had been sent to her by her recently departed grandmother, and nothing anyone could say had convinced her otherwise. So, of course, they'd kept the dog, who'd become Jess's constant companion, and when Pugsly had died of old age twelve years later, they'd all mourned and buried her in the backyard. That fall Jessie and Liddy had planted a bed of peonies, their shared favorite flower, to mark the spot.

Liddy stepped tentatively into the open living area, where the scent of ashes still lingered in the fireplace and folded magazines rested atop a pile of four-year-old newspapers on the coffee table. Rings on the table's wooden surface remained where cups or bottles had left their mark. The shades on the front windows were all the way up, and light from the full moon inched its way across the wood floor. The door to Jess's studio was half-open, and Liddy hesitated before pushing it aside. She stood in the doorway, her heart beating loudly, before turning on the light.

The room was as she'd left it when she and Emma had gone through the canvases Jess had left leaning against every wall and every piece of furniture. As far as Liddy knew, her daughter had not attempted to sell one piece while she'd been living there. It had been left to Liddy to decide what to do with the work Jessie had painted over the course of the three years she'd lived in the carriage house.

"You did it, girl. *Sold. Out.* All five pieces we sent to the Toller Gallery. Sold," Liddy announced to the silent room and took the check from her pocket and unfolded it. "See here? I hope you're proud of yourself. I'm proud of you. And I'm grateful to you. Unless you find a way to tell me otherwise, this money is going into the bookshop, like money to order books from the publishers. I wasn't even sure of how any of that worked, but I'm learning. I can't thank you enough. I know you're looking out for your mama, and I appreciate it."

She walked around the room, from time to time stopping to study some of the paintings that had not been sent out the first time.

"Now the Toller wants more of your work. I hope you're okay with that." She added wistfully, "Your reputation is growing, sweetheart. I only wish to God you were here to enjoy it." She paused. "I don't know what you can see or hear where you are. Sometimes I feel so strongly you are right here, right in the room with me. Other times, I don't feel you at all, and I don't know where you are. Are there other places you need to go? I mean, I know I've asked this before, but I don't understand whatever dimension you're in or where, exactly, it is. I guess we're not supposed to know that, right, while we're living this earthly life? I just know sometimes it feels like you're around, and I love those times. Sometimes I imagine your beautiful spirit is like Tinker Bell, only invisible, hovering around me and sharing my space.

"I've pretty much reconciled myself to never knowing why you had to leave us. Why you made that decision, why you kept to yourself whatever was hurting you so much. I would have moved heaven and earth to help you, to keep you here with us." She stared at a smear of paint on the floor for a long time.

"Oh. I almost forgot. There's something else I need to talk to you about. Those wonderful, fanciful, beautiful greeting cards you used to make. You know people still remember those? Emma and Maggie still have the ones you sent them, and Emma thinks Chris still has some of his somewhere. And Grace still has hers."

She walked to the back wall, where the enormous window looked out into the night.

"Grace is back—I'm guessing you know that. She's been helping me a lot with the shop. You probably know that, too." Liddy smiled. "So here's the thing about the cards you used to make. I'm thinking about having a few of those made into posters to hang in the shop. I'm pretty sure you'd approve. But Emma thinks I should go a little further and have the cards reproduced to sell. You know, like a whole line of greeting cards. Holiday cards and birthday cards. I like the idea. I like having more of you out into the world so your work can be admired by more people. I just don't know how you'd feel. I mean, would you feel I was exploiting your memory by turning those beautiful bits of you into something commercial? Would you rather we keep those private? I don't know. I need you to let me know, okay?"

With a glance at the closed door of Jessie's bedroom—the one room in the apartment Liddy had not been able to enter since the morning

Jim had found their daughter's lifeless body on her bed, the note she'd written clutched in her hand—Liddy left the studio and walked straight back to the kitchen, turning off lights as she passed from one space into the next. "Love you, Jess. Always," she said before she went down the steps. She locked the door behind her, then took the path back to her waiting house, sadness trailing behind her like a shadow.

Chapter Three

Moonlight flowed through Liddy's bedroom window and cast angled shadows on the bed, where sleep had eluded her since she'd lain down three hours earlier. Finally, she got up, turned on the lamp next to the bed, and reached for the notebook and pen on the table. She'd long since learned not to trust to memory those brilliant ideas that came to her in the middle of the night. For more than an hour, a seemingly endless stream of things she needed to do in the shop had wound and rewound through her brain, and she knew she wasn't going to sleep until she wrote them down.

Her to-do list spilled over onto the pad as she scribbled on a clean page. There was so much to do before opening day, and since she was determined to have her grand opening on the Tuesday after Labor Day—the traditional move-in day for the students at Alden Academy as well as the first day of school for the locals—she had a lot to accomplish in a very short period of time. It was important for her to attract the attention of all those wealthy parents who dropped their kids at their dorms before they headed back to the highway. She knew exactly what she had to do to call attention to her shop when the families stayed for lunch at Mimi's or the Harbor House, or stopped for coffee at Ground Me. And, of course, there were the local parents who would want a little me time after having deposited their kids at school on opening day. She needed to bring them in as well. After all, while the out-of-towners might be her bonus customers, the residents of Wyndham Beach would be her bread and butter if she could attract their attention and assure them Wyndham Beach Reads was not the old Wyndham Beach bookstore. While she wouldn't be selling textbooks, she had put in a request to both the local public and private schools' English departments for a list of required reading, and she planned on setting up that big front window with current bestsellers.

Liddy made a list of all the places she wanted Grace to leave flyers announcing the grand opening. The bulletin board in the general store. All the shops on the Stroll. Three B&Bs. Ground Me. The art center. Her mind was racing faster than her ability to think, so she started abbreviating. CS for the cheese shop. RP for Ray's Pizza. SFS for Simmons Fine Spirits. She only hoped she could remember what all those initials stood for when she got up in the morning.

She'd had Grace add a coupon to the flyers, promising a one-time twenty percent discount on all purchases made on her grand opening day. She was banking on the discount to provide additional incentive to the local customers to give the revamped shop a try.

She needed a new sign to replace the old one that had hung over the shop's front window for as long as she could remember. Wyndham Beach Books was the official name of Fred's shop, but she needed something new and different. Not that there was anything wrong with the name, but it was associated with years of Fred's neglectful ownership in the minds of the locals, and she had to change that. She'd played with any number of names. Liddy's Books. Jessie's Corner, which was her sentimental favorite, but everyone in town knew about Jessie, and Liddy was afraid it would feel like a sad place to the people who'd known her daughter. Plus, as Maggie had pointed out when they'd discussed the possibilities, people who weren't local might ask who Jessie was, which meant Liddy could find herself repeating the story over and over, because if anyone asked, Liddy'd be inclined to tell it all rather than offer the short answer, "My daughter." Instead, Maggie suggested

Wyndham Beach Reads, which Liddy loved. She'd designed the sign on paper and had given the mock-up to Tuck, who'd promised it would be in place on opening day.

Liddy had put a star next to all the things she wanted to discuss with Tuck, starting with an update on the sign. She knew she was going to end up owing him a small fortune, but there was no one else she'd trust to do things exactly as she wanted them done. Through the years, he'd been the go-to guy for projects large—like the deck and the remodeling of her master suite and the carriage house—and small, like the repairs on her back-porch steps, and they'd always seemed to be on the same wavelength. He was always booked, though, so she was grateful he'd carved out some time for her.

She thought about Grace again, and wondered if she was still thinking about moving out of Maggie's house. Recalling Jess's need for privacy, Liddy was of the opinion Grace should be on her own. Her guest suite should be reserved for guests, Liddy reminded herself, and the apartment in the carriage house was and would remain off limits.

But there was the little house.

She added that to the list of things to discuss with Tuck. Even if Grace decided not to move out of her mother's house—which would be a mistake in Liddy's opinion—Liddy should consider the possibility of using the little house as a rental property. Jim had used it as offices for years, so she could rent it out commercially. Or she could remodel it for living quarters, if not for Grace, then perhaps for someone else looking for a small house. The floor plan would require some reconfiguring— *How much would it cost for walls to be moved?* she wondered—but she should consider it. She double-starred *little house* on her list.

Just thinking about all she still had to do and the narrow window of time in which to do it exhausted her. She leaned back on the pillows and, without bothering to turn off the lamp, closed her eyes, and having moved all those *musts* from her brain onto paper, she fell into the best sleep she'd had in weeks.

~

"I need to have the exterior as attractive as I can make it in a week's time." Liddy stood on the sidewalk outside the shop, her hands on her hips, and shared her vision with Tuck. "The building already has that Tudor look—though you have to wonder why in a town of seventeenth- and eighteenth-century clapboard houses, so many of the shops were built in that style."

"A lot of these old shops were built by the same guy who designed the academy. All that Tudor brown and half-timber there on the harbor? Wouldn't do it that way myself, but then again, I wasn't around back when the school was built." Tuck stepped to the front of the shop and flaked off a bit of white paint from around the window. "Yeah, you do need new paint out here. The mullions all need to be repainted. Washing the glass on both sides would probably help, too."

"It's on the list."

"And the door . . ." He inspected it closely. "The wood's not in bad shape, but God knows how many coats of paint are on it. I'd recommend taking it off, sanding it down, and repainting it."

Liddy frowned. "How long would that take? I can't leave the shop without a door."

"I can have it done in one day if I start early enough in the morning."

"Okay, so you have my list. Want to take it home and price it all out and give me a call?"

"That's what I intend on doing." He folded up the paper she handed him and stuck it in the back pocket of his work jeans.

"I know you must have a ton of work this time of year, especially after that storm a few weeks back. I heard a few houses caught some damage, falling tree limbs and water seeping in, like I did. So I appreciate you coming right over and taking a look at things here."

"Not as busy as I used to be since I passed on most of the jobs to my son. Construction is a young man's game, Liddy."

"You're not that old, Tuck."

"Old enough I can't kneel and bend and lift the way I used to without something giving me pain. Knees, shoulders, back, neck . . . everything's taken a beating over the years. Linc is young and strong, and he loves the work and is good at what he does."

"He learned from the best."

Tuck grinned. "I like to think so. I spent my entire life building up Shelby and Son. I'm grateful Linc wants to take over."

"You're telling me you're retiring?"

"Semiretiring."

"So you do still work."

"Only the light stuff, and projects I find interesting or challenging." He took a few steps closer to Liddy and lowered his voice. "Or for people I like."

"Well, I guess I'm lucky you like me, because I have an endless list of projects." Liddy met his eyes, and for a moment she wondered if he might be openly flirting with her.

Tuck Shelby? Nah.

"Of course I like you. We've been friends for years, Lid. I haven't forgotten when I was first starting out, you and Jim hired me for one of my first big jobs."

"The carriage house." *We've been friends for years.* Yeah. Not flirting. Was she just a teeny bit disappointed? Um, yeah, she was.

He nodded. "Converting that second floor into an apartment for Jim's mom. Shame she didn't get to live there very long."

"After her stroke, we had to move her to an assisted care facility, and the apartment sat vacant for years until you came back and fixed it up for Jessie."

"That job was a godsend for me. After you guys told other people I'd done a good job—"

"A great job," she corrected him. "You did a great job, and we were happy to serve as a reference for you."

"That reference opened a lot of doors for me, Liddy. So whatever you need, whenever you need it, I'm just a phone call away. Retired, semiretired, or spending my days fishing, I'm always here for you."

"Well." Liddy cleared her throat. "Good to know."

"So I'll start on the front on Monday. The guys can do the painting, I'll take care of the door myself." He ran a hand over the wood. "I'm wondering what I'll find under all this paint."

"I'm curious myself. By the way, how's the sign coming along?"

"It's almost done. It just needs another coat of paint, and it'll be ready for hanging next week."

"I can't wait to see it." She pictured the front of the shop with the brand-new **WYNDHAM BEACH READS** sign out front, and another vision popped into her head. "Tuck, if I bought a flower box for under that window, could you install it for me?"

He looked at the space she indicated. "You mean a window box? One that would go the entire length of the window?"

She nodded.

He pulled a tape measure from a pocket in his tool belt and measured the length, then whistled. "A window box that long is going to have to be custom made, and it should probably be freestanding, since the window is so low, and God only knows how much weight that lower section of stucco could handle."

"Hmmm. I guess that would be pretty expensive."

"Custom has its price."

"So I guess I'll stick to planters on either side of the window. That should be doable, right?"

"Doable, sure." He stared at the front of the store as if seeing something she couldn't see. "Really would be pretty with planters at either end and one long window box spilling over with flowers."

"Overkill?"

"No such thing when you're talking about flowers."

"Flowers in season, then maybe some gourds and pumpkins and purple cabbage in the fall," she said. "Greens and holly in winter. Things that create a little interest, you know?"

"Color to draw the eye to the shop. Then they'll see the window and all those books, and they'll be hooked."

"That would be the idea. Everything I have is invested in this place, Tuck. I have to make this work. So that custom window box is going to have to wait. Maybe next year." Her eyes traveled the length of the window longingly, but she knew her money was going to have to be spent elsewhere.

"Well, then, let's go inside, and you can show me what else needs to be done in there so you can open on time, and we'll see how much we can get done today."

"Tuck, I can't ask you to do any more for me than you already have."

"You're not asking, I'm offering."

Liddy switched on the overhead lights after they stepped inside. She still didn't like the fluorescent glow, but until she knew what the must-haves—updating the heater and installing air-conditioning, for example—would cost, she didn't want to get ahead of herself.

"So what do you still need?" Tuck gestured to take in the entire shop. "Looks pretty good to me."

"Well, I was thinking maybe a coffee bar over here." Liddy walked to the open space to the left of the counter.

"Why?"

"Why what?"

"Why would you want a coffee bar?"

"I thought it might encourage people to browse. You know, grab a cup and walk through the store to get acquainted. Plus I think it would be nice once I get a book club or two rolling."

"Let me ask you this: How would you feel if Ground Me started selling books?"

Without hesitation, she said, "I'd be pissed off."

"Might want to think about that."

She nodded again, more slowly this time.

"You've got the best coffee in Massachusetts right across the street. Why would you want to compete with them?"

"I wasn't thinking of it in those terms, but yeah. You're right. So we'll scrap the coffee bar, maybe use that space for something else. A display of some sort, maybe the current week's bestsellers."

Liddy bit her bottom lip. All along she'd been sold on the coffee bar, but Tuck was right. For a shop as small as this one, a coffee bar wasn't the best use of the space. Especially since she herself relied on Ground Me for their excellent coffee. "Maybe for the opening I'll just send across the street for some carafes."

"A much better idea if you're determined to offer coffee on opening day and if you want to keep the peace on Front Street. You can just set up a little table there when you want to offer coffee or whatever." He gazed around the room. "So what were you planning on doing in here today?"

"I was going to start putting the books back onto the shelves, now that the floors are cleaned up and the shelves look so good."

"Just cleaning them up, adding a little shine, was all the floors and bookcases needed." Tuck ran a hand over the nearest shelf. "Nothing like beautiful wood grain, Liddy."

"It's pretty, all right." She walked to the back of the store and picked up one of the boxes of books waiting to be returned to their shelves.

"You're going to pull your back out doing that." Tuck took the box from her hands. "Tell me where this goes."

She pointed to a bookcase, and he carried the box over.

"Next?" he asked, his hands on his hips.

"Tuck, you don't have to cart all these boxes around. I know you have other things to do."

"You're right, I do. So let's not waste time arguing about what I can and can't help you with. Just point."

She sighed. She knew Tuck well enough to know he wasn't a man to argue with once he set his mind to something. Today he'd obviously set his mind to giving her a hand in the shop, so she was going to have to let him do just that.

Tuck finished hauling all the boxes of books to their destinations, and Liddy began sorting them so she could stock the shelves.

"Liddy, I'm going on upstairs to take a look at the water damage on the third floor."

"Check the back wall on the second floor, too, while you're up there," she called to him as he disappeared into the back hall.

As the morning progressed, Liddy accepted a shipment of new releases from a distributor for several of the big publishers. She stacked those boxes by the back door while she decided where and how to display them. Grace had designed price stickers for the shop, but Liddy still had to go through the books and decide on pricing. She'd need to discount the hardcovers, and the stickers would have to reflect the discount. She sighed. If she thought too much about everything she still had to do before opening day, she'd probably run screaming down Front Street as if her hair were on fire.

"At least then I'd be working off some of this tension," she muttered.

Tuck appeared at the back of the shop, wiping his hands on a checkered cloth. When he drew close to the counter where she stood, he shoved the cloth into a back pocket and announced, "Well, there's good news and bad news. Which do you want first?"

"Give me the good news." Liddy rested her elbows on the counter.

"Well, the good news is your roof isn't leaking."

"That is good news." She narrowed her eyes, expecting something even worse. "What's the bad news?"

"The bad news is the pipes are all original, and one's rusted out. Water's bled down inside the wall to the second floor. I'm surprised you don't see any damage down here." He glanced up at the ceiling.

"That can be fixed, though, right?"

"Sure. Just about anything can be fixed. But you're going to need some of the pipes replaced and the ceiling in that back room on the second floor repaired. Without taking out the wall, it's hard for me to know just how extensive the damage is."

"Damn it. Just when I thought I was getting a grip on things around here."

"You just need to give Jim a call, and he can put in a claim for you."

"Why would I call him?" she snapped sharply enough for him to take a step back as if he'd been slapped.

"I'm pretty sure insurance will cover the damage from the results of the leak, though the pipes might not be covered. Depends on how your policy is written, so . . ."

"Jim is my ex-husband."

"Well, I know that, but . . ."

"I did not buy any insurance from him. Why would I give that man any of my business?"

"Oh. Okay." He looked slightly taken aback. "So who's your agent?"

"Joan Galvin, over in Mattapoisett."

"Give her a call. Look, I took some pictures of the damage on my phone." Tuck took his phone from his back pocket and proceeded to share the photos with Liddy. "I'll just send them to you, and you can send them on to Joan, and she'll submit the claim for you."

"Thanks, Tuck." Liddy shook her head, wondering what else could go wrong. Then again, she was sure if you asked out loud, the cosmos would respond by showing you *what else*. Not that she was superstitious, but, unwilling to tempt fate so close to her opening day, she bit her tongue.

"Anything else I can do for you today?" he asked.

Liddy caught his subtle glance at his watch.

"Nope. I'm good." The sound of the door opening drew her attention to the front of the store. "Ah, Gracie's here. There's my second pair of hands. Thanks for everything, Tuck. I appreciate your help."

"You need me, don't be afraid to call." He turned and smiled at the young woman making her way toward them. "Morning, Grace."

"Hey, Tuck. Hi, Liddy." Grace dropped her bag behind the counter. "My mom said she'll be down this afternoon. She's doing a Zoom call with Daisy at noon."

Grace turned to Tuck. "My sister's four-year-old daughter started preschool last week in Pennsylvania, and she's dying to tell her nana all about it."

"I get that. I have three grandkids, and I try to be in their lives as much as possible. School, sports, dance. Whatever it is, I try to be there." Tuck smiled at Liddy, and she forced a smile she didn't feel in return. She tried really hard not to feel bitter, but sometimes it was difficult to share the enthusiasm of her friends for their grandchildren.

"Good for you they live close," Liddy said.

"'Bout as close as they could be," he replied.

"I know you're happy Linc moved back out there with you, Tuck." Liddy brushed imaginary dust from the top of the glass counter.

"Don't know what I'd do without the boy, that's the truth. He's a big help with my dad, not to mention he takes care of those kids pretty much by himself even while he's taking over the business."

"How is your dad doing these days?" Liddy asked.

"Not long for this world, I'm afraid. He does have good days and bad days, but he's been using a wheelchair for the last couple of years. That accident he had took more than his mobility. It for sure accelerated the Alzheimer's. The doctors have all said that's to be expected—he is eighty-nine years old, and he's been declining for years."

"I'm sorry. I know it has to be an emotional burden for you."

Tuck nodded. "It's harder for Linc. He and my dad have always been best buds. Dad was the one who taught him how to fish, you know, and that's my boy's first love. Sometimes I think he got into construction mostly to pay for his boat so he could go out on the water whenever he pleased. He still takes my dad out from time to time when Dad's up to it."

"And he has the three kids as well," Liddy murmured, thinking it a heavy load for a young man.

"I'm real proud of him for stepping up and taking care of them the way he's doing. It's not an easy task, raising kids on your own. You don't have much of a life. I know that for a fact. My kids were in high school when their mom died, and I had my hands full, believe it. Linc wasn't much of a problem, but that sister of his . . . ooh-whee." He shook his head. "Brenda's given me fits from the day she was born."

"I can't remember the last time I saw her," Liddy remarked.

"Yeah, well, that makes a whole bunch of us." He slapped his hand on the counter. "I'm gonna run. Don't forget to let me know if you need anything." He turned toward the door, then paused. "You here early every day?"

Liddy nodded. "Most days by seven. Why?"

"I'll want to get an early start on that door if it's going to be finished in one day. I'll look at the schedule, and I'll let you know which day."

"Thanks, Tuck. I really appreciate it." Even to herself, Liddy sounded like a broken record.

"Sure thing. And don't forget to call in that claim. I'll be ordering the replacement pipe and get that taken care of for you as soon as I can."

Tuck waved to Grace as he headed out the door and closed it behind him.

"He's around a lot," Grace noted.

Liddy shrugged. "There's been a lot to do around here."

"So there's a problem with the pipes upstairs? It's not the roof?"

"Tuck said that's the good news. Just replacing some pipes and some walls and a ceiling upstairs. Oh, and he reminded me to call my insurance agent. Which I'm going to do right now." Liddy looked in her wallet for the agent's card, put in the call, reported the damage, and forwarded Tuck's photos. The entire process would have taken about five minutes if Liddy and Joan hadn't gotten into a discussion about the Patriots' prospects for the coming NFL season.

"Liddy, I'm going to run upstairs and work on the website. I have it almost ready to go. Once I'm finished, I'll go over it with you, and you can tell me what you want added, or what you want changed." Grace took a sip of the coffee she'd brought with her, then made a face. "Ugh. Cold."

"Watch out for the ceiling up there," Liddy cautioned as Grace made her way around the boxes of books on the floor.

"I think I'll be okay. I set up my workspace on the back of the room under the window. There's a nice view out over the harbor."

"Still, just be mindful."

"Okay. If you need me, leave a message with my assistant, and if I can fit in a minute for you, we can chat." Grace headed up the stairs.

Liddy laughed. Grace's "office" was an old table they'd found under the second-floor eaves and cleaned up, and there was no assistant. They'd finished outfitting her office with a folding chair she'd brought from Maggie's garage. As long as Grace had internet access, she didn't care about her surroundings, quite a change from her former life, when she'd had a fancy office in a highly desirable building in Center City, Philadelphia, and as daughter of the owner of the prestigious firm, Flynn Law, Grace had had it made. Until she didn't.

Liddy hummed as she arranged the books on the shelves, beginning in the children's section and moving forward toward the front of the store. Literary fiction. Mystery and thrillers. Romance. Women's fiction. And so on until she reached the halfway mark in the shelves and it was time for a rest. Outside the temperature had begun to rise, and inside the shop, the air was becoming increasingly stuffy. She turned on the two ancient window air-conditioning units and prayed for the best. When she realized one was blowing warm air and the other barely cooling, she turned them off with a growl.

"Is it warm in here or is it me?" Maggie said by way of a greeting as she came into the shop. Her hair was pulled up into a ponytail, much like her daughter's, and she wore navy shorts and a yellow-and-white-striped tee.

"It's warm. Thank you for noticing. Damn it. Now I'm going to have to replace these." Liddy felt like kicking something.

"Have you thought about central air?" Maggie asked.

"I have invoices coming in from publishers for books I've ordered, and I owe a staggering amount to Tuck. I'm not exactly sure how much, but it has to be a lot. I had him here again this morning because there's a cracked pipe upstairs, and he's going to have to replace it so the ceiling doesn't come down. So while I have thought about having central air, I'm going to have to put it on hold."

She pulled a book from the shelf and threw it across the room. "This place is a money pit, and I was so enamored of the idea of being the one to save the town's bookshop I ignored what my accountant was telling me. I'll be lucky to still be in business come Christmas."

"Whoa. I'm sorry if I pushed a button. I didn't mean to." Maggie raised a hand as if to halt whatever Liddy was going to say. "That wasn't an attack. I get you're overwhelmed right now. I do. You've taken on a big project. I know you, and I know you want to make everything perfect. That the store has to represent you. It'll get there."

"The temperature is going up to ninety today, and the forecast is for more of the same for the next ten days. If it's this hot on opening day, people will be walking in and walking right back out again. I can't afford that. I need people in the shop spending money."

Liddy went to the front of the store and, leaning both forearms on the counter, slumped dejectedly. "I've worked so hard, and I've put so much into this place, Mags."

"I know you have." Maggie walked around the counter and rubbed Liddy's shoulders. "And it's going to be fine. Better than fine. We'll make it work. If you need money, I'm good for it. I sold Art's firm, so I can help out. I'd be happy to give you a loan—no interest—or invest and become a silent partner."

"Ha. You? Silent?" Liddy forced a laugh.

"It could be written into any deal we might make that I only give advice you ask for."

"Thanks, Maggie." Liddy gave Maggie's hand a squeeze.

"Hey, what are best friends for? Besides, I figure I owe you. I never did properly thank you for giving me your turn with Derek Demarco in the kissing closet in seventh grade."

"Are you kidding? I'd have died before I kissed him. He always smelled like garlic."

"Which is my favorite thing to cook with." She paused. "Which could trace back to Derek. Never thought about that, but maybe."

Liddy laughed. "Old debts aside, I appreciate the offer. I do have an emergency stash since Emma arranged to sell some of Jess's paintings, so I'm not desperate. Yet. But I'd like to hold on to as much of that as I can, because I don't know what other expenses I'm likely to have. It just seems there's no end to it—and I haven't even opened the shop yet. What was I thinking?"

"You were thinking it would be the perfect business for you, and it will be. You're just having a little down moment because it seems like everything is coming at you at once, but you can't resolve everything at once. My advice—and since I haven't signed an agreement not to offer it—handle each issue one at a time. You said Tuck's taking care of some work for you?"

Liddy nodded. "He's fixing the pipes and the water damage, and the insurance will cover most of that. And he's going to work on the front of the building for me. You know, paint, spruce it up."

"So you can wipe all that off your plate. What else?"

"Well, the obvious. It's like a freaking oven in here. The one air conditioner isn't working at all, and the other one is rolling on its back with all fours up in the air."

Maggie walked to the back of the shop and opened the window overlooking the harbor, and moments later a light breeze made its way in.

"The people I bought my house from had central air installed, but for years, my mom had window units upstairs and down. There are several in the storage space in the garage. I'll test them when I get home and see if any of those work. If so, we'll bring them down. What else?"

Liddy ran through all the things that had been keeping her up at night, starting with not knowing if she'd ordered enough books and ending with not knowing how many employees she was going to need.

"I put in orders based upon what the salespeople suggested, but I don't know if that's going to be enough. Fred never kept detailed records of how much of which authors he sold, so I had to guess based on my own preferences."

"You have very eclectic tastes in books. If you've gone with your gut, you're probably okay. I'm sure you can reorder, right?"

Liddy nodded. "The publishers I ordered from said their delivery turnaround was pretty quick."

"Okay, then cross that worry off your list. You sell out of something someone wants to buy, you tell them you'll special order it for them. Next?"

"Employees . . ."

"You already have Grace. So that's two of you. It's a small shop, Liddy. This isn't the general store. Maybe bring back Evelyn Marshall. She knows the shop, knows the customers."

"I called her a month ago, and she said she didn't know if she wanted to come back, but I'll give her another call and see if she's changed her mind. Even if she could just come in part-time for the next month or so until I can get my feet on the ground, it would be helpful. If she's not interested, maybe I can find someone else."

"If worse comes to worst, I can fill in till you find someone permanent. Emma's really busy at the art center right now, but I know she'll help out when she can. So that's three big things knocked off your worry list. What else is there?"

Liddy tapped her fingers on the glass countertop. "I want to make this the best bookshop ever. I want something going on in here every night to give people a reason to want to come in. I want to do book signings with authors my customers love." She smiled. "Years ago, Emma and I went to a signing in Boston for Stephen King. It was just so much fun. I'd love for our residents to enjoy something like that.

"And I'm thinking book clubs. Romance. Science fiction. Mystery and thrillers. Fantasy like *Game of Thrones*. And nonfiction books as well." She pushed a long tendril of graying hair from her face and tucked it behind her ear. "How annoying would it be when you want to talk about the mystery you just finished and there are two people in the group who only want to discuss the latest political tell-all?"

Maggie nodded. "Can't cross the streams."

"Exactly."

"If you have all those book clubs, you could be here every night," Maggie noted.

"What, like I have somewhere else to be? Something else to do with my time? Someone waiting for me at home? Please. I have the time."

"Maybe you could use some of that time for something other than the shop." Maggie sounded cautious.

"Right now, I don't have anything other than the shop." Liddy tried to dampen her rising annoyance. "I don't have a long-lost love to reunite with and spend my nights cuddled up to. I don't have kids or grandkids. Right now, this is it for me."

"You have friends who love you and who love spending time with you," Maggie said softly.

"Well, I guess for a while, if you want to spend time with me, you're going to have to spend it here." Liddy softened, too. She never doubted Maggie loved her and only wanted the best for her. "It's going to take time for me to build up this business. It's my responsibility, so I have to be the one to put in the time."

"I like book clubs. Maybe I'll come in for the mystery one. If you could schedule that for Brett's night off, we could come together."

"I'll see what I can do."

"You're the best, Lids."

"You know it, girl." Liddy turned toward the door. "Speaking of the chief, what's he doing?"

"He's on his way in right now. I asked him to bring you a rug from my old house for you to use in the children's section. I thought you could use it for story time." Maggie went to the door and held it open for Brett, who planted a quick kiss on her lips as he went past her, a rolled-up rug on his shoulder. While almost forty years older than he'd been when he and Maggie were together the first time, he still carried himself with the same confidence and strength he'd had those years he'd played professional football. His blond hair had traces of silver, and his face was weathered from the hours he'd spent outside, but there was no denying Brett Crawford still maintained the golden-boy aura of his youth.

"Where would you like this, Liddy?" he asked.

"Oh, I can't wait to see it! Back of the shop, please." Liddy pointed, then led the way. "You're looking casual today, Chief. Day off?"

"Nah. Just bumming this morning." He dropped the rug on the floor, then looked around. "Wow, Liddy. This place looks a thousand percent better already. Looks like you're ready to roll."

"Not quite, but thanks. There's still a long list of to-dos before next week, but yeah. It's shaping up."

"Doesn't even look like Fred's store anymore, it's so clean and bright. 'Bout the only thing I recognize is the old cash register. I see you kept Big Red." He nodded in the direction of the counter.

"Local legend. Not going to be using it, but it looks good, right?"

"Like it belongs there," he agreed. "So how 'bout we open the rug and take a look?"

Liddy and Maggie took opposite sides of the rug and, with Brett's help, rolled it out.

"You know, if you don't like it . . . ," Maggie began, but Liddy waved her off.

"It's perfect. Thank you." Liddy beamed her thanks as she straightened out a corner of the rug, then stepped back to admire it. The background was dark green, and the design was a grid pattern in colors of yellow, blue, and red. "It adds just the right amount of color and texture to the space. Absolutely perfect for the kids' section. Thank you again, Mags."

"You're welcome. It looks so much better here than it did in my spare room back in Bryn Mawr," Maggie said.

"What else are you doing in here, Liddy?" Brett asked.

"Decorwise, I just need to hang some posters. Grace is going to enlarge the images from some of Jess's greeting cards, and we're going to place them around the shop."

"That reminds me. I brought down all the cards I kept and the ones she sent my mom." Maggie walked to the front of the store, where she'd left her bag, and Brett followed. One last glance at the children's corner with its newly laid rug and Liddy caught up with them at the counter.

"I'm going to scoot," Brett said. "I need to get home and change and get into the station." He turned to Maggie. "I'll see you later."

"Be careful," she said as he left.

"This is Wyndham Beach," he said over his shoulder. "Nothing ever happens here."

"And thank God for that," Liddy muttered and reached for the small box holding Maggie's cards. "So let's sort through these cards and see which would make the best posters. I'm thinking bright colors and fun subjects . . ."

Chapter Four

"The rug looks great." Grace stood in the back of the shop, her hands on her hips. "This will be perfect for children's story time."

She went to the nearest shelf of children's books and selected one. "Oh, I love this book. *Hannah's Garden*." She glanced up at Liddy. "I've read this to Daisy about a thousand times."

Grace lowered herself to the floor, opened the book, and began to read aloud.

"'One sunny day, Hannah looked out the window and saw her mommy in the yard with a shovel. What, Hannah asked Alfie, her stuffed hedgehog, was Mommy going to do with that shovel?'" Grace looked up at Liddy and said, "This is where I always say, 'Daisy, what would her mommy do with a shovel?' And Daisy says, 'Dig holes to plant flowers.'"

"And Natalie stifles the urge to say, *Bury your daddy*." Maggie joined them. There was no love lost for Daisy's father in the Flynn family. Jon, Natalie's live-in love of three years, had bolted for the door the day Natalie told him she was pregnant, and poof! Just like that, he'd disappeared. "Sorry for the interruption. Do go on."

Grace resumed reading. Liddy heard footsteps and looked over her shoulder as Linc entered with two little girls in tow. Liddy waved them back, a finger crossing her lips. "Shhh," she whispered. "Grace is auditioning to read for the children's book hour."

Grace looked up in midsentence and, seeing Linc, met his eyes for a long moment, then looked back at the page. One of the little girls crept forward shyly and sat next to Grace on the rug. She hung over the book to look at the pictures, then looked up at Grace expectantly.

"I think she wants you to keep going," Maggie said.

"Oh, hey." Linc crooked a finger at the girl. "Don't bother Miss Grace, JoJo."

"She's not bothering me," Grace said without looking up. She turned her attention to the girl. "Your name is JoJo?"

The girl nodded.

"Would you like me to read more?" Grace asked.

The child nodded eagerly, settled in, and stuck her thumb in her mouth. Leaning against Grace, she pointed to something on the page.

"I apologize for the interruption." He turned to Liddy. "I just need to run upstairs for a minute. Dad can't find his cell phone, and he thinks he might have left it here." Linc made his way to the back stairs and ran up to the second floor.

Liddy and Maggie stood side by side and watched Grace's interaction with the children.

Grace directed her attention to the other little girl, who had remained standing next to the bookcase. Like her sister, she had jet-black hair and startling blue eyes. They looked remarkably alike, their faces heart-shaped and their noses equally pert. Grace asked, "Are you twins?"

"No. Mama said I'm just small because I was premature," the girl replied. "I'm older than her." She pointed to her sister. "She's five. I'm seven."

"Would you like to sit with us?" Grace patted the floor next to her.

The girl gave her head a fierce shake.

"Well, if you change your mind, you're welcome to join us." Grace resumed reading.

Liddy watched for a few minutes, then nodded in Grace's direction and whispered to Maggie, "Looks like Gracie has a fan."

Maggie smiled as JoJo touched Grace's dark hair and told her, "You have pretty hair."

"Thank you," Grace said. "So do you."

JoJo nodded. "It's like my mommy's."

"Well, I'm sure your mommy is very lovely."

"I don't remember."

The child's eyes filled with tears, prompting her older sister to say sternly, "Stop being a baby, JoJo."

"What's your name?" Grace's inquiry addressed to the older girl was met with a defiant stare but no response. "What's your sister's name, JoJo?"

Her thumb still in her mouth, JoJo replied, "Bliss."

"I can speak for myself," Bliss said.

"Then you might have done so when I asked you directly." Grace softened her tone. "Sure you wouldn't like to join us, Bliss?"

"That's a baby book." Bliss wrinkled her nose disdainfully.

"I don't know," Grace said. "I like it. I've read it countless times."

Bliss muttered something that sounded like "good for you" but remained where she stood, leaning against the nearest bookcase.

"Suit yourself." Grace resumed reading to JoJo.

When she finished the story, Liddy said, "Looks like you've got yourself another job to add to your résumé."

"What does that mean?" Grace asked.

"It means don't make plans for Saturday mornings." Liddy smiled, then turned as Linc rounded the corner from the bottom of the steps. "You'll be bringing the kids for Saturday morning story hours, Lincoln."

"What?" He laughed. "What did I just walk into?"

"We're doing children's story hour on Saturdays. What do you think of eleven a.m.?" she asked.

"Not sure. Could be tight. The two older kids have sports, but we haven't gotten the final weekend schedules yet."

"Any idea of the time?"

"Not yet, but softball and soccer are usually in the afternoon for the younger kids, but the older kids play in the morning. If they're on a travel team, like Duffy is, it could take up most of the day."

"I don't want to play soccer," JoJo piped up. "I want to read books with Miss Grace."

"You don't have to play if you don't want to." Linc knelt next to JoJo and brushed her hair back from her face. "We talked about that, remember?"

JoJo nodded.

"If you want to come to story hour, we'll make sure you get here," he said gently. "If I can't bring you, we'll ask Pop, okay?"

JoJo smiled and put her arms around Linc's neck.

"I can read my own books," Bliss announced. "I'm going to play soccer."

"You're already signed up for soccer, Bliss." Linc cast a weary glance at Bliss.

"Kids can be tough," Liddy said. "So did you find your dad's phone?"

"No. He must have lost it somewhere else." Linc stood, JoJo still wound around his neck.

Liddy paused to remember where else in the store Tuck had been that morning. "Oh, maybe over here." She pointed to where she and Tuck had discussed building shelves. "Let's take a look."

Linc lowered the little girl to the ground, and she walked back to Grace, who said, "So JoJo Shelby, looks like you're the very first to sign up for Saturday's story time."

"Our name's not Shelby," Bliss snapped. "It's Brown." She turned her back on Grace and fell in behind Linc and Liddy, who'd started toward the front of the store.

Liddy glanced over her shoulder as Maggie and Grace exchanged a long, puzzled look. There'd be time later for her to relate the little she knew about the mixed-up situation with the Shelby family.

~

"Why is their name Brown and not Shelby?" Grace barely waited until the door had closed behind Linc and the two girls before asking. "I thought they were Linc's kids."

"The kids are his sister Brenda's. Brown's her husband's last name, apparently." Liddy sighed. "I'm not sure why they're here in Wyndham Beach, but I do know they are hers, and she isn't with them, but they're living out on the island. So it seems Linc has taken most of the responsibility for them."

"That's a lot for a young single man to take on," Maggie observed.

"Linc was always solid. Dependable. Worked hard, never got in trouble I heard about. Whatever happened that brought those kids to Wyndham Beach, I am not at all surprised Linc's stepped up."

"So what's Brenda's story?" Grace asked.

"Oh, that one. What a wild child she was. She took off at seventeen, and as far as I know, she hasn't been back. At least, I haven't seen her. Tuck doesn't say much about her, and I'm not going to be the one to ask. If he ever feels like talking about it, I'll be glad to listen."

"How long have the kids been living with Tuck and Linc?" Grace asked.

"The first time I saw them was about two months before you moved back in the spring," Liddy said. "But why they're here . . ." She shrugged.

"Well, I know I'm shocked." Maggie placed a hand over her heart.

"Yeah, it's tough to understand how a mother could just walk away from her children," Liddy agreed.

"That's for sure, but I was referring to the fact it's been months and you still haven't managed to get the whole story," Maggie teased.

74

Liddy laughed. "I can't deny I'm dying to know. But I just can't bring myself to ask. Tuck adored that girl of his, spoiled her, stuck up for her no matter what. I know she was a wild kid who got even more uncontrollable after her mother died—I guess Brenda was around thirteen or so then. I'm sure Tuck still loves his daughter, and whatever happened must hurt him deeply. But you don't share that kind of pain with just anyone, and I have to respect that. Even if it's killing me not to know.

"I don't know the circumstances of her leaving or her relationship with her children, her brother, or her father, or the kids' father. I'm not going to speculate." Liddy looked away for a minute, then turned to Grace. "So let's get back to the business at hand."

She spread Jessie's cards across the counter. "I like these with the little animals for the kids' section, and maybe these botanicals for the far wall. What do you think?"

For the next hour, they sorted through all the old greeting cards Emma, Grace, and Maggie had brought in, setting aside cards that would become posters for each section of the store.

"It's really hard to decide among them, because they're all so wonderful." Grace debated between two floral designs, one colorful, one muted.

"The colors and the designs are so lively and graceful. Maybe do more than what you need so you can change them out every month," Maggie suggested.

"Then when you change out, take the retiring designs and offer them as note cards," Grace suggested. "And greeting cards, just like Jess did. We could even use some of her handwritten greetings from the inside of the cards, omitting, of course, the name of the recipient. If you think that would be okay."

"I do. I like the idea, especially about reproducing her handwriting." Liddy picked up a card and opened it, reading to herself the greeting her daughter had penned for the recipient. "Can you find out how that could be done?"

"Already researched it. I have a file upstairs." Grace grinned.

"I should have known. So how soon for the posters?" Liddy stacked the cards up in the order in which the posters would hang throughout the store.

"I found a printer in New Bedford who can do them tomorrow. I'll ask about the cards as well, so I'll take one with me. I'll see what they suggest, what the pricing would be." Grace tapped her fingers on the stack of cards. "How many cards of each design, Liddy? You know, the more you do, the less expensive they will be in the end."

They ran through the designs again and discussed the number of birthday cards to start with.

"Let's do fifteen of each of three different designs and see if they generate any interest. If they fly, we'll take a look at the holiday-themed cards. Halloween isn't far off, and then there's Thanksgiving, Christmas, Hanukkah."

"I think you'll be surprised at how well they'll do." Grace gathered up the cards and placed them in a pocket of her bag. "Liddy, take a look at the website when you get a minute and let me know if you approve or if you want changes. Once I have your okay, Wyndham Beach Reads will go live."

Grace ran upstairs for her laptop, then ran back down again. She grabbed her bag and called her "See you laters" over her shoulder.

"Hey," Liddy called after her. "You really did a great job reading earlier. May I count on you for Saturday morning?"

Grace flashed a grin and gave her a thumbs-up as she left the store.

"That girl of yours has a lot of skills," Liddy remarked when Grace disappeared from view.

"She's found skills she didn't know she had since we moved here," Maggie said. "It's been a long journey from Philadelphia to Wyndham

Beach, but I think she's discovered a lot about herself. She seems happier than she's been in a long time."

Liddy put the cards from the counter into a paper bag and put the bag into her purse. "I'm glad she stuck around."

"Me too. She hasn't said anything about whether she's going to stay awhile or move on. I know she's been restless since Brett and I got together. It's been life-changing for me, but not so much for my kid. Sometimes I think . . ." Maggie hesitated, as if not sure whether to continue.

"Sometimes you think what?"

"Maybe Grace would feel more settled if she had a place of her own."

Liddy's heart skipped a beat.

"Have you mentioned this to her?" Liddy played with the keys on Big Red.

"No, of course not. She'll think I don't want her around, and it isn't that at all." Maggie shook her head adamantly. "I love her company. I just wonder if maybe she'd be more likely to see her own future a little more clearly if she wasn't living at home with her mother and her mother's sometimes live-in boyfriend." She paused. "If you're nearing sixty, do you still say 'boyfriend'?"

"What are the alternatives? Lover? TMI. Gentleman friend? Too formal and old fashioned. Manfriend? Awkward and somewhat, I don't know, sleazy. I say stick with boyfriend regardless of your age and tune out any noise to the contrary."

"Boyfriend it is." Maggie took a bottle of water from her bag and unscrewed the cap. "Anyway, I don't want Grace to think I'm trying to get rid of her. I just want her to be happy."

"Let's assume she is thinking about wanting to move. Maybe she hasn't brought it up because she's afraid you'll think she's tired of being around you."

"You've had this discussion with her, haven't you?"

77

"It might have come up she was thinking about looking for a place of her own so you and Brett can have some privacy."

"And neither of you thought to bring me into the conversation?"

"I really didn't want to get in the middle. I didn't want you to think I was telling her what to do or giving her advice contrary to what you might want, and she isn't sure how you'd take her wanting to move out."

"I can appreciate that. But she's thirty-three. She shouldn't feel she needs to tiptoe around her mother."

"You turned fifty-nine at the beginning of the month. You shouldn't feel you need to tiptoe around your adult daughter."

"Touché." Maggie laughed. "All right. So what was the bottom line of your conversation?"

"She was going to think it over. I did caution her rentals in Wyndham Beach are few and expensive." Liddy smiled. "I'm not paying her all that much, Mags. I can do better once the shop opens, but right now, not so much."

"She has money from her father. If she wants to move out, she should be able to afford something nice. But you're right. I haven't seen anything at all for rent advertised outside of one of those big houses out on Ellis Road, which are several thousands of dollars monthly."

Liddy debated whether or not to bring up the little house. She hadn't even mentioned it to Grace as yet, and she hadn't had time to go through the place to see if it was suitable. The kitchen had been the break room for Jim's staff, the bathroom a powder room, and she wasn't sure if Jim had removed all his office furniture.

"What are you thinking, Liddy?"

Liddy hesitated before telling Maggie about the house and her reservations about its suitability. "I haven't mentioned it to Grace, so don't say anything until I know if it's workable."

"I won't mention it until you've made a decision, but it sounds like a good idea to me. Let me know what you think after you've gone through it."

"If you want, you can come with me. Oh, we might as well all go. If Grace thinks she might be interested, she can come along. I'll carve out some time."

"That would be great, thanks." Maggie leaned on the counter. "So Tuck was here again today, eh?"

"This morning. I had to call him about the leak upstairs."

"And he came right over?"

Liddy nodded.

"You know, when my roof leaked, I had to wait twelve hours for someone to call me back, then almost another whole day before someone showed up."

Liddy smiled smugly. "Hey, some have it, some wish they did."

"Well, it sounds like Tuck thinks you do."

"And he wouldn't be wrong."

Maggie laughed.

"What can I say? Aging hippie is still a look that turns 'em on," Liddy said nonchalantly.

"So what are you going to do about it?"

"What do you mean?"

Maggie rolled her eyes. "I'm pretty sure you're the same Lydia Bryant who was whining not too long ago about wanting to have sex again before she died."

"I'm not ready to die yet, and I don't whine. I was stating a fact. Not everyone has a still-hunky high school boyfriend in their back pocket, at their beck and call, ya know."

"What about Tuck? He's still looking good, and he's such a nice guy. Don't tell me you haven't noticed. And it sure sounds as if he's interested in you. Enough, at least, to drop what he's doing every time you call him."

"I wouldn't even know how to bridge the gap between old friends and bedmates. I've been out of the game for so long."

"If you want some advice, start by not treating it like a game. You're already spending time together. Switch it up. Invite him for dinner. Ask him to go with you to the opening of the new exhibit at the art center." Maggie snapped her fingers. "I know. Bring him to the cookout at my place on Monday. It'll be a nice, nonthreatening time to spend together that doesn't involve work. See how you two relate on a strictly social basis."

"I need to be here, in the shop, on Monday. You all are going to have to cook out without me."

"Uh-uh. Wrong answer."

"Did you not get the notice? This place opens on Tuesday. Therefore I will be putting in all the little finishing touches on Monday."

"Nope. All those little last-minute things will be done on Sunday. I'll help you. Grace will help, and we'll bring Emma in." When Liddy began to protest, Maggie said, "You've been working every day for weeks. You're going to be working every day for the next forever, and you're already exhausted. We are going to do everything that still needs to be done on Sunday, and on Monday you're going to rest and relax." Maggie took another sip of water. "You're going to hit the ground running on Tuesday morning, but on Monday, you're going to take a day off to appreciate all you've accomplished in such a short period of time. Maybe we'll spend a few hours on the beach, drink a few margaritas— which I'm counting on you to make because no one does it better—eat some delicious food, and spend the day with the people who love you." Maggie waggled her eyebrows. "And who knows, if you play your cards right, Tuck might make a move before you do."

"But—" Liddy protested.

"Nope. No buts. That's how it's going to be."

"Remind me again who put you in charge of my life."

"Executive decision." Maggie pointed to the back of the shop. "Now let's unpack a few more of those boxes."

~

"Good thing you got here when you did." Tuck stood on the sidewalk in front of the shop, his hands on his hips, watching Liddy cross Front Street early on Thursday morning. "I was starting to think I was going to have to pick the lock."

Liddy hastened across, wishing she'd worn something other than her cargo pants with the swath of paint that wouldn't come out and a white tee that clearly had seen better days.

"When you said you'd be here early, I thought you meant seven." She dodged a slow-moving sedan, waved to the driver, and hopped onto the curb. His crew was already set up, ladders against the exterior of the building. "They look like they mean business."

"Time is money, girl." Dark glasses hid his eyes. He wore a Shelby & Son T-shirt and khaki shorts. He wore them well.

"Well, then, I guess I better get moving." She unlocked the door and swung it open, but Tuck didn't come inside. "You coming?" she asked.

He squatted next to the door and studied the hinges, then the doorknob, then the plate surrounding the knob.

"These are old. Original, and I bet they're solid brass." He looked up at Liddy. "Be real pretty shined up."

"Wouldn't you have to take them off to polish them?" Liddy frowned. "I don't like that there'd be no door because of the mosquitoes and those damned man-eating flies that come in from the marsh."

"We talked about this. I have to take the door off to strip the old finish. That's what the sawhorses over there are for. I'm going to lay the door across them while I work."

"But then you have to put a new finish on it." She was still thinking through the process. "Can you do all that today?"

"If I can't, I'll rehang the door, and I'll take it off again in the morning." Tuck stood. "You're overthinking this. Just go about your business and let me go about mine."

Liddy watched him run a hand over the fancy doorknob.

"Yeah," he murmured, his fingers tracing the scrolling edge of the plate. "We'll get you polished up . . ." He looked up at Liddy. "Was there something else?"

"I guess not." Liddy went inside.

Heat hadn't built up in the shop yet, and with the door open—soon to be missing entirely—and the back window, the temperature would be tolerable for a while. Liddy made a mental note to call Maggie and ask if she'd had time to check out the window air conditioners she'd mentioned. The aesthetic wouldn't be quite what Liddy was going for, but it was better than sweltering. Besides, she reminded herself, cooler weather was just around the corner. She took out her list of things to do and went to work, occasionally looking out the front window to watch Tuck. Maggie was right. It might be nice to spend a few hours with Tuck away from the shop. Time to take things into her own hands— pun intended. The next time he came inside, she'd ask him to join them at Maggie's on Monday for the cookout.

But the next time she saw him, three members of his crew in blue Shelby tees were following him.

"I'm going to get these guys set up on the third floor to replace the leaking pipe; then by tomorrow we should be able to take down the ceiling on the second floor and replace it." He walked past her and through the shop without stopping.

She heard heavy footsteps on the stairs and listened, waiting for Tuck to come back down. But when he did, he wasn't alone. He and one of his guys passed by the bookcase where Liddy was shelving cookbooks, and they went out to Tuck's truck. She took a deep breath when she heard the front door open, but when she stepped into the aisle, one of the workers sidestepped around her, nodding pleasantly.

From time to time she looked out the front window, but Tuck never seemed to look up from his task of refinishing the front door. At one o'clock, he and his workers stopped for lunch, with Tuck getting into his truck and leaving. Around the same time, Grace arrived, framed posters in hand.

"They look fantastic, and the framing is excellent. I think you're going to love how they came out." Grace unwrapped the brown paper covering the posters.

One by one, Grace lined them up along the front of one of the bookcases.

"What do you think? Aren't they fabulous?" Grace clapped her hands in her excitement.

Liddy stood stock-still and stared. Each of the posters they'd chosen to enlarge joyfully bloomed with color and energy.

"Oh . . ." Liddy's hands crossed at her heart, and her eyes filled with tears. When she found her voice, she said, "They're more wonderful than I could have imagined. Oh, Gracie, you've brought my girl into the shop in the most glorious way. I don't know how to thank you for doing this." She went to Grace and embraced her. She wiped away the tears and then, all business again, said, "Let's hang these today, shall we?"

"We'll need the ladder." Grace gave Liddy one last squeeze. "And I'll have to go to the hardware store to get picture hangers and wire, but that won't take long. Let's place them around the shop where you want them hung. These with the baby animals, obviously, for the children's section . . ."

Liddy nodded, then picked up a poster of birds perched on the many branches of a birch tree, their vibrant colors a stark contrast to the white bark and the pale blue of the background. She leaned it up against the counter in the front of the store.

"I'd like this one right behind the counter," she told Grace. "It's cheery and bright and it's one of the first things you'll see when you come inside."

"Perfect." Grace picked up her bag where she'd dropped it and searched inside for her car keys. "I'm going to run out and pick up the hangers. I won't be long."

"Oh, Grace," Liddy called after her. "When you get back, let's talk about an idea I had for a rental."

"A rental for what?"

"A place for you."

Grace stopped abruptly. "A rental for me?"

Liddy nodded.

"Here in Wyndham Beach?"

"Yup."

"Hold that thought. I'll be back in a flash." Grace continued on her way out the open doorway. Liddy watched as she paused to speak with Tuck, who'd returned from his break and appeared to be showing off whatever he'd done to the door he was working on.

Liddy was thinking she should go and check out his progress when the guys who'd been working on the upper floors of the building returned and went directly upstairs, their work boots clumping on the wooden steps, thumping across the second floor, and reverberating through the ceiling. She walked to the front of the store and watched through the big window as Tuck sanded the paneled door by hand. The hardware had all been removed and was soaking in a bucket nearby his workstation. Every few minutes, a car horn would beep, and he'd raise a hand in greeting to whoever was driving past. After a while, Liddy went outside. Before she could open her mouth, Tuck said, "I'm thinking this door would look best painted red."

"I thought you loved the natural grain."

"I do. But it's not raising up the way I thought it would." He stepped back and left the piece of sandpaper he'd been using on the flat panel of the door. "Stand over here and look at the front of the building, Liddy. It's all stucco and timber. Dark cream and brown. A stained door is going to fade right in. You need a little something to give the facade a kick. I'm thinking a red door would be just the thing."

She took a few steps and stood where he'd indicated. Now that he'd mentioned it, the front of the building bordered on monochromatic.

"You could be right," she agreed. "Red's just the right touch."

"Yeah, it'll spiff this place up. I have some red paint at home. I'll bring it in tomorrow, and we'll give it a try. It's a good shade, a blue-red. Nice with the brown."

"Okay. Go for it."

"I don't think you'll regret it." He stood with his arms folded across his chest, his Red Sox cap shading his face, his dark glasses hiding his eyes.

They stood there staring at the front of the building for a few moments, Liddy wondering how best to broach the subject of Monday's cookout. Finally, she chastised herself—*Oh for crying out loud. It's a cookout. With a friend. What is your problem?*—and said with more non-chalance than she actually felt, "Oh, by the way. Maggie's having a cookout on Monday. Labor Day, you know? She told me to ask you if you'd like to stop over. If you're free."

"She did, did she?"

"Ah, yeah."

"Well, please tell Maggie I appreciate her invitation, but I have plans for Monday."

"Oh. Well, maybe another time." Liddy shrugged and went back inside, trying to ignore what felt like a burn of rejection. So he had other plans. No big deal.

No big deal at all.

~

True to her word, Maggie had sent Brett down to deliver the window air conditioners: two large ones for the shop, two smaller units for Liddy's office and the second floor. It had taken almost an hour to install them; then, as Brett was leaving, Evelyn called to let Liddy know she'd thought it over and would like to work part-time if that was okay with Liddy, which it was. Tuck had yet to put the door back when Liddy was ready to leave at six forty-five, having agreed to meet Maggie and Grace at the little house at seven.

"I need to leave," she told him.

"Some reason you can't?" Tuck straightened up, one hand on the small of his back as if to hold in pain.

"There's no door on my shop." She stated the obvious with no small touch of exasperation. "I can't leave it open like that."

"You think I'll let people wander in off the street and help themselves?"

"Of course not."

"Then what's your problem? The paint's dry, and Jack over there has the brass fittings all polished up." He turned toward the man he'd pointed out. "Jack, hold up that doorknob. Check it out, Liddy. Tell me that's not gonna knock 'em dead when they reach out to open the door and realize what they're looking at."

She walked over and picked up the shiny brass piece. "It's gorgeous. Wow. Who would have suspected this was under all that tarnish?"

"A trained eye suspected." He took off his ball cap, ran a hand through his hair, and put the cap back on. "Why don't you leave me the key and go on and do what you need to do? I have to clean up out here, and I need to run upstairs and check on the work up there. After I finish up, I'll drop it off. If you're not home, I'll leave the key under the mat by the front door." He paused. "You still have that welcome mat on the porch, right? Fake green grass, spells out *welcome* in daisies?"

"Yeah, it's still there." *But not for long.* She'd been meaning to get rid of that thing for months, but it hadn't been a priority, and lately she'd been mostly using the back door. Jim had bought the mat on sale at one of the big box stores the summer before Jessie died. Liddy'd thought it was tacky when he'd brought it home, and she still thought it was tacky. Mentally she added *toss front doormat* onto her list of things to do.

"So? That work for you?" he asked impatiently, apparently wanting to get back to the job at hand.

"That would be fine. Thanks." She paused, thinking about that mat. "On second thought, just put it under the flowerpot on the wicker table on the front porch if I don't answer the bell."

"Got it. Maybe I'll see you later, then." He went back to what he was doing.

It took Liddy only ten minutes to walk home. She went up the front steps and stared down at the welcome mat, which now seemed to offend her even more since Tuck had mentioned it.

"You really are ugly, and you're not adding anything to the curb appeal," she told it as she picked it up. "But I have just the place for you."

She went inside, picked up the mail from the floor inside the front door, and left it on the hall table, then went through the house and out the back.

"I should have made Jim take you with him when he left. No one liked you but him," she said aloud as she dropped it into the trash can.

She went back inside to look for the key for the little house, which was just next door, muttering to herself. "Yes, it's come to this. I talk to the trash."

The little white house stood at the end of a long paved driveway. Once upon a time, it had been a dirt path, but when Jim had decided to use it for his insurance business, he'd had macadam put down. He'd had sod brought in to replace the wild grasses growing around it, and he'd had a big sign installed out by the sidewalk. Now the sign was gone—she'd made him take it with him when he'd left, since the Bryant Agency was leaving town with him—and the tall grasses and wildflowers he'd tried to eliminate had reclaimed the property. As Liddy walked along the winding driveway, she wondered if all that pricey sod was still under there somewhere.

The door unlocked easily, and Liddy went inside. The air was stifling, and the room was dark. She brushed away a spider's web from one of the front windows, tossed aside the desiccated remains of what had been several flies and a yellow jacket, and pushed up the sash to let in some air. Her left hand searched the wall for the switch for the ceiling fan with its light fixture before she remembered the electricity had been shut off. But she knew the building well enough to know the front room led into a hallway off which were four doors. The break room and powder room were on the right, Jim's office and the big room housing his assistants on the left.

"Well, crap, Jim. You couldn't take your old banged-up file cabinets with you?" Liddy walked into the first office and kicked the bottom drawer of the closest cabinet. "Ugh, and I hate those venetian blinds. They never did work very well. Those gotta go, regardless of who ends up here. Even if no one lives here." She stared at them. "Off with their heads."

"Liddy?" Maggie called from the front room. "Who are you threatening to behead?"

Liddy went into the hall. "Jim. He left some stuff here I'm going to have to deal with now."

"Why don't you just call him and tell him to come get his shit?" Grace poked her head into the first room on the right.

"Because I don't speak to him."

"So send him an email." Grace disappeared into what had been the break room. "So this would be the kitchen?"

"Yes, if your idea of a kitchen is a small sink, an under-the-counter dorm-size refrigerator, and a hot plate," Liddy said from the doorway.

Grace went from room to room, occasionally commenting on the size of the room or the number of windows.

"I don't remember the rooms being so big. Of course, I was only in here a few times," Maggie said. "It's actually a nice-size little cottage."

"*Cottage* is a bit of a stretch." Liddy snorted. "*Cottage* makes me think of a cozy place with lots of charm. *Cozy* and *charming* are not words that come to mind here."

"It could be cozy and charming. And it's not all that small," Grace pointed out.

"I guess it looked smaller when Jim and his staff were here because there were desks and office equipment everywhere. The front room had the receptionist's desk and a sofa and a couple of chairs. That second room on the left had three desks in it and a bunch of filing cabinets. Empty—except for the damned cabinets—it's actually quite a nice space."

"I remember this place. Jessie and I used to come down here on the pretense of visiting her father. But that was just a cover to grab a can of soda and a Popsicle from the freezer. Then we'd go out back and play around the pond. Catch salamanders." Grace rejoined them in the hall. "I was so obsessed with salamanders my science project for school that year was titled 'All about Salamanders.'" She turned to Liddy. "Are you aware Massachusetts is the home to eleven different species of salamanders? Oh yes—several are on the state's concerned and endangered list: the blue-spotted salamander, the marbled salamander. One species is all female—they reproduce without fertilization of their eggs—though at ten, I didn't really understand what that meant. And some don't have lungs. They—"

"Breathe through their skins, like the Eastern red-backed salamander." Maggie finished the sentence for her daughter.

"How'd you know that?" Grace asked.

Maggie rolled her eyes. "Please. I was your audience every night for a solid week while you practiced the oral presentation of your report. I remember as if it were yesterday, the same way I remember the words to

'American Pie,' 'Crocodile Rock,' and 'The Cremation of Sam McGee.' Who knows why?"

"Oh my God. Songs from the past and Sam McGee." Liddy laughed. "What were we, in fifth grade or so then?"

"Something like that. My sister had a radio, and she played it all day, every day, after school." Maggie fell silent, and Liddy suspected Maggie was recalling that Sarah had passed away within a year or two of that memory. When she saw Grace give her mother's shoulder a squeeze, she knew Grace, too, was aware how the aunt she'd never known had died at fifteen after she'd ridden her bike over a yellow jacket nest. Highly allergic to their stings, Sarah hadn't even had time to call for help.

To change the subject, Liddy gestured with one hand to encompass the entire building. "So. What do we think?"

"It's quite a project." Maggie understated the obvious. "For starters, the gold wall-to-wall carpet is, in a word, hideous."

"Absolutely. It needs to go. I wonder if there's nice wood underneath." Grace knelt and tried to pry up a corner of the carpet, but it was firmly affixed to the floor. She gave up and stood, brushing dirt and dust from her knees and her hands. "The entire place needs reno. Like, a lot of reno. A full bathroom. A real kitchen."

"No argument. Putting in a kitchen and bath would require walls being moved. I guess I could consult an architect, but that's an expense I can't take on right now."

"I'd like to try my hand at reimagining the interior. Maybe it wouldn't be as much as we think. If I have questions about moving walls, I can always call Joe, since he's an engineer," she said, referring to her half brother, Maggie and Brett's son, who'd been adopted by a childless couple from Maine right after his birth.

"Grace, I'm putting what I have into the shop, and I need a cushion because I don't know what expenses might pop up. I don't know if I can scrape up enough to move walls in this place."

"Let me play with this for a few days on paper. If none of the walls I'd want to move are weight-bearing, maybe Tuck can do something."

Liddy and Maggie exchanged a long look. Finally, Maggie said, "So does that mean you like the house?"

"Oh, I love it, are you kidding? It's adorable," Grace exclaimed.

"Adorable? Really?" Liddy raised an eyebrow. "Don't quite see that myself, but okay."

Maggie wandered into the kitchen. "I think you have a little built-in prejudice." She leaned down and opened the door of the refrigerator. "At least Jim didn't leave anything in here."

"Yeah, the remains of a three-year-old tuna sandwich would have ensured him a long, painful death. As it is, I guess I'm lucky he only left some old filing cabinets and a few spiders."

"So if I could make this place livable, could I rent it from you?" Grace leaned against the kitchen counter. "This place could be perfect for me. If I could figure out a way to make it work, maybe I could do the renovations in place of paying rent."

"The plumbing alone could be more than you'd pay in rent for a year. I can't let you do that," Liddy protested. "It wouldn't be fair. And think of this—supposing you do all the work and a year from now you decide you want to live somewhere else."

"We'd work something out," Grace said. "You could rent it to someone else and pay me back monthly for what I put into it, less what I would have paid in rent while I was living here."

Liddy frowned. "That seems like a lot of math and record keeping. How much you spent on renovations. How much I should charge for rent once it's finished. How much I'd owe you monthly out of someone else's rent checks."

"Let me just play around a little, okay?" Grace put an arm around Liddy's shoulder. "Where's the harm in that, huh?"

"Play all you want, kiddo. But I think you're going to get a shock when you find out how much this little project would cost you. I should have looked at this place before I even mentioned it to you. Maybe it wasn't such a good idea after all."

"Maybe. But maybe not. Maybe having a place of my own, set up just the way I want it, could be worth it." Grace held up one hand to stop the protest her mother was about to make. "I understand I might not be in Wyndham Beach in another year. Who knows? But right now, I'm here." She glanced at Liddy. "On our way over, Mom and I talked. She knows I love her, and I know she loves me, but we both agreed it would be better for everyone if I have my own home. I think this could be perfect." She looked around the room. "I can already see how this room and the powder room and that storage closet at the end of the hall could be combined into a great kitchen. The two rooms across the hall could be made into one bedroom and a bath. The front room . . ." She walked down the hall, Liddy and Maggie following. "Living room on this side, dining area on the other. I don't need anything more than that." She stood in the middle of the space she'd designated for dining. "Actually, with the closet gone, I could have room in the kitchen for a small table if I wanted. I could use this area for an office."

"I still don't think this would be a good deal for you financially." Liddy pointed out what she thought was obvious. Grace would have to live in the house rent-free for several years before it would be profitable for her. "You might want to buy a place in a few years if you stay in town, and then you'll regret having tied up your money."

"I'm happy to take that chance. Besides, maybe I'd want to buy this place. Did you ever think about selling it?"

"I hadn't, really, but I'd sell in a heartbeat to you if you really wanted it."

Grace pulled up one of the blinds and peered outside. "Nice outdoor space." She craned her neck as she looked to the left. "Oh, I forgot just how close to the pond we are. It seemed farther away when I was a kid. I always loved the idea of having my own pond."

"I don't think it's much more than a home for a couple of frogs. Maybe the occasional duck." Liddy walked to the window. "There used to be a stone patio where Jim and his staff would eat lunch occasionally when the weather was good, but I don't need to look outside to know it's overgrown, which is a shame, because it's a pretty spot with a nice view of the woods and the pond." Liddy remembered weekends when Jim would work alone, and she'd take lunch to him and they'd eat outside on a glass-topped table. Apparently, Jim had thought he'd have more use for the table than he had for the filing cabinets, because the table was no longer there.

"It shouldn't be a problem to uncover the stones." Grace smiled. "Perfect."

"Well, I admit I don't see the perfection, but you do you, Gracie." Liddy turned to Maggie. "What do you think?"

"I think Grace knows what she's doing." Maggie glanced at her daughter. "If you believe you can make this work, go for it."

"It's already done inside my head. Now all I have to do is make it happen IRL." Grace grinned. "That would be *in real life*, Mom." Before Maggie could respond, Grace said, "Liddy, could I get a copy of the key made? I'd like to come back over the weekend with a measuring tape, so I have all the dimensions before I start planning."

"You can take this one and have a copy made for me." Liddy took the key from her pocket and handed it over to Grace.

"Thanks, Liddy." Grace slid the key into her own pocket.

"I have things to do tonight, so I need to get going," Liddy told them. "You can stick around as long as you like, but be mindful of when it starts to get dark. There are no lights between here and the street."

Grace tapped her phone, and a bright beam of light appeared. "Flashlight app. Very handy."

"Suit yourself, but it's a long driveway." Liddy patted Maggie on the shoulder as she started to the door. "I guess I'll see you over the weekend."

"I have to get home, so I'll walk out to the street with you. I told Brett I'd pick him up at seven forty-five at the police station. We want to check out the new sushi place that just opened in Wareham." Maggie called to Grace, who was headed toward one of the back rooms: "Grace. Sushi?"

"No thanks, Mom. I'll grab something on my way home," Grace called back.

"See you when you get there," Maggie told her daughter. "And for the record, I knew what *IRL* means."

"Thanks again, Liddy. This is going to be fun." Grace's voice faded slightly as she disappeared into what had once been Jim Bryant's office.

Liddy and Maggie left the front door open behind them and walked along the path leading to the driveway.

"You didn't say a whole lot in there." Liddy bent forward to avoid a low-hanging branch of a crab apple tree.

Maggie shrugged. "There wasn't a whole lot to say. Grace is on a mission to find her way after having her entire world blown up. For the first time ever, she's in charge of every aspect of her life. She's established her own business. She's getting more clients who want websites set up every week. She'll do a bang-up job on that house, and she'll love doing it. I think she'll stay in town longer if she has a place she's made her own. So she might decide to buy it after all."

"I'll leave that option on the table for her." Liddy paused to pick a stem of cornflowers hanging over the edge of the driveway. "By the way, I invited Tuck to your place for Monday, but he said he had other plans and to thank you."

"He's welcome." Maggie looped a hand through Liddy's arm. "I guess we should have thought of asking him earlier. It was a sort of last-minute invite."

"Or maybe he's just not interested in anything but a working relationship."

"Or maybe he really does have other plans." Maggie good-naturedly bumped Liddy's shoulder with her own. "He does have a family, you know. Linc. The kids. His dad."

"Maybe. Or maybe he's seeing someone else. He's probably having sex with someone else," she grumbled.

Just as well, she rationalized. She had plenty on her plate with the shop opening in a few days. She really didn't have time for the drama of a relationship with anyone.

Still, she couldn't help but wonder if someone was getting lucky, and who that lucky lady might be.

Chapter Five

Maggie had been right, Liddy thought as she mentally drifted just above her near-sleeping self. Today—Labor Day—should be her day of rest before tomorrow and all the stress of opening day. An hour or so on the beach in the warm midmorning sun, surrounded by nothing but blue water and bluer sky, luxuriating in a quiet marred only by the occasional cry of a gull or the sound of a passing boat's motor, was exactly what she needed. Resting, relaxing, refusing to let worry seep beneath the margins of her mind, which at that moment floated free. She pictured it like a kite rising over the water, high over the harbor and over Buzzards Bay, higher still over the three prone bodies on the hot sand of Cottage Street Beach, the waves rolling gently to the shore, the sail of a Sunfish billowing as the wind took it toward Shelby Island.

Shelby Island. Home of the Shelby clan for longer than anyone could remember. Liddy had never set foot on its rocky shore. She'd heard there was an old rambling house there and a barn where boats were stored. What else, she didn't know.

"Either of you ever been to Shelby Island?" Liddy asked her companions, her eyes still closed.

"Nope. You, Em?" Maggie leaned up on her elbows.

"Never been. Chris has, though. He and Linc were friends when they were in school," Emma replied drowsily. "Have you, Lids?"

"No. I was just wondering if what they said about it was true." Liddy, whose towel lay between the other two, adjusted the wide brim of her hat so it completely covered her face. "You know, about the haunted graveyard and the treasure hidden by the pirate who'd settled the island. All that stuff they used to talk about when we were in school."

"Oh, that. And, like, the Shelbys are descended from the pirate? I even remember his name. Claude-Rene Rousseau. When I was little, I thought it the most romantic name I ever heard." Emma laughed.

"I think it was stuff Tuck made up to keep people from wanting to come home with him after school," Maggie said sleepily from beneath her own wide-brimmed hat. "I remember Brett telling me things were not good at home for Tuck and his siblings, but I'm not exactly sure what that meant."

"I heard my parents talking about the Shelbys one time." Emma sat up and searched her bag for her water bottle. "I think Mrs. Shelby—Tuck's mother—had some sort of mental illness. My dad, as their pastor, counseled Mr. Shelby—Tuck's dad—a couple of times. As far as I know, Dad never went to the island, though. Mr. Shelby always came to the manse. I guess Mr. Shelby is still alive and living on the island."

"He is, but he isn't well," Liddy told them. "He's been in a wheelchair ever since that boating accident he had a few years ago. And he has Alzheimer's. Tuck mentioned him the other day."

"Now you've brought it up, I remember overhearing my mother talking to someone on the phone once. She said the family was cursed," Maggie said. "I guess she was referring to Mrs. Shelby's illness."

"I don't believe in curses." Liddy dismissed the idea. "But I can't deny the family has had some bad luck. Not just Mrs. Shelby's illness and Mr. Shelby's accident, but Tuck's wife died young. His daughter's run off and left her kids."

"But Tuck's solid, and Linc seems to be as well, so there's that," Maggie pointed out. "Maybe the curse was only put on the women."

"But that wouldn't explain Mr. Shelby's accident," Emma said.

"Will you two listen to yourselves? Talking as if you actually believe in curses." Liddy rested her arms over her abdomen.

"Maybe Linc broke the curse when he took in his sister's kids." Maggie ignored Liddy. "Tuck certainly appears to be doing well these days, curse or no curse."

"Not to mention the fact he's looking pretty good for a guy who's sixty-two. I saw him in the bank the other day." Emma glanced at Liddy pointedly. "Jeannie Brightcliffe was seriously checking him out. As in flirting with him while she was taking care of his business."

"Jeannie Brightcliffe is in her thirties. He's too old for her," Liddy grumbled.

"I don't know, Lids. She didn't seem to be thinking about the age difference."

"A lot of younger women like that silver-fox look," Maggie pointed out.

Liddy refused to react to the thought of thirtysomething, lithe, red-haired Jeannie flirting with Tuck. Her own feelings regarding the man still being somewhat jumbled, Liddy did what she always did when she didn't want to think or talk about something. She changed the subject. "So, Emma, what do you hear from Owen?"

"I've been so busy I haven't had much time to think about him. But I'm pretty sure he's still in London on some sort of business. I still don't know what he does, exactly." Emma tugged on the bottom of her classic one-piece black bathing suit, which matched her sun hat, black leather sandals, and black-and-white beach bag. As always, Emma was perfectly put together. When they'd first arrived at the beach, Liddy had been about to teasingly ask if she was wearing her pearls when she noticed Emma's pearl earrings. Of course. Not quite the same as that strand she always wore, but still. Pearls on the beach. Only Emma.

"Keeping track of all those Harrison investments, no doubt." Liddy opened her eyes and stared at the inside of her hat's brim until all she could see were concentric circles of brown and white, the colors of her hat. For her morning on the beach, Liddy had tossed her long hair into a topknot and pulled on a tank top and a pair of cutoff jeans. She'd topped it all off with the hat before grabbing her everyday handbag, into which she'd stuffed a bottle of water and a granola bar, and running out the door.

"I think they have a business there, but I never want to ask." Emma's potential new beau was the scion of the town's wealthiest family. Their mansion was for most of the year uninhabited, and the fabled carousel was brought out every few years on the Fourth of July for the local children to enjoy before it was returned to storage in one of the outbuildings on the mansion's grounds.

"Why do you feel you can't ask him?" Maggie's attire, while several notches above Liddy's last-minute, thrown-together choices, did not reach the level of Emma's beach chic. She wore a blue-and-green paisley one-piece bathing suit and bright-orange flip-flops, and her bag was a gray leather tote. Her blonde hair was pulled up in a high ponytail and held with a pink scrunchie, over which she wore a green WBPD ball cap she'd stolen from Brett.

"I don't want him to think I'm interested in his money or his status," Emma explained.

"Doesn't he know who your son is? Do you really think he'd be worried about you being interested in getting your hands on his investments, knowing Chris is worth a gazillion dollars?" Maggie sat up. "Em, can I borrow your sunscreen?"

"He knows, but we never talk about finances. Harry left me very well off, so I don't need anything from Chris." Emma dug in her bag and retrieved the sunscreen, which she tossed over Liddy's prone body to Maggie. "Not that I would expect my son to support me."

"Speaking of whom, where is the boy this holiday weekend?" Maggie squeezed lotion into her hand and proceeded to lather up her legs and arms.

"I'm not really sure. He was a little vague when I talked to him on Tuesday. Maybe off with that mysterious unnamed girlfriend I told you I think he has." Emma took a long drink from her now-warm water bottle. "What's Natalie up to? I figured she'd be here for sure."

"The community college where she teaches started two weeks ago, and she said she's up to her ears in paperwork already. She took on an extra remedial English class this semester, so she's really busy." Maggie finished with the sunscreen and tossed it back to Emma. "And Daisy has preschool on Tuesday, and Nat thought it might be too much for her to travel up here and back between Friday afternoon and today and then go to school tomorrow."

An old Bruce Springsteen tune began to play loudly from Liddy's phone.

"Oh." She sat up and grabbed her phone from her nearby bag. "It's Rosalita." Liddy stared at her phone for a moment before announcing, "She's still around the tip of the Cape."

"Who's Rosalita?" Maggie asked.

"She's the great white shark I'm tracking on this app I found online." Liddy held up the phone. "See the red icon there off Barnstable? That means there's been a confirmed sighting of her near the beach."

"Good call on the ringtone." Maggie high-fived Liddy and sang a few lines of the song.

Emma reached for the phone, and Liddy handed it over. "Oh, there she is on the map. I had no idea you were into sharks."

"I wasn't, but I saw something online about how they can be tagged with a sort of sonar thing that's used to track them. I thought it might be fun to see where they go, season to season. Last week she was a little further up the coast, but I guess she's going to be heading south soon and following the Gulf Stream now the water's getting cooler."

"How does one tag a shark?" Emma asked.

"There are a couple of different ways. They can shoot the tag onto a dorsal fin with a sort of speargun, or they can get it close to a boat and put it in a kind of sling, and then attach the tracker to the fin. The tracker sends a signal to a satellite whenever the shark breaks the plane of the water. I've been tracking Rosalita for the past few weeks, but this is the closest she's come to shore."

"Very cool." Emma passed the phone to Maggie.

"Yeah, there are different sharks you can track. I picked Rosalita because she wasn't first tracked until last fall, so she didn't have a lot of followers. At the time, she was in the Gulf of Mexico. She's not the biggest shark—only fourteen feet—but she seemed to have the most personality."

"Somehow when I think 'shark,' I don't think 'personality,'" Maggie said.

"The first picture I saw of her, she looked like she was smiling."

"Had she just taken a bite out of the guy who tried to tag her?" Maggie returned the phone to Liddy.

Liddy laughed. "Possibly. Anyway, it's a diversion for me. She's gotten around quite a bit. Nantucket, the Cape. All the way up the coast to Maine."

"Well, as long as you don't decide to bring her home and keep her for a pet, I guess it could be interesting." Maggie dug her toes into the sand.

"That would require one hell of an aquarium." Liddy put her phone back into her bag.

"So you're all set for your grand opening tomorrow, right?" Emma asked.

"I hope so. I can't think of anything I've missed. You guys have been great, helping me to set up the shop, hang the posters, put prices on the books. I don't know how to thank you."

"You thanked us last night with not one, not two, but three batches of your incomparable margaritas," Emma reminded her. "I'm amazed none of us are hungover."

"They were small pitchers. Besides, Grace was there to help. Four people, three small pitchers, no one gets hurt." Liddy adjusted her sunglasses, which had slipped down the bridge of her nose almost to the tip.

"Grace sounded excited about her proposed new living arrangements," Emma noted.

"She's going to talk to Tuck this week and see how much it will cost to make the changes she has in mind for the house. She said she wanted to wait until he was finished up at the bookstore, which he now should be." Liddy watched three old men cross the sand to set up their rods to surf-fish. "At least, I think he is. Maybe I should run down there and . . ."

"No," Maggie and Emma said in unison.

"No stopping at the bookstore. Tomorrow's soon enough. We agreed," Emma reminded her.

"I know. It's just so hard." Liddy sighed.

"Just close your eyes and relax for another . . . oh, let's give ourselves another thirty minutes out here on the beach. I can't remember the last time the three of us were here, sunbathing together."

"Remember that time right before high school graduation? The weekend before? Exams were over on Friday," Emma said. "I was still smarting over the fact Todd Hartman hadn't spoken to me since prom night. He'd taken me home when the evening was over, and I never heard from him again. I thought he liked me, and here he'd only wanted a date for the prom. It took me months to get over it."

"I remember that day. I was miserable. I'd just found out I was pregnant two weeks before graduation, and I had no idea how I was going to tell Brett. I couldn't bear to think about what I was going to say to my parents." Maggie's voice carried a trace of the confusion she must have felt back then.

Even though she was sympathetic to her friend's predicament, Liddy couldn't help but say, "I still am slightly pissed off over the fact you didn't tell Emma or me when you were going through it."

"I'm sorry. I just couldn't talk about it. Once the cat was out of the bag, it was all such a mess." Maggie sighed. "*I* was such a mess. Everyone was pressuring me to give up the baby. My parents and then Brett. His father was pressuring him. He was afraid Brett wouldn't be able to devote enough time to football when he got to Ohio State if we were married and had a child, and he'd lose his scholarship and have to drop out. He was afraid Brett would be overlooked in the NFL draft. Which meant he'd lose bragging rights about having a son who was playing in the pros. So he leaned on Brett, and Brett leaned on me, and my parents leaned on me, and eventually I cracked because I couldn't take any more. In the end . . . well, you know what happened in the end."

"Well, you and Brett have your boy back in your life," Emma pointed out, "and it seems like it's worked out for the best."

"He's been a delightful surprise. His parents—the ones who raised him—must have been wonderful people," Maggie agreed.

"It just goes to show you never know what's around the next corner," Emma pronounced. "Fate always seems to have another trick up its sleeve. You go along steadily for a while, then boom! Something you never expected pops up."

"True enough." Liddy nodded. "I never thought owning a bookstore was in my future."

"My point." Emma had been about to drop back onto her towel when she paused. "Oh, did you see the local paper this morning?"

"No," Liddy said. "Did I miss something?"

"There's an article about the coach's upcoming trial. Apparently, it's being delayed again because another victim has come forward, and the defense says it needs time to investigate." Emma rolled her eyes. "As if they don't have enough to convict that man already."

"What man? What trial?" Maggie asked.

"The former girls' basketball coach from the high school. Haven't you heard about it?" Liddy leaned up on her elbows. "Actually, I don't think you'd moved back when the story first broke, and since then it's been mostly legal stuff going on—appeals and discovery, that sort of thing, so it hasn't been in the news lately."

"So what's the story?" Maggie asked.

"A couple of girls came forward three or four years ago and told police their basketball coach had assaulted them. As in repeatedly raped them." Liddy sat all the way up. "They didn't report it at the time because he threatened them, said he had pictures of them and he'd send them to their parents if they told anyone, so they kept quiet. But one girl confided in her older sister, and it turned out he'd done the same thing to her two years earlier. They went to their parents, the parents called the police, and once the story broke, other girls who'd been abused came forward. It seems every year he'd picked out one girl on his team. Always a senior who wouldn't be around after graduation, which left him to cultivate a 'relationship'"—Liddy made the quotes sign—"with another girl the following year. Of course he claims it was all consensual, and the girls were all over sixteen. They said he continued the abuse and the threats right up to graduation; then he'd tell the girls to put it behind them and get on with their lives—or else the photos would be everywhere."

"Oh my God. That's disgusting. As the mother of daughters, I can't even imagine such a horror. Dear God, that's just terrible." Maggie visibly shivered. "I'm surprised Brett didn't mention it."

"It's not a Wyndham Beach case," Emma told her. "Since the regional high school is in Hastings, the police there handled it; then the state police got involved because the girls are from different towns. It's going to be tried in Fall River. And because the cases are still being investigated, all the action has been behind the scenes for a while. I heard they were still taking depositions from the victims. The judge has tried to keep a lid on it to avoid influencing the potential jury pool. There really hasn't been much about it in the news lately."

"He's an evil, sick man. He targeted the girls on his team and victimized them. They looked up to him and trusted him as their coach, and he abused them in the worst possible way. There's no punishment that would make up for what he's done to these kids." Liddy had been sickened by the sordid story, but at the same time, she'd been secretly just a little relieved all this had happened after Jessie's high school days had ended.

The conversation having taken a disturbing tone, all three women fell silent.

Finally, Emma said, "Guys, I'm starving."

"Me too," Liddy chimed in. "I say we go back to Maggie's and get started on lunch."

"Yeah, it's about time. I made a ton of food, thinking we'd have a crowd since Brett had invited a few of his officers, but they all bailed, and he's working. So it's just the three of us and Grace." Maggie stood and shook out her towel. "Besides, if you're eating, we don't have to worry about you running down Cottage Street to Front."

~

Liddy was awake at four on Tuesday morning, her nerves firing on all cylinders. She finally got out of bed at five fifteen and went downstairs, where she made coffee and talked herself into a real breakfast of waffles—frozen—and bacon. She stared out the kitchen window, watching for the sun to come up while she drank her first cup of coffee and practiced deep breathing to keep herself focused. Today was a big day, and she didn't want her nerves to dictate how it was going to unfold. She'd pondered her choices of opening-day garb, and decided to go with her perennial favorite: a long purple skirt, a white shirt, and miles of multicolored beads. It had been a while, she acknowledged, since she'd gone full-out Liddy, but there hadn't been much occasion for her to dress in anything other than work clothes for most of the summer. A business suit or tailored dress—she did, in fact, own one of each—might have seemed more apropos for the grand opening, but this was Wyndham Beach, and she was Liddy

Bryant, and everyone in town knew her, and most—okay, some—loved her just the way she was. Her trademark long skirt and what Emma referred to as her rainbow of beads around her neck were her statement: *This is who I am. Who I've always been.*

She paced herself on her walk to the shop, the sun just rising above the church on the corner. She stopped at Ground Me for coffee, a croissant, and all the congratulations the staff there had to offer. She gave them a thumbs-up as she left the shop and headed across the street. Traffic was almost nonexistent due to the early hour, so when she stopped dead in the middle of Front Street, there was no danger of her being run over.

"Oh." The hand not holding her coffee flew to her mouth.

There in front of her shop, right across the lower portion of the window, stretched a window box overflowing with flowers: daisies—white and painted—gerberas, baby's breath, low-growing zinnias, marigolds, petunias, nasturtiums, portulaca. The riotous circus of color lit up the entire front of the building.

"Oh . . . ," she exclaimed. "Oh . . ."

"You might want to move out of the way before someone mows you down," a voice behind her called. She turned to see Tuck leaning out the driver's side window of his truck.

"Did you do this?" She gestured to the front of her shop. "All this?"

"Guilty as charged." He eased to the curb and parked. "I got to thinking about how that long, low window box we talked about might look, and it kept nagging me." He got out of the cab and walked toward her. "So I nailed a few boards together, slapped some paint on them, and brought the whole thing down here last night."

"But the flowers . . . where . . . ?" She pointed but was still having a problem getting the words out. The front of her shop was glorious and looked so perfect she could barely believe it was hers.

"Oh, those. Well, you know Kathleen over at the nursery?" He joined her in the street, then took her elbow and guided her to the sidewalk. "I checked in with her on Saturday to see what flowers she had left. Since it's the end of the season, I wasn't sure she'd have anything, but as you can see, she had a bunch. When I told her what I was doing, she loaded me up with what she had. Said it was her grand opening gift to you. So if anyone asks you where the flowers came from, you be sure to direct them to Kathleen."

"I will. And I'll call her." Liddy nodded, still stunned at the sight of all that unexpected glory gracing the front of her shop. For one long moment, she was tempted to throw her arms around Tuck's neck, but good sense cautioned it wouldn't be a good idea for her to be seen hugging the man right there in the middle of town, gossips being what and who they were.

"Oh, the hell with it," she muttered.

If Tuck was surprised by having Liddy's arms wrap around him and hug him so tightly, he gave no sign. He hugged her back, so she figured he must have welcomed the gesture. His body felt solid and strong, and he smelled faintly of pine and WD-40, which brought a smile to her face. Jim had always worn a musky-scented aftershave he insisted was "manly." After he left her, the first time she caught a whiff of it on someone in the coffee shop, she'd almost thrown up. Pine and WD-40 were different but nice in their way, and infinitely better.

"Thank you, thank you, thank you. This just may be the nicest thing anyone has ever done for me." Liddy was so happy she had to stop herself from dancing right there. "It's all so beautiful. And look how gorgeous those flowers are with those tall urns on either side with the vines trailing down. Oh, the flowers are glorious, Tuck, and that sign! It's gorgeous! Perfect. I don't know how to thank you."

His dark eyes—pirate's eyes—stared into hers for what seemed to be a long time. "I could think of something."

Heat flushed her cheeks—*Was she actually blushing?*—and she slowly disengaged herself from his embrace and laughed uncertainly. "What do you have in mind?"

"Well, I remember all those times I was at your house, working on the carriage house or the back deck, and sometimes I'd check in with you before I left for the day." The corners of his mouth curved up just ever so much. "And sometimes I'd walk into your kitchen, and there you'd be cooking dinner, and wow, I'd be knocked out."

Liddy blinked. The sight of her cooking dinner had knocked him out? What kind of chauvinistic comment was that? Or maybe she'd looked better back then than she remembered, and he'd liked the way she looked.

"I swear I never smelled anything better than your beef stew."

"Beef stew?" It hadn't been her curves or her smile or her charm that had dazzled him? Disappointment washed through her.

He nodded. "Yup. Fantasized about it for years. So if you really want to thank me for this . . ." He gestured at the flower box. "You could invite me for dinner and make beef stew."

"Ah . . . well, sure. I could do that." She tried to cover up the fact she felt let down. "Maybe Sunday? I'll be here at the shop every night this week—first week, I need to be here, you know. But maybe Sunday I could get Grace to close for me."

"Sunday would be perfect."

"Great." She nodded. "I'll check with Gracie and let you know."

"I'll wait to hear from you."

"Okay, then. I should go inside and get ready to open."

"Wait. Stand over there next to the urn close to the door." Tuck directed her to the spot, then took his phone from his pocket. "We need to commemorate your big day." He took several pictures, then held out the phone for her to check the images. "Approve? Thumbs-up? Or down?"

"Definitely up for the first two—delete that third one, please. I look angry. Four is good. Five is perfect."

"I'll send them to your phone, and you can do what you want with them."

"Tuck, thanks for everything this morning. For just a few minutes, I forgot to be on edge."

"What do you have to be nervous about? Everyone in town has been talking about this for weeks."

"They have?"

Tuck nodded. "Sure have. Liddy, you have a lot of friends in this town. You've lived here all your life. Everyone knows you. And everyone remembers how you've supported every other business in Wyndham Beach and wants to return that support. Besides, we've been four, five months without a bookstore, so everyone's excited."

"Thank you. God, I hope you're right." She opened the door, and they went inside.

"Of course I'm right. Now, didn't I see a big 'Grand Opening' flag behind the counter?" Without waiting for her to answer, Tuck nudged her with his shoulder and said, "Let's put it out here for everyone to see. You want all those parents who are dropping off their kids today to know you are open for business."

The flag was flying over the newly painted red front door when the shop opened at ten, and by ten fifteen, there were more than a dozen shoppers. The carafes of coffee brought across the street from Ground Me were empty by noon, and the new-release table was almost sold out. For most of the morning and early afternoon, the checkout line stretched from the cash register in the front of the shop almost to the children's section at the very back. Emma had stopped in to lend moral support but quickly volunteered to do the bagging as Liddy rang up purchases. The lunch hour brought in more local residents, and later in the afternoon, there'd been an influx of well-dressed shoppers who'd stopped in because they'd seen the foot traffic, and they'd stayed to pick up a book or two. Jessie's framed posters drew a lot of interest, and Grace never failed to direct attention to the greeting cards, most of which were sold.

"How are you holding up?" Emma whispered to Liddy as she stuffed yet another bag with purchased books.

"Dead on my feet, thank you, but loving every minute of it." Liddy grinned from ear to ear. "Tuck said everyone in town would show up today, but I never expected all this. I'm going to have to make calls tonight to reorder stock."

"Uh-uh." Grace sidled up to the counter. "I'm checking stock, and I'll be emailing the distributors as soon as my mom gets here to relieve me as part of your sales force."

Liddy looked up from the register. "I didn't call Maggie."

"I did. She'll be here in fifteen minutes, and I'll take care of the reorders. You just keep smiling and chatting up the customers, and I'll take care of the floor." Grace's smile was almost as bright as Liddy's.

Maggie was there in ten, and she took over for Emma, bagging books at the counter. Around five things settled down to a handful of shoppers, and Emma sent Liddy to the back of the shop to sit in one of the wingback chairs in the children's section and rest for a few minutes. Grace ran the empty carafes back to Ground Me and returned with refills, anticipating an after-dinner crowd. She fixed a mug for Liddy and took it back to her.

"Hell of an opening, Lydia." Grace plunked down into the other chair.

"Indeed." Liddy smiled wearily. "If this kept up all week, I'll be able to actually hire someone full-time. You might even get a raise." She hastened to add, "Not that I expect this madness will continue, but just saying."

"I think you'll do really well. I put out those flyers we talked about, promoting all the things you're going to do, and the today-only twenty percent discount didn't hurt. The book clubs, the children's story hour on Saturday." She paused. "Though several people asked if we'd be doing the kids' readings in the afternoons."

"What did you tell them?" Liddy rested her head back against the chair and closed her eyes.

"I said we'd take it under advisement."

"That's up to you, if you want to do something extra like that. I'm too tired right now to make decisions on anything more complicated than when I will take my next sip of coffee."

"One of the people inquiring was a teacher at the elementary school. She said it would make a great field trip for her class if they could come in for a special story hour once in a while." Grace got up to offer her seat to her mother when Maggie joined them. "I said we'd think about it."

"Are you sure you want to take on something else?" Liddy opened her eyes. It would be a win-win situation for her, but Grace would have to deal with the additional work involved with selecting the books for each grade level and making sure there was sufficient stock for those kids who might want to purchase their own copy of whichever book Grace chose.

"We'll see." Grace wandered over to the shelf where Jessie's greeting cards were displayed. "We're going to have to reorder the birthday cards. There are only two left. And I think we should pick a few more of the designs to print up. We have lots to choose from."

"You do it." Liddy sat up and drank some of the coffee Grace had prepared for her. It was already lukewarm but tasted delicious and served to remind her she hadn't stopped for lunch. At least, she was pretty sure she hadn't. "I'm putting you in charge of the cards. Birthdays, holidays, just-to-say-hi cards. All in your hands. Whatever you want."

"Thanks. I'll go through them tonight."

Liddy heard the front door open, then close.

"Well, that was a short break." She stood, stretched, finished the last of the coffee, and headed for the front of the shop. "Hi, come on in. Are you looking for anything in particular, or just checking us out?"

By closing time, Liddy was exhausted. Grateful for the shop's smashing debut but more tired than she'd ever been.

At five minutes before nine, Tuck opened the door to let the last customer out, then came in.

"So how'd it go?" He came straight to the counter, where Liddy was leaning, hoping to hold herself up long enough to cash out for the night. "I drove by a few times and you looked busy."

"Busy is an understatement. You were right." She shifted her weight from one foot to the other. "I think I saw pretty much everyone I ever knew today."

"Foot traffic only or paying customers?"

"Some of each, but I think most people bought something. Grace spent much of the evening reordering some of the new releases. The new thrillers and romances were gone by three this afternoon."

"So all in all a good day?"

"All in all . . . a great day." Liddy couldn't help but smile in spite of her fatigue.

"I'm happy for you. You deserve this." He reached across the counter and gave her hand a squeeze. "If you're going to be here for a few more minutes, I want to run upstairs and check the work my guys did up there. Carlos said he finished the drywall this morning. I hope he didn't disturb your customers. I told him to come and go through the back door." He gestured toward the back of the shop.

"I didn't even know he was here." She frowned. That door had been locked. She'd checked it before she'd left on Sunday night. "How'd he get in?"

"He said it was unlocked."

"Oh, Grace probably unlocked it. Maybe she stepped outside for some fresh air and a few moments' peace at some point. It did get pretty wild in here for a while."

"I won't be long," he told her as he walked through the aisle leading to the back of the shop. "And then I'll drive you home. I don't know if you'd make it on foot tonight."

"No way would I make it all the way home to Jasper Street. Someone would find me sleeping on their front lawn in the morning."

"I think that's a given. You look like you're ready to crash." He disappeared around the corner, and she heard his boots thumping on the stairs as he headed up.

She was just finishing at the cash register when Tuck came down the steps at a fast clip.

"When I get my hands on those two. They know better than to ever leave anything on a job." He held up one hand. "Potato chip bags, candy wrappers, an empty soda can. I'm going to have their heads in the morning. No one who works for me leaves their trash on a work site."

"Oh, calm down. It's no big deal. Besides, maybe it was Grace. She's set up a makeshift office in that second-floor room." She reached for the trash and he handed it over.

"Somehow Grace doesn't strike me as the type to eat this crap. I could be wrong, though. I guess everyone has their weakness." He stood next to the counter. "Need me to take anything for you?"

"Aw, like carry my books home from school?" she teased, and he laughed.

"Something like that." He watched her drop the trash into a basket behind the counter.

"No, I've got it all. But I do appreciate the ride. I really am beat."

They walked outside onto the dimly lit sidewalk, and she paused to lock the front door.

"Oh crap, I meant to lock the back door," she said.

"I locked it with the dead bolt before I went upstairs." Tuck steered her toward his truck, which was parked at the curb in front of the shop, and opened the door for her. Liddy climbed in and buckled her seat belt.

"Think you can stay awake till I get you home?" he asked.

"I'll do my best." She stretched her legs out in front of her and forced her eyes to stay open.

Within minutes, Tuck was pulling into her driveway. When he looked as though he was about to get out of the truck, she said, "Thanks, Tuck. I can make it from here."

"You sure?"

Liddy paused. She'd have loved to invite Tuck in, put her arms around him and rest against his broad chest, be still, and share a moment of gratitude with him. But she simply lacked the physical strength to do more than tell him how much his thoughtfulness had warmed her heart. Whatever else she might say would have to wait for another time.

So she simply nodded and said, "See you later. And thanks again for everything. For all the work you did on the shop and the planting box and all the flowers and that wonderful sign. I can't tell you how much I appreciate all you've done to make this day special for me. So many people commented on how beautiful the shop was. Even the out-of-towners mentioned how all the color drew their attention to the shop. So thank you." She put a hand over her heart and added softly, "You're my hero, Tuck."

"Good to know. It's been my pleasure to help you. You've thanked me enough. Now go inside and go to bed." He put the truck in gear, and she slammed the passenger door. "Good night, Liddy."

She followed the path to her front door, wishing she'd had the presence of mind to leave the front light on. She climbed the steps, her heart full and her hand searching in her bag for the house keys. Tuck backed out of the driveway, pausing long enough for her to unlock the door and wave goodbye. Too tired to even eat, she somehow managed to strip out of her clothes and fall facedown on her bed. She was sound asleep in less than twenty minutes.

Chapter Six

Totally content to be exactly where she was at the moment, Grace sat in a rocking chair on her mother's front porch, her feet resting on the railing and her legs crossed at the ankles while she sipped the morning's first cup of coffee. Oh, sure, she'd rather be sitting on her own porch, but that was in the works. She mentally added *build front porch* to her list of things to do once she got the go-ahead on her plans for Liddy's little house. *Cottage* did sound cozier, but Grace liked the original name—the little house—and thought she'd keep it. Maybe have a plaque to proclaim it—in lowercase letters—somewhere on the property, like putting a name tag on the house. She couldn't wait for her plans to become reality. She could barely contain her excitement about her forthcoming meeting with Tuck after work. Having her own place again would be the best thing ever. Having a place of her own without memories of her failed marriage would be even better than best.

Not that living in her mother's home was terrible. It wasn't, not at all. She and Maggie had gotten along famously—for the most part—since they'd moved to Wyndham Beach. Grace suspected they owed their current compatibility to Maggie's being happy in her own life as much as to Grace's relief at having distanced herself from the life she'd left behind in Philadelphia with all its conflict. That flat-out, all-around mess was in the rearview mirror along with her law career, but she was okay with that, too. For ten years, she'd practiced at the firm founded by her father, but when it had all crashed and burned, she'd left the city with her tail between her legs, convinced she'd never practice again. Over time, might she have regained the respect she'd once enjoyed as part of the Philly legal community and the face of Flynn Law? Would she come to regret having moved on, miss the challenges, the courtroom sparring with opposing attorneys, the thrill of banking yet another big win? Maybe. But for now, she was fine with things just the way they were. Occasionally she did wonder how things were going at the firm, and how some of her old friends were doing, but did she miss her old life? She could honestly say she did not.

Grace liked Wyndham Beach, liked the life she was building for herself, and she had no desire to look beyond that. She loved the creative challenge of building imaginative websites for her business clients, and she enjoyed working with Liddy in Wyndham Beach Reads. After the pressure of making opening day a smash, things had calmed down at the shop, and both she and Liddy were settling into their roles. Grace's income had taken a nosedive, but she didn't need much to live on in the casual beach town, where the only occasion she'd had to wear one of her designer suits was to the funeral of a friend of her mother's a few months ago. These days, Grace lived in shorts or jeans and T-shirts. She found it liberating to not worry about her appearance the way she'd done in her previous life.

Grace's restlessness had only been seeping in since her mother had reunited with Brett. Not that she begrudged Maggie her newfound happiness. Not at all. Maggie smiled so much these days, and had a spring in her step Grace hadn't seen in ages. She deserved happiness after the pain of losing her husband—Grace and Natalie's father—and the fact she'd found joy with her first love, well, what could be better? Once upon a time, Maggie and Brett had dreamed of a life together, only to lose the dream, and now to have found it again? Priceless. That didn't mean Grace wanted to witness every moment of their happy life under the same roof. And it wasn't that Maggie and Brett were all over each other in Grace's presence. If anything, they were actually quite restrained. And that was part of what bothered Grace, sensing her mother felt she had to avoid showing too much affection for Brett around her daughter. Grace wanted her mother to feel free to be herself in her own home. As Grace had told Natalie, "If Mom wants to nail Brett on the kitchen table, I don't want her to feel she has to hold back because she's afraid I'll walk in on them and be horrified."

Natalie had laughed. "Scarred for life, for sure. But yeah, I see your point."

When Liddy mentioned the little house that stood empty at the back of her property, Grace couldn't wait to see it again. She hadn't been inside since she was a child, but as soon as she stepped across the threshold, she couldn't wait to make it her own. She just knew she could polish that little place into a perfect gem of a home. She'd been able to think of little else since she stepped inside.

Grace's phone rang, and she held the coffee mug away from her body lest she spill it while she searched her pockets for her phone.

"Hello?"

"Gracie, hi. Whatcha doing?" Natalie sounded unusually cheerful.

"Rocking on Mom's front porch, drinking coffee, and trying to talk myself into getting dressed to run down to the bookshop. You?"

"Walking from the parking lot to my first class," Natalie told her, which Grace could have guessed since her sister's words were punctuated by her huffing and puffing. "How're things in Wyndham Beach?"

"Great. It's a beautiful morning. If I hadn't promised Liddy to come in when she opened, I'd be walking on the beach right now. I don't know how many more beautiful, sunny, warm mornings we'll have here. I've never experienced a New England autumn or winter, so I don't know what to expect."

"Lots of color in autumn, lots of snow in winter. What else do you need to know?"

"Ha ha. Let me guess. You've been reading magazine articles about the glory of autumn in New England," Grace teased. "You'll have to make a trip up soon to see for yourself once the leaves begin to turn. We miss you."

"You can't fool me. It's my daughter you miss."

"Well, yes, Daisy first, then you. Seriously, when do you think you might be able to come for a visit?"

Natalie hesitated. "I'll check my schedule, and Daisy's school schedule, and I'll let you know."

"Please. You already know Daisy's schedule, and you said you only have one class on Friday morning." Grace took a sip of coffee. She asked, "What's up with you? Are you hiding something?"

"Nothing's up."

"Natalie, remember who you're talking to. I taught you the fine art of evasion. Now spill."

"No. If I tell you, you'll tell Mom. And she'll tell Emma, and . . ."

"Natalie Flynn, you're still seeing Chris, aren't you?" Before Natalie could respond, Grace said, "I don't understand why it's such a big deal, Nat. What do you think is going to happen if your mother and his know you're dating?"

"You know Mom and Emma are as close as sisters. They've been friends all their lives. What if Chris and I had a nasty breakup? Not that I'm planning on that ever happening, but you never know. Then Mom takes my side and Emma takes Chris's? Way to end a lifelong friendship. Uh-uh. I don't want that on my conscience." Grace could almost see Natalie shaking her head from side to side. "Besides, if Mom knew, she'd be hearing wedding bells, and every time I talk to her, it'll be, 'So how's Chris? Why don't you come home together this weekend so we can see you two? Are you thinking about moving in together? Will we see a ring anytime soon?'" Natalie sighed. "So then when we come home together, we'll have to deal with all that *and* sleeping arrangements. Mom's house or Emma's? His old room or mine? I just don't feel like dealing with all the ensuing drama just yet."

"Wait, are you saying you and the world's biggest rock star are sleeping together?"

"Duh."

Grace laughed. "Well, I can't say I blame you. Chris is adorable."

"He is." Natalie sighed again. "And he's still the same guy he was when we were little, and we used to spend summers at Wyndham Beach with Gramma, and we'd all play together. You and me and Chris and Jessie and the kids from the playground on Fifth Street, remember? Of course, since I was at least three years younger than everyone else, I got left behind a lot, but still, I have great memories."

"We did have some great summers growing up. You and Chris need to get your act together and bring Daisy up here so she can have fun summers at her gramma's house, you hear?"

"I hope by next summer we'll know where we're going," Natalie said softly. "Right now, it's too soon to tell, and I don't want to push it."

"It's not too soon to know you're in love with him, Nat."

"That obvious?"

"To quote my sister, *duh.*"

"It's complicated, Gracie. Our lives are so different. He is who he is, and he's traveling all over the world all the time; he has women flinging themselves at him constantly. I'm a teacher, a single mom with a four-year-old. I don't lead a very exciting life." She paused, then added, "Well, except for dating Chris. That's pretty exciting. But I can't compete with the women around him, models and actresses and women musicians. He just produced an album for Christal Ozanich. Christal Ozanich, Gracie!"

"So what are you saying? You think he had a fling with her?"

"I'm afraid to ask."

"Seriously? If you can't trust him that much, you need to rethink what you're doing. If it bothers you, you should ask him."

"I'm afraid he'll think I'm too . . . I don't know, clingy. Insecure. Possessive."

"I don't know about clingy or possessive, but insecure? Ya think?"

"The truth is the only time I don't feel insecure is when he's here with me and Daisy. Then it seems like there's nothing and no one else on earth. Like we're a tight unit. Then he's off for a couple of weeks doing God knows what, and I start to wonder if I shouldn't be dating someone else."

"Why would you want to date someone else?"

"I don't. But what if he is?"

"You're giving me a headache, Nat." Grace set her mug on the floor and wiped a hand across her face.

"I give myself a headache. So enough about that. Now you. What's doing with that house you looked at?"

"Nothing yet. But I will be going over my dream plans with the local contractor after work today. I hope he can do what I want done. He and Mom and Brett and everyone went to school together, and they all say he's the best around, so I have high expectations."

"It sounds exciting. I know how you enjoy a good makeover. Send me pictures tonight, okay? But right now, I've arrived at my class." The voices in the background were growing louder. "I gotta go. Talk to you later."

"Be careful, little sister."

"I will. Good luck with the house. And don't tell Mom. Promise."

"I promise."

"Pinky promise, Gracie." Natalie invoked the sacred oath of their childhood.

"Oh, for crying out . . . yes, pinky promise," Grace said, and the phone went silent.

Grace heard the door close, and Maggie stepped out onto the porch. "Who was that and what are you promising to do?"

"Oh. That was Natalie. She wants me to take pictures of the little house tonight and send them to her."

"What's she up to? I haven't heard from her since last week." Maggie sat in the chair closest to Grace.

"Just getting to know the kids, planning out the semester, that sort of thing." Withholding information wasn't really a lie, right?

Maggie nodded. "Did she say when she might be coming for a visit?"

"I didn't really have time to pin her down. She was on her way to class when she called." That much was true. Good so far.

"I know. Let's fly down to see her next weekend. We'll surprise her." Maggie smiled, obviously enamored of the idea.

"Ah, I don't think that would be a good idea, Mom."

"Why not?" Maggie narrowed her eyes.

Grace fought the urge to squirm under her mother's gaze. Maggie had always had a way of digging out whatever it was you were hiding.

"She might be busy with something at school. Or something with Daisy. She might have something lined up with her friends. You know, girls' night out." Grace forced herself to remain calm lest she set off her mother's truth-seeking radar.

"Then we could babysit for Daisy. Girls' night in," Maggie countered.

"Or what if she has a date?" Which she could have, if Chris was in town.

"Is she seeing someone? Did she say she met someone?"

"No, no, but that doesn't mean she might not by next weekend." Grace felt an overwhelming urge to cross her fingers behind her back, the way she had when she was a kid and she was lying. She'd always hated lying to her mother. This time she told herself it was Nat's lie, so it was on her.

"What do you know that you're not telling me?" Maggie stared at Grace, a stare intended to intimidate.

Grace almost caved, but she stayed strong. "Nothing. I just meant we don't know what her plans are. Suppose she decides to go see Elena and we fly to Philly and Nat and Daisy aren't there." Natalie could conceivably decide to drive to DC to see her college roommate for the weekend. It wasn't much of a stretch. "And no, she didn't say she was going to. I'm just saying we don't know what her plans are, and it would be foolish to make the trip to surprise her only to find out she isn't there or she's made other plans."

"You have a point." Maggie frowned. "I just miss seeing her and Daisy and wish they weren't so far away."

"I miss them, too. Why don't you call her tonight and see when she might be free?" Grace made a mental note to text Natalie to give her a heads-up.

"I'll do that." Maggie patted Grace on the knee. "Thanks, sweetie. Now don't you have to get ready to go to the bookshop?"

"I do." Grace swallowed the rest of her coffee, stood, and stretched. "Don't forget, I'm meeting Tuck at the little house tonight, so don't hold dinner for me. I'll probably grab something at Ray's after I leave the shop before I walk over to Jasper Street."

"Would you like to take my car?" her mother offered.

"No, thanks. I like walking around town." Grace leaned over and gave her mother a kiss on the top of her head.

Grace was almost to the door when Maggie said, "Gracie, are you sure you're not hiding something from me? For a moment there, before, you had that look about you."

"What look was that?" Grace skirted the real question.

"The look that says you're hiding something."

Grace shook her head. "Nothing to hide, Mom." She went inside and straight up to her room on the second floor. She sat on the bed and sent a text to Natalie: Mom knows something's up. She's turning up the heat. Trying not to break but the sooner you come clean, the better. And heads up—she's going to be calling you sometime soon. Get your shit together. xxox

   PS—you might not want Daisy to talk to Mom. She'll spill the beans.

~

Grace had spent much of her long but satisfying workday in the shop's second-floor office. She'd finished a website for a new client and emailed it for their approval, posted two more boxes of books for sale on the shop's site, and answered the day's emails and sales inquiries. She'd spent several hours working the shop's cash register while Liddy called in her book orders for the following week. When six o'clock rolled around, Grace said a cheery good night to Liddy and headed across the street to Ray's Pizza for his Thursday night special, advertised as soup and a slice: a cup of New England clam chowder, a slice of pizza, and a sixteen-ounce cup of soda. While she ate, she went over her notes and her sketch for the house, interior and exterior. She made a few last-minute changes, asked for a lid for her Diet Pepsi, and set out toward Jasper Street and the little house. She wondered if it had a separate address from Liddy's, and made a mental note to ask.

   It took less than ten minutes to arrive at her destination. She stood at the end of the driveway to take in the entire lot on which the little house had been built. The driveway was long and curved, the macadam in need of repair. The entire property was overgrown, the blue cornflowers, orange poppies, and wild daisies fought the knee-high grasses for space, and there were trees in desperate need of pruning. She thought the wildflowers were charming, but the grasses would have to go. She loved the look of the trees lining the drive, but the branches overhanging the house should be cut back. Window boxes below the front windows would be lovely. She sighed with pleasure at the mental image she'd fashioned of the newly painted house—maybe pale yellow?—with shutters and a front porch, a definite must-have. She slid the key into the lock and pushed open the door, trying to picture it painted something prettier and more distinctive than its current uninspiring muddy green. Maybe blue?

The house was as quiet as it had been on her previous visit, the air as still, but this time she felt its welcome. *It knows,* she told herself. *The house knows I want it and I'll do right by it, and it's happy I'm here.*

Grace went room to room, opening windows to let the breeze blow through from the front door to the kitchen. She opened the back door and stepped out onto the patio, which needed its share of attention, weeds having grown up between the flagstones. Moss covering a forgotten planter marked the end of the patio and the beginning of a path to the pond. She was just about to follow that path when she heard a truck pull up out front. She checked her phone and noted Tuck was right on time. She went back into the house and called, "Hi, Tuck. I was just out back, and I was . . ." She stopped midway between the kitchen and the dining room. "Oh."

"Sorry. Did I scare you?" Linc Shelby stood just inside the living room, his hand on the front doorknob. He had on well-worn jeans and a faded red short-sleeved Henley-style shirt with the buttons undone, and aviator sunglasses. His dark hair was slicked back and appeared damp, as if he'd just gotten out of the shower. He looked more *GQ* than small-town carpenter, and caught off guard, Grace felt she'd been struck by lightning.

"Oh. No. I, ah, I was expecting your father." An embarrassing flush spread from her chest to her face, clear up to her hairline. It was so unlike her to stammer.

"He pulled a muscle in his back this afternoon doing something he shouldn't have been doing, so he sent me in his place." He paused. "Is that okay?"

"Yeah. It's okay."

"You sure? You don't look as if it's okay." He removed his glasses and hung them from the V of his shirt. No longer hidden, his eyes appeared dark brown, almost bottomless, and too wise for a man in his midthirties.

"No, no, it's fine. It's just I expected to see Tuck when I came in, so I was surprised to see you, that's all. It's fine it's you. I mean, fine that you're here." Grace knew she sounded ridiculous, stumbling over her words. Where was the woman who had hypnotized juries with her spellbinding rhetoric?

Obviously, she'd stayed behind in Philly.

"So, what did you have in mind?" Linc looked around the front room, his hands on his hips.

"For . . . ?"

"The house. Dad said you wanted to completely renovate this place." He looked up at the ceiling. "Popcorn. I'm assuming you want that taken down."

"The popcorn ceilings." She got a grip. "They go all through the place. Yes, I'd like them gone."

"Dad said you were working on a sketch or a floor plan?"

"Yes."

"Want to show me?"

"Sure," she said, though she didn't move. "There was one thing . . ." She pointed to the far wall. "How hard would it be to build a fireplace there?"

"Woodburning?"

"Yes."

"It could be done, but you're talking a lot of money. You'd have to build a chimney and the firebox, the mantel. It wouldn't come cheap."

"I was afraid you'd say that." Grace shrugged. "Oh well. It would have been nice, but onward."

She motioned for him to follow her into the kitchen, where she'd left the sketch on the narrow counter.

"See, I thought if we could take down the wall here"—she pointed to the wall between the kitchen and the powder room—"then remove the closet at the end of the hall and combine it all into one, I could have a bigger kitchen."

Linc studied her drawing, then nodded. "As long as none of these walls are load bearing, that shouldn't be a problem. What else?"

"Over here . . ." Taking her carefully drawn plan with her, she gestured for him to follow her across the hall to the back room. "If we take out the wall between this room and the one next to it, I could have a big bedroom, a bathroom, and a walk-in closet."

"You think you have enough room for all that? How big a bathroom did you want?"

She pointed out on the sketch approximately where she'd like the proposed bath and closet. He walked off the footage he thought she'd need for the bath she had in mind, then nodded. "You'll have to have access to the closet through the bedroom because you'll need this wall"—he tapped on it—"for the vanity, but everything else looks good."

He looked around as if searching for something. "Basement door?"

"I don't think there is a basement."

"Which means the house should be on a concrete slab, so the slab carries the weight of the walls, which means we probably won't have to worry about which walls can and cannot be moved. If in fact that's the case, we should be able to do pretty much everything you've outlined without too much trouble and expense, but we'll check it out to be sure. The real money is going to be in moving the plumbing and the wiring."

Grace walked across the hall into the kitchen.

"Any idea when the house was built?" he asked as he followed.

She shook her head. "No. I never thought to ask Liddy. I thought maybe her husband—ex-husband—built it because he used it for his insurance business, but I don't know if that's true. The main house, where Liddy lives, is pretty old, so if this place was built around the same time—maybe sometime in the eighteen hundreds?—it's older than it looks. I'll see her tomorrow, and I'll ask her if she knows. Does it make a difference?"

"If some of the wiring is really old, as in knob and tube—you know what that is?"

Grace nodded. "My grandmother's house—the house my mom bought on Cottage Street—was built in the mid–eighteen hundreds. I remember seeing those white thingies when my sister and I used to play in the attic."

"Those white thingies—the porcelain knobs—are connected by wires enclosed in rubber tubing. Over time, the rubber can dry out and become brittle, and split, which can become a fire hazard. Some insurance companies won't insure a property that still has knob and tube."

"Jim—Liddy's ex—sold insurance, so I'm pretty sure he'd have known all that. Other than Jim using this building as an office, I don't know the history of the place."

"No big deal. We'll know when we start taking walls down. How soon did you want to start?"

"As soon as possible. I can't wait to move in."

"So no pressure," he deadpanned.

"None." She smiled. "Oh, I almost forgot. The outside needs work." She opened the back door and held it for Linc. Once outside, she pointed around the patio. "I would like this all cleaned up. The weeds pulled out from between the stones, the grass cut."

"I can give you the name of a landscaper if you want," he told her. "Our guys don't cut grass."

"Oh." For the second time since Linc arrived, Grace felt herself go red. "Sorry. I was thinking out loud. Of course you don't do that sort of work. Actually, looking at it now, there's no reason I can't do this myself."

"How much ground comes with the house?" he asked, graciously ignoring her evident embarrassment.

"I don't know. Liddy said it's on a separate lot from the rest of her property. I do know the house has a pond." She pointed straight ahead. "You can see the cattails from here, but they're hiding the pond itself."

"Nothing like a water view."

"I guess you'd know, living on an island."

"Yeah, there's no getting away from it. Water views from every window." He paused. "You might want to consider a screened-in porch if you're thinking about spending any amount of time sitting out here. So close to the pond, mosquitoes will be a problem in the summer."

Unconsciously, Grace scratched her arm. "Okay, add it to the list, maybe as a separate price."

"Sure." He was still looking at the back of the property. "You're probably going to want to hire someone to come in with a tractor to mow down all that tall grass."

"I couldn't do it with a regular lawn mower?"

"It would be tough. The grass is high and thick. Plus you don't know what's living there. Besides snakes, that is."

"What makes you think there are snakes?"

"For one thing, you're bound to have rodents—field rats and mice—snakes' favorite food group."

Grace eyed the grassy field with trepidation. "I'm not much of a snake fan. You really think . . . ?"

He knelt and pulled something long and transparent from the grassy section behind her. "Shredded skin. I'm thinking black snake because I haven't seen a garter snake this long in a long time. This has gotta be five feet." He held it up. "Almost as tall as you."

She felt the blood drain from her face. The thought of a snake of such size so close to her house—right by her kitchen door!—sent a shudder through her.

"They won't bother you," Linc assured her. "They'd be more scared of you than you are of them."

"No way would that be possible."

"They won't harm you, I promise." He glanced at his watch. "Was there anything else you wanted me to look at?"

"I'd like the exterior painted and a front porch added on. That's it, I guess."

"Let's take a walk around front and you can show me what you have in mind." He took a few steps toward the corner of the house, then stopped. He held up the snakeskin. "Did you want this?"

Was he serious? "Why would I want that?"

"It's kind of cool."

"Not in my world." When she mock shuddered, Linc laughed, the corners of his eyes crinkling. And dear God in heaven . . . the man had a dimple in his right cheek. She cleared her throat. "You're welcome to it."

"Thanks."

"Please. No need to thank me. I'm happy I don't have to dispose of it."

As they walked around the house to the front, Linc stopped to inspect a section of the outer wall. "You'll have to replace a bit of the siding, and you might want to get a termite inspection before we do any work."

"You think there are termites?"

"No, I think you just want to make certain there aren't any before you buy this place and put a lot of money into it."

No point in telling him she was renting, not buying, or her complicated financial agreement with Liddy. It wasn't information he needed to know.

When they arrived out front, Linc stood back to study the facade. "Tell me what you're thinking for out here."

"I'd like a covered porch running across the front of the house. Nothing fancy. Just a plain old covered porch."

He got a measuring tape from the truck and left the snakeskin hanging over the open window. "How wide do you want the porch?"

"Wide enough for chairs and maybe a small table."

He measured off several feet from the front of the house. "Out to about here?"

"Maybe just a little more."

He pulled the tape out another foot.

"That should be fine." Grace could picture it. "Perfect."

"Got it. I'll write all this up and get an estimate over to you in a few days."

"That would be great. How soon do you think you could start?"

"Depends on how soon we clear up a few other jobs and what my dad has promised other people we'd do without telling me."

"Oh."

"Grace, there are a few other contractors in town. Maybe one of them could fit you in sooner. I could give you the names of two or three if you're in a big hurry."

"That's nice of you, but I was told it had to be Tuck."

"By . . . ?"

"My mom and Liddy."

"Right up front you should know you won't get one hundred percent Tuck. You'll be lucky to get fifteen percent Tuck. He's not doing much of the work these days, so mostly you're going to get me." He slid his glasses back on, and once again his eyes were shielded. "Are you okay with that?"

"I'm fine with you." She was momentarily flustered but he appeared not to notice.

"I'll drop off some numbers to you as soon as I can." He took a few steps toward his truck. "I think your vision is spot-on. This'll look like an entirely different place once we're finished. Inside and out."

"That's the plan." She pointed to the snakeskin that hung like a white rope from the open driver's-side window. "What are you going to do with that?"

"Take it home. I think Duffy will love it."

"Duffy?"

"My ten-year-old nephew."

"Oh, by all means, please. Take it."

He removed the skin and opened the door, then climbed in. She assumed he'd laid the skin on the passenger seat but wasn't going to look.

"Thanks for coming out, Linc."

He waved and turned the truck around, then gave another wave as he headed for the street.

Grace stood right about where her new porch would be and watched the truck turn onto Jasper Street. She was curious about how he came to be raising his nephew and nieces but didn't know him well enough to ask. Actually, she didn't know him at all. What she did know was just slightly disconcerting. The first time they'd met, she'd been thrown off guard by a reaction to him she hadn't been able to put a name to. The instant attraction had been unexpected, and she could have sworn it had been mutual, but since that day, Linc had given her no sign he recalled first meeting her earlier in the summer. She'd seen him again at the town's July Fourth celebration. He'd been with the kids, and she'd assumed they were his, which had made her reaction embarrassing.

She went into the house and walked through it one last time. It was going to be perfect. One big bedroom, a lovely bath, a bright well-appointed kitchen, a spacious living room, and a dining space that would also serve as a home office. A patio out back where she could watch the birds—she'd have to get a feeder, and maybe a shepherd's hook to hang it on—and listen to the frogs in the pond while she drank her morning coffee. A front porch where she could sit and read in the evening. Next spring she'd plant flowers around the porch and in big urns next to the front door. And out back, around the patio, maybe an herb garden. Maybe even a small plot of vegetables.

Mariah Stewart

Grace sighed happily. The little house would be just the right place for her, and she couldn't wait until the work was completed so she could move in.

It was just perfect for her to settle in to while she tried to figure out the rest of her life.

Chapter Seven

By ten minutes before eleven on Saturday morning, the entire back section of the bookshop was filled with excited children. They ranged from age four to six or seven, the age group for the book Grace had chosen to read. Liddy had no doubt story hour would be a hit in Wyndham Beach, so she was feeling pretty smug watching the children stream into the shop. She pictured Jessie leaning against the doorjamb between the shop and the back hall as she silently cheered on Grace, her childhood friend.

Grace had dressed for the occasion in a white blouse with a black satin ribbon tied into a bow at the collar, a long dark skirt, and a straw hat laden with silk flowers à la Mary Poppins. She'd sent Liddy a text asking she open the back door of the shop so she could make her entrance directly into the children's section.

"Great costume. You look right in character." Liddy met Grace at the back door and ushered her inside. "Where did you find that outfit?"

"The blouse and skirt are mine, the ribbon was in my mom's stash of gift-wrapping essentials, and I found the hat in the attic." She lowered her voice to a whisper. "I pulled the flowers out of an arrangement my mom had in the dining room. I bet she doesn't even notice."

Grace sat in the club chair and smiled at the children who'd gathered. "Good morning, everyone. I'm Miss Grace, and I'll be your reader for today's story. Go ahead and find a place to sit, and when you're all ready, I'll begin."

"Your hat looks like Mary Poppins's," one of the girls told her.

"I'm so happy you think so." Grace winked at Liddy. "That's exactly the look I was going for."

Grace waited patiently as the children settled around her while Liddy welcomed newcomers.

"This is a wonderful idea, Liddy." Evelyn Marshall, who'd signed on to work part-time three days every week, shuttled her two granddaughters along the aisle to the children's section. "Just what we needed." She lowered her voice. "And look at the crowd. I hope all these parents and grandparents hang around and find a book to buy for themselves while they wait for their kids."

"One could hope." Liddy patted Evelyn on the arm and waved to Beth Benson, who was at the counter waving the sign-up sheet for the proposed book clubs.

"I'm all in for Thriller Tuesday," Beth told her.

"Great. I just selected the first book for this month." She took Beth by the elbow and steered her to the display of selections for the official launch of the book clubs and pointed to the top shelf. "Does John Sandford work for you?"

"Oh, he's one of my favorites." Beth grabbed a book from the shelf.

"There you go. The first meeting isn't for two weeks, so you'll have plenty of time to read it."

"Perfect." Beth headed for the cash register but was waylaid by the display of new romances. She stopped and picked up one, then another.

Liddy sighed happily.

The door opened, and Tuck walked in holding the hand of his youngest granddaughter.

"Are we late?" he asked somewhat anxiously.

"I don't think Grace has started reading yet, but you better hurry back there, JoJo."

JoJo took off down the aisle, dodging adults at every turn. Liddy and Tuck caught up just as she stopped at the display marking the children's section.

"What's wrong, Jo?" Tuck asked.

JoJo's eyes filled with tears, and she stuck her thumb in her mouth and pointed to the sea of children already crowded around Grace.

"We'll find a place for you to sit." Liddy lowered her voice and gently touched JoJo's shoulder to urge her forward, but the child did not move. "Look, JoJo, there's a spot right over there." Liddy tried to get her to move to her left, but JoJo stood firm.

Grace opened the book and appeared to be about to read when she looked up. She smiled at JoJo, who waved with just the fingers of her right hand. Even from a distance, Liddy was pretty sure Grace could see the tears on JoJo's face.

"You want to sit closer to Grace, JoJo? Is that it?" Liddy whispered, and JoJo nodded, her bottom lip quivering.

Liddy looked to Grace and silently formed the word *help*. Grace apparently got the message, because she scooted over on the chair and, looking directly at JoJo, patted the empty space. When the little girl took a few tentative steps forward, Grace nodded, and JoJo wove her way around the children seated on the floor. When she reached Grace, she climbed onto the chair, her thumb still in her mouth, her tears drying on her face. Grace whispered something in JoJo's ear, and the girl smiled.

Grace began to read, and even the children who'd been talking and laughing settled down and listened as the story was brought to life.

Liddy turned to Tuck and softly said, "She's a natural. Look at those kids. They're hanging on every word."

Tuck nodded. "Jo hasn't talked about anything all week except coming to the bookshop this morning because Miss Grace was going to read her a story. I don't think she realized there'd be so many other kids here."

When Liddy turned and headed to the front of the store, Tuck walked with her.

"She's awfully shy, and of the three kids, she's been the most affected by Brenda leaving them the way she did."

What way was that? The question burned Liddy's tongue, but she wasn't going to ask. Maybe he'd spill over beef stew at dinner tomorrow.

"She started school this week with the other kids, but she's so anxious over going to a new class with no familiar faces, she's having nightmares and barely talks unless Linc sits with her by herself and asks pointed questions. He said it's like pulling teeth, trying to get her to open up. I'm worried about her, to tell you the truth. I know Linc is, too. He's never been around kids, and then to take on these three." He shook his head. "He's doing the best he can, and he's afraid it's not good enough. I feel badly for him, but I don't know how to help."

"I'm sorry, Tuck," Liddy said. "I wish I knew what to tell you. Has Linc talked to one of the counselors at her school?"

Tuck opened his mouth to respond, but a customer grabbed Liddy by the arm and wanted to talk about the shelving of the nonfiction books.

"I don't know why true crime isn't shelved closer to psychology," the woman complained.

Liddy went into shopkeeper mode. "Excuse me, Tuck, while I help this customer."

"Sure. I apologize for monopolizing your time," he said.

"Maybe we can continue this conversation tomorrow over dinner," she said hopefully over her shoulder.

When the gossip was good, Liddy was right there with the best of them. But some things were sensitive—like your child abandoning her family and disappearing after turning her kids over to her only sibling. The subject was as tantalizing as it was disturbing and sad. Truth be told, Liddy was dying to know what had happened. But she wouldn't have asked, so the interruption when she sensed Tuck was going to say something definitive about the situation frustrated the devil out of her.

The story hour ended, and the counter was surrounded by parents wanting to pay for the books their kids had to have after Grace had read to them.

"I can see I'll be reading this one over and over for the next six months," one father muttered as he handed over his credit card for his purchases as well as his son's.

Liddy smiled brightly. "Come back next Saturday. New week, new book. You won't even have time to get tired of reading this one."

"Great idea. We'll be here."

Tuck was in line with JoJo, who clutched the book to her chest as if it were the most precious thing she'd ever had.

"So you liked the story, JoJo?" Grace came up behind her. JoJo nodded and hugged Grace's legs. "Will we see you next week?"

"I have a feeling she'll be begging to come back every week," Tuck told Grace.

JoJo nodded again but gave no indication she was ready to let go her hold on Grace.

"Jo, it's time to go. Thank Miss Liddy and Miss Grace and tell them you'll see them next week." Tuck knelt to JoJo's level after she hadn't budged. "Honey, you have to let go so Miss Grace can go home and get her lunch. You don't want her to be hungry, do you?"

JoJo seemed to think it over, then let go. She looked up at Grace, who hugged the child and said, "JoJo is my special friend. I hope you bring her back, Tuck."

"Of course I will." He ushered his granddaughter behind him so as to give the next person in line their turn to pay for their selections. "Oh, by the way, Grace, Linc showed me your plans for that little house over at Liddy's. Very nicely thought out but ambitious for a property you're merely renting."

Liddy half listened to Grace's response while she chatted with her customer. Grace easily sidestepped the comment about renting and addressed the compliment instead. "Thanks, Tuck. I spent a lot of time working on that floor plan, but I don't remember giving Linc my sketch to take with him."

"He sketched it out for me. From memory," Tuck explained. "It's going to be quite the place when all the work is done."

"That's the plan." Grace smoothed JoJo's hair back. "I'm going to run home now and change, but I'll be back in a flash. Liddy, if this keeps up, you're going to be exhausted by the end of the day."

"The thought has crossed my mind," Liddy told her. "But you don't have to change. You're a good advertisement for the story hour dressed the way you are."

"Well, then, I'll skip the trip home, but I would like to run across the street and get a sandwich and some coffee. I'm starving."

"Go for it. I'd say take your time, but—" Liddy's gesture took in the store. While the crowd had thinned, there were still a good number of people in the room. "Marion will be in soon. I'd wanted her for the entire day, but she had already agreed to give her daughter a hand at her flower shop this morning. Big wedding tomorrow." Marion was Emma's right hand at the art center and had been looking for part-time work. Liddy had been delighted when Marion had applied for the job and had hired her on the spot.

"I can wait till she gets here." Grace said goodbye to Tuck and JoJo and, summoned by a customer who needed help, walked off in the direction of the sci-fi shelves.

"I guess I'll see you tomorrow night," Tuck told Liddy over the head of the child who was counting out his coins to pay for his book. She nodded and helped the young boy to count.

It seemed most of the day saw a steady stream of customers, and even with the addition of Marion to work the cash register, Liddy was sailing on adrenaline. Around three, Maggie came in and shooed Liddy away from the counter.

"Grace says you haven't eaten all day, and you look beat." Maggie handed her a bag. "Sandwich. Salad. Dessert. Nice cold bottle of water. Go find a quiet spot and relax a bit. Brett's going to stop in later and bring us all coffee. And if you need us to, Gracie and I will close up for you tonight so you don't have to stay until nine. But right now—go."

Liddy retreated to her office without protest. She sat at her desk and took a few long, deep breaths before she opened the bag. She wanted to relax, but she was too keyed up from the day's events. There'd been something close to chaos around the cash register after Grace had finished reading, with all the children's books her patrons wanted to purchase. Brisk sales were always a good thing, but she hadn't realized how unnerving it could be to have so many people talking to her at once. She'd lived alone for the past three years, and she wasn't accustomed to dealing with so much activity, so many voices at the same time. She'd tried to ask her customers to form one line, but her request had been ignored except for the people closest to the counter. Next Saturday, she'd have signs made up—PLEASE FORM ONE LINE and PATIENCE, PLEASE—and she'd have someone near the front of the shop to make sure there'd be no bottleneck such as there'd been earlier.

She finished the ham-and-swiss sandwich, the salad, and the brownie Maggie'd brought and took her time sipping the water as she reflected on the day so far. She wouldn't know how many books had sold or how much was in the cash register until she closed up at the end of the day, but she knew they'd done well. That the store had not been empty since it opened in the morning was a clear statement from the residents of Wyndham Beach: they'd sorely missed having a bookstore in town and appreciated all the improvements since it had passed from Fred Lattimore's hands into her own. She'd received as many compliments on the exterior of the shop as she had on the interior, with Tuck's flower box getting rave reviews. She'd have to remember to tell him how much his handiwork had been admired.

Liddy stood and stretched, rejuvenated from the food and the rest, and eager to get back to work. She appreciated Emma's and Maggie's offer to stay until nine and close for her, but of course she wouldn't take it. They both had things to do. Grace insisted on staying till the end, and while Liddy needed the extra hands, she thought a young woman like Grace—beautiful, smart, funny, amicable—should be out having fun with other young people on a Saturday night, not stuck behind a cash register. Unfortunately, Liddy could count on the fingers of one hand the number of single people in Wyndham Beach who were Grace's age, which was one of the reasons she'd been so surprised Grace would want to put money into renovating a house she didn't own. She still wasn't comfortable with Grace putting so much of her savings into the house, though she wouldn't lose out in the end since Liddy was sure she'd be able to pay her back when the house was rented to someone else once Grace left. And wasn't it inevitable that Grace would eventually move on from Wyndham Beach? It was one thing for a woman like Grace to take some time to lick her wounds in a small town like this, another to dig in and stay for more than a few years. Liddy would bet money within two years—three at the very most—Grace would be gone to Boston or Pittsburgh, or maybe even back to Philly. She just didn't see her giving up her law career for good, and spending the rest of her life living alone in the little house, no matter how beautifully she fixed it up. Surely Grace wanted—and deserved—more out of life.

Liddy left her office and switched off the light. Customers still strolled through the aisles and searched the shelves for something that caught their eye. She was pleased to see almost everyone had at least one book in their hand, that her shop had brought all these people in on a sunny September Saturday when they could have been outside enjoying the perfect weather. At the same time, she wondered how long it would take before the novelty wore off.

It would be her job to give people a reason to keep coming back. She was working on that.

She was just about to step behind the counter when she noticed two men standing near the front door. Liddy blinked and stopped mid-stride. The tall gray-haired man wearing the Dartmouth sweatshirt was Dave Michaels, who owned a car dealership on Route 6. The shorter of the two was bald, wore dark glasses, and was dressed in a light-blue button-down shirt and khaki pants. He stood with both arms crossed over his chest, and their conversation appeared amicable.

It was the bald head that momentarily threw her.

Then Liddy saw red. What in the name of all that was holy was he doing here?

If Jim Bryant thought she'd greet him with a smile and open arms, he was out of his mind. She made a beeline for the pair.

"What are you doing here?" she asked sharply.

If the harshness of her tone surprised him, he gave no sign. "I saw the opening day sign earlier this week and thought I'd stop in to wish you well."

"Consider it done. Now you may leave."

"I, ah, think I'll go see what my wife's into," Dave said. "Jim, good seeing you again. I'll give you a call about the insurance we talked about. Congratulations, Liddy. Nice shop." Dave did a disappearing act.

"Why are you here, Jim?" She could barely stand to say his name.

"If you're asking me why I'm in Wyndham Beach," Jim replied calmly, "I had an appointment with a client."

"You still have clients in town?"

"Why wouldn't I? I was in business here for almost forty years. And I'm here, in your shop, because I wanted to see how you were doing."

"I don't want you here. This is my place. And how I'm doing is none of your business." Liddy was breathing fire. Her day had been going fabulously until he'd shown up. The welcome sign over the counter did not extend to him.

He stared into her eyes for a moment, then nodded slowly. "I guess I understand. I'll go. But I really do wish you all the best luck. I think it's terrific you bought this place."

"I have long since stopped caring what you think about anything." Liddy turned her back and went to the counter, where she relieved Marion. She greeted the next customer with the biggest smile she could muster.

At the end of the day, her hands were still shaking from the effort to control her temper, but she was proud she hadn't let it rip the way she'd wanted to.

How dare he kept circling around inside her head. How dare he come into her shop as if they were friends. They were not friends. They would never be friends. He'd walked out on her at the lowest point of her life, the point when she'd needed him to keep her from sinking under the weight of her grief. She could understand his withdrawal immediately after the shock of Jessie's death. Liddy had withdrawn, too. As time went on, it had become more difficult to get through the days. It was so hard to see past the pain and accept the fact she now had to live a life without her daughter, her sweet girl, her pride and joy. Months passed before she'd begun to feel even vaguely alive. And just when she was starting to breathe again, Jim had walked out on her.

After the double hit of her daughter's death and her husband's desertion, it had taken two full years for Liddy to understand that if she were to continue to live in this world, she needed to participate in life and make her days meaningful. Buying the bookshop was her investment in herself, her way of finding purpose in what had seemed, for a while, to be a life without direction. She had cleared a path for herself, and she owned it. Today had been the culmination of months of hard work and careful planning, and she took great pleasure in the success of her first week. But some of the day's shine had been tarnished by Jim's presence, adding yet another grievance onto the mile-high heap of things she'd never forgive him for.

~

Promptly at seven on Sunday evening, Liddy's doorbell rang. She dried her hands on the nearest dish towel, patted the long braid draped over her left shoulder, and smoothed the front of her blue-and-white-striped shirt. She held in her stomach as she went to answer the door, chastising herself for tucking her shirt into the waist of her khaki pants rather than leaving it out, where it could effectively hide her stomach.

She paused in the hall, muttered, "Oh, the hell with it," and pulled out her shirttails before opening the door and greeting her guest with a smile.

"Hey, Tuck. You're right on time."

"Are you kidding? I've been looking forward to this all week." His eyes twinkling, he handed her a bunch of colorful dahlias and a bottle of wine. "I brought red because I'm pretty sure that's what a good beef stew calls for."

"It does, so we'll go right into the kitchen and open this. And oh, what flowers!" she exclaimed. "I love dahlias. I don't know why I've never grown them. They're lovely, Tuck."

The flowers were beautiful, their glorious shades of reds, corals, golds, and pale yellows cheery. Liddy couldn't remember the last time anyone had brought her flowers, and she was touched by the gesture. She could have hugged Tuck for bringing them.

"Are these from Kathleen's nursery?" She touched the petals of a large flower the color of a sunset.

"No. They're from the nursery on Shelby Island."

"You grew these?"

"I did." He must have noticed her looking slightly drop jawed, because he said, "What? You think I don't do anything but pound nails and fish?"

Liddy laughed. "No, no. I just didn't know you were a gardener, that's all."

"There's a lot you don't know about me," he said, a hint of a tease in his voice.

"I'll bet there is," she murmured. "Next you're going to tell me you're a master gardener."

"Just an avid one. Actually, the dahlias started out with my mother. She grew them for as long as I can remember, but she never grew anything else. Even when she couldn't remember anything or anyone, she remembered how to tend these, when to bring the tubers in before the frost could kill them, when to divide them, when to plant again in the spring. The year after she died, I found a box of tubers in the barn, so I planted them in her memory. Fall came around, and I didn't want to be the one to let her dahlias die from the cold, so I dug them up, brought them in. It became sort of a thing for me."

"What else do you grow?"

"Nothing. Just dahlias."

"Well, if you're only going to grow one thing, you can't do better than these beauties. The colors are stunning."

They went into the kitchen, and Liddy gestured to the two wineglasses sitting on the counter. "Why don't you do the honors while I find a vase?"

"Your kitchen smells just like I remember, Liddy." Tuck sniffed the air and went to work on the wine bottle. "I can't wait to taste that stew."

"And in a few minutes, you will. Meanwhile, pour us some wine, and help yourself to some salsa and let me know if I've gone too far with the jalapeño." She pointed to the table, on which a blue bowl of salsa and a basket of chips awaited. "I've been told I have a heavy hand when it comes to seasoning."

He scooped up some salsa with a chip and took a bite. "Perfect. Just the right amount of heat."

Liddy opened a cupboard and found the tall dark-green pottery vase that would set off the colors of the dahlias perfectly. She placed the flowers in the vase and brought it to the kitchen table. She'd planned on eating in the dining room, with its formal dark furniture and Jim's grandmother's china, but somehow this round table surrounded by windows with its view of the pond at the far end of the property seemed cozier and more intimate.

He poured her wine and passed her the glass, tipping his in her direction. "Cheers, Lydia. Here's to the continued success of Wyndham Beach Reads. Judging by what I saw yesterday, you're off to a great start."

"Maybe it's just the novelty, because we haven't had a bookshop in town for months." She touched the rim of her glass with his, then took a sip of wine right before she sat in the chair next to his. "I'm hoping I can give people enough reason to come back on a regular basis. You know, book clubs, special sales, maybe some author signings." She grinned. "Not to mention a current inventory of bestsellers, something Fred could never keep on top of, even before he developed Alzheimer's."

"Well, I know the story hour for the kids was a big success. I heard people talking about it while I was in line to pay for JoJo's books." He took another chip and scooped up more salsa. "This is going to have to be my last chip. I need to save room for that stew. The aroma is driving me nuts."

"It should be done." She rose and took her wineglass with her. "Come here and give it a taste, see if you think it needs anything." She got out a big wooden spoon and handed it to Tuck, who dutifully dipped it into the pot. "Watch now, it's hot," she cautioned as he raised the spoon to his lips.

"Hot, but perfect. Damn, that's good, Liddy." He handed her the spoon.

"Want to eat in here or in the dining room?" she asked.

"Right here is fine." He proceeded to clear the kitchen table and set out the flatware she'd left on the counter. "I like this room. It's homey and cozy, just right for eating a big bowl of stew on a chilly evening."

"Here you go, then." She filled a soup bowl, piling it high with chunks of beef and pieces of potatoes and carrots, then topped it with the well-seasoned broth. She handed him the bowl, then prepared one for herself. She was about to sit when she remembered the salads she'd made earlier. She got those from the refrigerator and took a loaf of crusty bread from the oven, where she'd heated it. "I think that's it."

"This is quite a feast," he remarked as he dug into the stew.

"I hope you enjoy it."

"Every bite. Seriously, this is even more delicious than I'd fantasized."

"I'm glad you like it, and I'm glad you suggested it. I don't usually have company for dinner, and it's nice after a long week to have some-one to talk to over a meal."

"Did you work before? I don't remember."

"I worked for Jim for years. I did some light bookkeeping, followed up with his customers for payments, chatted with the insurance com-panies he dealt with, that sort of thing. That's how I reconnected with Jim after high school. He was working for his father—you know his dad owned the agency before Jim took over—and I got a job working for them after I graduated from college. I hadn't intended on staying in Wyndham Beach, but I needed to do something while I figured out where I wanted to go and what I wanted to do."

"And the rest is history."

"Ancient history." She dug into her salad.

"Well, while we're talking about ancient history, I remember you from school."

"You do?"

He nodded. "Oh, yeah. You hung out with Maggie and Emma Harper. You were the one who always stood out with your dark hair all the way down your back and your hippie clothes and your beads and your sassy mouth. I thought you were the coolest girl in your class."

Liddy laughed. "There are days when that description still fits. Except this"—she touched her braid—"is a lot more silver now. But I appreciate you thinking I was cool."

"You make silver look cool. You were the cool sophomore girl then, and you're the cool businesswoman now."

"Well, thank you. Flattery will get you anywhere."

He smiled in response. "I'll keep that in mind."

Liddy finished her salad and started on her stew. Noticing Tuck had finished his stew, she offered seconds. "My head says yes, but my stomach says better not. But thank you. It was delicious. Everything was delicious. Best meal I've had in . . . damn, I can't remember when I've had better."

"Surely someone is cooking out at your place. You all have to eat."

"Linc does his best to keep up now the kids are with us, and I try to get out on the water to do some fishing, catch something to put on the table once a week. But it's been a hard adjustment, having little ones in the house again. Linc and I used to be on our jobs by seven, work till we felt like quitting, but now we have kids to get breakfast for in the morning and get them to school on time. In the summer, it was camp. Now it's school, but it's over by three, and someone has to be there to pick them up, bring them home, oversee the homework, make dinner. Let them play and be kids. We're doing the best we can, but that girl of mine sure set a burden on the two of us." He hastened to add, "Not that we haven't come to love them, don't misunderstand. But we were a house of men for years. Then boom. Out of the blue we get this call." His eyes clouded over, and he fell silent.

Go on, Liddy silently urged him, but he just tapped on the side of his wineglass.

Finally, she couldn't help herself. "What happened, Tuck?"

"You know, I blame myself for the way Brenda is. I babied her and spoiled her and made excuses for her when I should have been making her take responsibility for her actions right from the start, so I feel a lot of this is on me. You know, you let a kid think she can get away with anything, and pretty soon she believes it. If I could do it over . . ."

"Hindsight's a bitch, Tuck. Everyone has something they'd do over if they could. And you're not responsible for the choices your kids make." Liddy had gone down that rabbit hole, blaming herself for whatever had made her daughter take her life. It had taken eighteen months of counseling for her to accept that while she might never know why Jessie had made that decision, it had been Jess's to make. *And keep in mind, Liddy, everything isn't always about you,* the therapist had said, but it had been months before Liddy had understood what that meant.

"Brenda was always hard to handle, but after her mother died . . ." Tuck shook his head from side to side. "I couldn't do a thing with her." He forced a weak smile. "It's tough raising a family on an island. And yet here we are, doing it all over again. Honestly, it's a miracle she graduated from high school. College? Out of the question. She took off for Boston right after graduation and I wouldn't hear from her for months. Then she'd call when she'd gotten into a scrape and needed help. And, of course, I always did what I could for her."

"Of course you did. She's your daughter. But what about the kids' father?"

"Brenda told Linc he's in prison for drug trafficking. Linc was going to try to find out more, but he's had his hands full between the kids and work."

"Did she tell the kids where she was going?"

"She didn't even tell the kids goodbye. Just put the kids in Linc's truck and drove off. I'm ashamed to admit she's my flesh and blood."

"I can't even imagine how difficult this has been for all of you."

"Linc's borne the brunt of it. He just pitched in, like, 'Okay, kids, it's just us now. We're going to do this thing.' And he has. I told him he was entitled to say, 'I told you so,' but he said that wouldn't solve anything, wouldn't bring his sister back or make things better for the kids. So he got them registered for school, helps them with their homework, got them into activities. Duffy and Bliss are in sports. JoJo wanted to take ballet lessons, but Linc was too late signing her up."

"How'd he register them for school? Didn't they need their birth certificates?"

"Thoughtful Brenda handed Linc an envelope," he said dryly. "Along with their medical records, sketchy though they were. Linc got them over to Dr. Clemmons, and she called the pediatrician listed on the vaccination list and filled in the blanks." He looked her in the eyes and said, "How can one kid turn out to be irresponsible and selfish and heartless, and the other turn out to be so responsible and kind and good-hearted?"

There was no answer, of course. She put both her hands over his on the table. "I'm so sorry, Tuck. I'm sorry for you and the kids and Linc—and I'm sorry for Brenda."

"Thanks, Liddy. Like I said before, we're all trying to adjust. Duffy's doing the best. I don't know how well the kids knew their father—I never met the guy myself so I don't know anything about him. But Duff seems like he's always been with us. It's like he looks to Linc as his dad. I don't know if that's good or bad, but for now, he seems okay."

"And the girls?"

"Bliss is definitely her mother's child. She's tough. Not as tough as Brenda, but that girl has some issues. Ironic name, huh?" He held on to Liddy's hands. "And JoJo—she never mentions her father, but she's the one who misses her mom the most. She's only five, so that's not a surprise, but she's not adjusting well at all. Sometimes she just curls up on my dad's lap in his wheelchair and she cries. Of course my dad doesn't know who she is. He calls her Brenda, which only confuses the kid."

"Maybe some counseling . . . ?"

Tuck nodded. "Linc has been in to see the school psychologist, and they're working out a plan."

"It sounds like you're doing everything you can for them."

He exhaled loudly. "We're doing our best."

"That's all anyone can do." She gave his hand a squeeze and, sensing he'd had enough for one night, stood and began to clear the table. "Now about dessert . . ."

"Liddy, I couldn't eat another thing."

"Guess I'll have to eat that fresh peach shortcake all by myself."

"Well, maybe I could force a little. Tell me what I can do to help."

"Not a thing." She smiled. "Coffee?"

"Decaf?"

"Sure. I can't drink the regular brew this time of the night. I'd be awake till Tuesday."

"Me too."

She started the coffee and got the peaches out of the refrigerator.

"I saw Jim yesterday after I left the shop." Tuck rested an arm over the back of the chair. "He mentioned he was going to stop in to see you."

"I wish you'd told him not to bother," she grumbled.

"Why would I have done that?" Tuck sounded genuinely curious.

"Because." She stabbed the knife into one of the shortcakes and sliced it open with a vengeance.

Tuck nodded slowly. "That's some highly mature reasoning."

Liddy fell quiet for a minute. Then: "I don't want him in my shop."

"I guess he thought it was a public place."

"Are you taking his side?" She turned to him, the knife still in her hand. "Because it sounds like you're taking his side."

He shrugged. "Why do there have to be sides?"

She slammed the knife onto the counter. "He walked out on me. One year to the day after Jessie died—the first anniversary of her death—he walked out. No explanation." She was mad at Jim all over again. "Do you know what he said? He said, 'Lid, I'm leaving.' That was it. Three words after nearly forty years of marriage. After everything we'd lost. Three words."

"Liddy, I'm so sorry. I had no idea. I never knew why the two of you split up. I just assumed it was one of those mutual things."

"There was nothing mutual about it. I never saw it coming." She turned back to the dessert, placing the shortcakes on the plates. Without turning around, she said, "You know, we buried two children."

"Two?"

"Before we had Jessie, we'd had a son. I'd had so many miscarriages, I was sure I'd never go full term. Then I did, but he was stillborn. What a kick in the ass that was. But we even got through that." She started to spoon the sliced peaches over the cakes, but paused, then threw the spoon into the sink with a vengeance. "I just would have liked to know why he left me."

"Did you ask him?"

"I asked him the night he said he was leaving." Liddy carried both plates to the table and set one in front of Tuck, the other at her place. "He just walked past me and out the door, like it was too much for me to ask of him. His stuff was already in the car—his clothes, personal items, and later, when the fog started to lift, I realized some photos were missing, a couple of books, his golf clubs. It was as if he'd never been here."

She paused as if she'd forgotten something, then remembered she'd made coffee. She poured it into two mugs and brought them to the table, along with the sugar bowl and a small pitcher of half-and-half.

"A week later, I got a call from a lawyer in Fall River. He said Jim had told him to give me everything, that he signed the house over to me along with our retirement fund. That's how badly he wanted to get away from me. He didn't even want half. He just wanted out."

She turned to Tuck, who was staring into his mug of coffee as he stirred in the sugar. "What makes a man do something like that?"

He shook his head. "I guess you'd need to ask Jim if you really want an answer."

"I don't want to talk to Jim." Hot tears formed in the corners of her eyes but did not spill.

"Then I guess you'll have to stay pissed off and in the dark for the rest of your life."

"You're not very sympathetic." Disappointed, she looked out the window rather than at him. She decided this dinner had been a bad idea, and she was starting to feel sorry she'd been reeled in when he was fishing for an invite. She'd just spilled her guts, and all he'd offered in return was logic. Why don't men understand that when a woman is teary and upset, the last thing she wants to hear—most of the time, anyway—is a logical response? She'd wanted to hear him say, "Damn, I never realized what a dumb SOB Jim is."

"I didn't realize you wanted sympathy, Liddy. I thought you wanted answers, and there's only one person who can give you that," he said softly as he reached for her hand. "Look, I am sorry—beyond sorry— you had to go through that, especially on the heels of losing Jessie. I know what it feels like to lose a daughter. Brenda still walks this earth, but she's lost all the same."

It was on the tip of her tongue to tell him it wasn't the same, that there was no comparison between Jessie taking her life and Brenda leaving. But gone was gone. They each had their own pain to deal with, and she had no right to judge or diminish his.

She sighed deeply. "Leave it to me to turn what had been a very pleasant evening into Liddy's melodrama, part one. I didn't intend to do that. I don't know why I . . ."

"Hey, stop. It's okay," he said. "We're friends, Liddy. We've been friends for a long time. You can talk to me about anything, anytime." He stood and pulled her gently from her seat and wrapped his arms around her. He felt solid and steady, and Liddy was pretty sure he wouldn't ever leave a woman he'd once loved without telling her why. "I'm here for part two, if you need me. I have the unfortunate habit of saying what I think, and the first thing I thought of was if you want to know why Jim left, you should just ask him. I guess that bluntness comes from living with my father and my son for so long."

"You might want to soften up a bit now you have two little girls living with you." She sniffed. "Or maybe not."

"No, you're right. They've had enough harsh realities." He held her tightly. "And so have you. I didn't mean to make you feel like I don't think Jim is a thoughtless, heartless jackass, because he obviously is."

"Hmmm. Thoughtless, heartless jackass." She nodded slowly, then smiled. *Thoughtless, heartless jackass* was even better than *dumb SOB.* "I like it."

Chapter Eight

Liddy filled an empty water bottle in the small powder room off her office, then proceeded to water the plants scattered throughout the shop. She started in the children's section, where she'd placed ivy and pothos in colorful pots along the wide windowsill. She refilled the bottle and went up front and watered the tall fiddle-leaf fig tree Maggie had brought from her house to fill a front corner and the huge schefflera Emma had sent as a grand opening gift. There were several floral arrangements sent by friends the previous week that needed attention, the dead or dying blooms removed, the remaining flowers rearranged, and the water changed. Liddy enjoyed these early morning hours when she had the shop to herself. The sun came in through the front window, and she could enjoy a cup of coffee in the warmth and silence while watching the town come alive.

"What do you think, Jess? These roses have any life left in them?" Liddy stood back and studied the contents of the vase on the counter, a gift from Carl Lattimore. "I agree. Time to chuck 'em. Nice gesture on Carl's part, though, don't you think?"

She took the vase back to her office, pitched the sad remains of the once-beautiful white roses into the trash, and emptied the vase into the powder room sink. She set it on the windowsill to dry, then settled at her desk to go over the inventory report Grace had run after they'd closed the night before.

"I don't know what I'd do without your old friend, Jess. She figured out how to integrate everything so all the sales can be tracked by the computer. I'm sure it's no mystery, but if I had to learn how to do all this, along with everything else I had to do, we wouldn't be open for about another year." Liddy raised her eyes from the report, then closed them and went to a place where she could see Jessie and Grace playing on the beach. They'd collect shells, splash in the surf, and toss tidbits of their lunch into the air to lure the gulls. Their mothers would sit on their beach towels, watching their daughters play, best friends, as Liddy and Maggie had been, as Liddy and Maggie had hoped they might be. And every August, Art would come to Wyndham Beach and collect his family, and Jessie would cry.

"Why does Gracie have to leave? She's my bestest friend," Jessie would sob into Liddy's chest after the Flynns' car disappeared from view.

"You know she lives somewhere else, Jess. She only comes here in the summer to stay with her grandmother." Liddy would wipe away Jessie's tears and smooth back her hair. She knew exactly how her daughter felt. Maggie was her oldest, dearest friend, and she hated having to say goodbye till next summer. Liddy felt like crying herself. "But you know she'll be back when summer comes again, right?"

"But she's not here now," Jessie would wail. "I want her to be here now, for all the time."

Liddy looked to the open doorway, where she pictured her daughter, and said aloud, "And now she is, sweetie."

As if summoned, Grace called from the front of the shop. "Liddy?"

"In the office. Would you bring my coffee when you head back this way?"

Less than a minute later, Grace handed Liddy the large cardboard cup from Ground Me and tossed a linen shirt onto what was supposed to be the visitors' chair. It was stacked with books, which was fine with

Liddy since she really didn't want anyone visiting her when she was in the office. Unless, of course, it was Grace bringing coffee.

"The stuff you had is probably cold by now. This is a new one." Grace handed her the to-go cup. She was dressed in one of her favorite outfits, a blue tank top and a denim skirt, her nod to the time she was scheduled to spend at the register later today, when she'd layer on the linen shirt. Till then, she'd be spending the morning on the second floor, where there was only a small air conditioner in the back window and a small fan to keep the air circulating.

"Thank you. There wasn't much left in the other one anyway." Liddy took a sip, then looked up at Grace. "I was just going over these reports you ran last night. We did really well last week."

"And you are surprised, why?" Grace leaned against the doorjamb, right next to where Liddy imagined Jessie. It brought a smile to her face to see the two old friends reunited, even if no one else saw them.

"People love books," Grace went on. "They need books. Everyone in town liked Fred and wanted to support him, but from what I've heard, he just couldn't keep up the store. We served a lot of very happy patrons last week, Liddy. People are glad to have a real bookstore here in town again. Everyone I talked to was excited."

"I hope all that glad and excitement wasn't used up the first week, because we're going to have to keep it going if the shop is to survive."

"It'll survive. Did you see the sign-up sheets for the book clubs? You might want to take a look at the sign-up sheet for romance and consider separating romance from women's fiction. I think there are too many people on the list to have good group discussions. Too many voices—some of them we know to be very opinionated."

"Huh. Okay, I'll take a look and see what I can do. Thanks for the tip."

"Sure. I'll be upstairs if you need me. I want to put this month's new releases, along with those for the next two, on the website. Anything else you want me to do?" Grace asked.

"Maybe reorder some of the books that sold out last week. Most of the thrillers we had on display are gone, and we sold a lot of children's books, no small thanks to you."

"You're welcome." Grace paused in the doorway. "Are Marion or Evelyn coming in today?"

Liddy shook her head. "I'll give you a shout if I need help on the floor, but I don't expect to be busy this morning."

"You know where to find me." Grace started up the steps to the second floor, then stopped and came back to the doorway. "Before I forget—I've had a number of inquiries about some of those old books we thought we'd try to sell online. The ones where we only had one dusty old copy?"

"Right. Some stuff Fred left on the shelves alongside new releases." Liddy rolled her eyes. "He had a complicated system."

"Some of those books are apparently quite rare. First editions and some obscure titles in the mix. I think we can cash in big-time on a few of them."

"How did you price them?"

Grace smiled. "I didn't, because I had no idea what they were worth. I listed the titles under a broad category and said, 'Send me your best offer by such and such a date.'"

"Sort of like eBay. Yeah, go for it, Gracie." She paused to consider whether they should be thinking about having several of those old books appraised by an expert in rare books, then reconsidered. But that would take more time than it might be worth, and if collectors were willing to bid on those books, they'd probably come close to their value. A bird in the hand . . .

"I'll let you know how it works out." Grace resumed her climb to her office.

Liddy had fifteen minutes before she was to open the shop, so she made her way to the front of the store, straightening books on a shelf here and there as she went by. She tidied the stack of greeting cards and rearranged the display of new paperbacks. At the counter, she turned on her iPad and checked Rosalita's migratory progress. The great white shark was currently moving toward the southern tip of Martha's Vineyard, brazenly close to the coastline. She'd just set the iPad on the counter when the door opened, and Tuck came in.

"Morning, Liddy." His smile was bright, and as always, his very presence made Liddy smile in return.

He has a great smile, she thought. *It reaches his eyes, which means he's glad to see me—unless I'm reaching and seeing something I want to see.*

"Hey, Tuck. What brings you in so early?"

"Early?" He scoffed. "It's almost nine o'clock. I want to run upstairs and take a quick look at the drywall my guys put up, make sure there's nothing else we need to do up there."

"You know the way."

A few minutes later, he came back down, a fistful of paper trash in his hand.

"I'm going to throttle those two guys." He held up a wad of empty corn chip bags and candy wrappers. "I told them never to leave this stuff behind on a job. I told them again last week after I found that first pile of empty snack bags up there."

Liddy held up the basket she kept behind the counter and Tuck tossed in the trash.

"Maybe Grace—"

"It wasn't Grace." He pulled his phone from the back pocket of his pants and speed-dialed a number. "I just asked her, and she said— yeah, Jack, this is Tuck. What did I tell you about leaving your trash on a worksite? I'm over here at the bookshop and I found . . . You sure? Who was working with you? Huh. Okay, I'm taking you at your word. Thanks." He disconnected the call and put the phone back into his pocket. "He swears he didn't leave anything up there, and the guy working with him didn't, either. He said they didn't bring anything with them—no snacks, no lunch, nothing."

"Maybe the stuff was left there from when Fred owned the store." Liddy searched her memory for the few times she'd gone onto the third floor. She didn't remember seeing empty chip bags or candy wrappers, but then again, she hadn't been looking for them.

"No. I was up there to inspect the leak when it was first discovered, and there was nothing on the floor."

Liddy shook her head. "Then I have no idea where it came from. But honestly, it's not a big deal."

"It is to me if my guys left it there." He frowned. "Jack's been with me a long time. He knows better, and I can't believe he'd lie about it."

She shrugged. "Let it go, Tuck. I'm not concerned about it."

"Yeah, but . . ."

"Let it go. Now tell me you had that leftover peach shortcake I sent you home with for breakfast this morning."

He grinned. "I had to fight my son for it, but yeah, I did, and it was delicious. Just as good the second time around."

"Good. Next time I'll make extra so I can send you home with some for Linc and the kids."

He rested his forearms on the counter. "So you think there'll be a next time?"

"I'm game if you are."

He narrowed his eyes. "Even after my unsympathetic display of manly ignorance?"

"Even after that." Liddy couldn't help but smile. He brought out the happy in her.

"You name the day and the time." His voice was low and rumbly, and it resonated somewhere deep inside her.

The front door opened, and Liddy's first customer of the day entered the shop.

"I'll get back to you," she told Tuck.

"I'll remind you if you don't." He tapped his fist lightly on the counter and winked at Liddy before nodding at the woman walking toward them. "Morning, Johanna."

"Morning, Tuck," the woman said sweetly. "How're things out on Shelby Island?"

"We're all doing fine, thanks for asking." He opened the door, and as he moved through it, the woman came into view. Liddy inwardly groaned. She'd known Johanna Hall since kindergarten. In a secret poll she and the other girls had taken, Johanna had won the title Most Annoying Person hands down. Back then, Johanna had been pushy and bossy and had had a mean streak, and from what Liddy had seen of her over the years, she hadn't changed much. She was one of those people who always rubbed Liddy the wrong way. Johanna flirting with Tuck definitely rubbed Liddy wrong.

Still, this morning she was a patron in Liddy's shop, and she had to be treated courteously.

Liddy took a deep breath. "Good morning, Johanna. Welcome to Wyndham Beach Reads."

Johanna watched through the window as Tuck's truck drove off. The fingers of one hand fluttered over her heart. "God, I swear that man gets better looking as he gets older. I can't believe I let him get away."

"You let who get away?" Liddy frowned. What was the woman talking about?

"Tuck. He had a thing for me back in high school. We went out a couple of times. You probably don't remember."

"No, I don't." Liddy raised an eyebrow. She probably would have remembered that.

"Oh, he was crazy about me junior year, begged me to go to the prom with him. But I was an idiot and took up with Brad Norton. When I realized what I'd lost, it was too late. Tuck had moved on. My big loss."

The woman was lying through her teeth. Liddy knew this for a fact because she knew (a) Tuck was already out of school by the time she and Johanna were juniors, since he was three years older, and (b) Tuck had dated Doreen Rick all through high school, and if anyone should be suffering from pangs of remorse, it should be Doreen. And (c) Liddy doubted Tuck Shelby had ever begged a woman for anything.

"Do you think two years after one's spouse has died is enough time before you start dating again?" Johanna leaned on the counter as if she and Liddy were besties.

"Has Ed been gone for two years already?" Liddy could have sworn it had been just a little more than a year since Ed Hall passed.

"Close enough. So where's your cookbook section, Liddy?"

Liddy showed her the way. "Are you looking for anything in particular?"

"*The Lascivious Dish*. It's the sequel to *The Sensuous Cook*. I heard about it on the radio the other day." Johanna skimmed the titles. "Ah, here we go."

She pulled the book from the shelf and held it up. On the cover was a beautiful young woman whose impressive cleavage was well showcased in a low-cut dress. Under the title was written, *Take it from the dining room to the bedroom in one fabulous meal.*

"Oh, yeah. Definitely this one." Johanna giggled as she flipped through the pages.

"Planning a big night for someone?" Liddy had a sinking suspicion she knew who Johanna's proposed victim would be.

Johanna didn't look up from the book. "I'm going after what I passed up the first time around." She glanced up at Liddy. "That man who just left?" She waved the book in Liddy's face and giggled again. "I'm going to invite him to dinner. He won't know what hit him."

Liddy didn't know what perturbed her more, that Johanna Hall planned on cooking a seductive dinner for Tuck, or that the woman giggled like a ten-year-old.

"Anything else?" Liddy's jaw was clenched so hard it ached.

"Nope. I've got all I need right here." She held the book against her chest and patted it.

"So when is this gastronomic seduction to take place?" Liddy asked casually.

"Well, I haven't asked him yet, but I'm hoping for this coming weekend. Not sure if Friday or Saturday night is best for this type of thing. What do you think, Liddy?" Not waiting for an answer, she said, "I'm guessing Saturday. Friday nights he's probably tired out from work, and we wouldn't want him tired out *before*, would we?"

Liddy didn't ask why the emphasis was on *before*. Johanna had made her intention perfectly clear.

Johanna walked to the counter and placed her bag next to Liddy's iPad. "What's this?"

"Oh, that's Rosalita. She's a great white shark I'm tracking." Liddy went behind the counter.

"I guess that's as good a way as any to pass the time if you're not busy." Johanna looked around. "And since I'm your only customer, I guess you're not."

She put the cookbook on the counter and handed Liddy her credit card. After the card was returned to her, Johanna began to flip through the pages of the book.

"Ooh! Lamb Is for Lovers—I wonder if Tuck likes lamb. And Kiss Me, Kale—that looks interesting and healthy." She made her way through the book, oohing and aahing while Liddy rang up the sale. "Oh, some of these are naughty," she exclaimed. "I'll have to mark this one with a sticky note."

"Would you like me to bag you?"

"Excuse me?" Johanna's left eyebrow rose.

"Bag the book." Liddy smiled. "Or would you like to take it as is?"

"I'll take it as is. If anyone's looking for me, I'll be in the parking lot next door, planning my menu. Oh, this is going to be fun!" Johanna dropped her credit card into her wallet, plunked the wallet into her bag, grabbed the cookbook from the counter, and headed out. "Wish me luck," she called back to Liddy.

"Right. Break a leg," Liddy muttered.

Over the next two hours, several customers—some longtime town residents and two women Liddy didn't recognize—came in to shop. Still stewing over Johanna's blatant pursuit of Tuck, she had to force a cheeriness she didn't feel. She thought she'd covered her foul mood, but when Emma stopped in later in the morning, she took one look at Liddy and asked, "What?"

"Don't ask," Liddy grumbled.

"I just did. What's going on?" Emma leaned over the counter.

"You remember Johanna Deasey from our class?" Liddy lowered her voice so as to not be overheard by the customers browsing the new-release table.

"Sure. Short, petite, brown hair. Annoying. Obnoxious. She married Ed Hall from the class behind us." Emma paused. "Didn't he die last year?"

"It was sometime before our reunion last September. I remember because Johanna wore black to every reunion event and constantly talked about how hard things were for her because Ed died without any warning, so she didn't know where to bury him."

"The cad. How dare he be so insensitive." Emma rolled her eyes. "Where did she bury him?"

"She had him cremated."

"Well, if that's what he wanted—"

"He didn't. He told Jerry Bach, and Jerry told me Ed was terrified of fire."

"Well, I guess . . ." Emma paused, then shook her head. "I don't know what to say. I know you can get a little thrown off balance when your husband dies."

"Oh, you're too damned nice, Emma. Would you please just one time agree with me without making excuses for someone who's on my shit list?"

"Well, I already called her annoying and obnoxious, but okay. What did she do to land on your list this early in the day?"

"She came in and bought a cookbook."

"I can see where that might set you off. She bought a book from you? The very nerve."

Liddy sighed deeply, then led Emma to the cookbook section. She found the title Johanna had bought and held up the cover. "This one."

Emma took the book, read the title, and began to page through it. "Hmmm. Steak with a Side of Spice. Daring Duchess Potatoes. Ooh La LaSagna. Cute. Lick My Ladyfingers. Oh, gag—no thank you. Sex with Your Sushi? Ah . . . raw fish and sex? Not so sure about that one, either. Oh, look at this, Cream My Brûlée." Emma laughed. "Well, that's pretty blatant." She held up the accompanying photo for Liddy. "It does look quite yummy, though, with the Razzle Dazzle Raspberry drizzle, doesn't it?" She took one look at Liddy's face and closed the book. "What?"

"Johanna came in here looking specifically for that book. She said she heard about it on the radio, and wanted to check it out because she's planning a seduction dinner for this weekend."

"So who's the lucky guy, and why do you care?" Emma tilted Liddy's face toward her own. "And why are you so pissed off?"

Liddy blew out a long breath. "It's Tuck. She's planning on seducing Tuck. She went through this whole thing about how he'd been crazy about her in high school and had wanted to go to the junior prom with her, which we both know is a crock, because Tuck was already out of school by then and was off somewhere with the army."

"Right. He joined up right after graduation, since he wasn't going to college, and he left town before the end of the summer. But the rest of it? Uh-uh. So what was the point of her telling you she and Tuck had this big romance going back then, since we do know it's not true?"

Liddy shrugged. "She made it sound like he'd been the one for her all along, and she shouldn't have let him go, and now she plans to reclaim him. Or something along those lines."

"And I repeat: Why do you care, and why are you pissed off?"

Liddy felt Emma studying her face and figured she was watching her body language as well.

"Oh. I get it," Emma said softly. "You . . ."

"Had dinner with Tuck last night. At my house. He sort of invited himself." Liddy related how the dinner had come about. "And I think we're going to do it again. But I probably won't be making Daring Duchess Potatoes and serving Steak with a Side of Spice."

Emma laughed at Liddy's cranky tone. "It sounds to me like you're doing just fine with beef stew." She rubbed Liddy's shoulders. "So you and Tuck . . . ?"

"I don't know. He's been a good friend for a long time, but lately it seems as if he's becoming a little more. I'm not sure where, if anyplace, this might go, but I do know I want to find out, and I don't want Johanna or anyone else getting there before I do. You should have seen the way she was practically drooling over him this morning."

"Liddy, I don't think you have anything to worry about."

"She's had work on her face *and* her boobs, and she's thirty pounds thinner than me."

"She's also five inches shorter than you. If she weighed the same amount, she'd look like a beach ball."

"One could only hope."

"Is this where I pay for my books?" A woman approached the counter.

"Yes, it sure is. Did you find everything you were looking for?" Liddy slipped back into her bookseller role.

"I'm around if you need me for anything." Emma excused herself and waved a quick goodbye as she left the shop.

"I found this"—the woman held up a book of poetry by a local poet, Graham Christy—"but I was also looking for a novel. I don't know the name, but the cover is blue, and it has a sort of sunburst on it. It's a new book, and I guess you'd call it general fiction."

"I know exactly the book." Liddy stepped from behind the counter and went directly to where the book was shelved spine out. She handed it to the customer. "Is this the one?"

"Oh, yes. Thank you. I'd like to take this one as well."

While Liddy rang up the purchase, she chatted with the woman, who related she and her family had just moved to a new development outside Mattapoisett. Her husband was a lawyer, and they had three children. Liddy mentioned the story hour on Saturday and the book clubs, and the woman took information on both.

"I'll try to be back on Saturday with my five-year-old," she told Liddy when another customer arrived to pay for their selections. "And I'll think about the mystery book club."

"You have a mystery book club?" An older gentleman handed Liddy his book for her to ring up. "My wife and I used to be in a book club, but after she passed away, I stopped going. Maybe it's time for me to join a new one."

"We'd love to have you." Liddy handed him the flyer Grace had made, and he looked it over.

"Wednesday night." He nodded. "I can do Wednesday night at seven." He smiled at Liddy. "I'll see you at the first meeting."

"I'll be sure to watch for you," she told him. "My name's Liddy, by the way."

"Augustus, but call me Gus. It's nice to make your acquaintance," he replied. "I just moved into the retirement village out on Route Six. I'll see if any of my new neighbors would like to accompany me."

"All will be welcome," Liddy assured him.

He picked up his package and had turned to leave when the iPad caught his eye. "What have we here?"

Liddy explained how she had signed up to follow Rosalita's journey.

"Oh, that's wonderful. In my past life, I taught marine biology at Holy Cross," he told her. "I'm delighted to see such interest in the great whites."

Another customer, overhearing, engaged Gus in conversation, and eventually ended up purchasing two books about sharks Gus recommended.

"You're hired," Liddy called to Gus as he left the shop, and he laughed.

"Wow, he was interesting," Liddy's next customer commented. "I could have listened to him all morning."

"Maybe sometime we could ask him to lead a discussion on sharks," Liddy thought aloud.

"I'd be there," the customer said. "And I think I'll look into the mystery book club. Thanks. I love your shop, and I'm so glad it's here. My husband is the new tennis coach at Alden Academy, so we've only been here since June. It was disappointing to find the nearest bookstore was a half hour away. Not that it's so far, but there's something nice about walking to your local shop, then maybe taking your book to the coffee shop across the street." She added, "It would be even nicer if there was a park close by where you could sit and read outside in good weather."

"There is a park about four blocks north of here, but I do have plans for a patio out back with maybe a few small tables next spring." Liddy hadn't had such plans until just now. "You'd have to bring your own coffee, though."

"I would love that." The woman brightened. "And I'll bring my son to the story hour next Saturday."

"Please do."

Liddy leaned on the counter and rested her back for a moment. It had been an interesting morning. She'd received good feedback from her customers and a few ideas on how to make a visit to the shop even more enjoyable. As the day progressed, she found her patrons loved watching Rosalita's progress, so she decided to leave the iPad on the counter every day.

Around four, some kids from the local high school began to filter in. There were two girls, who looked about sixteen, who both wore their white-blonde hair in high ponytails and were dressed almost identically, and a tall, gangly, dark-haired boy carrying a backpack, whom Liddy judged to be maybe a year or so older than the girls.

"Can I help you find something?" Liddy asked the girls as the boy walked past them. Out of the corner of her eye, she saw him sit in one of the wingback chairs in the children's section. He dropped his backpack at his feet, removed a book, and began to read.

"Do you have the new book by Janet Friesner?" one of the two asked.

"Maybe." Liddy tried to think if she'd seen that author somewhere. "Is it a YA?"

"Young adult, yes." The girl's ponytail bobbed up and down.

"That section is down here." Liddy led the way to the back of the store. The young adult section was right behind the children's books. She checked the shelves. "F . . . yes, Friesner." She pulled out a book. "The Hollow Hills High series?"

"Yes!" The girl reached for it eagerly. "I've been waiting for this book for months."

"I apologize for not being more familiar with this series." Liddy selected another book from the series and read from the back cover. "The continuing adventures of Angelet and Karyl."

"It's pronounced *Carol*, not *Carl*," the girl told her. Her companion rolled her eyes.

"Oops. Sorry. As I said, not familiar with it, but I am now." Liddy started back up the aisle. "Thanks for calling it to my attention."

Halfway to the counter, she heard one of the girls say, "Dylan, why's your hair wet?"

"I took a shower after gym class last period," the boy who'd earlier seated himself replied without looking up.

The girls exchanged an amused look and followed Liddy to the cash register. They chipped in an equal amount to pay for the book.

"Sharing?" Liddy asked.

The girls nodded.

"Smart. That way you can buy twice as many books," Liddy said.

One girl elbowed the other. "See? That's what I said."

They took their book and left the store. Minutes later, Maggie and Emma came in.

"We've come to whisk you away for dinner," Emma told her. "It's after five."

"Is it?" Liddy glanced at her watch. "Damn, it is. I guess time really does fly when you're having fun. Which I am. But I can't leave the store unattended."

"Grace is coming back in," Maggie said. "She'll be here any minute. I hope you don't mind, but I told her to park in that space right behind the shop. I didn't want to take the one space out front in case a customer needs it."

"My customers thank you, and I don't mind at all. I'll go unlock the back door." Liddy walked past them but returned in a moment. "I must be losing my mind. The door was already unlocked, but I swear I didn't unlock it. I can't imagine how that could have happened."

"When was the last time you went out back?"

Liddy shook her head. "I haven't gone out there in days." She tried to remember who might have done so. "Maybe Tuck's guys took some leftover drywall or something out back before they left the other day."

"Has anything been missing?" Emma asked.

"Not that I can tell." She looked around the shop. The books appeared to be in place, and she knew the money in the cash register was all there because she'd made a quick count earlier.

"Then maybe Grace opened it this morning for some reason. I'm sure there's a reasonable explanation. There she is now." Maggie pointed to the back of the shop. "Ask her."

But Grace hadn't used the back door in weeks.

"I'm not going to lose sleep over it." Liddy grabbed her bag. "Gracie, thanks so much for coming in. I appreciate the chance to step out for a bit. I won't be long."

"Take your time. I don't have plans for the night." Grace shooed the three women toward the front door.

"I've had some interesting people come in today," Liddy told them as they crossed Front Street. "I got some good ideas for the shop from some new customers."

"You can share those over dinner." Maggie linked an arm through Liddy's. "But first things first. Emma tells me Johanna Hall is on the prowl, and she's set her sights on Tuck, who might have his set on you. Spill it, Lids."

Over dinner, Liddy spilled.

"I could see Tuck as a companion for you." Emma touched her white napkin to the corners of her mouth.

"Companion, hell," Liddy scoffed. "I'm not looking to Tuck for companionship. I have you two for that, not to mention a steady stream of customers to talk to."

"Maybe *companion* wasn't the right word," Emma said. "You may fill whatever you prefer in the blank. Doesn't change the fact I could see you two together for something more than 'Hey, Liddy.' 'Hey, Tuck.'"

"I guess we'll have to wait to see what comes next. I'm just hoping it isn't Johanna."

"Tuck isn't stupid, and I'll bet he's had his pick of women to date for years," Maggie said. "If he had his eye on her, he'd have done something about it by now. I think she was blowing smoke."

"Why would she do that?"

Maggie shrugged. "Maybe because you're both single, and she saw him coming out of your shop at an early hour and was wondering what he was doing there."

"Could be," Emma said. "Maybe she was thinking there was something going on between the two of you, and she wanted to let you know you had competition. She wouldn't come right out and ask you, because she's sneaky."

"Not to mention petty and jealous. I agree with Em." Maggie drank the last of her iced tea. "She told you she was going to invite Tuck for dinner on Saturday night, maybe to see if she could get a reaction from you."

"She didn't. I was cool as a cucumber." Liddy checked the time on her phone. "I need to get back. Let's get the waiter to bring the check."

Emma left them at the corner to walk back to her house on Pitcher Street while Maggie and Liddy returned to the shop. Grace was at the register reading when they came in.

"How's it going?" Liddy asked her.

"Two customers while you were gone." Grace nodded in the direction of the children's section. "The kid is still here. I think he must be doing his homework."

"He could go to the library for that." Liddy glanced at the boy—Dylan, the girls had called him—who was writing in a notebook that was propped up on his backpack. "I thought kids did all their homework on computers these days."

"Maybe some subjects, maybe not some others." Grace shrugged. "And maybe he doesn't have a computer at home. He's not bothering anyone."

"Well, I wasn't going to give him the boot, Grace. I was just saying . . ." Liddy gestured for Grace to vacate the area behind the counter. "Are you done upstairs for the night?"

"I am. Mom, want a ride?" Grace dug her keys out from her bag.

"Sure. I could probably use the walk, but I'll make it up tomorrow with an early run."

"I'll run with you," Grace told her.

"Are you two still thinking about running a marathon?" Liddy asked.

"Mom is; I'm not."

"You could train with me, Lids," Maggie suggested. "I've been working with Dee Olson. She started running marathons after the last of her five kids left for college. She's done Boston and New York. I run with her on Monday, Wednesday, and Friday mornings." Maggie laughed. "Of course, so far, I've only been able to go three miles, but I'm working up to it slowly, which Dee said is the best way to go. Build up gradually."

"Well, it sure sounds like a good time to me, but I think I'll pass." The shop phone rang, and Liddy answered it. Maggie pointed toward the back of the shop to indicate they were leaving, and Liddy acknowledged their departure with a wave.

With twenty minutes left before closing, Liddy's neighbor, Bernadette Sikorski, strolled in.

"I meant to come in earlier, but I had my grandsons after school, and time just got away from me," Bernie told her. "I wanted to pick up the new book about the army nurse who was in Vietnam right at the end of the war. You know the one I'm talking about?"

"I do. It's right over here." Liddy led her to the general fiction bestseller table, but noticed the book was sold out. "Oh, maybe there's one left on the shelves."

The two women searched the shelf for the book and found it, out of place.

"It's unbelievable people can't put things back where they found them." Liddy held up the book. "Bernie, I'm pretty sure this is the one you want."

"Yes, that's it. That's the cover they showed on TV this morning. Thanks, Liddy." As she paid for the book, Bernie said, "I saw Maggie's daughter over by your place this afternoon."

"She's thinking about renting out the little house. You know, the small place down by the pond where Jim used to have his insurance agency."

"Oh, sure. Is that place even livable?"

"Grace has plans to make it so."

"Tell her to call my niece in Fairhaven if she needs insurance."

"I'll mention it to her." *Anyone but Jim.* Liddy's phone chimed nine o'clock, as she'd set it to do. "Did you walk over, Bernie?"

"I did. You ready to leave? We can walk together."

"Just let me check the back door to make sure it's locked and turn out the lights in my office. And there was one customer here . . ." Liddy looked around when she reached the back of the shop, but the boy who'd been doing his homework there for hours was gone. "Closing time. I'm locking up," she called just in case he or someone else might still be in the shop. When there was no response, Liddy locked the back door and got her bag from her office. He must have left the shop while she was helping Bernie.

She decided to leave her iPad and Rosalita on the counter for the morning, and she and Bernie headed off toward Jasper Street. They took their time, discussing Grace's plans for the shop and Bernie's grandson's soccer game along the way. The streetlights were a hazy glow overhead, the cicadas hummed in the background, and the very first faint hint of fall settled over the town.

Chapter Nine

Hope momentarily fluttered in Liddy's chest when her doorbell rang at seven in the morning, but a glance through the glass panel in the door brought her back to reality when she saw a thirty-three-year-old woman where she'd hoped to find a handsome man of sixty-two. She opened the door with a slight sense of disappointment.

"Liddy, I just came from the little house, and I had a thought." Grace stood on the front porch dressed in dark-gray sweatpants and a white UPenn sweatshirt, a colorful striped bag over her shoulder, and a bottle of water in her hand. "May I come in?"

"You didn't sleep there, did you?" Liddy opened the door and Grace went inside.

"No, of course not. No bed. Critters galore—did you know there are snakes down there?"

"I never thought about it, but it doesn't surprise me." Liddy led the way into the kitchen. "I was just going to have coffee. Want some?"

"I'd love some. Thank you." Grace sat at the table and hung her bag on the back of her chair.

Liddy poured coffee into two mugs and set them on the table, where she'd already placed the sugar bowl and a container of cream.

"You know, seeing you sitting there makes me think of all the times you had dinner with us when you were younger," Liddy said. "All the time you spent here with Jess during the summers when you were still a kid."

"I was just thinking the same. Jessie and I used to ride our bikes out to the point and back, or we'd play at the playground with the other kids all day till we had to come home for dinner. In the beginning of the summer, I always felt like a fifth wheel because they all went to school together and knew each other so well. By August, I felt right at home, like I belonged here, but by then it was time to go home. The following year, rinse and repeat." She put a scant bit of sugar into her mug and followed it with a healthy dose of half-and-half. "I'd start crying as soon as my dad got here because I never wanted to leave."

"Jessie always cried, too, when she knew you were leaving."

Grace held up her index finger on her left hand. "Someone told us this finger was the one that had the blood right from your heart. Jess and I decided one time we wanted to be blood sisters, so we cut our fingertips and mixed our blood together. We thought that would mean my parents couldn't take me back to Pennsylvania." Grace took a sip. "We were so bummed when my mother told us it didn't work that way." She stared at her finger. "If you look real close, you can still see the tiny scar." She smiled and looked up at Liddy. "We obviously had no conception of anatomy or where veins were. We cut a little too deep, and we both bled profusely."

Liddy reached for Grace's finger and studied it, then ran her thumb over the barely visible scar. "Did Jess have a scar, too?"

Grace nodded. "Not more noticeable than this one, I'm sure."

"I never saw it." She stared at the scar for a moment longer, then released Grace's hand. "Gracie, did my daughter ever tell you she'd thought about taking her life?" When Grace drew back in apparent shock at the unexpected question, Liddy said, "I'm sorry. I should have led up to that better. It's just, seeing you here, remembering how close you two were, I just wondered maybe . . ."

"No, Liddy. If Jess had ever given me any hint she was thinking about doing something like that, I'd have talked to her, I'd have told my mom, she would have told you." She shook her head. "Uh-uh. But please remember, we didn't see much of each other after high school. I came up here in the beginning of the summer with Mom and Natalie after graduation, but I only stayed for a few days before I left for the study program in Spain. After that, we both went to college, and I hardly ever saw her again. The few times we did see each other, it was sort of like ships passing in the night. She was living in Boston, and unless she happened to be home for the weekend when we were here visiting my grandmother, we just didn't connect. I'm very sorry. If I knew something, I'd tell you, but by then, we'd really grown apart. If she'd confided in anyone, it wouldn't have been me."

"I just had to ask." Liddy patted Grace's hands. "So tell me why you were at the little house at seven in the morning."

"Actually, I was there at six," Grace confessed. "I couldn't sleep, so I got up and got ready for work, but it was still so early, and I'd had this idea about some furniture of Mom's from the Bryn Mawr house. So I walked to the little house, and I was mentally placing those pieces around, you know how you do?"

Liddy nodded, wondering where this was going.

"So, I started thinking . . . oh, but first, does the little house have a separate address from your house?"

"Yes. I'm pretty sure I told you it's deeded separately, and Jim didn't want business mail coming to the house and family mail going to the office. So he arranged to give that property its own number, which it would have had if a regular-size house had been built there. It's two-oh-eight, by the way."

"Two-oh-eight Jasper Street. Got it." Grace took a deep breath. "I'm thinking I would like to buy the place rather than rent it. What do you think?"

"I have no use for it, Grace. And frankly, since you want to put so much money into it to fix it up, you should own it. I think I said that before. So, sure."

"How much would you want for it?"

"I have no idea what it's worth. I imagine most of the value is in the property." Liddy shrugged. "I have no idea how big the lot is."

"Let's get it appraised so I can make you a fair offer."

"Honey, I'd sell to you for one dollar."

"Uh-uh. Fair value. I'm not going to take advantage of you because our families are close."

"If I'm willing to sell to you for a dollar, you're not taking advantage of me. That's my price." Liddy folded her arms across her chest.

"So if I were Joe Blow from Rhode Island, the price would be one dollar?"

"Well, no, but . . ."

"My point. Let's get it appraised and see what it's worth, okay?"

"Were you this tough in court when you were practicing law?"

Grace smiled. "Much tougher. So how do we make this happen?"

"Let me check around and see who we can call."

"Great. Thank you. We'll go from there." Grace finished her coffee and stood. "I'm going down to the shop now. I still have some work from yesterday. I'll see you there."

Liddy saw her to the front door.

"Do you happen to know how old the little house is?" Grace asked from the porch.

"Not sure. It was already there when Jim's father inherited it from *his* father. One of the reasons he wanted to keep it was to have his business there. Jim and I bought it from the estate after his dad passed away so Jim could maintain the agency in the same place it started. But when it was built?" Liddy shrugged. "I guess there's some way to figure it out if you need to know."

"I'm just curious. Maybe I can find out by looking at old maps." She bit her bottom lip. "Maybe the library in town has some."

"That's probably the best place to start."

"I'll see you at the shop. Thanks for the coffee." Grace went down the steps, and was halfway to the sidewalk when she turned and waved.

Liddy waved back and watched the young woman swing her bag over her shoulder and cross the street. She stood in the doorway until Grace was no longer in sight.

Back in the kitchen, Liddy loaded the dishwasher, feeling once again the weight of all she'd lost. Seeing Grace here, seated in the same chair she'd sat on so many times as a child, broke Liddy's heart all over again. If only Jessie and Grace had been able to keep up with their friendship the way Liddy and Maggie had. Would Jessie have confided in Grace, told her why she had to leave this world, if they'd still been close? Would they have been able to stop whatever self-destructive train Jess was on?

Just one more question that will never be answered, Liddy thought as she slowly climbed the steps to the second floor to dress for work.

~

Between customers, Liddy put in a call to Gretchen Smith, who owned a real estate agency in town.

"Lydia Bryant. So nice to hear from you," Gretchen said in her usual cheery manner. "How've you been? I hear your bookshop is the place to see and be seen in Wyndham Beach."

"I've been fine, Gretchen. And yes, the store is going gangbusters right now. I'm hoping it continues."

"I apologize for not making it to your opening. With all the new construction on the old Wilson estate on the other side of Route Six, I've been busy as a bee in July."

"What new construction?"

"The new town house development. A first for Wyndham Beach, but a lawsuit was filed a few years ago, calling out the town for not having housing diversity—and let's face it, we've always been mostly single-family homes here in town. Anyway, the suit was settled some months ago, the Wilson property was sold to a developer, and the houses are going up quickly. Not many of them, because the settlement included a restriction on how many lots are permissible on less than an acre of ground. You should come over and take a look. They're really lovely, and the construction is top notch. You being in that big house all by yourself, a town house could be just the thing."

"I'm not thinking of moving, Gretchen, but if I were ever to put my house up for sale, you know the listing would go to you."

"I would hope so, Liddy. Now, if I can't sell you a town house, what can I do for you?"

"I need a property appraiser. A good one, and I need one fast."

"I thought you just said you weren't thinking of selling."

"There's a small house on our—my—grounds that's actually a separately deeded lot. That's the property I'm selling."

"Oh. You mean where the insurance office used to be?"

"Exactly. I already have a buyer, but I don't know what to ask for it, so I need it appraised. It's in dreadful condition, so I need a number as is."

"How much ground is it sitting on? Do you know?"

"No. I'm not really sure, but I think the property line is somewhere around the woods behind it. I think the edge of the driveway is the line on the left side if you're standing in the street, and the right side line is where the big holly bush marks the beginning of the Martins' property next door. Other than that, I don't know. Of course it's marked on the deed, which I do not have in front of me."

"Not to worry. I can check that easily enough." Gretchen's pen could be heard scratching on paper as she made notes.

"Gretchen, are you still writing everything with a fountain pen?"

"Ha ha. Only when I'm in the office. So I'm looking at my list of appraisers. Any of these familiar to you? Assuming you'd prefer someone you know." She began to read off a list of names, but Liddy stopped her.

"You just pick one. Whoever is fine."

"All right. Listen, you wouldn't mind if I stopped down there and took a look at the place, would you?"

"You're welcome, but Gretchen, I'm not listing it. It's already spoken for."

"I understand, but let's make sure you're asking the right price. I'll call someone to appraise and get back to you." Gretchen hung up.

"I'll set my own price, thanks anyway," Liddy said under her breath as she ended the call and placed her phone facedown on the counter.

Within the hour, Gretchen returned the call and confirmed someone would be there that afternoon to take a look.

"Can I pick up the key at the shop?" Gretchen asked.

"I'll have someone meet you there at four," Liddy told her.

She walked to the back of the shop and called up the stairs to Grace, who'd breezed in smiling fifteen minutes earlier. "The appraiser will be at the house at four," Liddy told her when she appeared at the top of the stairs. "Can you be there to open the house?"

"Sure, if you don't mind my leaving."

"If I'm telling you to go, I obviously don't mind. A Realtor is going to be there as well: Gretchen Smith. Do not tell her you're the buyer, and for the love of all that's holy, don't tell her what your plans are. She'll jack up the price and try to talk me into charging you more."

"You should charge me what it's worth, Liddy. But why would she care how much you charge for your property if she isn't handling the sale?"

"I suspect she's trying to keep the comps—the comparables in the neighborhood—high. We had this discussion. I will ask what I damn well please."

There was a customer at the counter, so Liddy returned to take care of him. "I love all the posters," he told her. "So colorful and imaginative. Are you selling reproductions?"

"We will be in the future, so stay tuned," she told him, then told him about Jessie. She mentioned she'd sold some of her paintings at the Toller Gallery in Boston.

"Oh, I know it well. I'll be in the city next weekend, so I'll be sure to stop in and check out more of her work. Thanks for the tip." He took his package and smiled at Liddy before leaving the shop.

Evelyn came in at noon and took over at the cash register to give Liddy a break, which she spent in her office, reviewing the orders Grace had placed over the weekend. After a half hour, she went across the street and picked up a pizza to share with Grace and Evelyn. She left the three remaining slices in the box on her desk, intending to wrap them up and put them into the small office refrigerator. When she went back onto the floor, she noticed Fred Lattimore talking to a customer in the nonfiction section. His white hair stuck up in tufts, and he was wearing khaki pants and a wrinkled blue shirt, some of the buttons missing their mark.

As she approached him, she heard him say, "Of course we can order that for you. Any book, really. I probably can have it in for you by Friday, if that's okay."

"Oh, that would be great, thanks. I'll stop back over the weekend." The customer, a woman who appeared to be Liddy's age, returned the book she'd been holding to the shelf, thanked Fred again, then left the shop.

Liddy watched Fred straighten out a shelf and then greet a new customer. His gait was uneven, and one look at his feet told the tale: one black shoe, one navy slipper.

"Oh, hello there. Come on in. This your first visit?" He shook the man's hand. "What can I sell you today?"

Dear Lord, he thinks he still owns this place.

Liddy caught Evelyn's eye, and Evelyn shrugged. Liddy waved her from behind the counter and took her place. She grabbed her phone and looked up the number for Fred's son. She was about to place the call when Fred came over to the counter.

"You're the new girl, aren't you? Sorry I got in a little late this morning, but thanks for opening for me. Have we been busy today?" He leaned on the counter, then looked around as if seeing the shop for the first time. "Are you the one who rearranged everything?" His voice began to rise. "I didn't give you permission to do this." He pointed at the walls. "What happened to my dog pictures? Did you throw them away? What are all those . . . those . . . what are those *things* hanging on the wall? All those crazy colors! I didn't put them there."

"Oh, Mr. Lattimore," Liddy said softly. She put a hand over her face and closed her eyes. What the hell?

"Mr. Lattimore, hello." Evelyn, who'd worked for Fred before Liddy bought the shop, sized up the situation and stepped in.

"Oh, Evelyn. I'm so glad you're here." Fred lowered his voice. "Keep an eye on the new girl. I think she stole all my dog pictures. She's trying to steal from the cash register."

"No, no, Mr. Lattimore. You know Liddy Bryant. Jim Bryant's . . . er, wife." Evelyn apparently decided the divorce was more information than the man needed at the moment.

"Jim the insurance guy?" Fred asked. "Took over for his old man after he died?"

"That's the one," Evelyn told him.

"Bought insurance from him, bought it from the old man before him." He turned to Liddy. "You're young Jim's wife?"

"Yes, sir," Liddy replied. *Close enough.*

"Do I know your people?" he asked.

"I believe you might. My dad was Alphonse Hess."

"He married a German girl. I remember her, all right." He winked at Liddy. "She was quite the looker."

"She certainly was," Liddy agreed.

"Come see how nice we made the children's section." Evelyn steered him toward the back of the shop, looking over her shoulder to mouth the words *Call Carl* to Liddy.

"Already on it." Liddy called the number for Carl's hardware store. Someone in the office picked up and asked her to hold while she located Carl.

"Carl, it's Liddy at the bookshop," she said after he came to the phone.

"Oh my God, is he there?" Before Liddy could respond, he said, "We've been looking for him for the past hour. I should have known he'd go there. I'll be there as soon as I can."

"It's okay. He's not bothering anyone, but he's obviously confused. He'll be safe till you get here," she assured him. She looked over her shoulder and saw Fred chatting with Evelyn and a customer. "He's okay. We won't let him leave."

"I'm on my way."

Liddy breathed a sigh of relief when Carl entered the store five minutes later. He looked like a younger version of his father, but his shirt was nicely pressed, and his shoes matched.

"He's in the back talking with Evelyn and Mayor Harper." Liddy pointed discreetly to the back of the shop.

"Thanks." Carl made a beeline for the children's section. Liddy watched him ease into the conversation, which he kept going for several minutes before addressing his father directly. Liddy couldn't hear what was being said, but she saw the elderly man rise from the chair, shake the mayor's hand, and walk toward the front of the store.

"Dad and I are going home for lunch now, Liddy," Carl said as they passed by. "We'll see you later."

"Okay. Enjoy yourselves." Liddy waved and Fred waved back. "See you later."

"Will you be working tomorrow, young lady?" Fred asked her.

"I'm pretty sure I'm on the schedule."

"Well, then, I'll see you tomorrow." He took two steps through the door, then stopped and turned around. "Oh. I'll be back at closing to count the receipts."

"Okay. We'll save them for you." Evelyn waved goodbye.

After the door closed, Evelyn's forearms sank onto the counter.

"Poor guy," she said. "It must be terrible to forget so much."

"I'm betting this won't be the last time we see him. I bet he'll be over here every chance he gets. Which isn't so bad, you know? He's not hurting anyone. I think he just spent so much of his life here, he thinks this is where he belongs. It's okay."

Liddy watched through the front window as Carl helped his father into the car. She felt an overwhelming sense of sadness. When she was old and forgetful, who would search for her if she wandered off? Who would find her and tuck her into the front seat of their car and drive her home? Where would home be, and with whom? The future was a great unknown for everyone, but maybe even a little more so when you had no significant other, no children, no living relatives.

She was having an "Is that all there is?" moment. If Jess hadn't died, would she and Jim have stayed together? Had he been intended to be her ever-after? Or was someone, somewhere, searching for her?

In her pocket, her phone buzzed to notify her of an incoming text from Gretchen, and she was grateful to turn her thoughts elsewhere.

There's a problem. I'll stop at the shop before I meet with the appraiser.

Liddy frowned. What problem could there be?

From the corner of her eye, she noticed the boy—Dylan—seated in the same chair he'd sat in the day before. And now that she thought about it, hadn't he been there the day before that, too? Was it odd a teenage boy would want to spend his after-school time in a bookshop instead of maybe with friends? She honestly didn't know a thing about teenage boys. Maybe both his parents worked, and he was a latchkey kid. He had to be at least sixteen, surely old enough to be alone until his parents got home. Maybe he didn't like being home alone. She was about to try to engage him in conversation when Gretchen arrived and waved to her from the front of the shop.

"I just read your text," Liddy said.

"Liddy, does Jim know you're selling the property?" Gretchen took Liddy by the arm and moved them both to a less busy spot.

"It's none of Jim's business. It's my property, and mine to sell."

"Not according to the deed."

"What are you talking about? Jim signed over everything to me in the divorce."

"Everything except his old office, apparently."

"Oh, hell. He must have overlooked it somehow." He wouldn't have deliberately held back on her, would he? Whatever else she might say about her ex-husband, she'd never known him to be duplicitous.

"Whatever. You're going to have to straighten this out, unless you want me to call him," Gretchen said.

"Oh, no. No. I'll take care of this." Liddy felt her blood pressure rise. Could he have done this on purpose?

Grace walked over, and Liddy took a deep breath intended to calm herself before she introduced the two women.

"Gracie, this is Gretchen Smith. She's a friend, a Realtor here in town, and she's arranged for an appraisal of the . . ."

Grace beamed. "Oh, great. I'll walk over with you and let you in. I'm Grace Flynn."

"Nice to meet you. I drove, but you're welcome to ride with me," Gretchen offered.

"Ah, Grace—I need to speak with you before you leave," Liddy told her.

"Grace, my car's parked right out front." Gretchen headed out. "Liddy, get back to me as soon as you talk to Jim."

Liddy nodded, then took Grace by the arm.

"Listen, Grace. For heaven's sake, don't prattle on about all your plans to make the house fabulous. The value of the house will go sky-high. Just remember, potential has no monetary value."

"Please. Ace negotiator here. Not my first real estate gig. I know when to keep my mouth shut. I hadn't planned on going in with her and the appraiser. I'll wait outside until they're done."

"I forgot who I was dealing with. Carry on, Gracie." Liddy gestured to the door.

Grace picked up the tote bag she'd brought in with her that morning. "If you don't need me later, I think after we're done at the house, I'll go right to the library to look for old maps."

"We've been slow all day. Go open up the house for Gretchen, then do your thing. I'll see you tomorrow." Liddy forced a smile at a customer who'd just entered the shop. Her fingers itched to grab her phone and call her ex. She looked around for Evelyn, and found her a few shelves down, helping another customer. She sighed and maintained the smile. "Can I help you find something?"

"The new romance by Cindy Bickley?" the woman asked.

"On the display to your right. You're in luck. I think there may be two copies left."

The customer picked up a copy and carried it directly to the counter. "I've been waiting for this. Cindy Bickley is my favorite author," she said.

"Oh, you might want to join our romance book club. We're reading *The Lady's Choice* this month. Actually, it's our first month, and our first selection." Liddy held up the sign-up sheet for the book clubs. "We'll be meeting on Thursday at seven."

"I'm in." The woman reached for the clipboard and signed her name: Deborah A. Allen. She paid for the book, and Liddy slid the paperback into the bag bearing a sketch of the store's facade and handed it over. "I'll see you then."

The minute the door closed behind her, Liddy waved Evelyn over. "Can you take over here for me? I need to make a call."

Liddy took her phone from her pocket and hustled to her office, dialing Jim's cell phone on the way. By the time she closed the office door, she'd worked up a string of expletives a mile long. Jim's phone rang six times, then finally he answered.

"Liddy! This is an unexpected pleasure. How are you?" The familiar voice struck a forgotten chord. She ignored it.

"I'm seeing red, that's how. I'm so mad at you I could . . ."

"Whoa, whoa. What's going on?"

"You told me you'd signed everything we owned over to me." Liddy forced herself to not sound as hysterical as she felt.

"I did. Everything we jointly owned," Jim said calmly.

"Well, you neglected one thing."

"And that would be . . . ?"

"The little house. Your name is still on the deed, Jim."

"You mean my old office? Well, yeah, my name probably is still on the deed."

"Why?"

"Because it wasn't jointly owned and never was. What's the big deal?"

"The big deal is that I want to sell it. I have a buyer and she's . . ."

"Slow down, Liddy. Why would you want to sell it, if you owned it?" He added under his breath, "Which you don't."

"I have no use of it or the land it sits on, and someone else does."

"It isn't yours to sell. It belongs to me, and I don't want to sell it. It's part of the parcel my great-grandfather bought at the turn of the last century. It's Bryant land, and it's going to stay Bryant land."

"For what purpose, Jim? There's no one to leave it to, no one who'll care it belonged to your family. Your sister has no children, and neither do you."

Jim went silent.

"That's what I thought you'd say." Liddy waited for his comeback. Finally, he said, "Why now?"

"Because there's someone who wants to buy it, and I want her to have it."

"How much?" he asked.

"To be determined. I'm having it appraised now. Today."

"I have to think about this."

"What's there to think about?" Liddy scoffed. "You planning on moving your office back in?"

"Oh, hell no. My business has tripled since I opened an office on the highway."

"So what's the point in holding on to it?" Liddy persisted.

"Because I don't see any particular reason to sell it."

"Well, I do, and I already promised Grace she could buy it."

"Who's Grace?"

"Grace Flynn."

"Grace Flynn." He paused for a long moment. "Jessie's old friend? That Grace Flynn?"

"Yes. She moved here with Maggie last year. I'm sure you've heard through the grapevine Maggie bought her family home last spring."

"I did. I'm sure you're happy to have her back, as close as you two were. But what's this got to do with Grace?"

"She needs a place of her own. I showed her the little house, believing it was mine, and mine to sell. She's totally in love with it and the idea of renovating it. She's already had a contractor look at it, and she has all these plans drawn up. I can't disappoint her." Liddy sighed. "Work with me on this, will you?"

"I remember Grace. She and Jess were joined at the hip during the summers when they were kids. They were best friends for a while." It was his turn to sigh. "What is it you want me to do?"

"I want you to sign the deed over to me so I can sell it to Grace."

"I'm surprised you're not giving it to her," he muttered.

"Believe me, I tried. She's insisting on paying market price, hence the appraisal today. I don't think the building is worth all that much—it could be a nice place for one person, maybe a couple at the most."

"True, but the land is probably worth a bundle. It's almost three acres."

"It is?" Why didn't she know that?

"It goes back into the woods and borders on the farthest point of the Harrison estate."

"I had no idea."

"Still want to sell it for the price of the building only? I mean, what's to prevent Grace from selling off the ground and making a huge profit for herself?"

"She wouldn't do that."

"You never know what people will do when there's a lot of money at stake, Lydia."

She hated when he called her Lydia.

"So put a clause in the deed that the parcel of land can never be split up or sold off, or however you want to word it."

"I guess I could talk to my lawyer about that." She could hear him wavering.

"Jessie would have wanted Grace to have that house, Jim." Liddy knew that was her ace. She couldn't remember a time when Jim had denied Jessie anything she really wanted.

He sighed again. "All right. I'll take care of the paperwork, and I'll get the new deed to you once it's done."

"Thank you."

"We'll consider this one of the last things we can do for Jess, right? To help her friend?" His voice sounded tight, as if he were close to tears.

When she realized she was nodding, tears in her own eyes, she said, "I think Jess would be delighted. Thank you again."

"I'll get back to you." Jim hung up without saying goodbye, same as he always did.

Liddy disconnected the call but remained at her desk, her emotions in a free fall. Knowing the property still belonged to Jim, and he'd benefit financially from a sale, she was grateful he'd come to see the situation through her eyes. Yet at the same time, she was still angry with him for, oh, so many reasons. She'd *wanted* to stay angry with him. But his generosity in their daughter's name touched her when she didn't want to be touched, made her grateful when she didn't want to feel any positive emotion for him. Yet there it was. He'd broken her heart, disappointed her to her very soul. And yet today he'd pulled through magnanimously merely because she'd asked.

Damn it. It was so much easier to be pissed off.

Chapter Ten

On Saturday morning, Liddy was showing a customer the greeting card selections when Grace came into the shop, wearing the same clothes she'd worn the week before.

"Sticking with the Mary Poppins look, I see," Liddy said as Grace walked by.

"If it ain't broke, don't fix it." Grace continued on to the back of the shop.

By ten forty-five, children were filing into the store like tiny soldiers on a mission. Their target was the children's section, where Grace would be reading from that week's selection, *Davey Wants a Dog*. Word of mouth since the first story hour must have been really good, because to Liddy's eye, it looked like twice as many kids as last week were crowding into the space. The thought of all those potential book sales put a big smile on her face.

Liddy noticed Tuck as he came in holding JoJo's hand, trailed by Bliss, who once again wore her too-bored-to-be-bothered expression. Which Liddy thought was silly since she was only two years older than her sister. Liddy suspected Bliss used her disdain as a means of asserting the fact she was older than JoJo, which she may have thought necessary since she and her sister were almost the same size. If JoJo liked it, it must be childish, whatever *it* might be.

"Hey, Tuck. I see you have book duty again today," Liddy noted.

"Yeah, Duffy has a travel soccer game this afternoon, and the bus is leaving at noon," he replied. "Linc volunteered to be assistant coach. As if he had nothing else to do."

"Pop, come *on*." JoJo tugged at his hand, her face marked with concern. "I don't want to be late again."

"God forbid you should be the last one there again." Tuck laughed and allowed himself to be pulled along to the back of the shop.

Five minutes later, Liddy was knee-deep in customers when she looked up and saw him standing about five feet away. He raised a hand to get her attention.

"Looks like you're going to be busy for a while. I'm going to run across the street for a cup of coffee. Can I bring you anything?" he asked.

"A coffee would be great. Thanks, Tuck."

Liddy assisted a customer who was looking for a book for her sister's birthday, and another who wanted "a mystery she wouldn't be able to solve before the end of the book." Liddy was pointing out several she'd found intriguing when Tuck returned with coffee.

"I left yours on the counter next to the iPad," he told her. "That shark of yours is making good time on her way south."

"She was already off the coast of Long Island yesterday."

"What's this about a shark?" Liddy's customer asked.

Liddy noticed a customer waiting to pay for her selection. She looked around but didn't see Evelyn, so she said, "Tuck, why don't you tell this nice woman about Rosalita?"

"I'd be happy to." Tuck launched into the information Liddy had given him about the shark tracker while Liddy stepped around another customer on her way to the counter.

The door opened, and Johanna Hall entered the shop with a small boy in hand.

"Oh, Liddy. Where's the children's story hour?" Johanna asked.

"All the way in the back, but it started about"—Liddy barely had the words out of her mouth when Johanna flew past her, dragging the boy, who looked to be about four—"ten minutes ago."

Liddy wondered if Tuck was having dinner at Johanna's tonight, and what seductive entrée Johanna might try to lure him with. Whatever that might be, how would it stand up against Liddy's beef stew?

Damn it, I saw him first.

Liddy rang up several more sales while watching Johanna corner Tuck near the gardening section. Well, at least she had good taste in men, because he did look fine in jeans and a dark-brown pullover the same color as his eyes.

She tried to focus on her customers and stay tuned in to their chatter, all the while trying to keep an eye on the duo moving toward the biographies. Tuck didn't appear to be saying much, she noticed. Johanna seemed to be doing most of the talking. He was just drinking his coffee and occasionally nodding.

She looked down at the transaction she was completing, but when she looked up again, Tuck and Johanna had disappeared somewhere between history and general fiction.

Story hour ended, and the rush of kids to pay for their books began. JoJo was pulling her grandfather into the single line Evelyn was enforcing like a trooper. Liddy noticed the little boy who'd come in with Johanna had begun tugging on her arm—Johanna's grandson, she assumed. Ever the gentleman, Tuck allowed them to get into the line before him.

"Was this your first story hour?" Liddy asked the boy.

He nodded.

"Did you like the story?"

He nodded again and held up the book, which Johanna took from his hand and placed on the counter. "We're going to read it again when we get home, right, Will?"

A third nod.

Johanna paid for the book and took the boy's hand. She turned back to Tuck and, in a voice that could have been heard in the back of the store, said, "See you tonight, Tuck. Don't be late. I have a special surprise hors d'oeuvre planned."

Liddy looked up in time to see Tuck's face turn beet red. He nodded to Johanna and forced a smile. Next in line, he handed over the book he was buying for his granddaughter.

"Hot date tonight, Tuck?" Liddy said under her breath.

Not raising his eyes to meet hers, he mumbled, "She invited me to some dinner thing."

"Well, bon appétit."

Liddy thought, to his credit, Tuck looked as though he wanted the floor to open up and swallow him whole.

JoJo tapped on the book impatiently, drawing Liddy's attention. "Did you enjoy the story, JoJo?"

"Uh-huh." JoJo's ponytail bobbed up and down. "I sat with Miss Grace again. She let me." Suddenly she yelped and jumped, and her small hand began rubbing her butt. Turning to her sister, she said, "That hurt. Pop said *don't pinch*."

"Miss Grace isn't your friend. She's just the lady who reads, JoJo." Bliss's expression had changed from bored to angry.

"She's nice. She lets me sit on her lap, and she lets me touch her hair like Mama did." JoJo had tears in her eyes.

"She's not Mama," Bliss snapped. "When Mama comes back, she'll be mad that you like Miss Grace so much."

JoJo burst into tears.

"Whoa." Tuck stepped in. "Bliss, that's unnecessary and it's unkind. What did we tell you about being mean to your sister? Come on, Jo." He picked up the weeping little girl, and she wrapped her arms around his neck. As he carried her to the door, he said, "We'll talk about this in the car. See you, Liddy."

"Tuck!" Liddy called to him. He'd left JoJo's book on the counter. She placed it on the floor next to her bag. If he didn't come back for it, she'd take it home, and voilà, she had the perfect excuse to call him and suggest he stop over tomorrow, when she could grill him about his dinner with Johanna.

"Did you find everything?" Liddy asked the woman who handed her two books and her credit card.

"I did. Do you think you'll be having any author signings here?" the woman asked.

"We've only recently opened," Liddy explained, then launched into her plans, which would hopefully include author appearances in time. The customer took information relative to the book clubs and left the shop, and another took her place at the counter, books in hand.

The children's story hour had brought so many customers into the shop Liddy had no time to brood over Johanna's big move on Tuck until late in the day. Evelyn relieved her at the register, and Liddy went back to her office. The coffee Tuck had brought her earlier was now cold. She poured some into the mug sitting on her desk, then put it into the microwave to reheat it.

Still tasty, she thought when she removed it and took a sip a minute later.

She sat in her chair and exhaled. There were so few things for the really young in a small town like Wyndham Beach, and the Saturday morning readings were a huge hit. The store had been packed, and while the children were falling in love with whatever book Grace had chosen to read that day, the waiting parents and grandparents, aunts, uncles, and family friends were finding plenty to read for themselves.

"A stroke of genius, if I do say so myself," she said aloud.

The store had been packed, and enthusiasm for Wyndham Beach Reads couldn't be higher.

All in all, it was a good day. Except for Johanna's plan to seduce Tuck. Would he fall into the snare Johanna was planning to bait with her "lascivious dishes"?

Would Liddy really want a man who was so weak he could be had for a gourmet meal? The image of Tuck in his jeans resurfaced, and she grudgingly admitted yes, yes, she would. And yes, she was that shallow.

She was spared further introspection by Grace knocking on the doorjamb.

"Liddy, have you heard from Gretchen or the appraiser?" Grace was still in her Mary Poppins garb.

"Only that the report should be ready sometime next week." That much was true. No need to let Grace know that, as it turned out, she didn't really own that property, or that she'd had to practically twist Jim's arm to sign it over to her. It would only complicate the situation.

"Oh, okay. I was just wondering. If you don't need me, I'd like to run home and then get to the library for a few hours."

"So I take it you didn't find the house on any maps?"

"No, I did find it. I found it on every map going back to nineteen hundred. I have a feeling it'll show up on earlier maps, but I didn't have time to pull those, because the library was closing."

"It'll be interesting to see how far back you have to go. But we're good here. I'm sure our busiest time is over." Liddy sat back in her chair and smiled. "The kiddies really do love your readings, Grace. And their parents seem to enjoy their time selecting books for themselves. We do a bang-up job on Saturdays, and I have you to thank."

"Aw, thanks, Liddy." Grace grinned. "I love doing it. The kids are so receptive and seem to enjoy themselves, so it's good for all of us."

"Tuck's granddaughter, Bliss, seems to think JoJo is becoming too fond of you, and somehow she sees that as being disloyal to their mother."

"You mean the mother who abandoned them? *That* mother?"

"Yes. And I share your disdain for the woman. But I only mentioned it to you because I think JoJo's very vulnerable right now, and while I'm not a child psychologist . . ."

"She's looking for a mother substitute. I get it. But she's a sweet girl, and she's hurting, and if it comforts her to sit on my lap and twirl my hair once a week while I read a story, I'm okay with that. It's not like I'm around her all the time. I don't think she's getting too attached. I think it just makes her happy to snuggle with someone. I don't know how snuggly the Shelby men are."

"You're probably right. You go on. We're good here. I didn't schedule you for tomorrow, so you have the rest of the weekend to haunt the online retailers for tile."

"I guess my mom told you I've been window-shopping on my laptop. I don't know exactly what I want, but it sure is fun looking." Grace hoisted her bag higher on her shoulder. "So you'll call me when you hear something from Gretchen?"

"Of course."

"Okay. I'll be patient." Grace rolled her eyes. "Who am I kidding? I can't wait!"

Liddy laughed. "You'll be the first to know. I promise."

"Thanks, Liddy. See you on Monday." Grace was half out the door when she stopped and turned around. "Oh, you know that kid who comes in here every day? The boy with the backpack?"

Liddy nodded. "His name is Dylan. What about him?"

"He was at the library when I was there after I left here yesterday. Which I thought was funny, because he was here most of the afternoon."

"He was?" Liddy tried to remember what time the boy left the shop yesterday. It was around six, she thought. "That's odd. I figured when he left here, he went home for dinner."

"Maybe he ate really fast and went back out. The library's a good place to study."

"He seemed to be doing that here," Liddy said. "He always has his nose in a book."

"Well, then, he must be an ace student. Good for him. And this time I'm really leaving."

Liddy heard Grace's retreating footsteps in the quiet of the shop. This time of day, there were few customers, and it was nice to sit in a quiet place and rest.

Rumbles from her stomach reminded her she'd skipped lunch. She was about to call in an order to the sandwich shop around the corner from the general store when she noticed the pizza box was still there from yesterday. There'd been three slices left, she recalled, and now she wondered if they were still good after not having been refrigerated overnight. She smiled, recalling how Jessie and Grace had used to enjoy cold leftover pizza for breakfast when they were kids. Cold pizza had never interested Liddy, but she did have the microwave there in the office, so why not?

She pulled the box to her and opened the lid, and found the box empty. Frowning, she questioned her memory. Hadn't there been pizza left over yesterday?

Maybe not. Then again, maybe Grace had heated it up for lunch earlier and forgotten to mention it. That was probably the case.

She folded the box in half and went out the back door to stuff it into the trash can. She glanced toward the harbor and saw a tall boy standing, looking out at the water. It took her a moment to realize it was Dylan, his ever-present backpack slung over one shoulder. He was leaning on one of the pilings shoring up the dock behind the doctor's office two doors down from the bookshop, his gaze fixed on a sailboat heading into the marina at the academy. Other than the two girls she'd seen him talking to the first day she'd noticed him in the shop, and the boy who'd stopped to chat briefly with him one afternoon, he always seemed to be alone, and that struck her as odd. Didn't most kids like to do things with their friends on Saturday night? What teenager preferred solitude to the company of his friends?

She went inside, closed the door behind her, and locked it. For some reason, the sight of the boy standing so still and staring so intently at the harbor bothered her. She wondered if he was having problems at home, or maybe with his relationships, problems that might seem insurmountable to him. If that were the case, she hoped he had someone to talk to. A chill ran up her spine as she contemplated what such a teenager might do. She promised herself she'd be more open to him, maybe even befriend him, just to keep an eye on him and watch for signs he might be thinking about doing something rash.

Not that Jessie had given any signs, she reminded herself. Still, maybe he needed a friend. She wouldn't pry, but she would try to be friendlier, to make sure he understood he was welcome there anytime.

She wandered through the shop, straightening shelves. Earlier Marion had come in to take Evelyn's place for the rest of the day. Liddy had thought she'd let Marion leave early, since the shop was slow, but now she thought better of it. She needed someone to talk to, to take her mind off the fact that right now, Tuck was arriving at Johanna's. Had she made Lamb Is for Lovers accompanied by some Daring Duchess Potatoes and some Kiss Me, Kale? Maybe some Lick My Ladyfingers for dessert?

"Ugh. I couldn't pull that off with a straight face," she muttered.

"Couldn't pull what off, Liddy?" Marion asked.

"Oh. Nothing. Just babbling to myself." But how, she wondered, did one serve such a thing? Did you announce in a sultry voice, *Tonight we're having Lamb Is for Lovers*? Or did you say, *I hope you like lamb*? She had to admit the latter lacked the drama and the pizzazz of the former, but gah! She could never get those words to come out of her mouth without laughing.

She was pretty sure Johanna could.

A couple came in and distracted her from the erotic images of Tuck and Johanna currently running amok in her head. By the time she finished showing them every new thriller and all the greeting cards, it was well after seven.

"Liddy, go home," Marion told her. "I can close up for the night, and Evelyn's on tomorrow. Seriously. Go home and get some rest."

Liddy was considering leaving when Gretchen arrived.

"What do you hear from Jim?" were the first words out of her mouth. No *Hi, Liddy*, no pleasantries. Gretchen was clearly a woman on a mission.

"He's taking care of it."

"Well, let me tell you something you don't know." She took Liddy's arm and guided her toward the window. "Liddy, you are sitting on a gold mine over there. That property is almost *three acres*. Do you have any idea what three acres of prime land is worth in Wyndham Beach? You could knock down that little old house and sell the whole thing to a developer. Or you could parcel it off in individual lots for custom homes. And oh, the views of the woods and the pond with that stream feeding it?" Gretchen apparently had visions of many high-ticket sales coming her way. "A gold mine, I'm telling you."

"I'm not interested, Gretchen. Besides, Jim has said he wants the entire parcel to remain intact, no subdivision ever. He's actually having a codicil attached to the deed to that respect, but thanks for stopping over to let me know."

Gretchen gripped her arm. "Liddy, you need to stop him from doing that. You could make a fortune."

"I don't know how else to say I'm not interested, other than to say, I'm not interested, and Jim doesn't want his family property broken up. End of story."

"Then I hope you're going to sell that little cabin for a bundle."

"Gretchen, we've been friends for years, so please don't take this personally, but it's really none of your business."

"Okay, I get that. I can understand you agreeing to sell to Grace—no, she didn't tell me, but it's obvious she's your buyer—before you knew the value of the property. But now that you know—okay, I don't have a solid number right yet, but trust me when I tell you it's huge—why would you go through with the sale?"

"Because I told her I would. And while I don't owe you any explanations, I'll just say Jim and I both agreed the house should be hers, and so it will be."

"Liddy, wouldn't this move faster if we just had Jim sell the property to Grace rather than have him sign it over to you, and then you sign it over to Grace?"

Liddy tapped her foot. Perhaps it had just occurred to Gretchen that if Jim were the seller, he might be more amenable to selling off at least part of the acreage, with Gretchen, of course, handling the transaction? Liddy could almost hear the argument, starting with, Does Grace really need three acres?

And if Jim knew how much the property was worth, might he be inclined to raise the selling price to Grace? It was too late, as far as Liddy was concerned, to change his mind.

"We're doing this my way. He will sign it over to me, and I will sell it to Grace. You, of course, will handle the paperwork for both transactions."

When Gretchen opened her mouth, Liddy held up a hand. "End of discussion, my friend."

"I'm only trying to look out for your best interests, Liddy."

Liddy softened. She believed Gretchen meant well. "I know you are, and I appreciate your concern. But this is a private matter between me and Grace."

Gretchen sighed. "Okay. So if I can't sell a bunch of houses for you, show me to a good book I can get lost in."

"I have just the thing." Liddy led her to the thriller section and handed her a book. "If this one doesn't do it, nothing will."

"Fine. I'll give it a try."

Minutes later, Gretchen left the shop, her new book under her arm, and Liddy all but collapsed against the counter.

"She's a tough one," Marion said.

"None tougher in this town. She sure worked me over."

Liddy went into her office and dialed Jim's cell. When he answered, she said, "Gretchen just stopped in. She didn't have a number, but she says it will be huge. I don't want you to change your mind, but I'd feel guilty if I didn't tell you."

"Pretty much what I already figured out. Thanks for letting me know, but I've never gone back on my word to you. I'm not about to start now. It is what it is."

"Thank you. You're being so reasonable about this."

"Well, you were right. There's no one to leave the land or anything else to." Suddenly Jim sounded very tired. "So if we can do something nice for someone Jess loved, that's what we'll do. Maybe Jess will know, wherever she is, and it will make her smile."

Liddy swallowed the lump in her throat, but before she could say anything else, he'd hung up. She turned off the light in her office and sat for a while in the dark. At eight thirty, she got up from her desk and walked up to the counter.

"I think I will take off a little early," she told Marion. "Are you sure you don't mind closing?"

"I don't mind at all," Marion said. "And I'll open in the morning. Come in when you're rested."

"Thank you. I don't know what I'd do without you." Liddy found her bag behind the counter, and left the shop. She crossed Front Street and walked the few blocks to Jasper Street, but at the corner, she paused. Johanna's house was one block up and another block over. She found her feet moving in that direction, and though she told herself it was a bad idea—a really bad, dumb idea—she kept walking.

Never ask a question you don't want the answer to, her father used to say.

And still, she kept walking.

When she came to the large two-story house with the big white pillars in front, she slowed. Yes, that was Tuck's truck in the driveway. She glanced at her watch, the numbers barely legible in the shadow of the streetlights. Johanna had announced to the entire shop that dinner was at seven, so he was probably past the hors d'oeuvres and into the main course.

She crossed the street and chastised herself for acting like the lovesick fourteen-year-old she'd been that summer she'd stalked Russ Watson. Having decided he was the love of her life, she'd done everything she could think of to get his attention. She'd shown up everywhere he went, as if by accident, when in actuality she'd eavesdropped on him and his friends every chance she got. She'd finally been caught hiding in a clump of forsythia while he was making out with Chery Thompkins in his backyard when the Watsons' next-door neighbor's dog sniffed her out and chased her across the yard. A picture of the chase flashed, and she saw herself screaming for help while the dog nipped at her ankles. She'd dashed across the grass and down the Watsons' driveway. The dog had chased her all the way to Beach Road before Russ caught up with it and took it home. He'd been so shocked at her appearance he hadn't said a word to her that night—or ever again. It hadn't been funny then—she was sure Chery Thompkins was going to tell everyone in school, but she hadn't because she'd told her boyfriend she was going to a sleepover at Adele Maxwell's, so she kept quiet. Liddy, of course, had not uttered a word to anyone, not even telling Maggie or Emma till the end of the summer. She'd thought they'd be shocked and horrified, but instead they'd both laughed, and she'd joined in, the three of them laughing until their sides hurt. Remembering made her laugh out loud all over again.

She laughed all the way home, at the absurdity of the situation and her foolishness at having reverted to spying on the guy she liked just as she had when she was a kid. And she did like Tuck, more than she'd ever liked any man—other than Jim, back when he was still a good guy and not the man who'd walked away when things got rough. She knew Tuck liked her, too. It was evident in the way he talked to her and the things he did for her. But if he chose a shallow, silly woman like Johanna over her, well, c'est la vie. There wasn't much she could do about that.

They could still be friends, which of course was second best in Liddy's eyes, and certainly not what she'd prefer. But she enjoyed his company too much to give it up should romance not be in the cards. He made her laugh, and he made her feel special, sexy, and smart. Who wouldn't want a man like that?

What she could do, she reasoned as she walked up the path leading to her front porch, was pour herself a nice fat glass of red wine and put her feet up. Of course, she'd rather have one of her world-famous margaritas, but it had been a long day, and margaritas were more work than she felt like tonight. Wine it would be, with a side of brie, crackers, and Netflix.

~

Having decided to take Marion up on her offer to open the shop in the morning so she could sleep in, Liddy set the alarm for seven instead of six. She took advantage of the extra time, treating herself to a longer shower than she'd had in weeks and making herself a real breakfast of poached eggs on toast and bacon. She'd just poured her second cup of coffee, which she'd decided to drink out on the deck, where she could admire the last of her summer flowers, when the doorbell rang. Expecting Emma or Maggie, she took her time getting to the foyer, wondering what could bring either of them out so early in the day.

She opened the door to find Tuck standing there.

"I hope this is okay—to stop over so early—but when we got home yesterday, we realized we'd left JoJo's book at the bookshop, and she was despondent. I thought I'd have time to stop at the shop last night, but you were already closed when I swung by."

"Ah, that's right. Dinner last night with the hot widow Hall."

Tuck looked at her as if she'd suddenly sprouted a second head.

"Hot widow?" He laughed. "I don't think so."

"Come on in and have a cup of coffee with me. Marion's opening up this morning, so I have time."

He followed her into the kitchen, and she poured him a mug. The cream and sugar were already on the table, so he fixed his coffee and took a sip. "You do make a great cup of coffee, Liddy."

"Thanks. I was just about to go out to the deck." She opened the back door and gestured for him to step outside. "Come join me."

There were three lounges on the left side of the deck, and a table with four chairs on the other. The morning air was crisp and scented with a faint hint of salt from the harbor mixed with the sweet autumn clematis that wound around an arbor.

"Let's take the lounges," she suggested.

"This is really nice out here." Tuck sat and put his feet up. "Your yard is beautiful. Do you have someone do your gardening? The flower beds look professionally done."

"Nope. That's all me, though I have to admit, lately the beds have taken a back seat to the shop. The weeds are out of hand, and pretty soon I'll have to find time to pull those canna tubers out and store them for next year."

"Running your own business can monopolize every bit of your life. I know all about that."

"I'm starting to understand just how much it takes. I don't mind, though. I love that shop, and I love seeing people find something to read that excites them. I love to read, so it's no hardship for me to read the new releases at night so I can recommend them to the right people. It's a fun job if you're a people person."

"Which you are," he noted.

"Yes, I am, but the past three years, I hardly saw anyone except Emma, and then Maggie moved back, so I was spending a lot of time with her as well. I didn't know how badly I needed the shop until Carl mentioned he was putting it up for sale. I knew right away I had to buy it."

"No regrets?"

She shook her head. "Not a one. How 'bout you? You sorry you're retiring?"

"Semiretiring, and nope. No regrets. I figured if I work less, I can spend more time with the kids, and Linc can start to have a life. I worry about the boy, you know? He has no social life. A man his age should be going out with his buddies, have a girlfriend, enjoy his life. Have his own place. All of which he was doing before he took on the kids. That girl he was dating took one look at those three kids and split. I can't remember the last time he did something for himself. It's not right he has to spend his life cleaning up after his sister."

"I'm sure he doesn't see it that way."

"No, he doesn't, and more's the pity. He'll never meet a nice girl, have a family of his own. Settle down here in Wyndham Beach. Unfortunately, nice girls his age are at a premium in Wyndham Beach."

"True enough. So how was dinner? What did Johanna make?" *If he says Lamb Is for Lovers, I swear I will roll right off this lounge onto the deck.*

"Some lamb thing."

The corners of her mouth began to twitch. "Was it good?"

"I didn't go back for seconds. I don't really like lamb. Never buy it, never order it out." He turned his head to look Liddy in the eye and said, "Johanna isn't a very good cook, Liddy. And she'd given me the impression it was going to be a dinner-party-type thing and there'd be other people there."

"Oh?" Liddy's eyes widened innocently. "And there weren't?"

"No. It was just me, and that made me uncomfortable."

"Why's that?"

"For one thing, she's a little . . . obvious. And for another, I never really knew her very well, so I didn't know what to talk about. I accepted the invitation because I thought it would be nice to see some people I might not have seen in a while. But"—he held his hands out, palms up—"it didn't happen that way. No one else to talk to. But since she talks so much, all I really had to do was keep myself awake."

"I thought someone said you used to date her in high school."

"What? No." He shook his head. "Nope. The only person I dated in high school was Doreen Rick."

"I guess I misunderstood." *Ha. You've been busted, Johanna.*

She tilted her head, listening. Was that the doorbell again?

"I don't believe this. Twice in one morning?" Liddy got up. "Probably one of the girls. Emma or Maggie. You stay put, Tuck. I'll be right back."

Liddy went to the front door with a smile on her face, imagining Emma's or Maggie's face at finding Tuck having coffee on Liddy's deck at just after nine on a Sunday morning. She'd let her friend speculate, but later she'd tell her the truth.

She opened the door and found herself face-to-face with Jim.

"Oh," she said, genuinely surprised to see him. "Jim. I wasn't expecting you."

"I hope it's not too early." He held up an envelope. "I know you were waiting for this."

"Is that what I think it is?"

He nodded. "Yup. All the paperwork you need. Duly signed and notarized. Just hand this to Gretchen. She'll know what to do with it." He passed it over. "As promised."

"Thank you. This is great, Jim. Really, I can't thank you enough."

"You can thank me by offering me a cup of your always-delicious coffee, since I skipped breakfast to drive this over before you went to the shop."

"Oh, of course. Come on in." She smiled to herself as she led the way into the kitchen, which of course he knew. He'd grown up in this house and had lived most of his married life here.

He helped himself to a mug from the cupboard and poured his coffee as if he still lived there, which sent a spike of pique up her spine.

The envelope still in her hands, she said, "I was just having my coffee out on the deck."

"I'd love to join you," he said, opening the door. "I always loved Sunday mornings, when we'd have our first . . ." He stopped two steps out from the door. "Oh. I didn't know you had company."

"Jim, you know—"

"Yeah. Tuck Shelby."

"Jim. Long time no see. How've you been?" Tuck said casually, as if it were the most natural thing in the world for him to be having coffee early on a Sunday morning with Jim's ex-wife, on Jim's ex-deck.

"Been fine. You?" Jim's eyes narrowed as he tried to figure out what Tuck was doing there so early in the morning.

Heh. Let him wonder.

"Never better." Tuck smiled.

Jim looked around as if not sure what to do. Sit at the table by himself, or on the third lounge, which was next to Tuck. He opted to stand, leaning against the deck rail, while he drank his coffee as if he couldn't get it down quickly enough.

"How're things at the bookstore?" Jim asked.

"Great," she said brightly. "I'm so lucky we have a town full of readers who were hungry for the store to reopen after months without it. It might not always be as busy as we've been since we first opened, but so far, so good." She held up crossed fingers.

"Great. I'm glad for you. That's great." He nodded and looked out over the yard—the yard, she recalled, where he'd watched her dig and plant and sweat, but never offered to help.

"So how's the insurance business going?" Tuck asked. "I guess you kept a lot of clients from Wyndham Beach."

"I did." Jim paused, then added, "Though I noticed you didn't renew any of your policies with me in June when they came up for renewal."

Tuck shrugged. "Frank Liddell offered me lower rates."

Jim looked about to say something, then apparently thought better of it. He finished his coffee and looked at Liddy as if seeing her for the first time.

"Well. I guess I'll be heading out." He pushed away from the railing and nodded at Tuck. "Tuck."

Tuck nodded back. "Jim."

"I'll walk you out." Liddy rose from the lounge.

"Don't bother. I know the way."

"Of course you do. I'll walk you out anyway." Liddy went into the kitchen behind Jim. He paused at the sink, as if about to rinse his mug, but she took it from his hands and placed it on the counter without saying a word.

At the front door, he paused. "So, you and Tuck . . . ?"

Liddy shrugged. "We had some things to talk about this morning." As much as she had enjoyed his obvious discomfort, she relented. "He stopped over just before you got here."

"He sure looked at home out on the deck."

"Well, as I said, we had some things to talk about."

"If you say so." He opened the front door and stepped out onto the porch. "Hey, my doormat's gone. Where'd it go?"

"Into the trash. Don't take this personally, but I hated that thing."

"I didn't know. Why didn't you tell me?"

She shrugged. "You liked it, and I didn't want to hurt your feelings."

He looked toward the driveway, then turned back to her and said, "Could I see you sometime? Maybe for dinner?"

"Sure. You know where to find me."

"I do."

"So, thanks again, Jim. Really. I'm grateful, and I know Grace will be, too."

"I'll be in touch." He crossed the lawn to the driveway instead of taking the path, his habit all the years he'd lived here. "Liddy, if you need anything—anything at all—I hope you'll call me."

"I'll keep that in mind. Thanks, Jim." She stood on the front porch until he got into his car and backed away, then went into the house and closed the door.

~

Tuck drove her to the shop at nine thirty, parked out front, and followed her inside to pick up JoJo's book. Liddy waved to Marion, who was at the back of the shop straightening books in the children's section, then stepped behind the counter for the bag she'd set aside for Tuck the night before.

"Thanks for holding this for me." Tuck flipped through the first few pages and held up the page where Grace had written a note to JoJo. "There's no way I'd have been able to take home a different copy." He held up the book so Liddy could read the inscription.

To my sweet friend JoJo. I love having you come to story hour on Saturday mornings! I hope you come back next week. I'll keep your seat warm! Love, Miss Grace

"That's nice of Gracie. I know she's fond of JoJo," Liddy said.

"I think we both know what Jo thinks of Grace."

There was much Liddy could say on the subject, but she merely nodded.

"Well, I better get going. I need to get the boat back for Linc, and he'll need me to watch the kids. He wanted to check something at that house of yours."

Liddy walked him to the door. "Thanks for stopping over this morning. It was nice having a few minutes to sit and relax over a cup of coffee with you."

"I don't think Jim appreciated me being there. I hope my being there didn't disrupt any plans you may have had with him."

"No plans with Jim. He was just dropping off some paperwork for me." Liddy opened the door and stepped out into the sunlight. "It's really none of his business who I entertain. Oh, looks like I need to water these flowers again."

"You take care of them, then. I'll see you." He drove off in the direction of Beach Plum Road, where he owned a building that housed his trucks and his equipment and where he had built a dock so he could tie up his boat.

Liddy watered the planters out front, then puttered here and there throughout the shop. Sales on Sundays were slow and customers few and far between until later in the afternoon, when the foot traffic in town picked up a bit.

"Liddy, what a lovely shop you have."

Liddy looked up from the publishers catalog she'd been thumbing through.

"Neva Kreger, how've you been?" Liddy was genuinely pleased to see one of Jessie's favorite teachers on the other side of the counter.

"I've been well, Liddy. I've heard so much about your shop I had to come see for myself." Neva glanced around the room as if trying to take it all in. "My goodness, such an improvement over the last time I was here."

"Not to disparage Fred . . ."

"Oh, of course not. But things had fallen behind. It's lovely now." Neva's kind face, framed with the wire-rimmed glasses she'd worn for all the years Liddy had known her, lit up when she smiled. A woman of roughly Liddy's age, she'd been voted the high school's favorite teacher many times for her warmth and her obvious love for her job and her students.

"Thank you, Neva. It's been my saving grace. I look forward to coming in here every day and talking to my customers."

"There's nothing like a new love to put a spark in your step. And when that new love is a book, oh my goodness. Books truly are the gifts that keep on giving. I envy you, being surrounded by all this every day. Aren't you tempted to read everything?"

Liddy laughed. "It's all I can do to keep up with the new releases, which I feel I must do, so when customers ask me about them, I can discuss the books and recommend them."

"An enviable job." Neva reached across the counter and gave Liddy's hand a squeeze. "Perhaps when I retire in a few years there will be an opening for me. I'd love to work here."

"There will always be a place for you, should you ever want one." Liddy stepped around the counter. "Now, what can I interest you in today? Or are you just browsing?"

"I wanted to talk to you about possibly ordering books for my senior AP English class." Neva took a list from her well-worn leather bag and showed it to Liddy. "I have several titles I want them to read this year."

"How many students?"

"There are eleven."

Liddy was looking over the list and nodding—she already had a few of the titles in stock but not eleven of any one of them. "When would you like to pick them up?"

"Would two weeks give you enough time?"

"More than enough. I'll have the orders go in first thing tomorrow, and I'll give you a call when to expect them. And, of course, I'll give you the friends-and-family discount."

"Thank you, Liddy. I'm sure the students will appreciate that."

"They'll be buying the books themselves?"

Neva nodded. "Some of the kids can well afford them, but for a few of them, finding money for books would be a stretch."

"Maybe we can come up with something to help out. Let me think about it."

"That would be great. The kids will welcome any help." She glanced at the new-release table. "Maybe I should pick up something for myself. Something that can help keep me focused next week."

"What's happening next week?"

"I'm having my deposition taken in the Bowers case on Wednesday, and I'm a nervous wreck about it. I don't know what they're going to ask me, so I can't prepare myself. I didn't know what that horrible man was doing." Neva looked as if she'd burst into tears at any moment. "And to think it was going on literally under my nose, and I never suspected. I feel so guilty. Most of those girls were my students at one time or another. I feel I should have known somehow something wasn't right. All those years he was getting away with it, and I never suspected."

"Why do you think you should have suspected something? Did one of the girls say something to you?"

Neva shook her head. "No, of course not. If anyone had said any-thing that even alluded to what he was doing, I would have gone right to the principal, and we would have called the police. But I guess when something like this happens, it's natural to look back and scrutinize everything and look for something you think should have been a warn-ing. But honestly, I can't say there was."

"I know it's easy for me to say, but don't beat yourself up over this. If you didn't know, you didn't know. There's nothing you can testify to."

"I suppose you're right." Neva's sigh seemed to come from the depths of her soul.

"Oh, hi. Welcome back." Marion's greeting drew Liddy's attention to the door.

"Dylan, hello." Neva's smile was warm and wide as she greeted the young man. "We were just talking about ordering books for your class."

"Hi, Ms. Kreger." Head down, and seeming to be surprised to see his teacher there, he nodded first to Neva and then to Liddy before he made for the back of the shop. He sat in the usual chair—Grace's story time chair—and opened his backpack, took out a notebook, and began to read.

"Dylan's one of my favorite students. Everyone on the faculty loves him," Neva confided. "He has such a quick mind. He's earning straight As in all-AP classes, and they say he's one of the best athletes we've had at Regional High since . . . well, since . . ."

"Since Brett Crawford?"

"That's what they tell me, but I only know what I've heard. I'm not into athletics, I'm afraid."

"Brett was in my class," Liddy explained. "He was drafted by the Seattle Seahawks and played something like five seasons before he was injured."

"Then that's who they were talking about in school."

"Dylan looks a little light to be a football player," Liddy observed.

"Oh, no, he plays baseball. He was all-state last year, and they say he's a shoo-in for this year as well. There are several colleges interested in him, and we're positive he can get enough financial aid that he can go to a top school. No question, the sky's the limit for that boy."

"So are you saying his parents can't afford for him to go to college?"

Neva's voice dropped to a whisper. "Well, it's no secret since it's been in all the papers. His parents were involved in that armed robbery over in New Bedford in July."

"The liquor store robbery?" Liddy searched her memory for details. "Three robbers, one shooter?" Her eyebrows raised. "One of his parents was the shooter?"

"No. Dylan's uncle, his father's brother, was the shooter, but because someone was badly injured, they faced the same charges. They made a deal with the DA and got fifteen years each. If the victim had died, it would have been a lot worse."

"Oh, that poor kid. Does he have family? Who is he living with?"

"The family's from Pike Creek, but he's staying with his grandmother here in Wyndham Beach."

"Oh, thank goodness he has someone." The amount of time Dylan spent in the bookshop was beginning to make sense. Surely it'd been hard for him to get used to living with an older relative. "Was he close to his grandmother before he moved in with her?"

"I don't know for sure, but I think maybe not. He doesn't seem to want to talk about it, or her. I don't wish to pry, of course, and certainly it's understandable if he just doesn't want to discuss his family. It has to have been devastating for him."

"What's his grandmother's name?"

"I think it's Linden. Margaret Linden. We all received notice when he moved."

Liddy frowned. She thought she knew everyone in Wyndham Beach, but Margaret Linden rang no bells. "Do you know what street she lives on?"

"Something Terrace. Devon, maybe? It wasn't a street I knew, so I'm guessing it's one of those new cul-de-sacs in that town house development on the other side of Route Six."

"As long as he has someone responsible looking after him," Liddy said. Not that it was any of her business. "Well, I'll let you wander around and see if something catches your eye."

"I'm sure I'll find something." Neva wandered to the new releases, then found her way to the cozy mysteries.

Liddy went back to the counter and turned on the iPad.

"Let's see what Rosalita's up to today," she said to no one in particular. Evelyn had come in minutes before, and Marion was getting ready to leave. Both women came to the counter to see where Liddy's shark was at that moment.

"She's smart to be heading south," Evelyn said as she buttoned up her cardigan in preparation for heading out. "It can turn cool here on a dime. I heard we're in for another cold, snowy winter this year."

"And that would be different from every other year, how?" Liddy asked.

Grace popped in to let Liddy know she'd found the first appearance of the little house on official town records.

"The earliest record I could find was on an 1843 map. Older than most of the other houses in that section of town," Grace announced.

"Can you find out who built it?" Liddy asked.

"No. The map had Robert Butler's name next to the house. Robert spelled *Rbrt*."

"Huh. There used to be a family named Butler on Roslyn Road. My grandmother used to play cards with a woman named Edith Butler. That's probably the same family."

"When you look at the early maps together, you can see where lots were sold off over the years. When the parcel of land your house sits on was sold, the little house—the original house—was included in the sale. Your house doesn't appear until 1908."

"That's about right. Jim's great-grandfather built it." Liddy smiled.

"At some point, the lots were separated, but I haven't found when. Cool, huh?" Grace glanced at the back of the shop. "Oh, I see your boyfriend is here again, and it looks like he brought his mother. Grandmother, maybe?"

"Oh, no. That's Neva Kreger. She teaches English at the high school. Jessie had her two years in a row. She adored her. All the kids do." Liddy hadn't noticed when Neva pulled the other wingback chair closer to Dylan's, but it appeared they were deep in conversation.

"Well, I'm going to head over to the house that will hopefully be mine someday soon," Grace said.

Liddy smiled reassuringly at her. "Don't worry. The little house will be yours very soon, and then you can order all the tile and appliances your little heart desires."

Grace laughed and headed out. Before she reached the door, Liddy said, "Hey, Grace, did you eat the pizza cold, or did you give it a turn or two in the microwave?"

Grace stopped, her hand on the door, and turned to Liddy. "What pizza?"

Chapter Eleven

As she turned the corner onto Jasper Street, Grace was humming "Happy," timing her steps with the beat, occasionally singing a word or two out loud. Even the threat of imminent rain didn't dampen her cheery mood. Up ahead, on her left, was her destination, her someday-soon-to-be home. *Soon*, she wryly acknowledged, was a relative term. Hopefully, Gretchen was as good at her job as Liddy claimed, and she'd manage to streamline the transaction.

Grace was eager for the work to begin, but since Linc had indicated he'd be busy on another job for a few more weeks, she figured it didn't so much matter she didn't actually own the place yet. Besides, she had work to do before Linc could get started. There were so many things the house needed—cabinets and bathroom fixtures, light fixtures, everything that goes into building a house. And this was almost like building a new house, since nothing presently in the building would remain once the renovation began.

She stopped at the foot of the driveway where it met the side-walk, picturing a cute mailbox there. Then she would line the drive on either side with flowers to make it look like a country lane. Orange daylilies, Queen Anne's lace, and blue cornflowers grew wild along many of the country roads around Philly, and that color-ful, random, blowsy look always said summer to her. Maybe the combination of the three would work here as well. She liked the idea, and made a mental note to add that to her list of things to do. That same combination of flowers would be lovely around the pond, she was thinking, as the house came into view. She slowed her steps when she saw the Shelby & Son truck parked next to a picturesque stand of white birch. As she drew closer, she saw Linc in front of the house, his focus on the phone in his hand.

"Hi," she called.

He turned at the sound and smiled, then dropped his phone into his back pocket.

"Hey, Grace. I was just looking up your number." He took a few steps toward her.

"Is there a problem?"

"No, I just wanted to check something. I'd made notes the last time I was here, but I have a question about the measurements of those back rooms where you want your bedroom and bath."

She held up the key. "Follow me."

Grace unlocked the door, and they went inside. The air was just as close and stifling as it had been every other time she'd been there, but this time a live wasp buzzed at the window in the front room. Linc opened the window to let it out.

"I was looking for something to smack it with," Grace said.

"Swatting at it would be a good way to get yourself stung. He wasn't bothering anyone. He just got trapped in here and wanted out." He closed the window and relatched it. "Looks like you need screens."

"I hope he didn't bring any friends with him."

"I'll check for nests when I start the reno," Linc assured her. "It's not unusual for insects to move in when a property is vacant for a while."

"Nests?" Grace grimaced and looked upward at the corners of the room.

The merest hint of a smile on his face, Linc walked past her and down the hall to the back rooms, a tape measure in his hand.

"I can't remember if you said you wanted a tub and a shower combined, or separate fixtures," he said when she came into the back room behind him.

She pondered the choices. She'd wanted separate—a big soaking tub for those times when she wanted a bubble bath and a good book, and a big shower wide enough for two, because you never knew.

"I can have both, right?" she asked.

"I'd need to take a little from the walk-in closet, but sure. You can have both." He stood with his hands on his hips, his gaze direct.

She was momentarily hung up on eyes that held her spellbound. How was it this guy was still single? *Had he always been?* she wondered. Maybe he had a girlfriend.

Oh, of course he would, she thought. How could he not?

"Grace?" He'd caught her mentally speculating on his status.

She hoped he wasn't psychic.

"How much off the closet?" she asked.

"Maybe a foot or so."

"So worth it. Yes, tub and big shower. I want a shower big enough for two."

He nodded and made a note without reacting. Well, of course, this wouldn't be the first time a client had made such a request.

"Now, when do I get to pick out the tub? And the vanity? And the shower surround? I like clear glass, and I like . . ."

"Whoa." Linc laughed. "Let's get the walls down to the studs and get the ceilings down, the carpet ripped up, and then take a look at the space. You should have an idea of what you want before those things happen, but we're dealing with limited space here. You want to be precise when you measure so you know, for example, what size cabinets to order. Taking down walls will change things slightly." He must have noticed her look of disappointment, because he added, "If you find something you feel you cannot live without, show me, and I'll do my best to make sure it works in your space, okay?"

"So I need to hold off on ordering anything?"

"You shouldn't be doing the ordering. Let me do that. As a contractor, I can get a better price, nine times out of ten." He walked across the hall to the kitchen. "Look at it this way. You can save enough to upgrade to designer tile for that big shower."

"Good point. I'll go over everything I want with you, and you can do the ordering. But fair warning: I want a lot."

"You're entitled. Your house." He knelt on one knee and tugged at a section of carpet. "Let's see what's under here."

"I tried to pull it up in the front room, but it wouldn't budge," she told him.

He yanked up the edge of the carpet to expose the floor beneath. "Wow. Check this out." He leaned back and beckoned her closer. "Heart pine. I'll bet anything it goes through the entire place."

Grace leaned over Linc's shoulder. "Oh, that's lovely. Why would you want to cover that with this ugly gold carpet?"

"The carpet probably wasn't this ugly when it was put down. Remember, this place was an insurance office for years, so you had people in and out in all sorts of weather. Be happy they had the floors well covered. The thick carpet and the pad under it protected the wood. If it looks like this all the way through, we're only going to have to sand it lightly, then put a protective stain on it. It'll save you time and a lot of money if we don't have to do anything but clean them up." He licked a finger and rubbed the wood. The grain was beautiful. "There you go." He looked up at her. "Antique wood just waiting to be brought back to life. Assuming it's as old as it looks."

"Oh, it's really old. I found this place on a map from 1843 at the library. It could be on another even earlier one, but I ran out of time. I'll keep looking, though."

"Eighteen forty-three? Seriously?" Linc stood and brushed the dust off his hands.

Grace told him the story of how the house appeared to be the original structure on this side of town and how parcels had been sold off.

"Good detecting. I was wondering when this place was built." He looked around the room appreciatively. "I'd have been able to deduce the age to a certain extent when I start taking it apart. The old nails they would have used would be a clue. Now I can't wait to rip the old drywall off and see what's behind it."

"I'm afraid we're both going to have to wait a little longer until the sale is completed. But once that's done—rip away."

"In the meantime, you go ahead and start building a file of what you want. Cabinets for the kitchen . . ." He hesitated before asking tentatively, "If you don't mind me offering a suggestion?"

She shook her head. "No, go ahead."

"Maybe for the kitchen cabinets a natural wood. Something warm. Walnut would be perfect but pricey for the type of grain you'd want. Brass handles would complement the wood, but if you want a look that's a little more contemporary, you might go for chrome. Light-colored backsplash—something simple. I know everyone does white subway tile, but there's a reason for it. It's classic and unobtrusive. You'd want those walnut cabinets to take center stage."

She could see it. "I like that. Countertops?"

"You could go with one of the stones—granite, quartz, marble. There are other materials for the counters, though, besides stone. In the house we did last month out on the point, we did concrete. Looked great. It can be stained any color if you like a different look."

"I've seen that done on some of the reno shows on HGTV." She recalled having liked the clean look.

"Ahhh, HGTV." He smiled.

"What? It's one of my favorite places."

"I thought it was a TV channel."

"Well, yes, but it's where you go to get new ideas, see new products, and learn new lingo. I mean, how many people do you suppose used the word *shiplap* before HGTV?" Grace leaned back against the doorway. "It's also a good place to get tips on how to set up furniture in odd-shaped rooms and how to reuse things you find in thrift or antique shops." She grinned. "Or in my mother's attic, which is my personal favorite place to shop."

She thought of the antique dresser she'd mentally placed on the short wall under the window in the front room, and the farm table her dad had made for their Bryn Mawr house. It didn't fit in Maggie's kitchen but would be perfect here in the little house, where it could serve for dining and for a home workstation.

"Did you give any more thought to a screened porch out back?" Linc asked.

"I'm still thinking about it. I really pictured a patio out there."

"You have room to do both, but it's your house. I was just thinking you'd be able to spend more time out back in the summer if you had a place to sit where the greenhead flies couldn't get to you."

"Oh my God, I hate those things. When we were kids, we'd be out on the beach, enjoying ourselves—then the wind would turn suddenly and unleash those vicious flying monkeys on us, and we'd be bitten everywhere. We'd run home all bitten up and itchy, and my gramma would put ice packs on the bites, then some kind of cream to take the itching away." She paused. "Do you have those flies out on your island?"

"Oh, sure. They can fly for miles. There's a section on one side of the island that's marsh, and if you know your greenhead flies, you know they breed in marshes. I've even been bitten on the boat in the middle of Buzzards Bay. There's no safe place outdoors from July to

September. Thankfully, it's already September. I haven't had a bite in at least a week."

The sudden sound of rain beating on the roof startled them both.

Linc looked out the window. "Damn. I was hoping to beat the storm home. I should get going. I have a few miles to go by boat."

"I'll close up. Go on." She turned off the lights and stepped outside in time to see Linc dash to his truck and hop inside. He had started the engine and begun to move forward when he looked back at the house.

He pulled directly in front of where she stood and rolled down the passenger-side window. "Where's your car?" he shouted over the rumble of thunder.

"I walked." She'd underestimated the rainfall and how quickly the temperature had dropped. Cats and dogs wasn't even close.

"Get in. I'll drop you off."

"No, it's okay." She declined the offer, knowing what she must look like, soaking wet with her clothes stuck to her and her hair plastered to her head.

"You'll get soaked. Come on."

The rain fell in an angry torrent. Linc was right. She'd be cold and waterlogged before she got to the driveway. She locked the door and ran to the truck. "Thanks," she said as she climbed in. "I didn't expect this."

"Don't you pay attention to the forecasts on the weather channel?"

"I never watch the news, it's always depressing, and I'm usually doing something else in the evening." Why oh why hadn't she been born one of those women who looked really good soaking wet?

"Enjoying Wyndham Beach's happening nightlife?"

"I had a beer at Dusty's one night with Chris Dean and Ted Affonseca. Does that count as nightlife? It was only once, and it was a few months ago, but still. The local tavern. Beer. A couple of guy friends. It should count as something."

He laughed. "How do you know Chris Dean?"

"I've always known him. Our moms have been best friends forever." *And he's sleeping with my sister, but that's probably neither relevant to this conversation nor appropriate.* "You must know him, too, if you grew up here."

"Yeah, we were in the same class all through school."

"He's a great guy. He sent Natalie and me tickets for his concert in Philly last year. Even sent a limo to pick us up."

"Natalie is . . . ?"

"My sister. Are you still friends with Chris?"

"I haven't seen him in years."

"He's still the same guy he was when we were kids."

"Good to know," he said.

There was a touch of something she couldn't define in the tone of his voice. It wasn't envy, the way some guys might feel toward an old friend who'd hit it out of the park the way Chris had. Nostalgia? Regret? She just couldn't put her finger on it.

"Were you friends with him?"

"Oh, sure. This is a small town, so all the kids got to know each other pretty well. The high school is regional, but each little town has its own K-through-eight school."

Before she could ask anything else, they were approaching the corner of Front and Cottage.

"Turn right onto Cottage?" he asked.

"Yes. It's the house with the cedar-shake siding about halfway up." She watched out the window until they neared the house. "This next one . . . yes, here."

He pulled into the driveway, close to the path.

"Hey, thanks for the ride." She reached for the door handle, dreading having to go out into the rain again.

"My pleasure. Grace—"

She turned to him, wishing she knew if her mascara had run, and if so, did she have raccoon eyes?

"I just want to say thanks for being so nice to JoJo. She's really having a hard time right now. She misses her mother a lot."

Grace nodded. "I know she does. I'm sorry she's hurting, and I wish I could do something to make it better for her. She's such a sweet little girl."

"She's very fond of you. All week she talks about going to the bookshop on Saturday to see her friend Grace and sit with you while you read. That little bit of special attention means a lot to her, you know? I try to give her as much attention as I can, but there are two other kids who need attention." His frustration came through in every word.

"And on top of that you have a day job and a company to run."

"My dad does as much as he can, but damn, it's tough for him sometimes, too. He's trying to retire, but he keeps getting sucked back into working. I can't devote as much time as I used to."

"You sound like several women I knew back in Philly. Women who worked outside their homes and were trying to do a good job raising their kids. Even those who had partners had a tough time of it, but the single moms had it the worst. It has to be really hard when your personal and professional lives are so demanding."

"I'm sorry. I know some people have no help at all, not even as much as I get from my dad." His face scrunched with concern. "Did I sound whiny?" he asked.

"No. You sound human."

"Thanks. Again, I'm sorry. I don't usually complain to my customers."

"Then consider me a friend."

"Fair enough. Anytime."

She opened the car door. "Thanks for the ride," she shouted as she jumped down, then made a frantic dash for the front porch. She splashed through a large puddle of mud on the way, dotting both legs with the evidence.

Grace knew Linc was sitting in the car, watching, as if waiting for her to get into the house, which was nice. She only wished she didn't look like an overgrown mud-spattered toddler who didn't know enough to come in out of the rain.

Chapter Twelve

Something had been nagging Liddy all the following week since her chat with Neva Kreger. It was the feeling you got when you knew something but couldn't really put your finger on it. When she realized what it was, she called Gretchen.

"Hi, Liddy. I was just going to call you. I went to the courthouse and filed the documents showing Jim sold you the cabin for one dollar. As soon as I get the duly recorded deed in your name, I'll let you know."

"Great. I'm glad it's moving along. Grace is so antsy to get things going. I swear she's there more than she's home." Liddy paused. "I didn't tell her about Jim's involvement, so I'd appreciate it if you didn't mention it. I just didn't want her to know how complicated things were."

"My lips are sealed."

"I appreciate that. Listen, the reason I'm calling—did you tell me you were the Realtor handling the sales of the town houses on Route Six?"

"I am." Gretchen's voice brightened. "Are you interested in one? I'd be happy to show you. Honestly, Liddy, you would love the floor plans. And the exterior maintenance is all done for you. And—"

"No, actually, I'm interested in knowing if someone else purchased a home there. The woman's name is Margaret Linden. Does that ring a bell?"

"Not offhand. Why?"

"She ordered a book, and it just came in. I wrote down her phone number and address, but I can't find the paper I wrote it on." Liddy laughed as if embarrassed at her oversight, but more so at her lie, which she told herself was for the greater good.

"Oh, I know the feeling. I do that all the time. I'll put something in a place I'm sure I'll remember, then immediately forget." Gretchen laughed, too. "Hold on, let me check the records. I don't recognize the name, but it's possible someone else in my office handled the sale, and I just don't remember hearing about it."

The phone went silent for a full minute. When Gretchen came back on, she said, "I don't see a Margaret Linden here. Is she maybe living with someone else? A relative maybe?"

"I don't know. I'm pretty sure she said the street was Devon Terrace."

"There is no Devon Terrace at that development. For that matter, there's no street with either Devon or Terrace in it. Trust me, I know every curve in every cul-de-sac."

"Huh. I guess I misunderstood. It was such a circus here on Saturday, with all the kids coming in for the story hour. I guess I'll have to wait till she contacts me again for her book. Thanks, Gretchen."

"You're welcome. I'll be in touch."

Liddy sat at her desk, tapping her pen on the blotter as several small incidents began to fall into place. The food wrappers. The pizza that disappeared. The back door being unlocked in the morning when she knew she'd locked up the night before.

She got up from her desk and went to the door and found it unlocked.

But she knew once the door was opened, it could not be locked or unlocked from the outside without a key. There were six keys for the shop, and she knew the location of every one of them. So someone had either found a way to pick a dead bolt, or they'd come into the shop and never left, then unlocked the door when they wanted to leave but couldn't relock it once they were outside.

Liddy waited until Grace left for the morning to run a few errands and Evelyn arrived to take over at the register. The foot traffic was light, but Thursdays weren't generally busy. Liddy went into the back of the shop as if going to her office, but she slipped into the back hall and tiptoed up the stairs to the second floor. She looked through each room but hadn't really expected to find anything out of place, because Grace used the area as her office and storage for books she was shipping out. Other than some printed copies of a page of text for a website she was working on, there was nothing on Grace's worktable and nothing on the floor.

Liddy climbed the steps to the third floor. At the landing, she took a deep breath. Out of shape or anxious? Maybe a bit of both, she conceded.

She went into the large front room that overlooked the center of town, but found nothing other than a few boxes of old books Fred had left behind. There was a small room to the left, and an even smaller room next to it. If she were to find anything to prove her theory correct, it would be in that room. It looked out over the harbor and had two small windows.

As soon as she went into the room, she knew her instincts were spot-on. Both windows were open just enough to let in a bit of fresh air—definitely not her doing—and a neatly folded pile of blankets was tucked under one of the eaves. It made a tidy, safe place for a hideout.

And that, she knew, was what Dylan had been doing: hiding out. Waiting until no one was looking at the back of the shop, then creeping up the steps to the third floor, where he'd sleep until the sun woke him through the window in the morning so he could get to school on time.

The question was why—and how he'd come to select her shop.

The bigger question: Now that she knew, what was she going to do about it?

~

"Liddy, isn't tonight the first romance book club?" Grace asked when she returned to the shop.

Liddy, whose thoughts had been elsewhere, had to stop and think. "Oh my Lord, I forgot all about it."

"It's not a big deal. But you probably need to decide right now where you're going to set up. I think the children's section is the obvious choice, since it has the most room. And I think we agreed on ordering a carafe or two of coffee and one of hot water for tea along with some cookies from Ground Me." Grace looked around. "Is someone bringing chairs from somewhere?"

Liddy groaned. "I meant to call Emma to see if she'd ask her brother if we could borrow some chairs from the church hall. It's right across the street, so we could run over and get them ourselves."

"I'll call her right now if you'll call for the coffee." Grace reached into her bag for her phone and looked up Emma's number, then hit send. "Any idea how many we'll need?"

"No. We could get fifty people, or it could be you, me, and Evelyn."

"I'll ask for . . . oh, hi, Emma. It's Grace . . ."

Seven o'clock rolled around, and the first meeting of the romance book club began right on time. Most of the eighteen members had purchased the book at least a week ahead of time—*The Lady's Choice* by Cindy Bickley—and were eager to discuss the story.

"I loved that Marianna had to choose between Nathan and Gerard." Tami Sellers took the lead, as Liddy had asked her to do. "I personally could not have made that decision. I'd have wanted them both."

Light laughter followed.

"I guess they never heard of a threesome," someone said, and more laughter followed.

"They don't know what they're missing," another voice popped up.

"Stick to the book, ladies." Liddy laughed as she returned to the front of the store.

"Where's the fun in that?" one of the ladies asked, sending a fresh wave of laughter around the group.

Someone from Ground Me delivered a box holding everything they needed for a coffee station. Liddy set it up on the table she normally reserved for the new children's books so the readers could help themselves.

"It's a rough crowd tonight, Dylan," Liddy told him when he came in a little after eight and appeared momentarily befuddled to find someone sitting in "his" chair and a group of women sitting around in a circle drinking coffee, eating cookies, and talking about a particularly hot sex scene. "You might want to cover your ears."

He turned red and headed to the front of the store, where he found a corner to sit in while he did what appeared to be homework. She wondered if his teachers wouldn't expect whatever he was writing to be typed and printed out. Where did kids go if there was no computer in their homes? She knew the library had only so many stations available, because last year she'd headed the fundraising drive to purchase eight desktops.

Since Grace had seen Dylan in the library one night after he'd left here, Liddy figured it might be his routine to go to the library after he'd left the bookshop at a time when someone might reasonably assume he'd gone home for dinner. If what she suspected was true, there'd been no dinner, just as there was no home and no grandmother named Margaret Linden. She had called Neva to double-check the name Dylan had given the school, and she'd called around to everyone she knew. She had not found one person in Wyndham Beach who'd ever heard the name.

It had taken Liddy a while to figure out her next step, even to the bait she'd use. Deciding what to do once the trap was sprung wasn't as easy.

She stepped outside the shop and made a phone call, completing her plan for the following night.

~

At eight thirty on Friday night, Liddy called to Grace, "If I call over to Ray's and order a large pepperoni-and-mushroom pizza, would you pick it up for me?" Liddy spoke just loudly enough for Dylan, who was in his usual place, to overhear.

"Sure. But pepperoni and mushrooms? You don't like pepperoni," Grace said as if she thought Liddy needed reminding.

"It's been a while since I had it, so I thought I'd give it another try. It always smells so good."

"Okay." Grace shrugged. "Just let me know when you want me to go."

Liddy waited until eight thirty to call in the order, so it wouldn't be ready until almost nine, which played into her plan. She walked the last customer to the door a little before nine and sent Grace to Ray's. She stood outside for several minutes and waited for Grace's return, giving Dylan time to dash upstairs.

"What are you doing out here?" Grace asked after she crossed the street, the large white box in her hands.

"Just getting a little fresh air," Liddy told her. "It's nice after being inside all day."

They went inside the shop, and Liddy locked the front door behind them and placed the **Closed** sign in the window.

"Your office?" Grace asked, and Liddy nodded.

The closer to the back steps the better. Liddy wanted that tantalizing smell of pepperoni and cheese to waft up the stairwell. In her world, pizza equaled bait.

"My sister's coming home for a few days next week." Grace helped herself to a slice and let it drop onto the paper plate Liddy handed her from the stash she kept in the bottom drawer of her desk. "Mom said Nat called this morning and asked if it was okay for her and Daisy to drive up for a long weekend. Duh." Grace rolled her eyes. "Mom's been having grandbaby withdrawal since the summer. She misses them both, of course, but she said she's had thirty years of Natalie and only four years of Daisy."

"You have to bring Daisy to story time on Saturday."

"She's already pumped. Mom told her all about it."

Liddy took a bite of her pizza and tried not to make a face. She really did not like pepperoni. She gave in and removed all the rounds of meat from her slice.

"No better this time around, eh?" Grace asked.

"No, sadly. I wanted to like it, but I guess I'll never develop a taste for it."

"What are you going to do with the rest of the pizza?"

"I'll wrap it up and put it in the fridge for tomorrow in case anyone wants it."

"Good thinking." Grace wiped the corners of her mouth, then her hands, with napkins. "Thanks, Liddy. Want me to help you lock up?"

"No, no. You go on home. I'm going to catch up on a little paperwork."

"Are you sure? This was supposed to be my night to close."

"Positive. It was a pretty quiet night, so there's not much to do."

Liddy stood in the doorway and watched Grace gather her bags.

"I'll see you tomorrow," Grace called.

"Good night, Grace." Liddy watched her leave, then relocked the door. As soon as Grace was out of sight, Liddy sprang into action.

She placed the pizza box in the middle of her desk; then she unlocked the back door.

Ten minutes later, she turned off the lights in her office and those in the rest of the shop. Then she sat in the dark and waited.

She didn't have to wait very long.

Liddy figured the boy assumed there was no one left in the shop, but he came down the steps quietly and cautiously, just in case. Once in the hallway, he peered around the corner and into the darkened shop.

From across the room, she heard his footsteps on the wooden floor as he made his way into her office and the rustling of the pizza box lid as he opened it.

She gave him a few minutes—after all, the kid had to be hungry—before she slipped into the hall and into her office and turned on the overhead light.

"Hello, Dylan."

He froze, the slice of pizza suspended halfway to his mouth, his eyes wide with surprise. Then he dropped the pizza onto the desk and bolted past her and swung open the unlocked back door.

"Ah, not so fast, son. Dylan, is it? Let's go back inside and talk to Mrs. Bryant, shall we?"

Brett marched Dylan into the office and gestured to him to sit in the chair facing the desk, where Liddy now sat.

"I didn't steal anything. I swear, I wasn't going to take anything. I just needed . . ." Dylan's eyes were wide and frightened, his voice shaky with fear at having to face not only his unwitting hostess but the chief of police as well.

"I'm pretty sure that's true, Dylan," Liddy said softly. She looked at Brett. "Nothing's been missing."

"Good to know." Brett stood blocking the doorway, his hands on his hips.

"Dylan, have you met Chief Crawford?" Liddy asked.

"No, I . . ." He turned in the seat and stared at Brett. "Are you Brett Crawford? *The* Brett Crawford?"

"I am Brett Crawford—not sure how the *the* got tagged on there, but yes." Brett appeared to be studying the boy. "Have we met?"

"No. I mean, *No, sir.* But I go to Regional High. Everyone knows about Brett Crawford. I mean, you. My coach—Coach Riley—has talked about you."

"Jason Riley's an old friend of mine."

"He told us about how you were all-state football in your junior and senior years and got a full scholarship to Ohio State to play 'cause you were the best linebacker in New England. And you got drafted by the pros. You played for Seattle, but he said everyone was hoping you'd go to the Patriots."

Brett smiled. "Yeah, especially my dad."

"Your picture's in the glass case in the school lobby," Dylan said. He looked as if he was torn between terror and hero worship. For those few seconds, hero worship won. Then the gravity of his situation brought the fear back to his eyes.

"I talked to Coach Riley tonight." Brett kept his voice low and steady.

"Oh, no. You told him . . . oh, no." Dylan covered his face with his hands, and his shoulders began to shake. "He's going to throw me off the team. I'll get kicked out of school."

Brett grabbed one of the folding chairs from the children's section and opened it so he could sit between Dylan and the door. Liddy didn't think Dylan was going to run, but Brett was apparently not willing to take that chance.

Liddy handed a box of tissues to Dylan.

"Take a minute, Dylan," Brett said softly.

Dylan nodded.

"So I want to tell you what Coach Riley told me tonight." Brett leaned one arm on the desk and turned his body toward Dylan in a friendly, nonthreatening way. "He told me you were the best third baseman he's ever coached, and you've been scouted by several top colleges as well as a few pro teams. He also said you were going to graduate at the top of your class. Probably number two. Congratulations on all that."

"Thanks," Dylan mumbled. "None of that's going to mean anything if I have a record for breaking and entering."

"Well, technically, you didn't break in," Liddy pointed out.

"I stayed upstairs," he said, though he knew she'd already figured that out and had shared the information with the chief. "But honestly, I wasn't going to do anything bad. I just needed a safe place to stay."

"Okay, back up." Liddy held up both hands, palms out, gesturing for him to stop there. "Take a deep breath—then tell us how that came about."

One deep breath later, he began. "My mom and dad went to prison over the summer. They and my father's brother robbed a liquor store, and my uncle shot someone, and they all went to prison for a long time." His face red with shame, he nervously glanced first at Brett, then Liddy, as if waiting for judgment. When none came, he continued. "I couldn't pay the rent on the apartment, but even if I could, I wouldn't have stayed there. Everyone knows what my parents did. I don't want to go into foster care, so I made up a story about my grandmother wanting me to come and live with her. I forged her name on the papers they sent home from school."

"Margaret Linden." Liddy tossed the name out. "Is that really your grandmother's name?"

He nodded.

"But she doesn't live in Wyndham Beach," Liddy said.

"No, ma'am. She lives in New Hampshire," he admitted. "But I didn't want to go live with her because I didn't want to leave school. I'm doing really well, and I need scholarships, or I won't be able to go to college."

"You could go right to the pros," Brett pointed out.

Dylan shook his head. "My dad never graduated from high school, so he could never get a good job because he didn't have an education." He shook his head again. "No way am I not getting a degree. I don't know everything, but I know you can't bet on playing for a pro team. Too many things can happen."

He looked at Brett. "You played ball for a while, but then you got hurt, and you couldn't play anymore. It can happen to anyone.

There's no guarantee I'd even make it in the pros. I need to go to *college*. Coach Riley said I could get enough financial aid to go to a big-time school." Tears filled his eyes again. "Now I'll be lucky to graduate from Regional."

"Why would you say that?"

"Aren't you going to put me in juvie?"

Brett ignored the question. "Finish your story. How you ended up homeless and sleeping in the attic of Mrs. Bryant's bookshop."

"I needed a place to stay. I'd been at the library to work on a paper, and it was late by the time I finished. I had to leave, and I walked down to the marina, but there were people milling around outside. People from the restaurant."

"Mimi's," Liddy said.

"Whatever. So I couldn't hang around there, and I didn't know what to do. The harbor is right there, and I thought maybe I should just . . ." He stopped and sniffed.

Liddy knew exactly what he'd thought about doing, and it sent a fireball to her heart and ice up her spine.

"Don't ever," she whispered. "Don't ever think that. Find someone to talk to. There are people who care about you. You will find someone who'll help, I promise you. Nothing is ever so absolute you can't find a way out. At the time it might seem like the easy way, but there's no coming back, Dylan. It's one and done. No college. No baseball."

Brett reached across the desk and squeezed her hand. An old friend, he'd been the one Liddy had called after they'd found Jess. He knew what she was thinking.

"I know. Going away for college, playing baseball and maybe making it to the pros someday—that's what's been keeping me going." He looked at Brett as if he wanted to plead with him to let him go, but he knew that wasn't going to happen.

"Go on, Dylan." Brett gave Liddy's hand another squeeze before releasing it.

"So anyway, I saw the back door of this place was open." Dylan's eyes were fixed on the floor.

"That must have been when we were painting, before we opened," Liddy said.

Dylan nodded. "There was a woman in here painting. She works here now."

"Grace," Liddy said.

"Yeah. That's what I've heard people call her. Anyway, I peeked inside, and the steps were right there, so I ran up to the top floor. It was nice and quiet and safe, so I stayed up there that night. Next day I hopped the bus to school at the corner. I'd taken some blankets when I left the apartment and stashed them in my locker, so after school, I put them in my backpack and brought them here. I took them upstairs to make a bed on the floor."

"I have about a million questions. Like, how are you doing laundry and how are you eating?" She remembered the pizza and pushed the box toward him. "I bought this to lure you down here, so you might as well eat it."

"'Cause you don't like pepperoni." He looked across the desk and almost smiled. "I heard Grace say it."

"I figured the aroma would drift up to the third floor."

"It did. I was dying. I still have a little money left from what I found in the apartment after my parents were arrested, but I try to spend as little as possible. I do go to the Laundromat on Fifth Street, though."

They sat silently and watched Dylan down two slices of pizza in about three seconds.

"There's Pepsi in the fridge behind you," Liddy told him.

"Thank you." He got up and took a bottle from the small refrigerator, then returned to his chair. "Why are you being so nice to me?" he asked.

"Why not be nice to you? From everything we've heard, you're a good kid. Smart and focused in spite of the bad hand you've been dealt.

You're not a thief, and you haven't hurt anyone. I understand why you thought you had to do things this way. I'm amazed you've gotten away with it, without anyone speaking to this 'grandmother' of yours."

"The counselor at school wanted her to come in, but I told them she hurt her hip and wasn't getting around well." He looked at Liddy. "Isn't that something old people do? Fall and hurt their hips?"

"Are you really asking me as if I would know this personally?" Liddy's eyebrows raised, and Brett laughed.

"Oh. No, ma'am," Dylan said hastily. "It's just something I heard, so I thought maybe you'd heard it, too."

"Good save," Brett told him. "So here's where we are. Dylan, you're underage, so you're going to have to go into foster care—"

"No. Please. I'll do anything." Dylan started to rise.

"Calm down and let me finish." Brett pulled him back into his seat. "Unless we can find a suitable placement for you." He paused. "I understand you turn eighteen soon?"

Dylan nodded. "End of October. That's one of the reasons I wanted to stay out on my own. I figured if I could keep my head down for another few weeks, I'd be too old for foster care, and I could stay at my school."

"So we just need a place for you to stay with a responsible adult until you turn eighteen. Fortunately, we know someone who's offering to let you stay until then."

"Who?" Dylan asked.

"Coach Riley. He and his wife have an extra room since their son is away right now. That's the good news. The bad news is when he comes home, he's going to want his room back. But maybe by then you'll be eighteen, and we'll look for another arrangement."

"Where would you go after you turn eighteen?" Liddy asked.

"I'll try to find a job and a room to rent. I'm a little on the skinny side, but honest, I'm strong and I'm not afraid to work." Dylan was so earnest and naive, Liddy didn't know whether to cry or to smile.

"Is the coach mad at me?" Dylan asked Brett. "I know he's mad at me."

"No, he's not mad. But I think he would like an explanation why you didn't come to him and tell him what you were going through. You'll have to have that conversation with him."

"So that's it? I just get to go to live with the coach for a few weeks?"

"We'll have to call DCF, the Department of Children and Family Services—" Brett caught Dylan by the arm when he launched himself out of his chair as if to run. "Sit down." Brett watched the wild-eyed boy until he sat. "We're pretty sure we can get them to go along with the plan we just talked about. I know someone there. Between the coach and your school counselor—with some input from me—I think we can work this out."

"You think. But you're not sure." Dylan sounded defeated.

"It's the thing that makes the most sense," Brett said. "Unless you have an idea better than living upstairs on the third floor and sneaking in and out?"

Finally, Dylan nodded. "Okay."

"If you're finished"—Brett pointed to the pizza—"we'll take off and let Mrs. Bryant go home. She's had a long day."

Dylan stood. "Can I go upstairs and get my things?"

"Of course. I'll be right here," Brett assured him.

He dashed up the stairs, no longer needing to tiptoe.

"Thanks, Brett. I knew you'd think of something," Liddy said.

"Thanks for calling me. You did a good deed, my friend. Dylan's right about what would happen once he got into the system. They'd place him wherever they had someone willing to take in a kid who was just about to age out. They'd look at the reason he's in need of a home, and that will turn many prospective foster parents off, particularly if they have other younger children in their home. They might assume he'd be a bad influence. Riley tells me the boy has endless potential. Said he's smart as a whip and has brilliant instincts when it comes to baseball.

His future should be wide open. He's never been in trouble. It's not fair for him to have his prospects snatched away because of events that are out of his control. His life has already been turned upside down, and he's dealing with it as best he can."

"Why do the kids have to pay the heaviest price when their parents screw up?"

"This—tonight—is only the first step. We probably will need to get Riley and his wife approved, unless we can get DCF to agree to let it slide. By the time they assign someone to the case, Dylan may have turned eighteen. Then step two is finding him a place to live after he leaves the Riley home."

"I don't know where he'll find a place in town to rent unless he has a lot of money."

"I'm pretty sure the state has a program to help with that sort of thing, but a home situation would be much better for him. I guess we'll worry about that when we need to." Brett stood at the sound of Dylan's footsteps banging their way down the stairs. When he came into view, Brett said, "Dylan, I think you have something to say to Mrs. Bryant."

"I'm sorry, Miz Bryant. For sneaking around and staying in your shop without you knowing. And for eating your pizza." Dylan met her eyes, and for the first time did not look away. "And thank you. For not being mad at me and having me arrested. I know you're trying to help me. I appreciate it."

"You're welcome, Dylan. I hope everything works out for you." Liddy walked him and Brett to the back door. "And I hope you come back to see me, so I know how you're doing."

"I will. But don't worry," Dylan said, "I won't pick your lock again."

"How do you know how to pick locks?" she asked.

His thin shoulders hunched. "My mom taught me."

The lump in Liddy's throat cut off any response she might have made.

She locked the back door and went to the window, where she watched Brett and Dylan get into the patrol car and, a moment later, pull away.

"Well, damn."

She was torn between feeling guilty over having turned him in and feeling relieved he'd be getting help to resolve his situation. She hoped the caseworker would be reasonable and would take the word of the chief of police, the boy's coach, and the high school counselor that Dylan would be in good hands for the few weeks until he turned eighteen.

If ever there was a kid who deserved a break, it was Dylan. She hoped with all her heart he'd find what he needed to get him through till he could graduate from high school and head off to college.

Liddy gathered up her things, stepped out onto the sidewalk, and, for the second time that night, locked the door. Her walk home was lit by the streetlights and the occasional passing car. She climbed her front steps, her door key in her hand, still wondering if she'd done the right thing.

Chapter Thirteen

Jessica Bryant was buried in an old graveyard that sat on a slight rise near a small church that hadn't been used for Sunday services in years. The congregation had grown to a size the church could no longer accommodate, so a larger plot of land had been purchased closer to the center of town, and a bigger church built, the old one now used only for small weddings and funerals. Because plots in the cemetery had been bought years ago by several of the church's earliest families—such as the Bryants—occasionally the gates were opened, and a new grave was dug to hold the remains of a child or grandchild or great-grandchild of someone who'd already been laid to rest there. So it was that when Liddy and Jim Bryant had to bury their daughter, they'd brought her to this small peaceful place to spend eternity between Jim's parents and her baby brother.

Liddy tried not to dwell on whether or not Jessie was actually there. She knew her body lay in a white casket with a pale-pink satin lining—something Liddy would never have chosen for Jessie, who'd have hated it. But Liddy had been incapable of making such decisions so soon after her daughter's death, so Jim's sister, Bunny, had stepped in and made the selection for her. Liddy preferred to think Jessie's spirit was around *her*, not trapped under the ground in pink satin, but Liddy often visited her daughter's grave and made sure the flowers she'd planted there were not in need of water or hadn't been mowed down by an inattentive groundskeeper.

Early on the Sunday morning after her confrontation with Dylan, Liddy left her house and walked three-quarters of a mile to the cemetery. It had rained overnight, and the air was still heavy, and a lingering mist hung over the town. She unlatched the gate, which had yet to be opened at this early hour, and walked to the third row from the back on the right side, where Bryants had been buried for over a century. She opened the tote bag she carried and unfolded the quilt that had lain on Jessie's bed and placed it on the wet grass. Liddy sat on the quilt, sipped coffee from her insulated mug, and rested her right arm on her upraised right knee. Leaning low, she spoke to her daughter, describing the events of the past twenty-four hours.

"I guess I'm wondering if I did the right thing," she said.

"It's not like you to have second thoughts," a voice from behind said.

Startled, Liddy jumped up, dropped her coffee, and yelled, "Jesus, Mary, and Edna, Jim! Did you have to sneak up on me? You can't announce yourself?"

"Sorry, Liddy. I didn't want to interrupt you." Jim walked toward her, his arms open as if to embrace her. In one hand he held a bouquet of Jessie's favorite orange roses.

"What are you doing here?" She took a step back away from him, her heart racing and her hands shaking.

"Same thing you're doing. Visiting our daughter's grave." He placed the roses on the ground directly in front of and as close as possible to the headstone. "You come here often?"

"Is that supposed to be funny?" Her heart was still racing, though at a slower speed.

"No. But I stop here every time I'm in Wyndham Beach, and I've never seen you here. So I was just wondering . . ."

"Yes, I visit often."

"I didn't mean to scare you. And I apologize for eavesdropping. I didn't hear you speaking until I was right here. Were you really expecting an answer from Jess?"

"I talk to her all the time, just like I did when she was alive," Liddy confessed.

"So do I," he admitted.

"You do?" For some reason, this surprised her.

"I do. So what did she tell you? Does she think you did the right thing?" he asked.

"Are you mocking me?"

"No. I'm just curious. You always did get yourself into the damnedest situations. This one must have been a real doozy."

"Ah, you do realize you sound just like your mother, right?"

Jim laughed. "Yeah, every once in a while, one of her expressions slip out. What's the dictionary definition of *doozy*, anyway?"

"I always thought it meant something singular. Not like anything else." Her wits were returning. "So what brings you into Wyndham Beach this morning?"

"Actually, I was coming in to see you, but I stopped here first."

"What did you want to see me about? I gave Gretchen the papers you signed, so—"

"Not about that. I don't care about that. We both agreed Grace should have that house if she wants it."

"Then what?" Did they have other business Liddy'd forgotten about?

"I just wanted to see you. I thought maybe we could go out to breakfast. Or lunch? Or dinner?"

"I have to open the shop at nine, and I close at six on Sunday," she explained.

"How about dinner?"

She thought for a moment. Did she really want to sit down with Jim and spend an hour or more with him? What did they have to talk about besides their daughter?

"Just dinner, Liddy."

It sounded almost as if he were pleading. "All right."

"I'll pick you up at the shop at six, then. Is that all right?"

"Sure." Her time here having been prematurely brought to an end, Liddy picked up the quilt and folded it, then tucked it back into the tote. "I'll leave so you can have your time alone."

"I appreciate that. I'll see you at six."

Liddy made her way over the uneven ground to the road, then onto the sidewalk. She'd planned on stopping at home to change before she went into the shop, but her encounter with Jim had left her unsettled, and the last place she wanted to be right then was in the house she'd shared with him for so many years. She made a quick detour into Ground Me for a large coffee to replace the brought-from-home brew she'd spilled when Jim had scared the pants off her and, once there, picked up one of their special only-on-Sunday cinnamon buns. She knew her hands would be sticky from the buttery, spicy syrup, but it would be worth it. She dashed across the street, dodging the cars headed for the tall-spired white church on the corner, where Emma's father had ministered to his flock when they were kids. Now Emma's brother's name was on the sign out front. Liddy hadn't been in that church since the funeral of a high school classmate the previous year, and since word on the street was that the son lacked the father's finesse with a sermon, she didn't figure she'd be going there anytime soon.

She unlocked the door, turned on first the lights, then the iPad to check Rosalita's progress—at present she was cruising toward Rehoboth Beach, Delaware—wiped down the countertop, and tried not to think about Dylan. What if Brett and the baseball coach were unable to convince DCF to permit the boy to stay with the Rileys until he turned eighteen? Surely, as Brett suggested, they'd agree the amount of paperwork and investigation wasn't worth the time it would take, because Dylan might turn eighteen before they even assigned a case-worker. Brett seemed to think it was a lock. Had he merely been trying to convince Dylan so he'd leave the shop?

Had she done the right thing? Would it have hurt her to have Dylan living above the shop for a while longer?

No, of course it would not have. But in her heart, she believed it would have hurt him. The boy belonged in a home, where he had real meals and someone to talk to. He was obviously conflicted about his parents. He knew they hadn't been good parents, but they were *his* parents, and he no doubt loved them. A wave of anger swept over her. His mother and father had had this wonderful child, who by all reports was an exemplary kid, and they'd left him on his own, homeless and without resources or money except what he could find in their apartment before he had to leave because he couldn't pay the rent. Had his parents given any thought to what would happen to him? Their neglect and lack of caring and concern was unforgivable. The kid deserved better.

Dylan's situation and her part in it had to be put aside when the first of the day's customers came in. Liddy found the Sunday crowd to be mostly browsers, where Saturday visitors to the shop were buyers. She was pretty sure there was something psychological at play there. Saturday was the first full day of the weekend, so you had all weekend to read a new book. But on Sunday the weekend hours were passing quickly, and you still had things to do besides relax and read.

There was a lull around two, and Liddy dug her phone out of her bag. She couldn't take it any longer—she had to call Brett to see what had happened with Dylan. She'd just begun to look up his number when Brett walked in the shop, dressed in jeans and a dark-blue sweater.

"Going casual today, I see," Liddy greeted him.

"I took a day off. Maggie's been after me to spend a day on the Cape. Walk the beach, stop at some small roadside place for lobster rolls. You know the drill, right?"

"Did you remind Maggie we have lovely beaches here in Wyndham Beach, and Captain Squiggy's out on Route Six does a fine lobster roll?"

"I was about to, but she told me not to bother." He shrugged, a smile on his face. "When the woman wants the Cape, you take her to the Cape."

"She wants the romance of the Cape." Liddy stated what she thought to be obvious.

"That too." Brett smiled at a customer who walked by. "Do you have a minute to talk?"

She called Marion over to operate the register, and she led Brett to her office, where she closed the door.

"So how's Dylan?" she asked.

"He's fine. His coach had a long talk with him after I left, and apparently it went very well. We agreed we'd call DCF tomorrow. I've had dealings with a supervisor there, and she's always been reasonable and understanding, so I'll call her first thing in the morning and see if I can arrange a meeting with her. We sure don't want to do anything unlawful, but at the same time, we all agree we don't feel Dylan should be removed from the school where he's had so much success."

"The kid's already lost so much," she noted.

"That's our thinking. So for now, anyway, things are good. I spoke with Dylan this morning, and he sounded almost relieved."

"I guess sneaking in and out of the shop morning and night was starting to wear thin. It had to be really stressful, wondering if he'd be caught and what would happen to him."

Brett nodded. "He's going to have to get a job so he can show DCF he's got roots here in the community besides school. We'll try to find him something that won't interfere with his studies or baseball once the season starts in the spring."

"Sounds like there's a solid plan for him. I'm glad. I was feeling so guilty, thinking, if he's forced into foster care and moved to another school district, what it would mean for him. New school, new teachers, new team where maybe they already have someone really good who plays his position—"

"Jason tells me he's never seen anyone like this kid. Plays his position really well, but he can hit like a pro, and for a tall, skinny kid, he has a strong throwing arm. The last thing Jason wants is for his star to go to a rival team." Brett looked at his watch. "I have to get going."

Liddy stood and opened the office door. Brett waited for her; then they walked into the store together.

"You did a good thing, Liddy. Dylan said to tell you he's grateful, but I suspect he'll be in before too long to tell you himself."

"That would be nice. I'd like to keep up with his progress."

Brett was nabbed on his way out by a local who wanted to complain about drag racing on Beach Plum Road on the weekends, so Liddy left him to deal with it and went to answer the phone. The rest of the day played out without incident, with a few sales to ring up, a few friends to chat with. At exactly 5:55, Jim walked in. He went right to the new nonfiction releases and skimmed the titles until something caught his eye. He took his book to the cash register, where Marion handled his cash sale, and Liddy observed from the back of the shop. She'd ducked into the bathroom off her office, tidied up the bun that sat at the base of her neck, and put on a little—very little—makeup.

"This is not a date," she muttered. "This is . . . dinner. Just . . . dinner."

Even so, she observed him as she would a stranger, and had to admit he was still good looking in a professorial way, with his glasses and gray cardigan sweater over a light-blue buttoned-down shirt and khakis.

She timed her walk from the back to coincide with six o'clock on the dot.

"Right on time, as always, I see," she said when she reached the counter.

"Oh, you know me, Liddy. Old habits die hard."

It crossed her mind that perhaps he saw her as an old habit. It was a disquieting thought.

"Give me just a minute," she told Jim, "while I close out the cash register."

"Don't you take the cash to the bank?"

"I have a well-hidden safe in my office," she told him. "I'll send the weekend's receipts to the bank in the morning."

"But they have a drop box," he told her. "You could—"

"Thanks, Jim, but I've got it under control." She gathered the cash and the credit receipts and took them to the office.

"Right. Of course you do," she heard him say.

She looked over her shoulder to see if he was being sarcastic, but he didn't appear to be, which was something in his favor. She went into the office, took care of her business, and was back up front in minutes.

"Where would you like to go?" Jim asked after she'd locked the shop and they were on their way to the parking lot where he'd left his car.

She hadn't given it much thought. Somewhere in town . . . no, that would only set off the gossips, and for the next two weeks she'd be answering the question, "So I heard you and Jim are back together?" No, thank you.

"No place fancy." She considered her attire, which was, she realized, not too different from his: khakis and a sweater, though hers was a pullover. "I'm not dressed for fine dining."

"I think you look terrific," he said.

"Thanks." She brushed off the compliment, wondering if he'd really looked at her at all, remembering all the times in the past when he'd answered the same when she'd asked how she looked. "You look fine," or, "You look great," even as she knew he wasn't seeing her at all.

"There's a new place in Mattapoisett," she said. "Their seafood is said to be amazing, but I don't recall the name."

"If you mean the Battered Cod, I've been there several times." Jim nodded enthusiastically. "It's excellent."

Liddy was looking around the lot for the gray sedan Jim usually drove, the one Jessie had named the Gray Goose, so she was caught off guard when he stopped at the passenger door of a new sleek black Mercedes.

"What happened to the Goose?" Liddy asked.

"She needed a new alternator, and given her age, I thought it best to retire her. Besides, I was ready for something new and exciting." Jim unlocked the door and held it for her.

Liddy slid across the soft-as-sin leather seat, a frown on her face. Were his remarks about the Goose really a metaphor for her? Had he found a newer, more exciting model? Would it be in poor taste if she asked? Would she care if he had?

"It's lovely," she told him after he got in and settled behind the wheel. "So how exciting is she? I mean, it."

"Very. Remember, the old Goose and I were a team for a long time. It was time for a change."

The drive to Mattapoisett was a short one, and in no time they were walking into the restaurant.

"Oh, Mr. Bryant. Nice to see you again," the pretty young hostess greeted him. "Your usual table?"

"That would be fine, Brandy." Jim took Liddy's arm and followed the hostess to a table overlooking the harbor.

"I'll send Nell over for your drink orders." She handed Liddy and Jim menus.

The twentysomething Nell was there in a flash to read off the specials and inquire about beverages.

"What do you say, Liddy? Shall we start off the evening with a nice wine?" Without waiting for her response, he ordered a bottle of something that sounded expensive to Liddy. She wondered when he'd abandoned his once-frugal nature.

Then again, she could be wrong about the wine. Or so she thought until she tasted it. She'd been right the first time. This was not the vintage Jim would have brought home in the past.

He poured into both glasses and handed one to her. "Let's have a toast."

"What are we toasting?"

"We're toasting us. To new beginnings." He tilted his glass in her direction.

She raised hers, touched the rim with his, and countered, "To Jessie."

He nodded slowly and said softly, "To Jess."

She took a sip, hoping to wash down the lump in her throat. Would a day ever come when she could mention her daughter's name without wanting to cry?

"What do you think of the wine?" Jim nodded in the direction of the bottle.

"It's delicious."

Jim held the glass in his hand and swirled it, then watched the slow whirlpool inside.

"It's local, from a vineyard about fifteen miles from here. They've become quite successful, even send their wines to a few of the top restaurants in Boston." He smiled. "They're clients of mine."

"Nice. Tell them we enjoyed their product." She turned her attention to the menu.

"I recommend the lobster thermidor. It's exceptional," he said without taking his eyes off the menu. "That's what I'm having. I think you'll like it."

He gestured for Nell to return to take the orders. "Two orders of lobster thermidor," he told her.

"Ah, actually, make it one." Liddy folded her menu and handed it to the waitress. "I'll have the scallops in citrus." When she looked across the table at Jim, he appeared slightly taken aback.

"I'll put your orders in." Nell went off in the direction of the kitchen.

"Thanks for the recommendation, Jim, but I am capable of deciding what I want to eat, and I can order for myself." She spoke softly, but there was steel in her voice.

"Of course. I apologize."

He didn't look contrite as much as injured, Liddy thought, but that was okay. All those years they were married, he'd always ordered for her without asking her preference, and she'd always let it slide. New day, new Liddy.

"So how'd things go at your bookstore today?" he asked, and she wondered if she didn't detect just the slightest note of patronizing in the question.

"It was fine. It's always a fine day in my shop, Jim."

"I think it's great you bought it, and anyone who'd ever been inside the place when old Fred owned it has to recognize how much work you've done there. It looks great now. I admit when I heard you were buying it, I had my doubts, but . . ."

"What doubts were they, Jim?"

"Well, let's face it, Liddy. You never owned a business before, and as far as I know, you never worked in retail. And I bet that shop hasn't made a profit in five years or more." He spoke slowly and, she thought, condescendingly, as if she couldn't understand the implications of buying a failing business unless he spelled it out for her.

She listened attentively, bit her tongue, and waited for him to finish tying the noose around his own neck.

"I was afraid you'd tie up all the money I gave you as our settlement in a shop doomed to fail."

"And yet, here I am, inexperienced me, with a shop doing bang-up business." Jim opened his mouth to speak, but she cut him off. "You're right, I don't have a background in any sort of business, unless you count the years I spent doing the bookkeeping for your insurance agency. Which I did learn a lot from, so thank you for the opportunity." She kept her voice low and tried to sound as rational as possible when what she really wanted was to dump her wine—delicious as it was—over his head. "But what I do have is a quick mind and a love of books. I know what people like to read and—"

"Because you were in book clubs for years?"

"Yes. Exactly. I know books. When I first looked at the shop, I admit I saw what you saw—a failed business, a depressing old shop that did not inspire flights of fancy, which is just what a great bookshop can do. And that's what my shop does." She sat back and, with some satisfaction, realized she'd done exactly that. "With some help from my friends, I've totally changed the character of the old building. I've made it inviting and welcoming, and it's on its way to becoming solvent for the first time in God only knows how long. It failed in the past because Fred was failing. He couldn't keep up physically with the demands of running a store, and his developing Alzheimer's, over time, meant he'd often forget to order books or keep up with the new releases and the bestsellers. I've talked to the salespeople from various publishers who lamented the loss of the old Fred, who once upon a time was a genius at doing what he loved." She paused. "Don't you remember how the shop used to be? How Jessie loved nothing more than going to the bookstore to pick out a new book?"

She was tempted to tell him how often she imagined she could see Jess there, leaning against the doorjamb at the back of the store. Liddy would smile at Jessie, and she imagined Jess would give her a wink or a thumbs-up before fading slowly until she'd disappeared.

"Jess loved that place. I bought the shop because I remembered what it once was, and I was determined to make it that place again. I can say with all confidence I've done what I set out to do. The people in Wyndham Beach remember what *they* loved about it, and are delighted it's open again and, if I may say so, better than ever. So please don't lecture me on what you obviously feel was a poor decision on my part. It was the best thing I've ever done for myself." She paused to reflect. "Maybe the only thing I've done strictly for myself in a very long time. I'm doing a great job, and I am happy. I'm working harder than I've ever worked at anything, and I'm having the time of my life."

"Well." It took him a minute to recover. "I can see I grossly underestimated you, and I am sorry if I sounded condescending."

"You were being condescending, and you've always underestimated me." Did he really think the fact they had a long-shared past gave him the right to question her decisions? Had he been so judgmental all those years they were married? And she had put up with it?

He nodded slowly. "Okay, yes. I guess I was. I applaud you for what you've done with that shop, and I acknowledge your success. I'm proud of you. But you have to agree, when you went into this, it didn't look like the best investment you could have made with your money."

"I disagree. It was the best investment ever."

"I can tell you're happy, and frankly, that's all that matters, right? You're happy and you're doing a great job, so I salute you." He raised his wineglass. "To your happiness and success. I hope your shop continues to do well."

"In spite of my lack of experience in running a business."

"It was a concern—of course it was. Be honest. You have to admit it's true."

"I will concede, yes, I never ran a business. But the rest of it—"

"The rest of it—I was wrong on all counts. I guess I'd forgotten how clever and resourceful you are. How determined you are when you want something."

"Thank you. I accept your apology."

"Good, because our dinners are about to be served, and knowing you were angry with me would make it hard for me to enjoy this beautiful lobster dish."

Liddy laughed and leaned back in her chair while Nell placed her plate on the table. Jim topped off her wine before she could object, so she asked the waitress to bring her a glass of water.

"The wine is wonderful," Liddy told Jim when she felt his eyes on her. "But I rarely drink anymore, so I need to pace myself. Unless I'm making margaritas. I make killer margaritas."

"I look forward to you making one for me sometime." He dug into his dinner. "So is Tuck going to do the renovation for Grace?" Jim asked without looking at her.

"His son, Linc, is."

Jim merely nodded.

"Is there something you want to say?" Liddy put her fork down.

"What? Nope." He shrugged. "Although I have to say I was surprised to see Tuck lounging on our deck early on a Sunday morning."

"Don't go there, Jim." She swallowed the urge to point out it was not *their* deck, but hers.

He nodded, then apparently thinking it might be a good time to change the subject, said, "So what's the latest on this boy who was hiding out in your shop?"

"How'd you hear about him?"

"I ran into Phil Thompson. He joined the police force about six months ago, and he heard Brett talking on the phone about the kid. So . . . ?"

Liddy told him.

When she was finished, he said, "You're lucky they got the kid out of there. Parents like that, who knows what he might have done."

"What are you talking about?" She put her fork down. "What do you think he might have done?"

"He was raised by criminals. He could have robbed you, or hurt you or Grace. He could have dangerous tendencies. Maybe even set the place on fire. It was smart of you to call the police, but I'm surprised you're not pressing charges. I think you should reconsider."

"I have to say I'm surprised at your attitude." Appalled was more like it, but she was trying to give him the benefit of the doubt. He didn't know Dylan, didn't know what a quiet, lost child he was. "What if, God forbid, something had happened to us and it had been our Jess in a situation where she had nowhere to go and no one to turn to?"

"We've never robbed a liquor store or shot someone in the process." He paused. "Did you want dessert?"

"I'll pass, but thank you."

He waved Nell over and asked for the check. She handed it over, and he passed her his credit card. As he did so, he told Liddy, "Just be glad he's out of your life."

He might not be, she thought, but decided to keep that to herself.

They left the restaurant and drove to Wyndham Beach under a beautiful almost-full moon. It was a perfect late September evening, and Liddy tried not to remember all the other perfect September nights she'd shared with the man behind the wheel. There'd been so many good times, but tonight had brought up some memories she'd buried. She'd forgotten how judgmental Jim was, how he always questioned her decisions and often tried to bully her into seeing things his way, to want what he wanted or what he thought she should want. And his attitude toward Dylan disturbed her.

He pulled into the driveway and turned off the ignition.

"Invite me in for coffee?"

"Sure." She got out of the car without waiting for him to open the door for her, something that had always peeved him when they were married and they'd go someplace together.

She unlocked the door and snapped on a light in the foyer.

"Hey, where's the table that used to be under the window here?" He pointed to the spot where his grandmother's Chippendale table had once stood. Before she could answer, he stepped into the living room. "And my dad's desk is gone." He turned to look at Liddy. "You know that desk belonged to my great-grandfather. What did you do with it?"

"I took an ax to it and burned the pieces in the firepit out on the deck," she deadpanned.

Jim turned white. "Why would you . . . ?"

"The desk and the table and your old rocking chair are all in the attic. Lighten up, Jim." She went into the kitchen to start the coffee, and he came in behind her. "Feel free to pick them up anytime."

"I guess I should make arrangements to do that."

They took their coffee to the screened porch off the dining room and sat at the round table where they'd sat a hundred nights before.

"I forgot how much I miss this." There was a touch of wistfulness in his voice.

"Drinking coffee on the porch or just the house in general?"

"Drinking coffee on the porch with you. Being in this house with you." He reached over for her hand. "We had a lot of very good times here, Liddy. I miss those times. I miss you."

"You apparently didn't miss them so much," she said, "since you left."

"I wasn't thinking clearly then."

"Then you probably should have just taken a break instead of walking away without looking back." She hadn't been prepared to have this conversation.

"Who said I didn't look back?" he protested.

"You left without even telling me why. You fell out of love with me? Okay, it happens. But you should have told me."

"It wasn't that. Tell me you didn't think I'd fallen out of love with you."

"What else would I have thought? You don't leave someone you love." She pulled her hand away slowly.

"I've never stopped loving you. Not for a day."

"Do you really think I could believe that? After you walked out on me at the lowest point of my life? The one-year anniversary of Jess's death and you pack your bags and leave with no explanation? Do you have any idea what I went through after you left? My only child dies by her own hand without so much as telling me why, and then my husband walks out on me?" Liddy stood, the words she'd never said boiling over and spilling out.

"Listen to me." He grabbed her arm. "I am sorry from the bottom of my heart. I wish to God I hadn't been such a coward. But I couldn't take another second under this roof. My girl was gone, and I didn't know why. I was broken by it, no less than you. We should have been comforting each other, but you went somewhere into yourself, and I couldn't reach you. I hurt every bit as much as you did. I missed her every bit as much. But you acted as if you were the lone victim, like no one else's pain mattered. My pain mattered. It still matters, just as much as yours."

Liddy inhaled sharply. Had she questioned Jim's right to the same agonizing pain she'd felt after their daughter's death? Had she ever considered what he'd been going through? She honestly didn't remember asking him how he felt. Had she even cared, or was he right in thinking she'd been oblivious to the fact that he was in pain, too?

She couldn't give him an honest answer because she didn't remember.

"Maybe you're right. I'm sorry, but I don't remember much of those first months after she died. I look back and all I see of my life is a big black bottomless hole. I'm sorry I didn't realize you were in a bottomless pit of your own. I'm sorry you feel I didn't care about your pain. Maybe I didn't if I'm to be honest. Maybe I couldn't. I'm sorry if I drove you away. I just wish you'd told me why."

"I'd tried for weeks, months, that entire year before I left. When I realized I was never going to get through to you, I didn't feel I had a choice. We should have been holding each other up instead of quietly watching the other sink."

"You realize this is a conversation we should have had long ago. When it would have mattered."

"You don't think it matters now?"

"Only in the same way it would matter to know why Jess killed herself. She'd still be gone, but at least we'd know why." Her voice had fallen to a whisper. "It still haunts me that I don't know why."

"It torments me, too. It always will, because the chances of us finding out . . ." Jim stood slowly, as if standing stressed every bone in his body. He went into the kitchen and rinsed his coffee mug and put it into the dishwasher. When Liddy came into the room, he turned to her and said, "I meant what I said. I still love you. I always will."

Did she still love him? She didn't know.

She followed him to the front door and opened it. He stood with his hand on the doorknob and turned to her. Without warning, he took her in his arms and kissed her the way he had a million times over the course of their marriage. She waited for the zing she used to feel when he kissed her like that, but it just wasn't there. She pulled away from him sadly.

"Could we try again, Lids? Just think about it. Think about all we had before Jess . . . before we lost her."

When she did not respond, he pulled away from her slowly, his arms withdrawing reluctantly.

"I'll be in touch." He went down the steps and got into his car. She heard the engine start, saw him wave before he backed out of the driveway. He tooted the horn once, then drove off.

Liddy stood in the doorway, feeling gutted. She closed the door, locked it, then turned off the outside light.

Chapter Fourteen

Grace loved working, loved the eye-catching, informative websites she created for her clients, and loved helping customers at Wyndham Beach Reads find the perfect book. She'd never considered a job in retail, but she loved it. Who knew?

But this Thursday morning, she was grateful to be off for three days. Natalie and Daisy were coming for the weekend, and Grace couldn't wait to see her sister, cuddle her niece, and spoil her the way only an aunt could do, and show Nat her little house. The sale had gone through quickly and easily that very morning. Oh, she and Liddy had haggled over the price. Grace knew the property was worth many times more than what she was asking, but Liddy had set her price, and wasn't going to take a penny more.

"You do realize how backward this is, right?" Grace had said. "Usually the buyer is trying to get the seller to take less, not more."

"I don't care. My way or the highway," Liddy had replied.

"I feel guilty, like I'm cheating you."

"You're not. If anyone is cheating me, it's me. So just stop. I don't have to sell it to you."

"You wouldn't sell that place to anyone but me, and you know it," Grace had countered.

"I could, or I could simply keep it. Are you willing to call my bluff?" Liddy had raised an eyebrow, challenging Grace, who'd had to admit Liddy looked steely eyed and resolute.

So Liddy had gotten her price, and Grace had gotten the house she'd been designing and redesigning in her head for weeks. She couldn't wait to tell Linc—and she hadn't.

"Linc, it's Grace. Grace Flynn. Please give me a call when you get a minute." She'd left a voice mail message on his cell phone as soon as she got into her car after she'd left the settlement table.

When she got to the house—her house!—she'd parked on the grass, where she'd decided she wanted proper parking for at least two cars, preferably in the same macadam she was going to use in the driveway. She stood in front of the house and pictured the front porch and the shutters and the window boxes as she'd described to Linc. She could see it in her mind's eye, and couldn't wait to see the vision become reality.

At the sound of a vehicle in the driveway, she turned around to see Linc's truck coming toward her slowly. He parked next to her and got out, and her heart flipped in her chest.

"How'd you know I was here?" she asked as he approached.

"I ran into your mother when I stopped for lunch, and she told me as of eleven this morning, this little bundle of sticks was all yours. Then I heard your message. It didn't take a genius to figure it out." He stood next to her and studied the house much as she had done. "So how does it feel?"

"Amazing. Honestly, I'm so happy I don't know what to do with myself." She held the key in her hand and flipped it from one palm into the other. "Want to come in?"

"Sure. I have to watch the time, though. I need to get back to work." Linc followed her into the house.

Grace went from room to room, opening all the windows. "I love the way it smells here when the windows are all open."

"It does blow out the scent of the ages."

Grace laughed. "Are you saying my house smells bad?"

"All old houses that have been closed up for a while have a certain smell. Not necessarily bad," Linc said diplomatically before adding, "Then again, not necessarily good."

"Well, I expect you to banish whatever odors there may be when you get down to business here." Her eyes were shining, and for a moment she caught him looking at her as if he liked what he saw. Then in seconds, poof! It was gone.

Interesting. And curious.

"I'll do the best I can." He turned away and walked to the window on the right side of the front room. "You know, I was thinking you might like to have that screened-in porch we talked about . . ."

"I thought about it, and yes, it makes sense."

"How about if we make it a four-season room? Insulate it, put in a heated floor, maybe. Double- or triple-pane windows so you can see out, but the cold winter air won't come in."

"I could sit and watch the snow fall," she mused. "Yeah. I like it. Put it into your estimate."

"Okay."

"You already did, didn't you? You knew I'd say yes."

Linc laughed, a relatively rare occurrence. Grace thought how sad it was he didn't laugh more often. He had a great laugh. It crinkled his eyes and brought out the dimple in his right cheek. Grace was a sucker for a man with dimples.

"I admit I worked it in at the end. Easy enough to remove if you'd nixed the idea."

"So is it done? The estimate?"

"It is. If I'd known I'd be seeing you today, I'd have brought it with me. If you're around tomorrow . . ."

"I will be. My sister and her daughter are coming for the weekend, so I know I'll be showing off my soon-to-be home."

"What do you think she'll say when she sees it?"

"She'll love it. Nat has a good eye. She's really creative—she'll see the potential. I've already sent her some pictures, and she can't wait to see it." She noticed him checking his watch. "You have to get back." She walked outside with him. "So when can you start?"

"I have probably another week to finish up the job we're on now. But maybe I could stop over on the weekends and do a little of this, a little of that. Knock out some of the little things."

"That would be amazing. Thank you, Linc. You don't know what this house means to me. It's the first house I've owned by myself."

"Then we have to make sure we get it right." He paused to look back at the front of the house. "One more thing. I'm wondering if you might want to remove the vinyl siding."

"You say that as if you find vinyl siding personally offensive. Like you should be holding your nose when you say the words." She lowered her voice. "Vinyl. Siding."

That brought a smile to his face. "To tell you the truth, it's not my favorite. It has its place, but not on historical buildings."

"What do you think the original siding looks like?"

"We can pull back a piece of the vinyl when I get a few minutes to take a look. It's probably clapboard, which is how most of the early homes were built."

"You think the original wood survived all these years?"

"It could have. There may be some sections that will need replacement—some might require some repair, but sure. The original wood construction is probably under the vinyl."

"Okay, then. We should definitely look."

He nodded and walked to his truck.

"Make sure JoJo comes to story hour on Saturday. I'm bringing my niece, and they're around the same age. Daisy's a little younger, but still. They could hang out a little in the bookshop."

"I'll remind my dad. Though JoJo will remind him, I'm sure. She counts down the days."

"A girl who loves books." Grace sighed. "That's one of the best things you can give your kids, so someone got that right."

"It must be your influence. I never saw any of my sister's kids pick up a book before JoJo started going to the bookstore on Saturdays, and the other two still don't. My sister wasn't the type to read bedtime stories." He opened the driver's-side door and looked back at her.

"I'm sorry."

"Yeah. Me too." He got into the cab and drove off.

~

Grace offered to do the shopping for the weekend, since Maggie was determined to make all Natalie's favorite foods. It was late afternoon by the time she finished all the errands and returned to the house on Cottage Street. She was delighted to see Natalie's car in the driveway.

"Hey, anyone home?" she called out when she went inside. "Where is everyone?"

"Aunt Gracie! We came to see you!" Daisy dashed through the kitchen screen door and hit Grace at the knees, almost knocking her over.

"I see you have." Grace hobbled to the counter and set down the bag she was carrying so she could hug her niece. "I'm happy to see you. I missed you."

"I missed you, too." Daisy tugged Grace's hand. "Mommy and Nana are in the garden. I helped Nana pick flowers to put in a vase. She's going to let me help her pick up leaves tomorrow, 'cause they're falling off her trees . . ."

Daisy continued her happy chatter all the way to the backyard. Grace and Natalie hugged and sat together on the deck, bringing each other up to date on their lives.

"Tell me more about this house you're buying," Natalie said.

"Bought. We settled this morning. I was over there earlier, and my contractor stopped by." When Maggie joined them on the deck, a bouquet of flowers in her hands, Grace said, "Mom, thanks for letting Linc know about the settlement. He stopped over and gave me some really good ideas."

"When is the work going to begin?" Natalie asked.

"Not sure. He and his crew are finishing up another job. He'll give me a heads-up when he's ready to start."

Maggie called to Daisy, who was busy picking up yellow leaves from the ground. "Daisy, leave those for tomorrow. Right now we have to arrange these flowers in a vase, and I'd like you to help me."

Daisy came running, and she and Maggie disappeared into the house.

Grace repeated Linc's suggestion for the four-season porch, and the more she talked about it, the more she liked the idea. "This little house will be, well, *little*, but it's going to have everything I ever wanted. And it will be all mine."

"I'm delighted for you. I'm sure it's going to be wonderful. Can we go tomorrow?"

"We can go first thing in the morning."

"I'd rather go later in the day, if it's all right with you."

"Sure, but—"

Natalie leaned in. "Chris is coming tomorrow, but don't say anything. He wants to surprise Emma, so don't even tell Mom, in case she slips."

"I think the only one you need to worry about slipping is your daughter."

Natalie laughed. "She doesn't know, for that very reason. Daisy hasn't yet learned how to keep a secret."

"Which is why you need to tell Mom you and Chris are dating. If you don't, you know Daisy will."

Natalie shrugged. "Daisy doesn't even know what dating means."

"Don't underestimate the child," Grace warned. "She's going to blow the whistle on you two, just wait."

~

Chris showed up at the Flynn house just before noon on Friday.

"Chris!" Maggie hugged him. "Does your mother know you're here?"

"She does now. I just came from the art center." He hugged Grace before he hugged Natalie.

Anyone with eyes could tell Nat got a different kind of hug. If Maggie was curious, she didn't let on.

"Where's the sprite?" he said, looking around.

"She's out in the backyard picking up leaves," Nat told him, her face shining with happiness.

Watching her sister, Grace thought Natalie couldn't help herself. She just couldn't. She was in love with this guy. She sighed and glanced at her mother, who was watching Nat drag Chris out the back door to find Daisy.

Maggie met Grace's eyes and said merely, "Oh, dear."

"I know. She's over the moon."

"And headed for a fall, I'm afraid," Maggie told her. "Emma said she's pretty sure Chris has a girlfriend, though he hasn't said much about her, but Em said she thinks he's seeing someone on a pretty regular basis. Oh, when Natalie finds out, it's going to break her heart."

"Mom," Grace said. "Natalie is the girlfriend he hasn't told Emma about."

"What?" Confused, Maggie tilted her head as if trying to make sense of what she'd heard.

"Natalie and Chris have been seeing each other for months."

"Oh, the little sneak! And she told you, but she didn't tell me?" Maggie looked offended.

"She didn't come out so much and tell me. I figured it out and told her I knew."

"Well, why in the world haven't they said anything to Emma and me? You know we'd both be delighted if they were to—"

"Don't say it, because that's exactly why they haven't told you two. They don't want to be pressured; they don't want you and Emma to be asking them when they're getting married or whatever."

"But we wouldn't—" Maggie protested, and Grace laughed.

"Mom, you were just about to say it a moment ago."

"Oh, well, it just slipped out."

"It can't slip out when you're talking to Natalie. Maybe they're going to tell you this weekend; maybe that's why Chris flew in this morning, so they'd be here together. I don't know. But don't make a big deal of it if they say anything, okay?"

Maggie rolled her eyes. "No, it's not okay. But I'll try really hard not to yell *yahoo*. Is that what you're afraid of? Or I'll start humming the wedding march?"

"I think that's what Nat's afraid of. I think she wants Chris to make the decision when to do what."

"That doesn't sound like your sister."

"It does if you take into consideration who Chris is."

Maggie appeared to think it over for a moment. "You think Nat doesn't want Chris to feel she's pressuring him because she thinks he'll feel cornered and break off with her and take off with some model or whoever it is he used to date that Emma hated?"

Grace laughed. "I believe that may be the longest sentence I've ever heard you speak. But yes, I think that's it. There's a bit of insecurity at play there for sure. Nat compares herself to all those beautiful women Chris knows and has dated in the past, and she doesn't think she measures up. So I'm thinking we just respect her feelings and let them decide what and when."

"But she's foolish to compare herself to anyone else. She's a beautiful girl in her own right, and I'm sure Chris knows that." She paused. "You think Emma doesn't know they're dating?"

"I'm pretty sure she doesn't."

"Damn. She's one of my two best friends. I hate knowing something I can't tell either of them." Maggie grumbled a bit under her breath, but Grace knew her mother wouldn't discuss her sister's secret with anyone until Nat wanted her to.

A few minutes later, Natalie and Chris came into the house, holding hands.

"Gracie, I heard you bought a ramshackle old house that needs about a bazillion dollars' worth of repairs," he said.

"It actually *needs* very little. I mean, it's not in terrible shape. The layout just doesn't suit me, and I want a real kitchen, and a killer bathroom, and . . . you'll have to see it. But to do everything I want probably will run in the area of a bazillion dollars. I found out this morning I might be removing the vinyl siding. I have no idea what that will cost."

"Let's go take a look. I'm dying to see it." Natalie looked around. "Where's Daisy?"

"Upstairs with Mom," Grace told her.

"I'll be right back." Natalie gave Chris a starry-eyed smile and headed for the front stairs. "Gracie, it's getting a little chilly out. Do you want me to bring a sweater down for you?"

"Yes, please and thank you." To Chris, Grace said, "I'm going to make coffee to take with me. Would you like some?"

"Sure. Thanks."

Grace made coffee and searched the cabinets for a couple of insulated mugs, all the while feeling Chris's eyes on her.

"So you decided to come visit your mama on a whim, huh?" she asked.

"Yeah. What a coincidence Nat's here at the same time." His lips twitched as he tried not to smile.

Grace laughed. "You say that almost as if you expect me to believe it."

"A for effort?"

"More like a D-minus."

"What did Nat tell you?"

"She just confirmed you were seeing each other. I figured it out."

"You ever think about a career with the FBI?"

"I did, actually. At one point in my life, I thought I'd finish law school, practice with my dad for a few years, then apply to the bureau. That was plan A." The coffee finished dripping, and she poured some into a mug, which she passed to Chris. "We all know how that worked out." She rolled her eyes. "I should have stuck with that plan."

"But you're working for Liddy, and you started your own business. Nat says you're happy here."

"I am happy. It's a nice change after practicing law for ten years. It's sure a lot less stressful. Especially since my lying, cheating ex-husband is totally out of my life."

"If you'd stuck with plan A, you wouldn't be here, and you wouldn't have your new house to look forward to," he pointed out.

"Way to rationalize."

"Thank you. I think."

Natalie came down the back steps, holding two sweaters. She tossed one to Grace, who slipped it on over her shirt. She filled another mug with coffee and handed it to Natalie.

"Where's the munchkin?" Grace asked.

"She's going to stay here with Mom. They're looking at old photos of us in an album Mom had in her room. She won't even know we're gone."

Grace poured cream into her coffee, added a little sugar, then snapped on the lid.

"Drive or walk?" she asked.

"Walk," Natalie and Chris said in unison.

"It's a good day for a walk," Grace agreed, and the three of them set out.

At the corner of Cottage and Front, Natalie stopped to look across the street at the bookshop.

"Wow, it looks great! Remember how grungy it looked for the last few years? It looks glorious now. Can we stop in, maybe on the way back?" Natalie asked.

"Sure, but you know you're going to have to bring Daisy in tomorrow morning for story time."

"Mom said you were like the pied piper, getting all the kids in town to come in to listen to you read to them so their parents have to buy the book when you've finished. Very clever ruse, sister."

"Not all the kids, but yeah, we get quite a crowd. No one has to buy a book, but a lot of the kids want to take a copy home with them. The shop sells a lot of books on Saturday morning, which is what I think Liddy intended when she decided to do the story hour," Grace said as they turned up Front toward Jasper. "And if you think the outside looks great, wait till you see the inside."

When they walked past Liddy's house, Chris stopped, and Nat asked, "What?"

"Every time I go by this place, I think of Jessie. She was such a great girl. Funny and clever and creative, and a hell of a good friend." He nodded in the direction of the carriage house. "I hate she had something so heavy on her heart she just went and ended it. So many people loved her. She could have talked to someone, maybe gotten some relief from whatever was weighing her down. Sometimes I still can't believe it."

"Same," Grace said, touching Chris's arm. "We were friends for so long; then we just grew apart. I've often wondered if we'd remained close, if she'd have told me what was going on in her life that was hurting her so much."

"I never knew her as well as either of you, but I remember her coming to the house for Grace." Natalie turned to Chris. "And I know the two of you had been friends since nursery school."

"She was the sister I never had. I wish I'd been around more for her. Maybe she'd have confided in me." He left the thought unfinished.

Grace began walking, and Chris and Natalie finally caught up to her at the end of her new driveway.

"This way, friends."

"Nice long driveway," Chris noted.

"Lots of holes to fill," Nat said.

"I'm going to have the driveway paved," Grace told them. "I kind of like the rough country lane look, but it's hell navigating past all those potholes, especially when it rains, so I'm going to sacrifice charm for function. At least outside."

"Oh, it's . . . small," Natalie said when the house came into view.

"Hence the name, the little house," Grace said. "The plan out here is to have a porch. Can't you see it with a couple of rocking chairs and some big containers of flowers?"

"Uh-huh. Lots of flowers." Natalie nodded.

Grace turned the key in the lock and pushed open the door. She led Chris and Natalie through the interior, describing her plans for each space.

"I can see what you're seeing, Grace, and you're right. It's going to be perfect." Natalie hugged her sister.

"I know, right?" Grace opened the back door. "Come see what I'm planning out back."

She walked them through the plans for the porch, and pointed out where the little patio would be.

"It's going to be beautiful. The view of the pond is the best. And look at those woods, with all the leaves turning colors." Natalie stood with her hands in her pockets. "It's so peaceful here. I'd love to wake up in the morning and look out on all this."

"Not much room for guests," Grace said. "You'd have to bring sleeping bags or an air mattress."

"I'd totally do that. It would be like camping."

"Or we could bring a tent," Chris said. "Set it up down near the pond."

"Snakes," Grace said pointedly.

"No tent." Natalie shook her head. "But all in on the air mattress."

Grace finished the tour in the kitchen. "I have this room pretty much set up in my head, so I'm hoping my contractor can make it happen. I think he can. We're pretty much on the same wavelength."

Chris picked up the card Linc had left on the kitchen counter and read aloud, "Shelby and Son. Tuck's still in business?"

"Yes, do you know him?" Grace asked.

"I used to know Tuck's son," he replied.

"Linc. He's my contractor."

A shadow crossed Chris's face, but he merely nodded and looked at his watch. "We should probably get back to your mom's. I'd hoped to get up to the beach to take some photos while we're here, and it's a good day for it."

Natalie and Chris ambled along the drive, holding hands while Grace locked up.

"So what do you think of my little house?" Grace asked when she fell in step with them.

"I love it. I told you I think it's perfect for you. I can't wait to see it after all the work is done." Nat looped an arm through Grace's.

They walked back to Maggie's at a brisker pace, and when they arrived, Natalie and Chris went down to the beach while Grace went inside. Daisy had fallen asleep on Maggie's bed, and had slept the entire time her mother was gone. When she awoke, she wanted a snack, then to walk to the beach to find her mom and Chris.

"Is tomorrow Sunday?" Daisy asked as she bit into a banana chocolate chip muffin Maggie had made that morning.

"No, tomorrow's Saturday," Grace said. "Remember I told you I'd take you to the bookshop for story time, and I'd read a book for you and all the other kids who come in?"

Daisy nodded, her twin blonde ponytails bobbing up and down.

"The day after tomorrow is Sunday," Maggie told her.

"Good."

"I think you're going home on Sunday. Is that why you're asking?" Maggie wet a napkin and wiped the chocolate from Daisy's face after she finished her muffin.

"Uh-uh. I like Sundays best."

"Because you and your mom get to stay home together?" Maggie asked.

"No, because Chris makes us blueberry pancakes for breakfast on Sunday." All innocence, Daisy looked up at her grandmother.

Maggie paused while she processed the information before she said, "Oh, that's nice of him. Every Sunday?"

Daisy nodded enthusiastically. "Yup."

Maggie got up slowly. "I think I'll start dinner. Grace, did I tell you I invited Emma and Chris to join us for dinner tonight?"

"Chris brings us dinner on Fridays," Daisy went on, "and Mommy cooks something special on Saturday."

"Well. That's . . . nice, too." Maggie looked at Grace, who shrugged and said, "No filter. I've been telling Nat—"

"You might want to tell her again."

"Right. I'll walk down to the beach," Grace said.

"Me too." Daisy climbed out of the chair she'd been sitting in and raced to the door.

"Jacket, miss," Maggie called after her.

"I'll get it." Grace helped Daisy into her jacket, and set out with her niece, who chattered the entire time.

When they arrived at the beach, Grace scanned the sand, but she didn't see either Natalie or Chris until she looked up at the lifeguard stand. The two of them were wrapped around each other, making out.

"Oh, for crying out . . ." Grace called Nat's cell phone. "Clean it up. I've got your kid here."

"We're coming down." Natalie stood and pulled Chris up with her. He climbed down the ladder, then waited at the bottom for Nat.

"I found a pretty shell," Daisy called. "I'm going to find one for Nana."

"Stay right around there, sweetie. No closer to the water, okay?" Natalie turned to Grace. "What's going on?"

"Just a heads-up. Mom invited Chris and Emma for dinner, and there's no controlling the uncontrollable." She pointed to Daisy, then turned to Chris. "Within the space of two minutes, she told Mom and me that Chris makes you guys blueberry pancakes every Sunday morning and brings dinner on Friday nights."

Chris laughed. "That's our girl."

"So just decide what you're going to say. And now I'm heading back to the house because I'm freezing. That wind coming across the bay is cold."

"Thanks, Gracie. We'll bring Daisy back," Natalie said. "We've got it covered."

Grace nodded and headed toward home.

Dinner went surprisingly smoothly, with Chris taking the lead at the beginning of the meal, announcing he and Natalie had been seeing each other, but explaining they'd been trying to keep it quiet because he didn't want the distraction of the press or gossip magazines bothering Natalie.

"For myself, I don't care. I'm used to it. But Natalie is not, and we don't want Daisy's life disrupted." He turned to his mother. "Do you remember when that reporter tracked you down a few years ago? He followed you around, took pictures of the house."

"I couldn't leave home without someone trailing behind me. Though why anyone would have wanted to take pictures of me . . ." Emma shrugged.

"You're the mother of a superstar," Grace said. "There was a market for those pictures because fans want to know everything. Where he grew up, where he went to school . . ."

Emma bit her bottom lip. "So what does this mean, exactly? You're 'seeing' each other?"

"It means we're dating, Mom." Chris added, "Exclusively."

"Really? You and Natalie?"

"Yup." Chris draped an arm around the back of Natalie's chair. "Me and Nat."

"Why, that's . . ." Emma scrambled for a word. "It's wonderful. I couldn't be happier."

Emma turned to Maggie. "I told you he had a girlfriend. I had no idea it was someone I already love like a daughter. Why . . ."

Grace cleared her throat and looked at her mother.

"Now, Em." Maggie placed a hand on Emma's arm, and Grace suspected she may have given Emma a tap with her foot under the table. "Let's not get ahead of ourselves. I think it's wonderful Natalie and Chris are dating, but let's give them some room to find their way through this. After all, they've been friends for so long, this is uncharted territory for them. Am I right, Natalie?"

"That's it exactly, Mom. Thank you."

"Well, we can still be happy they're . . . whatever it is they're doing." Emma looked across the table. "Together."

"Yes. Absolutely." Chris stood. "Be happy Nat and I are together. I · brought a bottle of champagne so we could drink a toast—to all of us."

Natalie produced the bottle and handed it to Chris, who opened it. He poured the wine into everyone's glass except Daisy's, who was busy counting the flowers on her napkin.

After dinner, Chris suggested he, Natalie, and Grace walk down to Dusty's for a beer or two. Grace could tell her mother and Emma were happy to be left alone to discuss Chris's announcement and what it might mean for the future, and to plan, no doubt, a wedding that might never happen.

Dusty's Pub was the only true old-time tavern in Wyndham Beach. It had a long polished wood bar with a long mirror behind it and rows of liquor in front of it. It was dimly lit, and had several booths bearing the initials of the countless men and women who'd sat there over the ages. A few round tables seated four in the back, and off to one side there was a pool table, on the other, a dartboard. A modest-size television hanging over one end of the bar was set only to sports—and only to a Bruins, Patriots, Red Sox, or Celtics game. If none of their teams were playing live, they reran championship games their teams had won in the past.

Chris greeted several of the men seated at the bar, then looked around for a table or a booth, but they were all occupied.

"We can sit at the bar until a table or a booth frees up." Grace pointed to three stools at the end of the bar.

After a friendly chat with the bartender, Chris ordered beers for the three of them. After they were served, they clicked the necks of their bottles together, and they each took a drink.

"So that went well, right?" Chris said. "My mom, your mom— they're good with us dating."

"I think they may be too good." Grace chose her words carefully. "Just don't let them push you to . . . you know, move your relationship to a place you're not ready to go."

"I'm not worried about it." Chris nudged Natalie with his shoulder. "You worried?"

"If you're okay, I'm okay," Natalie said.

"Relax, Gracie. We know where we're headed," Chris told her, his voice low, his eyes first on Grace, then on Natalie. "We have a master plan."

Grace covered her ears. "Well, don't tell me. That way I never have to lie when Mom starts grilling me."

"You know I don't worry about you. It's Daisy."

"I told you: she's a spill machine. Something happens, or she over-hears things, she's gonna talk about it," Grace said.

Chris laughed. "Oh, yeah, she's tough, but we have a great time together. I couldn't love her more if she were my own."

"I'm happy to hear it, Chris. She deserves . . ." Grace bit her lip. She was about to say *a father who loves her*. Would he be that father for her?

Chris got off his stool and placed one arm around Natalie, the other around Grace. "She does deserve. And she'll have everything she deserves, Grace, I promise you. I don't want you to worry that we'll be this happy family pod for a while, and then I'll leave, and Daisy will be hurt. That isn't going to happen. I would never let things go this far if I didn't know for sure where we were headed."

"I wasn't going to say—"

"You didn't have to. Trust me. Trust Natalie. We know what we're doing." He turned and kissed Natalie on the cheek. "Right, babe?"

"Right." Natalie touched his face.

"You guys are sickening." Grace rolled her eyes, and they laughed.

"Oh, before I forget, would you happen to have a phone number for Linc Shelby?" Chris asked casually.

Maybe a little too casually, Grace thought. "I have it. Sure." She found her phone in her purse, read off Linc's number, and watched Chris save it in his phone.

Chris went back to his stool and leaned on the bar, staring at his phone, a distant look on his face. After several minutes passed, he hopped down and said, "I'll be back. I need to make a call."

He touched Natalie's back as he walked past, a somber expression on his face.

"What's that all about?" Grace turned and watched Chris leave the bar.

Natalie shook her head. "I swear I have no idea."

Chapter Fifteen

Fred Lattimore was greeting shoppers as they came into Wyndham Beach Reads on Saturday morning. He was wearing his usual khakis with a neatly buttoned shirt—which Liddy figured someone else had buttoned for him—and a tan bucket hat with a few fishing lures fastened on.

"Come on in. Nice to see you brought the kids. We have a whole section of children's books, sonny," he told one little boy, who ignored him completely in his race to the back of the shop for story time. "Slow down, little fella!" Fred called after him. "No running!"

He later complained to Liddy and Evelyn: "Why are all these kids in my shop? This is a bookstore, not a playroom. What are these parents thinking, letting those kids go off on their own like that?"

"Ah, Fred, they're thinking the kids might like to hear a story," Evelyn told him.

"Well, that's what bedtime is for. Bedtime stories," he grumbled. "And what's with all of 'em crowding into the back of the room like that?"

The back door opened, and in walked Grace in her Mary Poppins dress and hat, holding Daisy by the hand. The kids who'd already gathered grew animated and excited at the sight of their story reader.

"And who the devil is that?" Fred demanded. He started to totter toward the back of the shop, and Liddy stopped him.

"Fred, we do a story hour every Saturday. People bring in their kids and we have someone"—Liddy nodded in Grace's direction—"read a book aloud to the children."

"Well, I'll put a stop to that." He tried to get around Liddy, but she blocked his way.

"Fred. It sells a lot of books."

"Huh?" He stopped fighting her for a moment.

"We sell a ton of books on Saturday because of the story hour. People bring in their kids or their grandkids, and the kids listen to a story. Then nine times out of ten, the kids love the story so much they want to buy a copy of the book to take home so they can read it again."

"They do?"

Liddy nodded. "They do. And while their parents are here, waiting for the story hour to end so they can take their kids home, they wander around the store and pick up books for themselves."

"Well." Fred stood stone-still while apparently trying to process this information. "Well then. All right."

Carl showed up five minutes later to take his dad home. By then, Fred had forgotten how lucrative the children's story hour was, and he complained to Carl about his shop being overrun with kids.

"I hate what's happened to Fred," Evelyn told Liddy. "He was the best guy to work for. It's so sad to see him like this."

"It is, for everyone. I don't mind him coming in and thinking he owns the shop. But I'm not gonna lie—I would mind if he started chasing people out, the way he was going to chase out the kids earlier."

"Yeah, that would be bad," Evelyn agreed.

"Bad for the store's reputation, bad for our bottom line."

A few stragglers came in and raced to the children's section. The last one in was JoJo.

"Did Grace start reading yet?" Tuck asked.

"No, but she's just about to," Liddy told him.

"Hurry, then, Jo. Go on back." He shooed his granddaughter along, then leaned an elbow on the counter and gave Liddy a smile. "How's your day going so far?"

"Good. But it's early." She found it easy to smile back.

"How about you and me—" Tuck was interrupted by a furious JoJo, who hit his legs like a torpedo.

"I want to go home." Angry tears poured down her face. "I . . . want . . . to . . . go . . . home."

"Jo, you just got here. Grace is going to read you all a story," Tuck told her.

"No! I don't want a story. I want to go home now!"

Liddy came out from behind the counter and knelt next to JoJo, who was sobbing, her face hidden in the side of her grandfather's leg.

"JoJo, what happened? Tell me and we'll—"

"No." She mumbled something else, and Tuck gave up.

He lifted her in his arms and said, "All right, Jo. I'm taking you home. But can you tell us what happened?"

She shook her head and stuck her thumb in her mouth.

"I'll talk to you later," he told Liddy, and left the store with JoJo in his arms.

Liddy walked back to the children's area, mystified. What could possibly have happened in the few seconds JoJo had been in the back of the shop?

When Liddy rounded the corner, the source of JoJo's despair was clear as Liddy looked upon the scene through JoJo's eyes. Another little girl was in her place on Grace's lap, turning the pages.

Another little girl was Grace's special friend, too.

It had never occurred to Liddy that JoJo would see Daisy's presence that morning as a betrayal of the special bond she'd thought she and Grace shared, that the coveted place on Grace's lap was hers and hers alone.

"Well, damn," Liddy muttered, drawing a disapproving glance from a father standing nearby. She pulled her phone from her pocket and called Tuck's cell, and left a message. "I think I figured out why JoJo was so distressed. Give me a call when you can."

~

Maggie came into the shop around one, looking for Grace and Daisy.

"Grace said she and Daisy were going to have lunch at Beach Fries," Liddy told her.

"That's nice they're getting to spend a little time together." Maggie paused at the shelf where the new biographies were displayed. "How are your book clubs doing? I keep meaning to ask, but then when I see you, we get to talking about something else, and I forget."

"They're doing really well. Almost too well. We've had so many show up for the mystery group we're splitting off thrillers as a separate group. And romance has already splintered off women's fiction. Nonfiction is growing, and I may have to start a second group for just biographies."

"Wow, it sounds great. So much interest in town."

"Well, it's not all sunshine, Mags. Some members of the romance group seem to think it's true-confessions night. Like when someone commented on a particularly hot scene, LeeAnn said something like, 'If you think that's hot, let me tell you about the time . . .'"

"She did not." Maggie's eyes widened.

"Oh, yes, she did. She just went on and on, no one saying a thing. I mean, you could have heard a pin drop in this place. You could hear her all the way up here, and everyone in the shop just stopped in their tracks. I don't know if the other ladies in the book club were too shocked to speak or if they were living vicariously through LeeAnn. Either way, it had a lot of people talking." Liddy reflected for a moment. "Which could result in more readers showing up next week."

Maggie laughed. "Hey, if it means more book sales . . ."

"Yeah. Maybe not necessarily a bad thing." Liddy leaned on the counter. "So how's it going with Natalie home? I'm sure you're happy to see her and Daisy."

"You should probably be sitting down, but since you're not, I'll just lay it out there. Natalie and Chris are 'together.'"

Liddy frowned. "Chris who?"

"Chris Dean."

Liddy's jaw dropped slightly. "Emma's Chris? Rock and roll Chris Dean, international rock star and sex symbol Chris Dean? That Chris?"

Maggie nodded. "That Chris."

"Well . . . wow. How 'bout that?" Liddy searched her friend's face for a sign of approval or disapproval, and wasn't sure what she was seeing. "So how do you and Emma feel about that? And how did you find out?"

"Chris showed up yesterday afternoon at my house, and right away, I knew there was something between him and Nat. Just the way they looked at each other. It was just so pure and so loving. I knew Natalie had feelings for him. It worried me because I had no idea how he felt about her, and I didn't want her to have her heart broken. But seeing them together, well, it's obvious. I looked at Grace, and I knew she knew because she didn't look at all surprised at the way those two hugged each other. I'd invited Emma and Chris for dinner, and Chris made this very sweet announcement about how they were seeing each other exclusively and how they were trying to keep things quiet, so Natalie and Daisy weren't overrun with gossipy press following them around."

"Huh. Natalie and Chris." Liddy thought about that pairing for a moment. She'd never mentioned it, even to her best friends, but she'd always hoped someday Chris and Jessie would have seen each other as something more than friends. But this—Chris and Natalie—was almost as good. Almost, but not quite, though no one would ever need to know. "Well, I can see it. They're alike in so many ways, and, of course, they've known each other for so long. But you haven't said how you feel about it."

"I'm happy Natalie has found someone she loves who loves her after the horrible way Jon treated her when he found out she was pregnant with Daisy." Maggie's expression grew dark. "Forcing her to make a choice between him and their child."

"Obviously he didn't know Nat as well as he thought he did."

"Obviously," Maggie agreed. "We've both known Chris since he was a baby. We know what a fine and wonderful man he is, and I couldn't love him more."

"And yet—" Liddy sensed there was more.

Maggie sighed. "And yet I wonder if his lifestyle is conducive to the sort of life she wants. She's not a jet-setter. She's home and family, and I don't know if Chris is ready to put his life as a big star behind him."

"I don't think he's let it go to his head. Remember when he flew us and Emma down to Charlotte last year to see his concert? I hadn't been around him in a while, and I was impressed by how much he *hadn't* changed." She grinned and quoted Emma. "He's a good boy."

Maggie laughed. "Yes, he's a good boy. And he's a good man. I just worry because . . ."

"Because she's your baby girl and you don't want to see her hurt by anyone."

"Not that I think Chris would deliberately hurt her, but still . . ."

"But still, she's your baby girl."

Maggie nodded. "Emma's over the moon, of course. She'd always said if she could pick a wife for Chris, it would be Natalie."

"Wait, wife? Are we talking marriage?"

"No. Not yet anyway. But you know how Emma wants so badly for him to settle down and move back to Wyndham Beach and have a houseful of kids for her to spoil. I think they both want to take things slowly. Nat's been burned before, and Chris has never had a long-term, serious relationship, at least as far as Emma knows. It's plain to see he loves my daughter, and he's wonderful with Daisy. She adores him, and he clearly loves her. So I guess we'll have to see where it goes."

"I had an interesting week, too," Liddy said, then proceeded to tell Maggie first about Dylan, then about Jim's declaration of love.

"Wait, what? Jim said he wants to try again? As in, marry you again?"

"He didn't say that, but yeah. He wants us to get back together."

"What did you say?" Maggie took a bottle of water from her bag and drank.

"I didn't really say anything. I was taken completely off guard."

"How do you feel about him? How did it feel to see him again?"

"It felt strange, to tell you the truth. I don't know how I feel about him." Liddy sighed. "There's so much that happened between us. He left me, and I cannot think about the night he walked out without feeling like I'm going to throw up. It still hurts like hell. But"—she took a deep breath—"I understand a little better how he felt and why he did what he did. I have to acknowledge my own part in that. In the aftermath of Jess's death, I let him down as much as he let me down. I should have been more mindful of the fact he'd lost his daughter, too, and he was grieving as much as I was, but I didn't. I have to own that." Liddy's shoulders slumped. The admission was painful, and she let it sink in for a moment.

"How'd you leave it with him?"

Liddy shrugged. "Up in the air, I guess. I felt such an overwhelming sorrow, Maggie. Sorry I'd been so blind to what he'd been going through. Sorry we weren't able to help each other. Sorry we paid with our marriage for not being there for each other."

"Do you still love him?"

"I think there's a part of me that will always love the best parts of Jim. But little things keep coming back to me. The things he did all through our marriage that annoyed me back then, I'm finding

287

unacceptable now. Like the way he always talked down to me, as if I couldn't understand things unless he explained them to me."

"Mansplaining," Maggie said.

"In the worst possible way. And I used to hate when we'd go out to dinner and he'd order for me, but I always just let it ride. It didn't seem like such a big deal to me back then. Now that I've been on my own for a while, I find it insulting and demeaning. Like he doesn't think I know what I want unless he tells me. It's infuriating. He did it again last night, can you believe it?"

"Did you let him?"

"No, I didn't let him. I ordered for myself. He seemed surprised, but I bet he doesn't do that again."

"Well, good for you. One bad habit broken."

"I should have spoken up a long time ago."

"But at least you're doing it now."

"Yeah, but I'm pretty sure now's too late."

~

Tuck returned Liddy's call just as Maggie was about to leave. She waved goodbye so Liddy could have some privacy.

"I think I know why JoJo was so upset at the shop this morning and why she wanted to leave." Liddy told him about Daisy sitting on Grace's lap. "Someone was in her place, and she didn't like it."

"Aw, geez." Tuck exhaled loudly. "I'm too old to figure out how to handle all this stuff."

Liddy laughed. "No, you're not. You just haven't had to deal with a little girl's feelings in a long time. Look, I understand it's tough . . ."

"Tough? That kid cried all the way back to the island. I couldn't take it, Liddy. I didn't know what to do."

"There was nothing you could have done. She thinks she's lost something, and she just had to cry it out."

"So what do I do?"

"I'll talk to Grace. Maybe she could talk to JoJo. If nothing else, Grace needs to know. I just spoke with Maggie. I should have brought it up then." *But there were other pressing things to discuss,* she could have added, but somehow she didn't think Tuck would want to hear about Jim's declaration of love.

"I'd appreciate that. Maybe Grace'll know what to say." His voice faded away for a moment.

"Tuck, I think there's a bad connection."

" . . . happens out here on the water and . . ." He faded out again.

"Why don't you call me later?"

"Why don't I stop by?" She heard that loud and clear.

"I close the shop at nine."

"I'll be at your place at nine-oh-one."

Liddy smiled and dropped her phone into her bag, and headed into the shop. She noticed the tall, lanky figure standing at the counter, watching Rosalita make her way into the North Carolina waters.

"Hey, Dylan." She smiled. "I'm glad to see you." She was surprised by how much she'd missed him around the shop.

"Hi, Miz Bryant." Dylan looked happy to see her, too.

"Come on back to my office for a minute, so we can have a little talk in private." She paused. "I'll be right back," she told Evelyn as she passed her in the aisle.

"So how are things working out for you at the coach's? Are you okay there?" Liddy asked.

"It's okay. Coach's wife is nice, and she's a good cook."

"So I guess dinners are a little better than a bag of chips, a candy bar, or leftover pizza?"

He nodded, an embarrassed smile on his face. "Yeah. A lot better."

"Dylan, if I'd known what you were going through—"

He shrugged. "It's okay. I mean, I wouldn't blame you if you'd been mad at me for crashing in your shop and eating your leftover pizza and using your computer."

She hadn't known about that last one, but it didn't matter now.

"I swear, I never looked at your files or anything. I just typed a couple of papers and emailed them to my teachers."

"I understand. I'm just glad you've got a place to stay and you're able to stay in school."

"Yeah, me too. I'm going to have to get a job so I can save some money, because I can't live at Coach's house much longer. Miz Riley's mom fell yesterday and broke her leg. She's in a hospital in Providence, but they're going to move her to a nursing home, and they're going to be bringing her to live with them as soon as she can get out of rehab. They're going to need the room I'm staying in, but that's not for another month or so, and by then I'll be eighteen and no one will have to supervise me, so it's okay." He shrugged as if it didn't matter, but she could see the uncertainty of his future weighed heavily on his mind. "I knew I wouldn't be staying there for too long."

"Is there someone else you could stay with until you've finished high school?"

Dylan shook his head almost apologetically. "There really isn't anyone. Unless I want to go out of state, like to my grandma's, for real. That would mess me up with baseball, and that's my ticket, you know?"

Liddy's heart sank. It was so unfair that this good kid was going to be uprooted again. She wished she could have done more for him. On impulse, she said, "Dylan, maybe after you leave the Rileys', you could stay with me if nothing else comes along. I have room, and you could stay until you start college next fall."

He blinked, then stared as if he hadn't understood what she'd said.

"And if you still need a job, you could work for me in the bookshop." The words fell from her mouth even as the thoughts were forming.

"Wait, what? Live in your house? Work here?" He looked confused. "Why would you do that for me?"

"Because you deserve to finish out your last year of high school without worrying about where to live and whether you'll have enough left at the end of the week to do your laundry." Once she'd decided she was in, Liddy was all in. "I could use another person here, and I don't know anyone else who knows their way around the shop like you do."

"I know it pretty well, yeah. I loved being here, Miz Bryant. I like books a lot."

"I suspected as much, since you always had one in your hands."

"Yes, ma'am." He still appeared dazed.

"Now, if you stay with me, there will be rules. Curfew. Keep your room clean. Maybe help out with some yard work. And it goes without saying: no drugs, no alcohol. And no kids—especially girls—in the house when I'm not there."

"Yes, ma'am, I will. I mean, I won't. I don't smoke and I don't drink and I'd never do drugs. And I'll be happy to do yard work and anything else you need done. I'm stronger than I look, and I'm a real hard worker."

"So what do you think? Want to fill out a job application?"

"I would. Thank you."

She opened her bottom desk drawer and took an application form from a file. She handed it to him with a pen, and said, "You can leave this here on my desk when you're done. I'll be up front."

"Thank you, Miz Bryant," he said. "Miz Bryant . . . I don't know what . . . how . . ."

"You're welcome. You can have your coach call me. Tell him he can check me out with Chief Crawford. He's known me since we were fifteen." As she left the room, Liddy said, "Oh, one more thing. If you're going to live in my house and work for me, you're going to have to call me Liddy."

~

There'd been a few late customers, which meant Liddy didn't get to close up until almost nine fifteen. By the time she walked home, it was almost nine thirty. Along the way, she thought about what she'd done, the offers she'd made to Dylan. All her instincts told her she'd done exactly the right thing. She'd called Tuck to let him know she'd be late, but he assured her he didn't care. He offered to come pick her up, but she declined. He was comfortable, he told her, in one of her rocking chairs on the front porch.

And that was where she found him. When she came up the front walk, she could see him, the rocker he was sitting in moving slowly back and forth, his feet up on the rail, and his head resting against the back of the chair.

"Well, don't you look comfy," she said as she came up the steps.

"I am, thank you." He sat up and lowered his feet from the railing. "These are great chairs. I might have to get a few for the porch at home."

"Your house has a front porch?" Liddy lowered herself into the chair next to his.

"Sure. Rockers and porches go together like chocolate and peanut butter." He rocked for a moment. "You've never been to our island, have you?"

"No, but I'd like to. I don't know anyone who has been, so there's always been this sort of mystique about it. Like those stories about pirates that used to go around."

"Those stories were true," he told her. "My three-times great-grandfather was a bona fide pirate. When he got tired chasing ships around the Caribbean and had stashed away a fortune, he sailed up north here and landed on the island, claimed it for his own. At the time, there was no house, so he built one. When he needed a wife, he went into Boston and found one, brought her back."

"Sounds like something some little boy made up."

"Nope. He wrote it all down in a journal. When he died, his wife put it in a metal box and left it in the top of a closet, where it stayed for probably a hundred years. My granddad was the one who found it."

"Huh." She smiled in the dark. "I guess that's where you and Linc got your swagger."

Tuck laughed.

"So the house you live in is the one he built?"

"There's only one house on the island, and yes, he built it."

"What was his name?"

"Nicholas Shelby. His wife was Marcy King before she married him. Her people were wealthy Bostonians, her father an investor. I always wondered if some of those ships old Nick robbed had been owned by her father." He looked at Liddy from the corner of his eye. "Would have made for some tense family dinners."

"Did her family know who he was?"

"Doubtful. I think he probably sold himself as a merchant of sorts. After all, he did own a ship."

"I wonder what she thought of him, assuming she ever learned the truth."

"If she didn't know while he was alive, she sure knew after he died. That journal of his was pretty explicit."

"You read it?"

He nodded. "I did. Some of the ink has faded, but enough of it is still legible that there's no doubt what he was. He must have been good at pirating, though. He never worked at anything for the rest of his life, and he and Marcy had nine kids. I don't know what happened to all of them—a few are buried on the island—but I do know there were a few doctors and lawyers in the bunch. The girls made good marriages, so he must have tucked away a whole bunch of plundered goods. When we were little and we'd act up, my father would tell us to grab a shovel and see if we could find the buried treasure. Kept my sister and me busy many an afternoon."

"Are he and Marcy buried there as well?"

"She is. He was buried at sea, as was his wish." He lowered his feet from the rail. "Almost all the Shelby men who lived on the island have been buried at sea. My great-granddad, my grandfather, I know for sure. Others before them, I have to assume. I had a brother who died when he was three. He's there in the graveyard with Marcy, but my dad will probably join the others in the water, sooner than later."

"And you?"

"I hate to break with tradition," was all he said.

"How is your dad?"

"Not well. He has late-stage dementia, so we know he won't be with us much longer." He rocked for a moment, then said, "I read something once that, after you die, any sickness you had while you were on earth is gone. You're restored to the way you were when you were young and healthy, and you are reunited with the people you loved here on earth. I don't know if that's true, but it would be nice if my dad met up with my mother, and remembered her."

"Dementia is a terrible thing." Liddy thought of Fred, suffering from Alzheimer's, his son trying so hard to keep him safe. "Who takes care of him when you and Linc are both working?"

"There's a nurse who stays with us through the week, and another on the weekend. It's not easy convincing someone who's lived their entire life on the mainland to make that crossing every day, especially when the weather acts up. We couldn't keep my dad at home without them. He requires a lot of care, and neither Linc nor I is trained to do everything he needs."

"I'm sorry. It has to be hard on you, but it's really sad for him."

"The only positive thing about his condition is that he doesn't remember my mother. He doesn't remember how lonely and heartbroken he was all those years he lived without her." Tuck cleared his throat. "Can we go inside?"

"Sure. Come on."

She unlocked the door, and they went inside. As they walked toward the kitchen, she noticed a paper bag in his hand.

"What's in the bag?" she asked.

"Something I've been saving for a special occasion." Once in the kitchen, he set the bag on the table.

"Is this a special occasion?" She turned on the overhead light.

He took her in his arms and kissed her. The long, deep kiss had been totally unexpected, but was met with much enthusiasm. Tuck was solid and strong, and Liddy enjoyed every second of that first lip-lock.

And there, she thought. *There it is. That zing . . .*

He stepped back, his hands on her shoulders, and looked into her eyes as if searching for something. Liddy thought he must have found it, because he smiled.

"That made this a special occasion." He released her, opened the bag, and took out a bottle. He set it on the table. "Glasses?"

Liddy pointed to a cabinet and picked up the bottle. She read the label, then turned to him in shock. "Pappy Van Winkle bourbon? Are you serious?"

"As a heart attack."

"But I read it's impossible to find."

"Damn near is. And insanely expensive if you do."

"Then how . . . ?"

"I have a friend who owns a liquor store in Connecticut. He called me a while back and asked me if I wanted to buy a bottle at the retail price. He had five bottles, and he was saving three for his daughter's wedding, so I bought the other two."

"Wow. He must be some friend."

"We go back," Tuck said simply.

"We have a book in the shop about the man who started the company. And I read a magazine article about this stuff."

"Please don't call the best bourbon in the country 'stuff.'"

"Oh. Sorry. All I know is that a bottle can sell for thousands of dollars. I don't think I've ever had bourbon, so I wouldn't know the difference between it and a bottle off the shelf."

"After tonight, you'll never be able to say that again." He handed her a glass containing a small amount of the richly colored liquid. He lifted his own and made a toast. "To fine friends and fine bourbon."

She was about to refuse the glass, but he seemed so happy to share his good luck at having scored a bottle of the precious liquor, and he'd said he'd brought it to mark a special occasion. Their first kiss had been a wowzer—and *first* meant there'd be more to follow, right? She'd definitely drink to that. Liddy raised the glass to her lips and took a sip. "Oh. This is . . . different."

"Like it?"

She nodded. "It's not at all what I expected. It's good."

"I'm glad you like it. But sip it slowly, because that's all you're getting tonight." He was looking into her eyes as he recapped the bottle, but she wasn't totally sure he was referring only to the bourbon. "Now, maybe we could sit out on your deck again, and you can tell me about your day."

She told him about offering Dylan a place to live and a job.

"Good for you, Liddy." He beamed his approval. "There's a kid who needed a break, deserved a break—and you made it happen for him. You'll never be sorry for having helped him to keep moving toward his goal. From all you've said, this kid has had everything stacked against him, and yet he's been working his tail off at school. I saw Jason Riley at the drugstore the other day, and we got to talking. He says this kid is the best baseball player he's ever coached. He has a bright career ahead of him, and with his grades, he's guaranteed to get into a top school. Him having a stable place to live and a job is going to make all the difference in the world to that boy. You're an amazing woman, Lydia, and I'm proud of you."

Somehow *Lydia* sounded a lot better coming from Tuck than it did from Jim.

Later, after he'd kissed her good night—another zinger—and she'd locked up the house, she lay in her bed and thought about the two men in her life. She and Jim had almost forty years of history, and he'd declared his love for her in no uncertain turns. Tuck had brought her rare bourbon and asked her about her day. Jim had criticized her when she'd told him she hadn't pressed charges against Dylan. Tuck had praised her for those same actions. As flattering as all the attention was, she'd never been comfortable juggling relationships. Sooner or later, she'd have to choose one.

~

Two days later, Tuck came into the shop right around twelve thirty. He came up behind her while she was straightening out the mystery section.

"Any chance you could take a long lunch?" he whispered.

Liddy kept her cool. She glanced around the shop as if debating. "Well, we haven't been really busy today, and Evelyn and Grace are here, so sure. What do you have in mind?"

"How does a picnic on the beach sound?"

"That sounds great." Not to mention romantic.

"How 'bout I come back for you in about twenty minutes?"

"I'll be here."

Her heart pounding, Liddy went back to the powder room in her office and checked her appearance. She'd worn a denim skirt and a white long-sleeved cotton tee, over which she wore a dark-rose cardigan. Tennis shoes. No makeup. She looked at herself closer, then decided a little mascara would be good. She tucked some errant strands of hair back into the bun she wore. She pictured the two of them on the beach at the end of Cottage Street, sitting near the rocks on a patchwork quilt, eating cheese and fruit and drinking wine. Or should she make that bourbon? But no. That was for special occasions. Would today be special? She went back out to the floor and tried to act busy until Tuck came back.

"So where are we going?" she asked after they'd driven past Cottage Street in his truck. She'd assumed that was where they were headed. When she said *beach*, she meant Cottage Street Beach. Apparently, Tuck had something else in mind.

"We're taking a ride." He continued to drive in the direction of the bay. He pulled up in front of the old warehouse he used for the business and turned off the car.

"I thought you said we were going to the beach," Liddy said, a little confused. A warehouse was no place for an afternoon tryst, if in fact that was what he'd planned. Her hopes were fading fast.

"We are."

He opened the driver's door and got out, then grabbed a bag from the space behind the cab. He walked toward the passenger side and pointed to the Boston Whaler tied up at the dock. Delighted, Liddy jumped out of the truck and stared at the boat. It had been years since she'd been out on the bay. Her father had had a catamaran when she was growing up, and she and her sister, Ruth, had spent many an afternoon gliding over the water from the bay to the harbor and back again.

But then she'd grown up and gotten married. Jim got seasick, so eventually she'd sold the catamaran.

"Good thing I wore sneakers today," she commented as he helped her step over the side of the boat onto the deck. She found her balance easily and felt a stirring of something familiar growing inside. She was happy to be on the water again. She hadn't even realized how much she'd missed it.

She helped Tuck untie the boat, then watched as he took his place at the wheel.

"You might want to come stand here with me," he told her. "There's a good deal of chop further out, so it's going to get a little rough. Not to mention you will probably get wet."

"It's okay," she said as the boat pulled away from the dock. "I don't mind."

He turned the boat toward the open bay, and increased the speed. When their destination became clear, she broke into a grin. He was taking her to Shelby Island.

Water flew up from the sides of the boat, spraying but not soaking her. She wouldn't have cared if it had. She was out on the water again and, for a few minutes, remembered how it felt to be young and have the wind in your face and not a care in the world. It was exhilarating. As they approached the island, it became obvious it was larger than it looked from the mainland, and what she could see of it was mostly green. She felt like Wendy, getting her first glimpse of Neverland. Tuck cut the motor and let the waves roll him toward the dock, where he tied off the Whaler.

He picked up the bag and jumped off the boat and held his hand out to Liddy and said, "Welcome to Shelby Island."

She took his hand and stepped off the side of the boat onto the dock.

"Tour first or lunch first?" he asked.

She tried to look like she was thinking it over, though there was really no question. "Tour first."

"Somehow, I knew you'd say that." Tuck took her hand, and they walked over a dune where beach grass grew in untidy clumps and beach plums were prolific.

"My grandma used to make beach plum jam," Liddy told him.

"My grandmother and my mom did, too. A ton of it grew this year. It's a shame to see the fruit go to waste, but no one has the time to make jam these days."

They rounded a stand of scrub pine, and up ahead, the house Nicholas Shelby had built for the wife he'd yet to meet came into view. For some reason, Liddy had expected to find it weather-beaten and grayed, the paint worn off by sun and wind, maybe even a sagging front porch. But the large house with all its gables rising beyond the dunes was pristine white, with a door the color of peaches and shutters painted black. Morning glories twined along the front porch, the last few flowers holding on to the hope of a few more sunny weeks.

"It's beautiful, Tuck."

"Thanks. It's a lot of work to keep up. We end up painting the exterior every couple of years, but it's worth the effort. The old girl's hung in there for a long time. I don't want her falling apart on my watch. Come on in and say hi to my dad if he's awake."

Inside, the front hall was spacious and cool, the floor a natural wide-plank pine. The stairs from the second floor flowed elegantly from the right side into the foyer. A chandelier hung solemnly, and a vintage piano stood against one wall. She caught a glimpse of the dining room as she followed Tuck into the house, and noted the formal furniture, which she suspected might have been in the house for a very long time. They passed through the kitchen and the sunporch and out through a screened door into the garden, where a man wrapped in a blue blanket sat in a wheelchair. His eyes were fixed on the dahlias swaying in the breeze.

"Dad." Tuck spoke softly and touched his father on the shoulder, but there was no response to either his voice or his touch.

Tuck gestured for Liddy to step into his father's line of sight.

"Dad, this is my friend Lydia. You used to take her father, Alphonse Hess, out on your charter boat to fish for tuna, remember? Do you remember Alphonse Hess?"

That was news to Liddy. She did recall her father going deep-sea fishing, but she had no idea Tuck's father had captained that boat.

"He's not having a good day, Tuck." The nurse Tuck had mentioned came outside with a glass of water in her hand. "I've been trying to get him to take some water, but I'm not getting through to him. I hate to hook him up to an IV again, because it agitates him, but I can't let him get dehydrated."

"Do what you have to do, Irene." Tuck introduced Liddy to the nurse, then gestured for Liddy to follow him through the garden. He stopped midway and said, "Wait here a sec."

He ran back inside the house, giving Liddy an opportunity to check out the backyard. The dahlias grew in a bed along one side of the garden. They reminded her of an artist's palette, the glorious flowers planted in pods of color—shades of red in one place, yellows in another, pinks in yet another. They stood tall and swayed on their thick stalks in the breeze. But Tuck hadn't been kidding when he said he hadn't planted anything else. There were beds in which nothing grew but the unidentifiable brown and brittle remains of whatever flowers had once grown there.

Tuck emerged from the house with a quilt draped over his arm. He picked up the bag from where he'd set it on the ground, and caught up with Liddy at the far end of the garden.

"Forgot we needed something to sit on." He held up the quilt, then held up the bag. "I guess a picnic basket would make this feel more like an actual picnic than just lunch on the beach."

"It's fine, no apologies necessary. And for the record, I have a picnic basket that hasn't been used in years. Available," she said as she leaned into him slightly, "for future outings."

"I hope there will be more to come." He reached for her hand.

They trudged over a dune that was higher than it appeared, and by the time they came down the other side, Liddy was a little out of breath, though Tuck seemed to take it in stride.

"How about right here?" He nodded in the general direction of a section of beach off to their left.

"Perfect," she said.

She helped him spread out the blanket, and then sat near the middle, looking out toward the water. "I'm disoriented," she told him. "Am I looking at Buzzards Bay here?"

Tuck nodded. "And if you look off that way far enough"—he pointed to the right—"eventually you'll see the Atlantic."

"I didn't realize you were out this far."

"Sometimes distance over water can feel different from that over land. It doesn't for me, but then again, I've never known anything else."

"Your island is beautiful." She couldn't stop looking around at the landscape. "It's wild in its own way, and yet it feels—I don't know, friendly."

"That's because I told it to behave today, that I was bringing a friend over, so no tossing big waves onto the beach, no shark sightings—though you might like that—no greenhead flies, no midges. No swarming gnats or yellow jackets."

Liddy laughed. "It's sounding less like paradise when you put it that way."

"We have the same challenges you have in town, sometimes more because we're more vulnerable to the weather. We have an extra-large generator that runs on gas—that's delivered by boat—and we have several fireplaces. I buy a lot of wood and stockpile it for the winter. I've thought about a windmill, but I worry about birds flying into it. We have to keep the freezer stocked from November right on through to April, because a really bad nor'easter can keep us huddled here for days. But most of the time, like today, it really can feel like paradise." He smiled. "Not a tropical one, but still . . ."

"Paradise all the same," Liddy agreed.

Tuck began to empty the contents of the bag. "I told Tom at the general store to make us some sandwiches and to cut them in quarters in case you don't like one, you can try one of the others. He said he made up some turkey, chicken salad, roast beef, and ham and swiss."

"Were you expecting a crowd?" She stared at the pile of sandwiches.

"I figured the kids would eat whatever we don't." He unwrapped a few. "What's your pleasure?"

"I love Tom's chicken salad," she said, and he offered her one with the paper still wrapped around it. "I will probably eat this whole thing."

"Go ahead. I'll do the same with one of the roast beefs."

"I think this is a happy place," Liddy announced between bites. "There's so much to see."

Tuck pointed up to the top of one of the pines. "There's a nesting pair of osprey up there. They've been here for as long as I can remember. They migrate south—Central America, South America, as soon as the weather starts to get cool. Every year in the spring, they come back to the same nest—they're monogamous—and have a chick or two; then you see them out there fishing, bringing food back for their little ones. At times this beach has been covered in parts of dead fish, which Brenda hated. For one thing, you can probably imagine what a beach full of dead fish smells like. And of course then the gulls come to pick over what's left."

"I've never been close enough to osprey to watch them feed their young."

"They add a bit to the nest every year, and about three years ago, that one up there got so heavy, it fell right out of the tree. They had to start over, build a new nest."

"Wow, that's rough."

Tuck shrugged. "Just like people, something happens to bring your house down, you start again." He reached over and eased a loose strand of her hair behind her ear. "Isn't that what you're helping your friend Dylan do?"

"Isn't that what you're helping your grandchildren do?"

"That's what you do for family."

"Well, Dylan's not exactly my family."

"Sure he is. You saved him. You took him under your wing." He pointed upward toward the nest. "No pun."

They finished eating, and Tuck rested back on his elbows. Liddy could feel his eyes on her, so she turned to look at him, and he pulled her closer to lean against him. She closed her eyes and lifted her face to the sun and let it warm her all the way through. For just a moment, she was seventeen again, having a picnic on the beach with the cool older guy who liked her. There was no Jim, no decisions hanging over her head, no lost children, no heartaches, and for just those few minutes, that was enough.

Tuck sat up when Liddy did, and he kissed her as though he meant it. She kissed him back and thought how free she felt, alone on an island beach with a man who really *saw* her, who didn't hesitate to let her know how much he liked her—no Kiss Me, Kale necessary.

After they'd made the ride back through the waves, the sun beating down in earnest, the spray a salty shower flinging up from all sides, she returned to her bookshop feeling different than when she'd left. Today, for the first time, she'd set foot on Shelby Island, and she'd fallen a little in love with the place, if not also the man.

Her last thought before she fell asleep that night was while Jim might be the sentimental favorite, the newcomer might have the edge. It was a hard lesson to learn, but a true one: you can't live inside your memories. You can only make new ones.

Chapter Sixteen

Grace paced a little, hoping Linc would return her call sooner rather than later. She'd left a voice mail asking him to call, without going into detail. She hoped he didn't blow off the call, thinking she was bugging him about when he was going to start on the house or something equally annoying.

"How's JoJo?" she asked when he called back.

"Ah, well, now that you ask, she's been a little quiet this week, maybe a little more so than usual," he replied. "Why?"

In the background she could hear men talking, laughing, and yelling back and forth. She looked at the phone and realized it was right around the time he'd be sending his crew home for the night.

"Linc, something happened at the bookshop on Saturday that upset her." She took a deep breath.

"I heard. My dad told me. I know she likes to sit with you, but my dad said there was someone else in her seat, so Jo wouldn't stay for the story."

"The someone else was my four-year-old niece, my sister Natalie's daughter. After I sat down, she climbed into my lap. She was feeling a little shy and insecure because she didn't know anyone, and there were a lot of kids gathered around us. So when JoJo arrived, expecting to sit on my lap, there was a little girl in her place, and I think it hurt her. I don't want her to stop coming for story time. I know she enjoys it very much. I'm very fond of her, and if I hurt her, even inadvertently, I need to make it up to her."

"Tell me what you have in mind."

"I'd like to talk to her and explain no one's taking her place. She could have sat on the chair next to me, even if Daisy were on my lap. And she needs to know Daisy wasn't just some random kid. She's a member of my family."

"Look, I'm just wrapping up here, and I have to head home. Let me think about this and see what I can come up with." He paused. "Are you going to be around later?"

"Yes."

"I'll give you a call."

She hit "End" and slid the phone into the pocket of her jeans. In the kitchen, she scrounged for something to eat. Her mother and Brett were having dinner in town, so she was on her own. Leftover spaghetti looked promising, and since there was little else to choose from, she reheated it and ate standing up, looking out the window at her mother's flower beds.

They'll have to be cleaned up soon for winter. I can help with that, she was thinking when the phone rang.

"Have you had dinner?" Linc asked.

"Just finishing."

"How long's it been since you were at Jackson's?"

"Jackson's the ice-cream parlor?" She tried to remember the last time. "Not since I moved here, so gosh, I guess it's been years."

"I'm taking JoJo out for a treat, just the two of us. Maybe you could stop in while we're there."

"What time?"

"I'm just heading out to the boat now. We should be there by seven."

"I'll see you there."

Grace rinsed her plate and loaded it into the dishwasher, then went upstairs. She stood in front of the mirror in her mother's bedroom and took stock of her appearance. It had been months since she'd been concerned about how she looked. Correction: how she looked to a guy she was interested in. The truth was she hadn't been interested in anyone since Zach, and that seemed like a long time ago. Linc was different from her ex in a thousand ways, she thought as she hopped into the shower. Actually, she couldn't think of one way in which they were similar, and she took that as a good sign.

She dried her hair and stood in front of her closet, trying to decide what to wear. She picked out a nice pair of jeans and a pink-and-white-striped shirt with the sleeves rolled to her elbows. She put her hair up into a ponytail and tied it with a pretty scarf. A little more makeup than she usually wore. Sandals. She was early, so she went downstairs and called Natalie.

"Nat, when Chris left the bar the other night and went outside to make a call—did he call Linc?"

"He did. He's been pretty closemouthed about it, though. I asked him, and at first he just sort of shrugged me off, which he never does, though later he did acknowledge the call. I didn't press him. So I have no idea what's going on there, if that was going to be your next question."

"It was. Thanks. Gotta run."

Grace walked into town, and arrived at Front Street in time to see Linc's truck park in the municipal lot. She slowed her steps to a near crawl and watched as he crossed the street, hustling JoJo along, holding her hand. Grace waited until they disappeared into the ice-cream parlor before picking up her pace. When she entered the old-fashioned shop, she scanned the room and found them in a booth near the back. She walked over and pretended to be surprised to see them.

"Linc! How are you?" she exclaimed.

"Hey, Grace. I'm fine. How're you?" he returned the greeting. "JoJo, look who's here. Our friend Grace."

"Oh, JoJo's here, too. I'm so happy to see you."

"Want to join us? We were just looking at the menu."

"I'd love to. Thanks, Linc." Grace slid into the booth next to JoJo. "Do you love ice cream, like I do? What's your favorite flavor?" Not only did JoJo not respond, she didn't acknowledge Grace, who looked across the table at Linc for guidance. But he shrugged. He wasn't going to be much help, because he obviously had no more of a clue than Grace had.

"Okay, you two, listen up. This is what they have today." Linc read the list of the shop's special concoctions, but in the end, they each opted for a simple one-scoop dish. Linc went to the counter to put in their order.

Grace turned to JoJo. "I missed you on Saturday at the bookshop, JoJo. I brought someone to meet you, and she was disappointed you weren't there. So was I."

"Who?" she asked quietly.

"My niece was here just for the weekend. She's only four, so she's not as old as you. But I told her all about you, and she couldn't wait to meet you."

JoJo didn't respond.

"She doesn't know anyone in Wyndham Beach, so she was feeling shy and a little scared. So I told her she could share my chair with you, so the two of you could sit with me. I told her you were a special friend."

JoJo looked up into Grace's face as if wondering if that were true. "What's her name?"

"Daisy."

"That's a flower." JoJo almost smiled.

"It is. But it's also a name for a little girl."

"Is Daisy special, too?" JoJo looked up into Grace's eyes.

"Sure she is. She's my niece. Her mother is my sister."

Grace thought she could see wheels starting to turn.

"Like I'm Uncle Linc's niece because my mama is his sister?"

"Yes. Exactly like that. How clever of you to figure that out."

"Did your sister 'bandon Daisy so she had to come live with you?"

Grace wanted to put her head down on the tabletop and weep.

"No, sweetie. Daisy doesn't live with me. She lives far away, in Pennsylvania."

"Will she come back here?"

"I hope so but probably not for a while. I want her to because I want her to meet you. Then she'll have a friend here in Wyndham Beach, and she'll have someone to play with when she visits."

"It's sad when you feel like you don't have any friends," JoJo told Grace, whose heart cracked just a little more.

"It's very sad, Jo. You're right."

Linc returned to the table, his eyes first on his niece, then on Grace.

"Everything all right here?" he asked.

"I think so." Grace gently ran a hand over JoJo's hair. "Are we all right, JoJo?"

The little girl nodded and told Linc, "Grace has a niece, like I'm your niece, but she doesn't live here. When she comes to visit, we're going to be friends and play together."

"I think that would be great, Jo." Linc winked at Grace, and mouthed the words *thank you*. She winked back.

Linc's name was called, and he rose to get their orders. Chocolate for him, strawberry for Grace, mint chocolate chip with gummy bears for JoJo, who was chatting normally by the time they finished their ice cream.

Linc asked if Natalie was still there.

"No, they left this morning." She was dying to ask about that phone call from Chris, but she bit her tongue.

They were just about to get up to leave when an older woman walking past stopped and smiled at them. For a moment, Grace thought it might be someone Linc knew, but apparently not, because the woman said, "How nice to see such a beautiful family out together. My husband and I used to bring our daughter here. She's grown and moved away, and my husband's gone now, but thank you so much for the memory." She smiled at Linc, then at Grace, who'd opened her mouth to correct the woman, but before she could speak, Linc said, "Thank you for sharing that with us."

"God bless," the woman said before she walked away.

Grace looked at him as if to ask why he hadn't told the woman they weren't a family. He apparently read the question in her eyes. "It gave her a happy memory to see us the way she saw herself."

Grace nodded, wondering why she hadn't seen what he'd immediately recognized.

They walked out into the fading light, and Linc offered to drop her off on Cottage Street.

"It's a beautiful night, so I'll walk, but thank you."

"Thank *you*." He leaned over and placed a very soft, very tentative kiss, on her lips. "For Jo," he whispered.

"Glad I could help." Grace smiled. *For Jo? Right.*

~

Grace was at the shop two days later when her phone rang.

"Grace, it's Linc. I have your estimate here—I should have given it to you the other night when we were at Jackson's, but it slipped my mind. Do you have time to go over some numbers after work? Like around four thirty, maybe a little later?"

"I'm working until four thirty, but give me an extra fifteen minutes, and I'll meet you at the house."

"See you there."

She'd been working online for Liddy most of the day, filling orders that came in through the website and answering emails, so she'd worn dark-green cargo pants and a tan sweater with an old but very comfy pair of running shoes. At 4:36, she went into the powder room and brushed out her hair. She dabbed on a hint of lipstick and swiped mascara over her lashes.

"Well, where are we off to?" Liddy said when Grace passed the counter.

"I'm meeting Linc at the house, and he's going to give me the estimate for all the work I want done."

"Good luck. You might want to take a good stiff drink beforehand. You're going to need it," Liddy told her.

"Yeah, I know it's going to be a big number, but I'm prepared for it. I hope."

On Sunday afternoon, Grace and Natalie had taken Maggie's old patio set over to the little house and put it out back. The sisters had gotten to talk for a few minutes over a glass of wine, while Chris had taken Daisy to the pond to look for frogs and salamanders, but they'd left the small glass-topped table and the chairs on the patio.

While she waited for Linc, Grace put her laptop on the table, then opened it. She pulled up the photos of bathroom tiles she'd saved, still debating between the dark-blue and the dark-gray accent tiles, when she heard Linc's truck. She walked around the house to greet him, waiting while he got out of the truck's cab, a file in his hand.

"Hey." She watched him cross the ground between them. She liked the way he walked, tall and straight, a no-nonsense kind of walk, as if he always knew where he was going and what he was going to do once he got there. She liked a man with purpose.

He held up the file. "Ready for some pain?"

Grace laughed. "Come on back to the patio. I've been looking at some accent tiles for the bathroom and can't decide which would look best."

They rounded the back of the house, and she gestured to the chairs. "We have seating. And a little table. Would you like a glass of wine before you deliver the news?"

"You have wine? Here?"

"My sister and I have been known to share a bottle or two. The glasses are even clean."

"I'll pass, but you go ahead. You're the one who's going to need something to help soften the blow."

"Ouch."

Linc sat in one of the chairs and leaned over to look at the laptop's screen. "These are the tiles you're looking at?"

Grace nodded.

"Those are some pricey tiles."

"A girl can dream." She sat in the chair closest to him. "So give me the good news."

"Sorry, but I'm not here to give you good news," he quipped. "I'm about to give you a number that might break your heart."

"Hand it over." She held out a hand and he gave her the file. She opened it and skimmed the itemized numbers. She liked that he'd listed every single thing they'd talked about, how much each would cost, the charge for labor, and an estimate of how long each phase should take.

"I tried to trim it where I could, but honestly, it's a lot of work. And keep in mind that's an estimate. There's no telling what we might find once we get started."

"You did add the screened porch we talked about with the energy-efficient windows." She didn't like the additional cost, but she knew she'd be sorry if she didn't do it.

"Anything you want to take out? Any questions about anything?" he asked.

Grace shook her head. "No. It's about what I figured. We're going with it. I'm assuming you want a deposit."

He looked surprised she seemed okay with the bottom line. "I usually ask one-third up front, but we can make it a little less if—"

"No, it's okay, but thank you. I have my checkbook. Let me run inside." She got up and opened the door. "You sure you don't want a glass of wine? A beer?"

"A beer would be great, thanks."

She came back with her bag over her shoulder, a glass of wine in one hand and a bottle of beer in the other. Linc held the door for her, and took the bottle.

"How'd you keep this cold?" he asked.

"Cooler with a lot of ice." She put her wineglass on the table and got her checkbook from her bag. "I'm so excited, Linc. This is the first house that will be just mine." She dug around the bottom of the bag until her fingers located a pen. "I make it out to . . . ?"

"Shelby and Son."

She wrote out the check and handed it to him. He looked it over, then folded it and put it in his shirt pocket. "Can I use your pen?" he asked.

Grace handed it over, and Linc signed the contract attached to the estimate. He gave the pen and the paperwork back to her, and she signed it as well, then handed his copy to him.

"Bookselling is more lucrative than I thought." He slipped the piece of paper into the folder. "Sorry. None of my business."

"I don't mind. I'd be curious, too, if I owned a business like yours, and I had a contract for six figures with a customer whose only visible means of income was a part-time job in a bookshop." She put her copy of the contract into her bag and looped the strap over the back of the chair. "I have savings, some from the proceeds of the house I sold in Pennsylvania."

"I thought you said this was your first house?"

"I said it was the first place that was just mine. The house I sold was the house I'd bought with my ex-husband."

"I didn't know you'd been married."

"Almost ten years. We met in law school. Started dating, fell in love, married, and my dad hired us both at his firm after we graduated. Dad was a hell of a lawyer, a great man. An incredible father." Tears formed in the corners of her eyes, remembering him.

"Your dad passed away a few years ago, right?"

She nodded. "And that's when the shit hit the fan. He was barely in his grave when my husband told me he wanted a divorce. He waited until after my father died to tell me, because he was hoping Dad would pass the firm directly into my hands. When he realized that wasn't happening, he walked."

"He—" Linc looked dumbstruck. "He left you because—well, any reason for leaving you would be a lame one. He must be the biggest asshole on the planet."

Grace smiled, enjoying Linc's indignation on her behalf.

"Yes, he is. Because that's not all." Grace took a long sip of wine. "Come to find out he was having an affair with one of our paralegals."

Linc appeared speechless.

"Yeah," Grace said. "And to top it off, I found out she had hacked into my computer and stole some files. Long story I won't go into now, but suffice it to say she used the files to make me look badder than bad, like the most pathetic loser on the face of the earth."

"Holy—what did you do?"

"What could we do? We called the FBI and had her arrested."

Linc burst out laughing. "Remind me not to mess with you."

She took another sip of wine and watched him pick at the label on his bottle. "Anyway, my sister and I inherited some from the firm's sale, and he had a life insurance policy in our names, so I can buy my house and some pretty things for it." She grinned. "Plus I have my own business creating websites. Does your company have one?"

"We've never needed one. We've always gotten our business through word of mouth."

"You should think about it. I do one hell of a job."

"I just bet you do." He finished the beer, turning the empty bottle around in his hands for a long moment. "Grace, I'm sorry you had to go through all that. I can't believe any man is that stupid."

"Well, apparently there is one," she said.

"You're better off without him, if he's so blind he couldn't see—" Linc hesitated to finish the thought.

So of course she had to ask, "See what?"

"What he had in you."

"Thank you. That's very nice of you to say."

Then, because he may have thought he'd said more than he'd meant to say, he changed the subject. "So how was the visit with your sister?"

"It was great. And Chris came home. Chris Dean?" She watched his face for a reaction, but there was none. "They finally told the moms they were dating, and it's obvious they're serious about each other, to the delight of both said moms." She paused, then added as if she'd just remembered: "He asked for your phone number."

Linc nodded but didn't comment.

Grace couldn't let it go. Her curiosity was getting the best of her. "He called you Friday night from Dusty's, didn't he?" It really wasn't a question.

"Yes, he called."

"I think he was hoping you'd come out and join us. It sounded as if he wanted to see you again."

"I guess."

She stared at him, willing him to elaborate. When he didn't, she said, "I didn't realize you were such good friends."

Linc laughed. "Grace, you are about as subtle as a sledgehammer. If you want to know why he called, just ask."

"Okay. I'm asking. Even though we both know it's none of my business, which you could remind me, but you apparently have much better manners."

Linc took a deep breath and peeled a little more paper from the bottle he still held. "Chris and I were really good friends all through school. He and I actually started his first band together."

"Wait." Had she heard correctly? "You were in a band with Chris Dean? Seriously?"

315

"Yup. Sometimes we practiced out on the island, where the noise wouldn't bother anyone, other times in someone's garage. We wrote a bunch of songs together and played at parties, and it was all fun and games. Then we graduated, Chris went off to college, and I didn't. I stayed home because my mom had died three years earlier, and my dad was at loose ends, and my sister was in all kinds of trouble. Chris wanted me to play with them on the weekends, but I couldn't. I was going to community college at night and trying to help my dad during the day and trying to keep the lid on Brenda. So Chris found someone else to play in my place, and that's history. The guy who replaced me is still with Chris."

"So, in other words, if you had stayed with him, you'd be a member of DEAN now?"

"Yeah."

"Yow, that's heavy, Linc." She could hardly believe anyone would give up an opportunity like that and not be bitter over what could have been. She couldn't help herself from asking, "How do you feel about that?"

"How do you think I feel? Pretty crappy, actually, if I let myself go there, which I try not to do. And for the most part, I don't think about it. If I had to do it again, I know I'd make the same decision. I couldn't walk out on my dad. My mom's death was a real blow to him. I missed my mother, and I grieved for her, but my father was really having a hard time." Linc stared off in the direction of the pond. "And Brenda was being Brenda, with no regard for anyone but herself."

"I hope you don't think he called you the other night to rub it in, because that's so not who Chris is."

"What? Oh, no. Nothing like that." Linc grew quiet for a moment. "Actually, he wanted me to record a couple of songs with them. Some things we wrote together back in high school. He said he just ran across them in a folder he was going through. He said the songs were better than he remembered." Linc smiled wryly. "They must be, because I don't remember they were very good."

"Not Lennon and McCartney?"

"More like Beavis and Butt-Head. Anyway, he wanted to get together and maybe revise them a little, then record them in his studio. Maybe have me perform with them live sometimes, as like a guest guitarist."

Grace's jaw dropped. "I hope you said yes."

"I would have loved to, but I have three good reasons to say no. Four, if you count my dad's business, which I've pretty much taken over so the man can have a life. The next job up is yours, by the way. I'm sure you'd love to have me put that on hold indefinitely."

"You want to do it, though."

"Grace, I can't even go there."

"Wow. Just . . . wow." She stared at him with a combination of admiration and disbelief. Had she ever known anyone so selfless? She was beginning to think this may be a man worth having, worth keeping. "Okay, let's think this through. There has to be a way." She tapped her fingers on the side of her glass. "Where's his studio?"

"California."

"Maybe you could go for a couple of long weekends," she suggested.

"Sure." His guard down, he sounded glum, as he was entitled. "Because Chris has nothing better to do than to plan his life around me."

"You might be surprised. You know the old saying: if you don't ask, the answer is always no."

"Grace, even if he agreed to work with me Thursday through Monday . . . I can't leave my dad with three kids for four days."

"So leave him with Duffy and leave the girls with someone else."

"There isn't anyone else. That's the bottom line."

"You're wrong. There's your dad, and there's me." She bit her lip, thinking. "The kids are in school all day Friday and Monday, right? So it's just Friday night through Monday morning they'd need to be with someone. Duffy could stay with your dad, and I'll take JoJo and Bliss. My mom would love it."

"That's a lot to ask of someone." He forced a smile. "And besides, Bliss hates you."

"Pshaw. I'll win her over."

Finally, a genuine smile. "Does anyone really say *pshaw*?"

Grace laughed. "Listen, we could make this work for you."

"No way I could ask—"

"You're not asking. I'm offering. Let me be your bottom line." Grace grabbed his arm. "This is a once-in-a-lifetime opportunity to do something you've wanted to do for a long time. A chance to go back and say yes, like you wish you could have back then. Go ahead, Linc. Do it."

"You sound like the bad angel, you know that?" He tapped his shoulder where a bad angel might sit.

"Oh, I'm a very good angel. Linc, the only thing holding you back is you."

"I haven't played in a long time."

"Then I guess you'd better go home, dust off that guitar, and start practicing."

He stood up and put his arms around her, and she leaned into him. He just held her for a while, and she knew he was trying to decide if he could make that leap of faith. She decided to take a leap of her own. She stood on her tiptoes and kissed him on the lips.

If he was surprised, he didn't show it. He kissed her without hesitation, as if he'd been thinking about it long before tonight.

When she finally pulled back, he looked down at her and asked, "You know if I do this, it'll take time away from working on your house."

"Do what you have to do. The house will be there, and so will I."

~

Grace was in an exceptionally good mood when she came into the bookshop the following morning.

"Something going on I should know about?" Liddy asked.

"Nope. Just in a good mood."

"Great. Would you take the register for me? I see Dylan's here, and I want to show him what I'd like him to do this morning."

"Sure." Grace turned the iPad around and hummed as she watched Rosalita. She greeted the two women who were the first of the day's customers with a big smile and pointed out the newest of the new releases that had come in over the weekend.

While the women walked through the shop, she opened the newspaper Dylan had left on the counter and scanned the front page. One article in particular caught her eye.

Motions Filed in Case Against Coach Accused of Assaulting Local Girls

Lawyers for Kenneth Bowers, the former girls' basketball coach at Mid-Coast Regional High School, have filed motions seeking additional time in which to complete discovery while the defendant undergoes psychiatric evaluation. Bowers has been accused of sexual assault by members of the team going back to 2010. So far, ten former students have come forward to make allegations against Bowers, who began coaching at the high school in 2000 . . .

Grace was on the verge of throwing up. Her hands shook, and she tried to turn off the voice in her head that repeated what she didn't want to know. She managed to get through the entire day, but immediately upon leaving the shop, she went directly to her mother's and right up to her room. She opened her laptop and pulled up every reference she could find to Kenneth Bowers and the case against him. She made notes as she read, and she wept. The alleged assaults were believed to have begun in 2010, but the first victim to accuse Bowers came forward in 2019. Once her story was made public, other victims came forward.

Grace stared at the screen, trying to put it all together. When everything finally came into focus, a terrible truth was staring her in the face.

The first *reported* assault occurred in 2010, but Grace knew an earlier assault had occurred in 2003, because she knew who the victim had been.

But what to do about what she knew?

She went downstairs into the kitchen, where her mother was making dinner.

"Oh, Gracie. I didn't hear you come in. I wish I'd known," Maggie exclaimed. "I just finished FaceTiming with Daisy. And she was so cute! She was showing me what she . . ." Maggie glanced over her shoulder and stopped in midsentence when she looked at Grace. "Sweetie, what's wrong?"

"Mom, did Jessie leave a suicide note?" Grace asked quietly.

"What?" Maggie turned around sharply. "Grace, what in heaven's name made you think about that?"

"Did she, Mom?"

Maggie nodded. "Yes. Jim found it in Jess's hand."

"Did Liddy tell you what it said?"

Maggie put down the knife she was using to chop onions. "It said, *It's all my fault. I should have told. I'm so sorry.*"

Grace covered her face with her hands and burst into tears.

"Grace, what is going on?"

"Mom, I think I know why Jessie killed herself."

Maggie sat on one of the barstools at the kitchen island and pulled Grace over to sit on the one next to her. "Tell me."

"Remember how when we were little, Jess and I were so close?"

"Of course. You two were inseparable in the summers."

"Until we got to high school. Then I'd only spend a week or so here because we either went somewhere on vacation with Dad, or I was on a study-abroad trip."

"Right. You went to France in your junior year and Spain when you were a senior."

"So I'd come up here with you and Natalie for the first week or so of the summer, and then I'd leave. That's when Jessie and I started to drift apart. I'd leave and she'd have a job, so even when I was here, we didn't spend as much time together. We still considered ourselves best friends, but the truth was, by senior year in high school, we didn't spend much time together. And after we both started college, we just didn't see each other at all. I started working in Dad's office in the summers, and when I was in law school, I interned with the DA, remember?"

"I do."

Grace got up and poured herself a glass of water. She leaned back against the counter.

"That last summer—right after we'd both graduated high school—I only spent one day with Jess. It was the day before I left for Spain. I called her and asked her if she wanted to go to the beach. We met up on Cottage Street Beach like we used to do." Grace nervously took a sip of water. Even talking about it made her feel sick. "We were talking about what we were doing for the rest of the summer, and how it felt to be out of high school and going off to college, and all of a sudden, Jessie burst into tears. She told me she'd had an affair with her basketball coach, how he'd told her he was in love with her, and always made excuses for her to come to his office after practice. How he talked her into having sex with him. She knew it was a mistake and regretted it as soon as it happened, but he wouldn't let her break it off. He told me he'd taken pictures of her while they were having sex, and he threatened to send the pictures to her parents."

"Oh my God, Grace. I can't even . . ." Maggie's face was white, and her hands shook.

"I told Jess she had to tell her parents anyway: 'You can't let him get away with what he's done to you.'"

"What did she say?"

"She said she would, that night. She promised me."

"But she couldn't have. If Liddy'd known Jess had been a victim, she'd have gone right to the police."

"Which means Jess lied to me and Liddy doesn't know. Mom, I think Jess was horrified when the story broke. I think she looked at the long list of girls who'd been abused by this guy and thought if she'd told back when it happened to her, he wouldn't have been around to assault anyone else. I believe she felt responsible for every one of them, and I think the guilt was more than she could bear." Grace stared at the floor. "If she couldn't face her parents with the fact it had happened to her, she damn well wasn't going to face them after all these other girls had been hurt. She wouldn't have wanted them to know she could have stopped it before it happened to someone else."

"So she started saving the pills she was given for her back pain until she could take them all at once. Poor Jess." Maggie pressed a hand over her heart. "Oh God, this is just all too horrible."

"Mom, do I tell Liddy? Is it better for her to know, or better for her to always be wondering?"

Maggie shook her head slowly, side to side. "I don't know."

~

Grace excused herself from dinner. She had no appetite. Restless, she walked to Jasper Street. She wanted to sit out back and watch the sun sink behind the pond and the trees and try to find some semblance of peace. But when she got there, Linc's truck was in the driveway. She went inside and found him in the front room.

"You're here late," she said.

"I hope you don't mind. You asked me about a fireplace, and it's occurred to me there should have been several. Given the age of the house, it just doesn't make sense there isn't one."

"Let me know if you find one."

He was staring at the ceiling. "I might be able to find some evidence of chimneys on the roof."

"Good luck."

Grace wandered outside and down to the pond. She stood with her hands in her pockets, thinking about Jessie. On the one hand, she felt an overwhelming sadness. On the other, she was infuriated Jess had taken her life and she'd broken her promise to Grace.

"You think you're at fault for what happened to all those other girls? You aren't responsible. *He's* responsible," she whispered as night began to close in. "You were seventeen years old, Jess. How could you have known he'd do this again and again?"

Grace remembered making her mother drive past the Bryants' house on their way to the airport for her flight the morning she left. She'd called Jess and told her to go out front so they could wave goodbye.

"Mom, slow down," she'd told Maggie when she saw Jessie standing at the foot of the Bryants' driveway.

Grace had rolled down her window and mouthed the words, *Did you tell her?* Jess had smiled and given her a thumbs-up.

But Jessie had lied. If Liddy had known the truth, Bowers would have been in prison a long time ago. Or he'd be dead, and Liddy'd be in prison.

Grace wrapped her arms around her middle and cried.

"Hey, Grace—you okay?" Linc stepped out the back door. "Stupid question. Of course you're not."

For a minute, Linc appeared to not know what to do. He stood by and watched helplessly, then slowly put his arms around her and held her until the tears stopped.

"I'm sorry. I'm really sorry." She looked for something to blot away the wet spot her tears had left on his shoulder.

"It's okay. I've gotten used to tears. JoJo cries a lot. She even cries in her sleep. I know she misses her mother, but I can't make it better for her. I can't make Brenda come back." His frustration was clear in every word. "But I hold her and let her cry, so she knows someone cares she's hurting. So I'm good at that. You can always cry on my shoulder, Grace."

"Do you think it's better for the kids to know or to not know why their mother left them? Would it be better for them to know the truth?"

"If I knew for certain, I would tell them," he said without hesitation. "Truth trumps lies every time."

"Even if the truth is very hurtful? Even if it makes the pain worse?"

"When something terrible happens to you, right off, there's going to be pain whether you're told the truth or a lie. If you're told a lie, it'll hurt all over again once the truth comes out, and sooner or later, it always does. If you know the truth, maybe you can begin to understand, and if you can understand, maybe you can forgive the person who hurt you." He leaned back and looked into Grace's eyes. "The kids might be a little too young to understand now, but they'll grow up. Better to grow up with the truth."

"Do you know where your sister is?"

"I have a gut feeling. I think she's in rehab, but I don't know where. Brenda's husband, Don—the kids' father—was a drug dealer. He was arrested and is serving a long prison term. I know Brenda has a heavy-duty addiction. When I saw her, I hardly recognized her. She looked like someone else. Brenda was a beautiful girl before she hooked up with Don Brown." His face told her exactly how much he'd been affected by her appearance. "Maybe him getting locked up was like a light bulb going off in her head. Like, if she didn't straighten herself out, she'd be in prison eventually, or she'd be dead. Either way, she'd lose her kids, and they'd end up in foster care. I don't know for sure, but I like to think she's somewhere getting herself clean so she can come back and be part of her kids' lives. Part of our family again." Linc held Grace close and rested his chin on the top of her head.

"You think she's in rehab now?"

"I want to believe that. The whole thing happened so fast, there wasn't much time for Q and A. First there's the phone call telling me to come quick, to meet her in a park. She sounded so desperate, I couldn't imagine what was happening. So I drove like a bat out of hell, and when I got there, she just told the kids to get out of her car and into my truck. No real explanation, just, 'You have to take my kids. Don't try to find me and don't contact Don. I don't want him to know where they are. I don't want him in their lives. He'll ruin them the same way he ruined me.' Then she drove away."

"Do you think they know their father's in prison?"

"I don't know what they were told. They've never mentioned him around me or my dad, so I have to wonder if maybe they're glad he's out of the picture."

"Would they be upset if they knew Brenda was in rehab?"

"I honestly don't know. But what if she's not? What if she's still addicted and out on the streets? What if she never gets clean and the worst happens, and she never comes back?" His anguish and fear for his sister's life came through loud and clear.

As much as Grace's heart grieved for Jessie, she couldn't help but feel pain for the Shelby family. For the kids who'd been sent to live with an uncle and a grandfather they barely knew. For Linc, who instead of chasing his dream had stayed home after high school to try to keep his sister out of trouble and help his father keep his feet on the ground. For Tuck, who hadn't been able to protect his adored little girl from her dangerous instincts. And for Brenda, whose bad decisions had ended with her passing off the responsibility for her children.

Grace stayed anchored in Linc's arms until she felt strong enough to do what she knew had to be done. She took a few steps back, and he let her go. "Thank you, Linc."

"For what?"

"For helping me understand what I have to do." She held his face in her hands for a moment, then kissed him before heading for home.

I should have asked him if he called Chris, she thought as she turned off Jasper onto Church Street. *I should have asked him if he'd found his guitar.* But all she could think about was the parallels between Jessie and Brenda, and how their choices had created such chaos in their own lives as well as their families'.

When she got home, Grace found her mother in the backyard. She went out onto the deck and announced, "I think we need to tell Liddy, Mom. It's eaten her alive to not know."

"I came to the same realization," Maggie said. "When will you tell her?"

"It might as well be tonight." Grace suddenly felt weary, overcome with dread, but determined to see this through.

"Want me to come with you?" Maggie didn't wait for Grace's reply to start toward the house.

"Yes, please, Mom. She's going to need you. And so will I."

Chapter Seventeen

When Liddy's doorbell rang at nine thirty at night, she assumed she'd find Jim or Tuck on the porch when she opened the door. She wasn't prepared to see Grace and Maggie, but she welcomed their company. Her first thought was to make a batch of margaritas to enjoy on the deck before the nights became too cold. But when they stepped inside, Liddy was taken aback at their appearance.

"You two look like you've lost your best . . ." She took in a sharp breath. "Oh God, what happened?" Both hands flew to her heart. "Did something happen to Natalie? Daisy?"

"No, no. They're fine," Maggie said.

"Emma, then? Chris?" Liddy couldn't imagine anything less that could put such sorrow on Maggie's face.

"No. Liddy, listen—"

"I'm listening, but hurry up. I've exhausted the list of family."

"Not exactly," Grace said. "Liddy, can we go into the kitchen and sit down?"

"Well, sure, but someone better tell me what the hell's going on." Liddy led the way into the kitchen, where Maggie and Grace each took a seat. Before joining them, Liddy asked, "Water? Coffee? Wine?"

"Nothing, thanks." Maggie reached over and took Liddy by the hand, and pulled her over to the vacant chair next to hers. "Liddy, just come sit here by me. Grace has something to tell you."

The first thing Liddy noticed was that Grace's eyes were red rimmed. The second was that her bottom lip was trembling. Obviously whatever Grace had to say wasn't good news.

"What, Gracie?"

Grace said in the softest voice possible, "Liddy, I think—I mean, I'm pretty sure I've figured out why Jessie felt she had to take her life."

"What?" Liddy snatched her hand from Maggie's. "What are you talking about? How could you possibly know?"

"Just listen. I saw a newspaper article today. It was about this coach who's been arrested for assaulting some of his students."

"Kenneth Bowers. What's he got to do with Jessie?"

"Jessie was on the basketball team. He was her coach the second year after he started at Mid-Coast Regional."

"So, what, you think he assaulted Jess just because she played basketball? That's a stretch." Liddy turned to Maggie. "I can't believe you brought her down here to toss out this supposition."

"It's not supposition, Liddy."

Anger built in Liddy. "You always did have an overactive imagination, Grace, but this time, you've taken it too far. It's hurtful." Liddy stared at Grace, who normally had such a kind nature. It was unlike her to do something like this. "How did you come up with something so outlandish? Why in God's name would you think Jess was one of his victims?"

"Because she told me she was." Grace's voice was barely above a whisper.

"Jess told you . . . what, in a dream?" Liddy scoffed and got out of her chair. She'd loved Grace like a second daughter, but she'd heard enough. She was just about to ask them both to leave when she saw the tears streaming down Grace's face. The room was so quiet she could hear cicadas hitting the overhead light on the front porch.

"Liddy, please listen. She told me when I was here that summer right after we'd both graduated high school. I was going in a study-abroad program, and I was only going to be here for a few days."

Liddy sat back down slowly. "I remember."

"Jess and I spent the day before I left at the beach, and it was almost like old times. Among other things that day, she told me she was happy to be out of school because it meant her coach wouldn't make her have sex with him anymore."

"Stop. Just stop." Liddy's face went white. "She told you this? She said . . . ?"

Grace nodded.

Liddy covered her face with her hands. When the anger hit, it hit hard. She exploded. "You've known about this all this time and *you didn't tell me*? You knew all along? You *KNEW*?"

"When she told me what happened, I asked her if she'd told you and she said no. He told her he had photos of her that she wouldn't want you to see," Grace said softly, trying to remain composed in the face of Liddy's anger. "I said she had to tell you anyway. That you wouldn't care about the pictures—you only cared about her. I made her promise to tell you that night, and she said she would. I had no reason to think she hadn't. Jess and I didn't see each other for years, and we grew apart, so we never spoke of it again. She was in Boston painting, and I was in Philadelphia practicing law. Liddy, if I'd thought for one moment she hadn't told you, I would have."

"But you knew she'd taken her life. You had to think it was connected to . . ." Liddy wasn't aware of the tears that were falling.

"Even if I'd thought there was a connection, I thought you knew. I had no idea what her life had been like, what other things might have happened during all those years we didn't see each other. It wasn't until I read the story in the newspaper I started putting things together. I still wasn't one hundred percent positive, so I pulled up everything about the case I could find on the internet. Jess could have been the first girl he abused, or there could have been someone before her who still hasn't come forward. I think when she realized how many others had been hurt after her . . . I think she sank under the guilt. I checked the date the story broke against the date of her death. She died a little more than two weeks after the story hit the news."

Liddy was speechless. Could Grace be right? Had that horrible man done to her daughter what he'd done to the others? She couldn't believe Jess hadn't told her, that she'd kept it to herself all those years. She was about to tell Grace she was wrong—she must have misunderstood—when she thought of the note Jim had found in Jess's hand.

It's all my fault. I should have told. I'm so sorry.

A sob broke from her throat, and she leaned against the back of the chair to keep from falling over as the truth became clear: Jessie had believed her silence had permitted Bowers to move on to abusing other girls in the same manner in which he'd abused her. If not for the bravery of the last girl he'd assaulted, he would still be getting away with it.

Liddy fought to control her anger and the terrible pain sweeping through her. She wiped her eyes with the tissue Maggie handed her and looked toward the heavens as if asking for strength. "But why didn't she trust us? Why didn't she tell us?" She looked at Grace as if expecting her to answer.

"I can only guess she was ashamed of what happened, that she thought somehow she was responsible for it. This guy Bowers groomed her very carefully. She told me he said he was in love with her, he couldn't live without her. Maybe at first she was flattered, but by the time she realized it was a mistake, he threatened her, and I guess she thought there was no way out.

"When I was between my second and third years in law school, I interned with the local district attorney's office. There were several cases similar to this one. These guys all follow the same pattern, and Bowers followed it to a T. Jess wasn't responsible for what happened to her, any more than any of the other girls were responsible for what happened to them. I wish with all my heart we'd remained close. She might have confided in me when the story broke. I could have been there for her."

"My poor baby. My poor girl. To have had to endure that abuse, and then years later to have it all come back in such a terrible way." Liddy crossed her forearms on the tabletop, rested her head on them, and wept, Maggie gently rubbing her back and saying all the things your best friend said when your heart was breaking. Finally, when she was for the moment cried out, she lifted her head and asked, "Did you catch the name of the woman from the DA's office who's prosecuting the case?"

"It started with a *P*. Perry? No, I think it was Priest," Grace said. "I don't remember her first name."

Liddy got up and looked for her phone. "I'm calling the courthouse."

"Liddy, it's almost ten o'clock at night," Maggie pointed out. "The courthouse is closed. There's time enough to call in the morning."

Liddy nodded and drank from the glass Grace had set out for her.

"I'm all right. Thank you, Grace, for telling me. I hated hearing it, but I believe you're right. It's the only thing that makes sense. Her dying within a few weeks of the story breaking—that can't be a coincidence. Up until then, she'd seemed really happy. She'd been painting more than she had been in a long time, and it was the best work she'd ever done."

"Liddy, I'm so sorry. I hated to tell you. But—"

"I know you did. I know it wasn't easy for you, but you were right to tell me. At least now I know the truth. It's going to haunt me as long as I live, but at least I know. Not knowing was harder." Liddy wrapped her arms around Grace and hugged her hard.

"Thank you for not shooting the messenger." A drained and weary Grace let Liddy hold on to her.

"Are you all right, Lids?" Maggie, too, looked worn out from the emotional hour that had just passed.

"I'll be okay." Liddy released her hold on Grace.

"Do you want me to stay with you tonight?" Maggie's face creased with concern. "Honey, you shouldn't be alone tonight."

"Thanks for offering." Liddy patted Maggie's arm and walked them to the door. "But I won't be."

~

She was still sitting at the kitchen table when the doorbell rang. Her legs felt like wooden sticks as she slowly walked to the front door and opened it.

"I got here as quickly as I could." An ashen-faced Jim took her hands. "What happened?"

"Come inside. There's something you need to hear."

Liddy repeated the story Grace had told earlier. Jim listened, never interrupting, but his face reflected the pain as he began to understand what had driven their beloved daughter to take her life. When she finished, Jim got up and walked outside to the deck. Seconds later, the sound of his sobs filled the room. Liddy gave him some time alone before joining him. He was seated at the end of one of the lounges, his arms hanging loosely between his knees, his head down. She knew his pain was as fierce and as sharp as hers.

"Jim, talk to me." Liddy sat behind him on the lounge and wrapped an arm around his middle.

He shook his head.

"You realize not talking is what drove us apart? Not sharing how we felt is what led to our divorce. For many people, it's infidelity, or money, or problems with jobs or the kids. For us, it was the silence. And you're doing it again, Jim. You're going off alone with your pain and leaving me alone to deal with mine." Liddy spoke quietly, but she was pretty sure he was getting the message.

"I don't know what to say."

"Well, that's a start. I can't think of anything that would make a difference, but maybe we can start with how we feel about Bowers."

"I want him to be put away forever. I want him to never see the light of day again. I want him to be in solitary for the rest of his life. No one to talk to. No one to give a shit about him. It might make me feel better on one level if all the fathers could get together with baseball bats and take a shot at him. But whatever pain he'd be feeling would eventually pass. I'd rather have him suffer for a longer time. So lock him up in a tiny room all by himself for as long as he lives. So he'll know that every day for the rest of his life will be the same. That's the worst punishment I can think of." Jim stared off into the dark night. "Pedophiles are the lowest of the low in the prison population. If he's ever out of his cell, he'll be a sitting duck. Maybe from time to time someone there will get to him, beat him up a little. Then he can go back into his little five-by-eight room and lick his wounds. Until the next time."

"You're surprising me. You're the most nonviolent man I ever met."

"What that man did to our girl . . . what he took from her . . . and all the others . . ." Jim's voice cracked. "What he took from us. I have no qualms about wishing the worst on him for the rest of his life. His victims suffered, their parents have all suffered. I think he needs to suffer, too." Jim sounded weary, as if merely putting words to thoughts was an effort. "So what do we do about this revelation? Where do we go from here?"

"First thing tomorrow we call the district attorney's office, and we ask to meet with the ADA who is handling the case. We tell her we've just discovered what Bowers had done to Jess so she'll add Jessie's name to the list of victims," Liddy thought aloud. "We can't bring Jess back, but we can seek justice for her."

"How do we get through the rest of this night?"

Liddy thought about it for a while. Then she stood and took Jim's hand and pulled him off the lounge. "By remembering how full and happy our lives were when we still had Jess. A few months ago, I found some photos from when she was in grade school. I'd like to share them

333

with you. Sometimes the only way through a bad time is to think about the good times. You up for that?"

Jim sighed. "I'm game if you are."

"Well, come on then. Maybe you could make a fire while I get us something to drink, and then we can sit on the sofa together and look at pictures and talk about our girl." Jim's hand still in hers, Liddy opened the back door and went into the kitchen. "I think she'd like that."

~

When Liddy called in the morning, the ADA's assistant told her to leave a message, and if there was time later in the day, she'd get a callback.

"We're calling about the Bowers case," Liddy explained. "We believe our daughter was one of his first victims."

There was a long pause before the woman on the other end told her, "That's ADA Priest's case, but she isn't in right now."

"We'd like her to return our call. Please. Tell her it's important."

Liddy and Jim spent most of the day pacing, waiting for the phone to ring.

"I might just as well have gone into the bookshop instead of paying Evelyn to open up and stay the day," Liddy complained after several hours passed without a callback.

The call came right after Liddy'd prepared a late lunch and Jim helped her take it out onto the deck.

"This is Linnea Priest from the county DA's office. I'm returning a call to Lydia Bryant." The woman spoke briskly, a right-to-the-point tone in her voice.

"Thank you. I'm putting this on speaker so my husband can be part of the call." Liddy took a deep breath, and launched right in. "Our daughter, Jessica Bryant, graduated from Mid-Coast Regional High School in 2004. She was a member of the basketball team coached by

Kenneth Bowers. We believe she may have been his first victim." Liddy spoke calmly and directly.

"Why do you believe that, Mrs. Bryant?" The ADA was still all business.

"Because she told someone she was."

"Recently?" The note of skepticism was apparent.

"No. Early in the summer of 2004. Right after graduation."

"If this is true, I'm going to need to speak with your daughter directly. Where is she now? Tell me how to contact her, and I'll have an investigator take her statement."

"That won't be possible. Jessica—our daughter—took her own life a few weeks after this story made the news. We think she took her life because she felt guilty about not coming forward earlier. That she could have prevented the trauma the other victims went through." Liddy's heart was pounding, and her mouth was dry. "We didn't even know."

Liddy related the story Grace had told her. When she was finished, she said, "We want her name added to the list of his victims."

The attorney was silent for a long moment. "Your story—your daughter's story—certainly sounds plausible, especially since she told someone the year it happened. But we won't be able to add your daughter—"

"Jessica. Jessica Bryant."

"Your daughter, Jessica, to the case. It won't be admissible."

"Why not? I know in my heart this is what happened. If you'd known my daughter, you'd know what a caring, responsible, sensitive young woman she was. She was happy, she was an artist, she—"

"Mr. and Mrs. Bryant, I'm sure she was all that and more." Linnea Priest's tone softened. "I understand completely, and I am terribly sorry for your loss. But without your *daughter's* testimony, the judge would never allow it."

"But her friend—the person she told—she'll testify."

"Without any evidence, it will still be viewed as hearsay, and the defense attorney will object, and the court will agree. I am so sorry. You have my deepest sympathy. But I cannot add her as a victim."

"I—we understand," Jim said. "But it's very difficult for us not to have justice in our daughter's name."

"I appreciate your position. I sincerely do. But I hope you will find some small measure of comfort in knowing that justice will be served. For all the young women who have come forward, as well as those who have chosen to remain silent, or who for whatever reason will not be heard in court." Priest paused. "But I can tell you this, and it will come out at trial: I don't believe Jessica was his first victim. He coached at a high school in Michigan, and before that, in Indiana. He left both schools in haste."

"So someone knew what he was before he even came here?" Jim asked, incredulous.

"We're still investigating." She put her hand over the phone for a few seconds, then said, "I apologize, but I have a meeting, and I'm already late. I appreciate your call, and I will remember your daughter when this case comes up for trial. If there is any way to bring this before the court, I'll be in touch. Take care."

"Thank you. And thank you for taking the time to speak with us," Liddy said right before the line went dead.

Liddy and Jim stood facing each other, their silence another obstacle between them. Finally, Liddy said, "You know what this means, right? If it's true Bowers did this before, that Jessie wasn't the first victim . . . it means she didn't have to feel guilty. She didn't need to . . ."

"You can't think that way. She had no way of knowing if she'd been the first. She believed her silence was the reason other girls were hurt. Knowing what we know now, maybe she was right."

"The girls he'd assaulted before he came here—if they'd told—he wouldn't have been at Mid-Coast Regional and Jessie—"

"We can't go there, Liddy. We can't blame them any more than the girls who filed the lawsuit should blame Jessie."

"But if—" Liddy protested.

"There are no ifs. These are kids. Jess was seventeen, so I suspect the others were about the same age. Yes, of course they should have told their parents or a teacher or the police. That's obvious to us, as adults. But kids aren't known for always recognizing the long-term consequences of their actions. And something like this—I'm sure they felt embarrassed, ashamed, frightened. Jess told Grace he'd threatened her.

"I wish everyone had done the right thing—the first victim had spoken out, the schools where he'd taught before had blown the whistle on him instead of protecting their district from lawsuits." He paused to think. "Of course, we don't know they weren't sued, or threatened with a suit and maybe settled out of court. There's a reason he was terminated at two schools before he came here, and I think before this case is over, the truth will come out. We have to trust that ADA Priest will let us know." Jim brushed away a tear. "But the bottom line is, nothing will make a difference. Jessie will still be gone."

Liddy decided to go to her shop. She needed to focus on something other than herself, and, she had to admit, she wanted Jim to leave, and there was no graceful way to ask him to go. She'd gone upstairs to take a shower, and when she came back downstairs, she was dressed for work. She found Jim on the front porch.

"My granddad used to sit right here in the afternoons and watch the birds build their nests in the maple trees that used to grow along the driveway. He always said it was relaxing, made him feel like he didn't have a care in the world. Now I know what he meant," Jim said when she closed the door behind her.

"Yes, it's peaceful here. Listen, Jim, I need a distraction. I'm going to the bookshop. I'll call you if I hear anything from the DA's office, but I don't expect to. Not for a while, anyway." Liddy tried tactfully to make it clear it was time for him to go. "Thanks for coming last night."

"Thanks for calling me and letting me crash in the guest room." Jim leaned back against the rocking chair, his eyes closed. Evidently, he didn't take the hint.

She was trying to find a way to let him know he should probably leave.

"I want you to know I meant what I said. I still love you. I never stopped." His eyes still closed, he said, "Can we try again? Do you think it's too late to go back to what we had?"

He opened his eyes and sat forward in the chair. "Don't answer now. Please just give it some thought before you make a decision."

Liddy hadn't really wanted to get into a discussion just then, but she knew Jim deserved an answer. "I thought about this most of the night last night. I just can't get past what I felt when you left me. Every time I think back on that day, I feel that pain all over again, that sense of desertion."

"So you're saying you can't forgive and forget?"

"I can forgive, but I don't know how I could ever forget. I just don't think it would work, Jim," she said softly. "I'm sorry."

"So you're saying this is it?"

"I'm afraid so."

"I guess I understand. I just wish things were different." Jim stood and moved toward the front steps, ready at last to leave. He'd taken his one last shot. He kissed her as if he knew it was the last time. He went down the steps, paused on the sidewalk, then turned back to her. "You know where to find me if you change your mind."

"Thanks, Jim, but it's not likely. We both need to move on."

The sound of music drew their attention to the driveway. They both watched as Tuck parked his truck behind Liddy's car.

Jim glanced back at Liddy. "Looks like you already have."

He cut across the lawn to his car and got in without looking back.

～

"This will probably be the last time this year we'll be sitting here in shorts and T-shirts, so let's enjoy this warm spell while it lasts. It's supposed to be in the mid to low forties tomorrow." Liddy poured from a pitcher of margaritas into glasses that she then passed around. One to Emma, then one to Maggie. She lifted the third in a toast. "To the three of us. Long may we wave."

"Was that a pun?" Emma turned her left arm to show off her tattoo, the three waves that represented the three of them and all they'd been through together.

"Well, we are as unchanging and as deep as the sea," Maggie said solemnly, then laughed. "Sorry. I can't say that with a straight face."

"We have our deep moments," Liddy said. "And in some respects, we haven't changed at all in the years we've known each other."

"True. Here's to us." Emma raised her glass and took a sip.

Maggie unwrapped the platter of goodies she'd brought to share: a round of brie encased in puff pastry, a layer of raspberry jam under the pastry, toasted slices of baguette, and some green grapes. Liddy set out small plates and a stack of napkins, then added a knife to the cheese plate. "Help yourselves. The cheese is still warm. I just took it out of the oven before I drove over."

"Oh, yum." Emma dived in. "This is the best. Drinks and snacks with my besties on this beautiful deck."

"Em, I don't think grown-ups say *besties*," Liddy told her.

"Lids, I don't think adults say *grown-ups*," Maggie noted.

"I don't care. That's who you are. You're my people. My bestest people," Emma told them.

"Oh, well, *bestest* is much better." Liddy nodded. "Much more acceptable for a woman of your age and station."

"I have no station, and I'm feeling old as Stonehenge," Emma grumbled.

"What have you got to be cranky about? We know you're over the moon that Chris's secret girlfriend turned out to be Nat." Liddy spread brie on a slice of bread. "Isn't that what you always wanted, Em?"

"Yes, of course. I'm just feeling out of sorts because the plans I had for our little artists' colony here in Wyndham Beach are getting all mucked up."

"No applicants?" Maggie asked.

"Too many applicants. Excellent prospects and nowhere to put them all. Which means I have to choose among them, and I just can't." Emma took a sip of her margarita, then took another. "I hate to be the one who has to shatter someone's dreams. They're all worthy." She waved her hand as if to dismiss the subject. "I'll think of something." She turned her attention to Liddy. "So have you heard from Jim?"

Liddy shrugged. "Not since he left last week. It made me so sad to hear him say how much he loved me and wanted to try again. I've thought long and hard about it, but I can't get past what I felt when he left me."

"You can't change the way you feel, Lids. Your life, your call," Emma pointed out.

"I did make the call. I'll always have feelings for Jim, but I need to move on. Which is just what I told him." Liddy's grin spread slowly. "Just before Tuck pulled into the driveway."

"Way to make your point," Maggie said. "So let me guess. Jim drove off in a huff, and Tuck carried you inside, and you spent the rest of the afternoon in a sex-induced coma."

"No, he drove me to work. But Jim did drive off in a bit of a huff."

"Better he should know the truth." Emma sipped her drink. "You still make the best margaritas in New England."

"Thank you. I do, don't I? Guys, I have another announcement. A small one, but still . . ."

"What? You're giving up your house to run off to Shelby Island and live with Tuck," Maggie suggested.

"No, but that may be on the table at some point. More immediately, I have an appointment tomorrow at Making Waves."

Maggie and Emma looked at each other, then back at Liddy.

"What for?" Maggie asked. "Manicure?"

"Facial?" Emma guessed.

Liddy grabbed her braid and held it up. "Do you have any idea how long it's been since I had my hair cut? Or how many miles of split ends I have?"

Maggie glanced at Emma. "This can't be the real Liddy. She must be a pod person."

Emma nodded. "Let's look in her basement. I bet the real Liddy is down there."

"I understand your skepticism, but I'm serious. I'm long overdue. Like, years overdue." She dropped the braid on her chest, then looked down at it hanging there. "I will probably miss it, but it's time."

"When is this momentous event going to take place?" Emma helped herself to a few more grapes.

"Friday afternoon at two. Felicia is blocking off a full hour for me."

"Has she seen how much hair you have?" Maggie asked.

"She has."

"So how much are you having taken off?"

"I told her I want enough left to make a decent ponytail."

"What brought this on?" Emma asked.

"I just feel like the hair—the braid, the big fat bun—is part of who I used to be but maybe not so much who I am now. I'm starting my life over, on my terms. I'm a different person now. I want to look like someone who's turned a corner in her life and moved on to better things." Liddy stared into her glass. "Does that make any sense?"

"It makes total sense, but you'll always be Liddy. You can't change your personality, and that's what we've loved about you for so many years. Cutting your hair won't make you a different woman," Emma said.

"But it will signal that I'm a changed woman. There's a difference."

"I get it. I think whatever makes you feel the way you want to feel when you look in the mirror—I'm all for it. But Emma's right." Maggie shook her head. "You're not going to change who you are."

"Well, I am a businesswoman now, you know. And I have a boyfriend. I think. Maybe." Liddy looked at Maggie. "Was it yea or nay on the term *boyfriend*? Did we ever decide?"

"What were the options? Gentleman friend? Sounds like an old man. Tuck isn't old. And we already agreed *lover* is TMI," Maggie said. "Age is only a state of mind, my friends."

"I'll drink to that." Liddy raised her glass and clinked the rim with Emma and Maggie.

"So. You and Tuck, huh?" Emma said.

"Yep."

"Never saw that coming," Emma admitted.

"Why not?"

"Wild island boy, town girl."

Liddy laughed. "I'm afraid he's not really all that wild. But he is an island boy. Did I tell you he took me to the island?"

"No! When?" Emma exclaimed.

"Yup. I met his dad, who isn't doing well, by the way. Tuck said yesterday the doctors don't expect him to last much longer. He has the option of moving him to the hospital, but Tuck thinks the trip would kill him. Besides, he said his dad wants to die on the island and be buried at sea, and that's the way it's going to be."

They tossed around the benefit of being dropped into the ocean far out at sea, or cremation versus traditional burial. When they realized how morbid the conversation was, they opted for a new topic.

"Brett and I are going to Maine to see Joe and the kids this weekend," Maggie told them. "Joe's son Jamey's last soccer game is on Saturday, and he invited us to come."

"Wow, that's progress. I remember when Jamey didn't even want to meet you or Brett," Liddy noted.

"He's okay with us now. He's bonded with Brett because of the sports thing, and he tolerates me because he wants Brett around. But I'll take it. Grandkids I never knew I had? Yes, please." Maggie smiled. "And they'll be here in a few weeks, because Grace has been texting Joe about her house. She wanted the opinion of an engineer, so she's sent him pictures, plus sketches of the old floor plan versus the new one. He wants to check it out before walls start coming down. Plus I think she wants Joe to meet Linc."

"Gracie and Linc Shelby? What's happening there?" Emma was obviously surprised.

"Oh, there's something brewing. She hasn't said a whole lot. But as always with Grace, it's what she hasn't said that's the tip-off. She spends a lot of time at her house after she leaves the bookshop. She says she just likes to keep up with the progress on the renovation. From what I've seen of Linc, he seems like a really nice guy. But I worry that . . ." Maggie seemed lost for words.

"That he has too much on his plate between running his father's business and raising his sister's children?" Liddy filled in the blanks.

Maggie nodded. "He's taken on a lot. Obviously, he's an exceptional young man to step up the way he has for those children and to work more so his father can work less. I just don't know if he has anything left to give to a relationship. Grace has had a few rough years. I'd hate to see her get involved with someone who can't give her what she needs emotionally."

"You have to let it play out," Emma told her. "If it's meant to be, they'll find a way to make it work."

"If it makes you feel better, he's stopped into the shop a few times, and yesterday he took Grace to lunch. It was just a trip across the street to Ray's for a pizza, but it was sweet the way they walk together. Not touching but bumping shoulders every once in a while."

"Liddy, did you video them as they left the shop?" Maggie asked.

"God knows I was tempted, but I had a customer."

"Next time excuse yourself and run outside with your camera." Maggie shook her head. "Really, Liddy. I expect better of you."

"I don't know what I was thinking." Liddy rolled her eyes.

"Of course, maybe they were just talking about the house and her plans," Maggie suggested.

"Um, no, this did not look like a business conversation."

"Well, that makes me feel a little better," Maggie said. "But video would have been nice."

Liddy picked up her glass and found it empty. A glance at the pitcher confirmed they'd finished it off.

"I'll be right back." Liddy went inside and whipped up a second pitcher of margaritas. When she came back outside, she said, "So, guys, I've been thinking."

"About?" Maggie tucked her legs under her.

"Thanksgiving."

"Thanksgiving is a month away," Emma pointed out.

"Always a big holiday in our family. It was one of Art's favorites," Maggie said. "This will be my first Thanksgiving in Wyndham Beach since I was a girl."

"Maggie, I know you and your family do a big Thanksgiving every year, and seriously, no one does a holiday better than you. But this year, I'd like to host Thanksgiving dinner for all of us. Your family and Tuck and his family and Emma and Chris. Oh, and of course Dylan."

Emma smiled. "You're such a good soul, Liddy. Taking him in, giving him not only a home but a job."

"It's nice to have someone in the house to talk to at night, someone to watch TV with. And he's no trouble at all. He's the best helper. He's raked the leaves in the backyard and helped me clean up the flower beds. He even ran the vacuum cleaner one night while I was making dinner. And he's only been with me for a week, but so far, so good.

He's working out so well in the shop, and he's keeping his grades up. Straight As, in spite of everything he's gone through. I admit I hadn't quite thought it through when I offered him a room, but it's turned out better than I ever could have expected."

"I love when things work out like that," Emma said. "Let's drink a toast to Liddy and her big heart."

Liddy topped off everyone's drink for a toast.

"To Liddy's big heart." Maggie raised her glass.

"I discussed it with Jessie, and she gave me a big thumbs-up, so we'll drink to Jess, too," Liddy said, and they did.

A moment later, Maggie said, "Liddy, about Thanksgiving. I already invited Joe and the kids."

"I figured you would have, but they're included in the invitation. I have so much to be thankful for, and I can't think of a better way to express how grateful I am to you for being my friends through these past few years."

Liddy could tell Maggie was torn between her quiet, elegant holiday dinner with her family and a big dinner that would inevitably be loud and chaotic, as dinners tended to be when more than two small children were involved.

"It's fine with me," Emma spoke up. "I love the idea. I can't remember the last time I cooked a turkey."

"Me either. Which is why we'll leave that job to Maggie." Liddy reached out and took Maggie's hand. "Please? This one time?"

"Of course. I think it's a great idea."

"Thank you. You do realize any big dinner at my house means you both are going to be doing some of the cooking, because I can't remember ever feeding this many people unless I called a caterer."

"No catering. We've got this."

Liddy went inside for a notepad and pen. "Let's figure out our menu, and then we'll divvy up the list, who's doing what."

"This will be so much fun!" Emma was visibly excited.

"We need rules," Liddy said. "No green bean casserole. No brussels sprouts."

"I love brussels sprouts," Maggie protested.

"Fine. We can have brussels sprouts." Liddy added it to her list. "But the green beans are not negotiable."

Chapter Eighteen

Liddy stood in the close, dusty attic, which still held the scent and the tail end of summer's heat, and knew it was fruitless to even try to remember which of the many boxes held her grandmother's wedding china. It had been packed away after her sister, Ruth, died and Jim had relegated it to the third floor because he had insisted his grandmother's china took precedence over anyone else's. Liddy was grateful when Ruth had bequeathed the lovely service for twelve to her. They'd squabbled over it from the time they were kids, both having coveted it, but Ruth had been born four years before Liddy, and their mother believed that to the elder went the spoils.

When Liddy had decided to host Thanksgiving for all the people she loved best in this year of changes and new beginnings, she'd thought back on last year's holiday and how drop-dead gorgeous Maggie's table had looked. There'd been the beautiful deep-plum tablecloth and the colorful centerpiece, the china and the crystal, and the gold napkins. Any Instagram influencer would have been proud to photograph the flawless decor. Liddy had never gone all out like that, had never tried her hand at anything she felt could stand up to Maggie's magic touch, but she was going to put together a table, an ambience that would make her guests feel special and would reflect Liddy's unique style.

She moved and poked in boxes until she was a liquid pile of sweat, but eventually she found the cartons containing the china she wanted, so she pushed them closer to the stairs while she poked around a little more. She was delighted to find a box of crystal wineglasses she'd forgotten about, several lace tablecloths—sizes unknown but she'd give them a try—and a wicker cornucopia, which she thought she could use as a centerpiece filled with fresh fruit and maybe a few pumpkins. She was grateful Dylan was on hand to carry everything to the first floor, and by the time all the boxes were in the kitchen, she wanted to walk into the shower fully dressed. She did manage to disrobe first, and after drying her hair, she felt like a new person. A glance in the bathroom mirror reminded her she was, in fact, a new person. The pounds of hair she'd shed were not missed. In their absence, a prettier Liddy had emerged. The shoulder-length cut was more flattering than she'd anticipated, and she found the new look more sophisticated, more suited to her life as a business owner and woman-about-town.

Tuck's face when he saw her had said more than any words. His eyes had grown wide, and he'd blinked. Then he'd grinned. Then he'd kissed her. He was one of the few people in Wyndham Beach who hadn't asked her if she "missed all that hair." He'd called her a knockout, which he'd followed with, "But you've always knocked me out."

Oh, yeah. The man knew what *really* constituted foreplay.

One night after dinner, after Dylan had gone to his room to study for a test, Liddy and Tuck had moved out to the deck. Bundled together in blankets against the chill, they cuddled on a single lounge and watched the stars blink overhead. Liddy sighed and said, "I keep forgetting—I want you and your family to have Thanksgiving dinner here with me and my family." She paused. "Do you think your dad could make the trip?"

"He'd never survive the crossing from the island, and that's assuming we could get him into the boat without him having a heart attack."

"In that case, we'll send dinner back to him and his nurse."

"That's very thoughtful, Liddy. Thank you."

"So you'll come and bring Linc and the kids?"

"You sure you're ready for all of us?"

"Please." She rolled her eyes. "You're talking to the woman who figured out how to keep a herd of four-, five-, and six-year-olds sitting quietly for an hour on Saturday mornings."

Tuck nodded. "True."

"So?" Liddy prodded him.

"On one condition."

She narrowed her eyes suspiciously. "What?"

"That you spend Christmas—including Christmas Eve—with us."

"On the island?"

"No. In the warehouse where I keep my trucks." He laughed. "Of course on the island."

She wiggled around to face him. "I'd love to spend Christmas with you. I may have to bring Dylan with me, though."

"Dylan's welcome, along with anyone else you'd like to bring." He raised an eyebrow. "Except maybe Jim."

Liddy laughed. "I think Jim has something of his own going on. I heard he was seen out to dinner twice last week with Jeannie Brightcliffe."

"Jeannie Brightcliffe the babe . . . I mean, the head teller at the bank?"

Liddy rolled her eyes. "Yes, that Jeannie Brightcliffe."

"Isn't she a little young for Jim?"

Liddy held up her hands. "None of my business." She closed her eyes and smiled. "Thanksgiving is going to be so much fun. I invited everyone I love. Maggie and her kids and her grandkids and Emma and Chris and Dylan. And you all, of course."

"Linc tells me Chris and Maggie's Natalie are an item."

"Indeed they are. Emma says it's the real thing. And speaking of Maggie's daughters, I've noticed your son hanging around my shop frequently and escorting one of my employees to lunch. I'm wondering if there isn't a bit of a real thing developing there as well."

"I sure hope so. Grace is a doll. Linc's been carrying a heavy load, and it looks like Grace is starting to carry a bit of that for him. You know, she takes the kids to dinner once or twice every week so Linc can have time to get his paperwork done, now that he's writing songs again with Chris."

"I heard about that. What an amazing opportunity for him."

"It is, but I doubt he'd have taken it if not for Grace. He said she's the one who talked him into working with Chris on some of those songs they wrote back in the day." He shook his head. "And to think, back then, I thought it was just a couple of boys playing rock star out in my barn or in the Deans' garage. I had no idea how far Chris was going to take it. Linc gave all that up to help run the business, and now he has Brenda's kids on top of everything else. But Grace is helping him keep everything in balance. He couldn't do it without her, and I couldn't be happier."

"So he's in a happy place, and he has a shot to do something he loves. Everyone doesn't get that second chance, you know?"

"I do. I might have to bring that bottle of Pappy's with me to Thanksgiving dinner. It'll be good to have a little time to catch up with Brett. We've both been so busy doing our own thing over these past few years, we haven't had much time to sit down and talk."

"Well, on Thanksgiving, you'll have all afternoon to sit out here and talk about old times."

He leaned down and kissed her. "I'm not so interested in looking back these days. I'm more interested in looking forward."

"You sound like a man with a plan."

He nodded. "Yes, ma'am, I am. I'm thinking we should take this relationship to the next level."

Liddy sat up. "What does that mean, exactly?"

"It means we should be thinking about our future together and what that's going to look like. You know, at our age, you can't be drag- ging your feet, because you never know . . ."

"Speak for yourself, bucko. I'm in my prime." She poked him in the chest. "Think you can keep up?"

"Or I'll die trying." He pulled her closer. "Seriously, do you think you could live off the mainland?"

"Maybe someday. I like the island. It might be a challenge for me to get to work some days, but I'd give it a go. Maybe not right now, though. I'm just starting to feel unfettered, you know? I've laid my daughter to rest for real now, and I've worked things out with Jim, more or less. I don't love him, and that makes me a little sad, I'm not going to lie. But I feel at peace about our divorce. I love having my own business. I love my shop and the energy I get from it."

She studied his face, loving what she saw there. "I just want you to understand. I care very much about you, but right now, I need my time."

"Take all the time you need. We'll do this any way you want, as long as in the end I can put a ring on your finger."

"I don't need a ring. I don't know that I'll ever want one again, but that doesn't mean I don't want to be with you."

Tuck grinned wickedly. "We can be Wyndham Beach's biggest scandal." He lowered his voice to whisper in her ear. "Did you hear about Liddy Bryant and Tuck Shelby? Shacking up on that island for days! Unmarried and practically living together! And at their age!"

Liddy laughed. "I would dearly love to be the town's biggest scandal for once in my life. It could be a lot of fun."

"However you want to play it, it's okay with me as long as we're together. It's your call, Liddy. All the way."

~

Beginning one full week out from Thanksgiving, Liddy began her preparations. She opened the dining room table and put in the two leaves that would extend it to seat twelve adults, and she set up an auxiliary table for the six children: Maggie's grandkids—Daisy plus Joe's two, Jamey and Lulu—and Tuck's three. She hand-washed all the china and her mother's crystal one night, finishing a little after ten thirty.

Three nights before the holiday, Liddy ironed the delicate linen napkins she'd found in one of Ruth's boxes, and hand-washed the only lace cloth that would fit the table once the leaves were added. Two nights before, she washed the crystal goblets that had been a wedding present to her parents. The night before, she set the table with her prized dishes—her grandmother's bone china with tiny yellow flowers painted around the border, edged in platinum. Maggie had loaned her six less fragile plates painted with pumpkins for the kids, so she set the children's table with those. The last thing she did before she went to bed was to pack up Jim's grandmother's china. Dylan carried it upstairs to the guest room, where Liddy was stockpiling other things Jim or someone in his family should have. Maybe someday he'd marry a woman who had children, and he'd have someone to pass those things on to.

Maybe he'd marry a much-younger woman and have another child. The thought of a geriatric Jim trying to keep up with the schedule of a middle schooler brought a smile to her face but no pang to her heart. And that was when she knew for certain, one hundred percent, no doubt in her mind, their years together were definitely in the rearview mirror.

∽

Early on Thanksgiving morning, Liddy picked Emma up, and they drove to Ground Me, where they purchased three large coffees and three croissants. From there, they drove to the beach at the end of Cottage Street, where they found Maggie wrapped in a blanket and huddled against the rocks.

"What are you doing all the way over there?" Liddy held her own blanket over one arm, the coffees in their carrier in both hands.

"The rocks are blocking the wind. Tell me again why we're out here in the cold on a holiday morning." Maggie reached for her coffee and wrapped her hands around the container.

"Because we're starting a new tradition. Coffee on the beach at sunrise before we go back to my place and start cooking."

"Why can't we start this new tradition on, say, Memorial Day? Or the Fourth of July?" Maggie took the croissant Emma offered her.

"Because Thanksgiving is in November, and it's the day we gather together with all those we love and be thankful they're with us," Liddy explained as if she were speaking to a five-year-old.

"That sounded like a Hallmark card." Emma selected a croissant for herself, then handed the bag to Liddy.

"We can gather and be thankful when it's warm again," Maggie grumbled.

"Someone got up on the wrong side of the bed." Emma nodded in Maggie's direction.

Liddy and Emma wrapped up in their blankets and sat with Maggie on the cold, damp sand. The breeze blew up around them, chilling them even more and pushing the whitecaps onto the shore.

"So what do you hear from your shark?" Maggie asked through chattering teeth.

"Rosalita? She's long gone. Right about now, she's enjoying those warm waters of the south."

"Shark's got more sense than some people I know," Emma muttered.

Hunched in her blanket, Liddy laughed. "Hey, we went south last November. Emma and I had Thanksgiving with you and the girls, and then on Friday, we went to Charlotte to see Chris and his band in concert."

"We got our tattoos at that little shop a few blocks from the hotel. We called to make an appointment, and the girl who owned the place said she was booked solid, so sorry. No tattoos for you," Emma recalled.

"Until Chris called and promised her backstage passes and tickets for his Saturday night show." Maggie smiled. "And the poor girl almost passed out when he walked into her shop to deliver the bribe."

"That was a really fun weekend. I can't believe it's been a year," Liddy said. "And oh, hasn't it been one hell of a year?"

"You're telling me! It's been a year of miracles for me. All these things I never believed would happen. Brett and I have grandchildren together. Fancy that!" She took a sip of coffee. "And Natalie—oh, Emma, remember when she and Chris were little, and he'd take her around the block in his wagon? And we dreamed about how we'd get them together when they grew up."

"It's so much better that they found each other on their own." Emma grinned. "Just think, I'm going to have a daughter-in-law who's always been like a daughter to me. Which would give me an automatic granddaughter." She turned to Maggie. "Will you mind sharing Daisy with me?"

"Of course not!"

"Have they made it official, then?" Liddy asked.

"No," Emma admitted, "but they're so much in love, I can't imagine him with anyone else."

"And Gracie really seems to have found herself." Maggie turned to Liddy. "Thanks to you, she has a job she loves and a house that's going to be totally Grace when she's finished. And she's found herself a new guy, and everything about Linc just feels right."

"I remember him from Chris's high school days, when the band would rehearse in our garage if Harry wasn't home. He was a shy kid, but always so well mannered. Chris tells me he and Linc are collaborating on some music again."

"How'd it go, having Linc's nieces with you while he was in California with Chris?" Emma asked. "You haven't said much about it."

"Grace was nervous because Bliss didn't like her, but it turned out fine. I kept her busy. Chopping fruit, loading the dishwasher, setting the table. Simple things like that. Giving her responsibility and letting her feel useful has made all the difference in her behavior. She even gets along better with Gracie now, so she's coming around."

"Well, speaking of big years—Liddy, what a year you've had!" Emma exclaimed.

"Oh my God, where to even begin? I bought a business! My shop has given me life. I never saw myself as a businessperson, but I enjoy all the work that comes with owning a business. I love books and I love the shop—it's anchored me. I feel like for the first time ever, I'm in control of my life. No one's expectations to meet except my own. If I succeed, it's my victory. If I fail, it's my failure. But either way, it's on me." Liddy smiled. "It's a nice change."

"Jess would have been so proud, Lids," Maggie said.

Liddy nodded. "And Jim and I have made our peace, such as it is. And the questions about Jessie's death have been resolved. I can never thank Gracie enough for putting all the pieces together. With Bowers's inevitable conviction, he'll be sentenced to more years than he has left. A small consolation, but at least justice will be done. Sort of. So that's a good thing, and more than I thought I'd ever see."

Emma said, "And look at you with a boyfriend."

Liddy smiled. "Yeah. Who'd have thunk it?" She finished off her almost-cold coffee.

"Not to mention a new look," Emma continued. "I love the shoulder-length hair, Liddy. It makes your eyes look bigger and brighter."

"Thanks, but that could be mascara."

"And Emma, you've gotten some funding for the center, so you can have that artists' colony you wanted," Maggie said.

"I'm still working out the details, but we'll get there." She brightened. "But my dream of Chris settling down here and raising a family has more of a chance to come true than it did a year ago, so there's that. Chris is happier than I have ever seen him, and that makes me happy."

Liddy glanced at her watch. "Hey, we should start back to the house. We're going to have to get that turkey ready to go in the oven. He's huge, so it's going to take forever to roast him."

"Remind me why you bought a twenty-eight-pound turkey?" Maggie stood and emptied the cold contents of her cup into the sand.

"When I went to pick it up at the farm, it was this one or a twelve pounder, which never would have been enough." Liddy folded her blanket. "I asked the farmer how it got so big, and he said, 'Well, it just kept eating.'"

Maggie laughed and shook the sand out of her blanket. "Lids, I've been thinking. If you married Tuck and someday Gracie married Linc, would that make you her mother-in-law?"

"And if Nat marries Chris, Maggie'd be his mother-in-law, and Emma, you'd be Natalie's."

"Oh my God, my head just exploded." Emma laughed as she gathered up the empty paper cups.

"Yeah, that all sounds incestuous." The sand back on the beach where it belonged, Liddy wrapped herself up again as the wind whipped across the beach.

"That would be an amazing turn of events." Maggie nodded. "We'd need another tattoo to commemorate if all that happened."

"That's a lot of what-ifs. Let's see how things play out. I don't know if I want to marry Tuck. I don't know if I ever want to marry anyone again."

They started walking in the direction of Cottage Street.

"So, what, you just plan on having a 'relationship' forever?" Emma's fingers made air quotes.

Liddy shrugged. "Maybe. I kinda like the idea. It'll keep everyone guessing."

"Especially Tuck," Maggie said.

"Well, it would keep him on his toes," Liddy acknowledged.

"It'll keep you on your toes if a certain pesky widow in town figures he's fair game. I read something online the other day," Emma told them. "'No ring? Not a real thing.'"

"Oh, it's a real thing, all right. But this time, it's going to be on my terms. My timeline." They reached the sidewalk, and Liddy stamped her feet, hoping to jiggle some of the sand from her shoes. She gave up, took off her shoes, shook out the sand, and put them back on.

"Tuck's okay with that?" Maggie stopped and waited for Liddy to catch up. "With you calling all the shots?"

Liddy smiled, a true Cheshire cat smile. "It was his idea."

"Aren't you lucky to have found someone who gets you so completely?" Emma grinned.

"No doubt about it. I'm the luckiest woman alive."

AUTHOR'S NOTE

As a parent, I cannot fathom any pain more devastating than losing a child, but to lose a child by his or her own hand must be soul crushing. If you've lost a loved one of any age to suicide, you have my deepest sympathy.

Through my own family research, I discovered my great-grandfather, a French immigrant—a onetime French professor at an Irish university, a business owner, and an apparent popular international sportsman who was well regarded and respected in his adopted home of Philadelphia— took his life on the first day of August in 1899 at the age of forty-nine. The available records give no hint as to why he chose to go down that path. I've often wondered how my great-grandmother coped with his death and all the questions she must have had while raising their seven children alone (and how she managed to talk her Catholic parish into permitting him to be buried in a Catholic cemetery, suicide being a grievous sin). Thinking about her, a woman whose name I carry, is what led me to create the character Jessica Bryant and to imagine the cause and effect of her actions. I have tried to handle the subject of her death as sensitively, respectfully, and realistically as I could. I understand that the reason an individual chooses to end their life is deeply personal, and may never be fully understood by their family and friends, but in this book, I wanted to give Jessie's grieving parents a path toward eventually understanding their daughter's choice.

The statistics relative to suicide in the United States are eye-opening. Did you know that suicide is the second-leading cause of death among individuals between the ages of ten and thirty-four (from the Centers for Disease Control and Prevention)?

Or that elderly people commit suicide twice as often as young people?*

Or that it's the tenth-leading cause of death overall in the United States?*

If someone you know—including you—is having suicidal thoughts, please, please, please call the National Suicide Prevention Lifeline 24-7 at 1-800-273-8255. (If you're a veteran, call that number, then press 1.) All calls are confidential. The Crisis Text Line offers emotional support 24-7—text HELLO to 741741.

*Statistics: The National Institute of Mental Health

ACKNOWLEDGMENTS

I have been most fortunate to have worked with amazing profession-
als at every stage of my twenty-six-year career, and I'm grateful for
every editor, publicist, marketing team, cover artist, production man-
ager, and salesperson—everyone who helped turn my manuscripts into
books. It's been pure pleasure to work with the entire Montlake team
on every phase of the process. From my acquiring editor to that final
proofreader—folks, this is a highly professional, author-friendly, hard-
working, talented, smart crew, and I love working with them. So many
thanks for all you do—Anh Schluep, Maria Gomez, Ashley Vanicek,
Jillian Cline, Lauren Grange—you're "the best of the best of the best"
(direct quote from Will Smith—*Men in Black*). Holly Ingraham, you're
a joy to work with—I couldn't have asked for a smarter, sharper, more
talented editorial partner for this book (and the last). And special thanks
to the art department for the gorgeous covers that exemplify the setting
and mood of my books!

Huge thanks for all the support to my readers—those who have
been with me since my first book was published in 1995 to those who
have just discovered my writing. In particular, to my Facebook friends
and family—you have been phenomenal! When I needed names for
some secondary characters for *Goodbye Again*, so many of you stepped
up to suggest names or to volunteer your own, I had to toss them all into
a hat and pull out names when I needed them! So a special shout-out

to Edith Faye Kosloski Butler, Doreen Jones Rick, Neva Kress Kreger, Bernadette Sikorski, Cindy Bickley, Janet Friesner, Gretchen Smith, Deborah K. Allen, Angelet Davis, Karyl Davis, Marcy King, Tami Sellers, Christal Gayle Ozanich, Linnea Priest, and Jeannie Brightcliffe (okay, I sneaked her in as a surprise). I hope you all enjoy the roles your names played.

Thanks to TLC Book Tours and all the bloggers and reviewers for their kind words about my books, and to the book angels who've helped spread the word on my behalf through the years, especially Maureen Downey, Helen Egner, Marilyn Rowe Harper, Jo Ellen Grossman, Maudeen Haisch Wachsmith, and Dede Frederick (with apologies to anyone I've missed). Writer friends who try to keep me sane—thanks to Robyn Carr, Dana Marton, Nancy Herkness, Chery Griffin, Terri Brisbin, and Marianne McBay.

And to my family: my husband, Bill; our daughters, Kate and Rebecca; their spouses, Michael and David, respectively; and their off-spring—Cole, Jack, Robb, Camryn, Charlotte, and Gethin—you have my heart.

ABOUT THE AUTHOR

Photo © 2016 Nicole Leigh

Mariah Stewart is the *New York Times*, *Publishers Weekly*, and *USA Today* bestselling author of several series, including Wyndham Beach, The Chesapeake Diaries, and The Hudson Sisters, as well as stand-alone novels, novellas, and short stories. A native of Hightstown, New Jersey, she lives with her husband and two rambunctious rescue dogs amid the rolling hills of Chester County, Pennsylvania, where she savors country life, tends her gardens, and works on her next novel. She's the proud mama of two fabulous daughters, who—along with her equally fabulous sons-in-law—have gifted her with six adorable (and yes, fabulous) granddarlings. For more information visit www.mariahstewart.com.